LOST
— TO —
TWO WORLDS

LOST TO TWO WORLDS *is a sad reflection of our times, when evil men do evil things yet flourish without misgivings, while good men can anguish a lifetime from childhood trauma that permanently defines them.*

The story unfolds over two centuries on three continents. It focuses on the lives of two men whose characters are diametrically opposed: Benjamin Boyd, a Scotsman and a real-life, historic pioneer who arrives in Australia in 1842, and a fictional character named Daniel Hannaford, a mining engineer born in Australia in 1953. A man with few redeeming qualities, Boyd stops at nothing, including murder and a form of slavery known as blackbirding, all to satiate his excessive personal needs and a driving ambition to restore his family's fortunes.

173 years later, Daniel Hannaford accepts an engineering contract on the small island of Lucaya in the Caribbean. Disturbed by a tormented past and an irresolute personality, Daniel meets Brianna, a Jamaican bartender at an island government party. That same evening, both are witness to a brutal attack on a woman, encouraged by the island's premier and perpetrated by the son of an influential British Lord and billionaire.

Separated by almost two hundred years, the two stories, narrated in juxtaposition, illustrate the good and evil of two very different men, one driven by greed and ambition and the other tormented by his past and the guilt of loving two women.

LOST

—·TO·—

TWO WORLDS

A Novel

J MICHAEL BAILEY

BOYDTOWN • VANCOUVER • SYDNEY

LOST TO TWO WORLDS

Ravello Publishing

PO Box 317, Princes Highway, Eden, NSW, Australia

Cover design – *germancreative*
Technical support – Simon Bailey
Cover idea – Michael Bailey
Typesetting – Sue Balcer
Editor – Scott Hurley

Australian First Editions
ISBN – Trade paperback – 978-0-6450635-4-7
ISBN – ebook – ISBN 978-0-6450635-5-4

A catalogue record for this work is available from the National Library of Australia

LOST TO A WORLD IN WHICH I CRAVE NO PART
I SIT ALONE AND COMMUNE WITH MY HEART
PLEASED WITH MY LITTLE CORNER OF THE EARTH
GLAD THAT I CAME NOT SORRY TO DEPART

Inscription at Mercury's Seat, Villa Cimbrone in Ravello, Italy
(Composed by the Latin poet Catullus around 60 BC)

For my family and friends and to all who provided the inspiration

PROLOGUE

His grossly obese body packed the small cabin as he continued to struggle and his lungs heaved from the exertion. Dressed head to foot in thick woolen clothing, he was already drenched in sweat from his efforts in the suffocating tropical heat.

His labours were eventually rewarded as he finally succeeded to return the heavy portrait of the woman to the ornamental nail embedded in the dark teak paneling. She had finally been retrieved after more than six years of his incredible adventures.

The portrait was of a severe and unattractive looking woman with a large, flat nose and a prominent wart in the centre of her forehead. Miss Emma Green was the only daughter of a wealthy banker in the City of London whose wife had died giving birth to her twenty-four years earlier. Eager to find her a suitor, Emma's father was hopeful that the entrepreneur would finally relieve him of the responsibility he had inherited upon the death of his wife. A rumour, encouraged by her obnoxious father, suggested that Emma was much in love with this Scottish adventurer.

Benjamin Boyd had originated the rumour, transmitting it subtly over time to family and friends prior to sailing from Portsmouth, in December 1841, aboard the Wanderer, RYC *(Royal Yacht Club). This false story was necessary for propriety of an age when men of Boyd's standing were either already married or investigating eligible candidates with pedigrees suitable to further their careers or replenish diminishing family bank accounts.*

The truth of the matter was that Emma Green had no interest in this amoral, self-absorbed and opinionated Scottish scoundrel already the shape of a cask of whiskey. She had been forewarned that he was a rogue, intent only on restoring family fortunes. His father, Edward Boyd, had declared bankruptcy after speculating unsuccessfully in a trans-Atlantic shipping venture.

She had been correct in thinking him a conniving reprobate but was wrong about his design on her fortune. He had no need of her money, for he had already been promised funding from the British government to establish the Royal Bank of Australia. Soon he would have unlimited access to upward of one million pounds to finance his enterprise on the far side of the globe. His relationship with her was purely a ruse to keep society's wagging tongues from confirming what many secretly believed, but none had dared speak.

He was wearing a pair of calf-length breeches and a dark purple, pull-over-hunting shirt, the very same outfit he had worn overseeing his ship's crew as they worked the goldfields of California – a time when his desperation knew no bounds. His futile quest for gold had begun eight months earlier. With none of the fanfare accompanying his arrival in Australia, he had quietly sailed from Sydney to escape jail for fraud and restore his finances in the American gold rush.

He laced up a pair of Monticello bootees over a thick pair of black socks, pulled on a Monmouth cap and knotted a kerchief around his neck. Tucked in the belt of his breeches was a brand-new Colt 1847 Walter revolver he had purchased before sailing from San Francisco with the grandiose notion of setting up a white republic in the Solomon Islands. He had also packed a leather portmanteau with supplies: a little food, an extra flask of water, a compass, and two short-barrelled, flintlock-hunting rifles he had brought with him from Merton Hall, his ancestral home in Scotland.

The jolly boat rocked gently against the hull of the Wanderer, *moored in a sheltered bay to the northeast of the island. Other than ripples fanned by the breeze, the water was calm; it was coloured a light blue, fading to turquoise as it neared land. A narrow white sandy beach with sentinels of bowed palms skirted the shore. Behind it, a near-impenetrable jungle spread over most of the island that a Spanish fleet had discovered under the command of Alvaro de Mendana in 1568.*

It was believed with some certainty that the island was still populated by small, isolated groups of Micronesian cannibals.

After years of indulgence hosting and attending grand society functions in Sydney, Boyd was no longer a specimen of good health. His ambitions to become the wealthiest landowner in all of Australia was financed by permanently borrowed money from the very bank he had been tasked to establish by trusting investors back in London.

He looked twenty years older than someone in his forty-eighth year. The thick greying beard he had grown did nothing to conceal the sagging jowls that accentuated a triple chin. He was a naturally large man who had an inclination to eat and drink to excess, until he seemed to be disguising more of a female form beneath men's clothing. The crew occasionally mocked him behind his back, laughing raucously over their evening potion of rum and proposing that their captain was about to deliver twins. His breathing was often laboured, and any exertion would soon raise pinprick beads of perspiration on his face.

Boyd was unable to climb the rope ladder down to the dingy below. Instead, the crew had constructed a harness solely for his use akin to a makeshift bosun's chair. Four of the ablest crew lowered him slowly down to the dingy where young Stevens undid the straps supporting him from the deck above. A single rope lowered Boyd's case with the two flintlocks. He felt beneath his shirt to check that the Colt revolver was still there.

Using one of the oars Stevens shoved the jolly boat from the Wanderer *and once clear of the schooner, he began to row. The twenty-one-year-old was strong; he pulled the oars expertly whilst gazing at Boyd, who sat smiling at him kindly. He had only been a scrawny young lad ten years ago* when Boyd had taken him on as his cabin boy. Boyd greatly admired the transformation and the young man's bronzed physique as the dingy drew further away from the Wanderer.

The pair continued to shore as the crew cheered their progress. They were happy to be rid of their captain for a few hours, waving and wishing them luck on their expedition; they were off to shoot birds for dinner, hopefully sufficient in number to feed the ship's complement of fourteen souls.

With some assistance from Stevens, Boyd managed to rise and climb out after the small boat nudged into the soft sand. He stood up to his ankles in warm water. Stevens then dragged the craft up the beach a short way as Boyd slowly trudged towards the dense jungle through the powdery white sand. Stevens followed, carrying the portmanteau and a machete. From the Wanderer the crew saw them as two specks disappearing from sight; they would never see either of them alive again.

Boyd already understood that it would the last time he would see the Wanderer or his crew. This was his sole reason for replacing the portrait of Lord Nelson with Emma Green, the lady whose painting would protect his reputation from that tinge of doubt. After all, had he not carried her picture always with him to remind him of a love lost long ago? Save one member of the crew, no one was aware that she had languished inside his cabin for more than six years. Stevens was the one who had helped him bury her beneath the bed when propriety was no longer necessary in a land where building fortunes was all that mattered.

PART 1

PART 1

CHAPTER 1

SAPPHIRE COAST – Australia

April 2017

What 'could have been' never is when dreams are scattered at dawn. It is only the exceptional and the courageous who rediscover them in days of sunlight and in the brilliance of a purposeful life. His tragedy was to have a locked box full of such dreams but not the courage to turn the key. Indecision had always been his true calling; the things that mattered most often resulted always eluding him.

Daniel Hannaford was frequently numbed by a sense of loss and utter loneliness. It had been this way ever since his mother had quite literally vanished from his life and he had ended up in a Catholic boarding school far from the sunshine of Australia. Incarcerated in a foreign and often bitterly cold country and isolated from everything he had ever known, he'd seen his childhood and innocence slowly and irrevocably stolen.

Grieving and suffering unwarranted feelings of guilt over his mother's disappearance, he often travelled in the company of anxiety and fear instilled by the nightmares fed by crippled human beings calling themselves the servants of God. These were the men commissioned to care for the boys at the school; instead, they plucked the souls from their young prey, leaving many on a long and lonely journey into darkness.

Daniel appeared not to hear his wife when she came from inside carrying a stained wooden tray with two mugs of coffee and a plate of biscotti. She had baked them the day before from a recipe her mother had brought to Australia the year of the Queen's coronation. That was sixty-four years ago. Her mother and father were now resting in a Sydney suburban cemetery thousands of miles from the mountain village in the Campania region east of Napoli where Mario and Anna De Luca had been born.

"You're not brooding again, I hope? I'll go back inside if you are," she warned, before giving him one of the special smiles radiating her genuine love for him. She lost her balance slightly as she was placing the tray on the table and Daniel reached out to gently steady her. Some of the coffee from the mugs spilled, adding to the collection of stains on the tray.

Pia would be sixty-one in a few weeks, three years younger than her husband. She worried that she was already displaying signs of old age, a looming yet unavoidable condition that occasionally petrified her just as much as any terminal disease. She was tall for a woman of southern Italian heritage, and slim besides. Even now she remained extremely elegant, more like a wealthy Milanese. There was certainly nothing to indicate she was the daughter of impoverished *contadini* who'd arrived in Australia with no money and limited education.

Most days she was content with her life, except on occasion when feelings of sadness coupled with a degree of anger would suddenly overwhelm her. This was when she would imagine how her life could have been, one of true purpose and meaning. She had always had an abundance of love to share, but Daniel had seemed to struggle with the concept from the time they had met. This was not to say he did not love her. She knew that he did in his way. Several years after they were married, she began to realize that because love and affection had been absent from his early life, it was impossible for him to process and express his emotions when he was older. Instead, he had smothered these feelings in order to survive what sixty years later would be considered a truly brutal way of raising vulnerable young children.

Sighing, Pia sat on one of the wicker chairs on the expansive pressure treated deck that encircled the house outside.

She was looking out over the shimmering crystal water of Twofold Bay. It was perfectly framed by eucalyptus and a range of hills cascading from the Great Dividing Range, formed three hundred million years ago when Australia collided with what are now parts of South America and New Zealand.

They had met briefly in 1978, at a Bob Dylan concert in Perth where both attended Curtin University. He was four months from graduating as a mining engineer, and Pia was completing her Bachelor of Nursing degree.

Shortly after Daniel finished his degree, he headed to Jamaica to gain valuable work experience for twelve months at Kaiser Bauxite in Discovery Bay, half an hour by road from Ocho Rios. Jamaica had been the largest producer of bauxite in the world but had recently relinquished that position to Australia, which nonetheless still had much to learn from the tiny Caribbean nation.

Meeting her again by chance in a coffee shop in Perth on his return to Australia, Daniel had asked Pia out and they had started dating. Seven months later they were married at the Victorian-Gothic Town Hall in Perth. The wedding was a small affair. Neither had family to invite, just half a dozen friends from their university days. Without contemplating thoughts of a honeymoon, they had left immediately for the Northern Territory where Daniel had accepted a job in Nhulunby, the site of the world's largest bauxite deposits. Pia had also found her first job at the Gove Hospital, about four kilometres from the mine.

They remained thirty-five years in Gove, living in a pleasant suburb until, quite out of the blue, Daniel was offered a job in the Caribbean by an old school friend in 2014. Daniel was sixty-one at the time but had never once contemplated an early retirement. They were both beginning to tire of living in the Northern Territory. It was much too hot and there was very little for them to do in a remote mining town except work and go to the pub, or occasionally to the local RSL club. They flew to Darwin for long weekends now and again, and returned to Perth a couple of times a year if for no other reason than to reconnect with so-called civilization. Until recently, three or four days of city life was all they needed, and they were happy to return home to Gove. It was only when they started approaching retirement years that they decided they wanted more from life.

They had bought a house south of Eden, a town in New South Wales they'd enjoyed visiting on one of their rare holidays. They loved the cooler weather of the Sapphire Coast. The house was only five minutes from the nearest beach and a number of national parks with plenty of bush walks. And they were also still far enough away from the big-city life they both disliked so much, yet closer to all the amenities that had been lacking in Nhulunby. Pia was only fifty-eight when they finally flew to New South Wales to move into their new house. She hoped to find some part-time work at one of the doctor's offices in Eden but was pleased to be leaving her hectic and often stressful life as Director of Nursing in what had become a very busy hospital.

Despite having more time alone to regret what she had wanted most in life, Pia still chose to remain in Eden when Daniel left Australia for the island of Lucaya, six hundred miles southeast of Miami. He had negotiated a contract including six weeks' annual leave, which was more than sufficient to head back to Australia to spend time with Pia. Anyway, it was only going to be for two years, three at most, after which he might be content to retire and potter around the house.

Daniel pulled out a chair and sat next to Pia, and they remained quite content in silence for a while. A warm breeze wafted the late afternoon calls of bellbirds, and they watched the aerobatics of the grey and pink galahs, first swooping then suddenly banking before climbing in perfect formation. It was late April and the weather was unusually warm, with just a few weeks remaining before the onset of winter. He drummed his fingers on top of the table, forgetting how much this annoyed Pia – it was a habit that told her his mind was elsewhere. She was quite concerned about him in these moments of cognitive absence. It was not something she had ever recognized in him until his return from the Caribbean the previous year.

Perhaps he was developing dementia, she occasionally worried. God forbid. What would she do, how would she cope? He appeared the same. He was still a handsome, solidly built man standing at 5'8," as he was when they had first met at the Dylan concert in Perth. He also remained the same solitary man in his relationship with the outside world, always striving to achieve perfection through hard work, while selfishly guarding his time off and allowing few to invade his privacy.

Daniel eventually returned Pia's smile, yet it overshadowed his enduring guilt for not providing what he knew she had always wanted. His inability to escape his inner isolation made it impossible to express the tenderness or love she deserved.

Another flock of galahs rolled in flight and landed in the field next door and started pecking through the grass. He barely saw them. His mind drifted elsewhere, back to the Caribbean where gentle trade winds brushed a pearl-drop paradise of islands. Dark histories were hidden there, now including his own. It was there that everything had changed for Daniel.

CHAPTER 2

THE JAMAICAN – Lucaya
December 2015

"What can I get you to drink, sir?" the black girl behind the bar asked cheerfully with a melodic and characteristic Jamaican lilt. She was to him unquestionably the most attractive and pleasant person at the premier's party, an observation Daniel made without consideration of anyone else in the brief fifteen minutes since he had arrived. This spontaneous decision surprised him almost as much as this pretty girl, who immediately noticed his confounded manner, as if he were in shock.

He had the kindest of eyes, and he was staring at her as if she were the most beautiful woman he had ever seen. She had never considered herself to be particularly attractive, but it seemed obvious this man believed so.

She suddenly shivered despite the warmth of the night. Then she smiled, displaying two tidy rows of perfect white teeth. To him they appeared as tiny beacons of light shining through the unblemished darkness of the most beautiful African face he had ever seen. Her large eyes absorbed him in a singular glance. For no reason he could explain, the way she had looked at him made him feel indescribably happy.

It was a large party by island standards, with perhaps four hundred people milling about the pool and garden areas. Winding paths were softly illuminated by moonbeam columns and rope lights wrapped around tall palm trees rustling from ocean breezes. The British governor was in attendance with his wife; he was chatting with the premier and Lord Geoffrey Elm, a ruthless seventy-three-year-old businessman lacking the slightest semblance of a moral compass who had used his tremendous wealth and influence to purchase a peerage. He had made no altruistic or social contribution to anything or to anybody other than himself. It was rumoured that those who promoted his peerage were leading Tory politicians, including the Foreign Secretary.

By way of a lucrative exchange, the Foreign Secretary was compensated with exotic holidays at several of the Peer's villas in the Caribbean, flown directly from the UK in one of a fleet of three executive jets; one he maintained for his personal use and the other two for the convenience of various executives working at his companies overseas. He also spent time aboard both of Elm's mega yachts; twice on cruises in the Mediterranean and once in the South Pacific. Money was also suspected of having greased the Foreign Secretary's already greasy palms on more than one occasion, but nothing which could ever be proved. The *Guardian* newspaper had published a story to this effect, which had to be retracted later with an apology. It was all true but the paper could not afford the cost of a libel suit if pursued by the highly litigious Geoffrey Elm.

The local and international press nicknamed Premier Walter Harrison's house Tara, the plantation mansion in Margaret Mitchell's epic novel *Gone with the Wind*. The island was small, but the premier had quickly earned himself an envious reputation, at least amongst those locals and their pastors who worshipped money, yachts and jet-set lifestyles. It was yet to be determined how someone who had little money two years previously could afford such trappings of wealth, despite the recent salary increase of three hundred and fifty thousand a year approved by his cabinet cronies, nearly all of whom were somehow related to each other. When the premier had first assumed office, he was receiving a salary of just sixty thousand dollars a year. And yet, including the massive increase, four hundred and ten thousand was still barely sufficient to pay just for the Tiffany jewellery he showered on his wife and on his various mistresses.

Recently, dark clouds had begun gathering on the premier's horizon with clamouring from the opposition party to establish a special investigation into government corruption. To avoid a cover-up the opposition were insisting that such an investigation be directed by the fraud squad in London and staffed by British police officers. The poorly paid local constabulary, drawn from police forces within the Caribbean, was simply not trusted.

Now that the British press had got hold of the story, it seemed likely that the Foreign and Commonwealth Office would have to recommend something to counter tales of the millions the premier, as well as members of his extended family and the cabinet, were rumoured to have pocketed from the dubious sales of Crown land. Lord Elm had been advising his good friend the Foreign Secretary to leave the matter alone, assuring him it was all quite trivial and could be dealt with by the local people themselves.

On the other hand, the Foreign Secretary knew full well that the British tabloids had started to smell blood. Stymying the public's appetite for salacious news of the playboy premier, without setting up some sort of formal inquiry to investigate the more serious accusations, could make matters worse – more importantly, it could raise serious questions of his own involvement and his future as Foreign Secretary.

"A Corona would be fine, thanks," Daniel replied, feeling a little embarrassed by how attracted he was to this woman half his age. He hoped she had not noticed. The Jamaican, though, possessed the intuition of all beautiful women and was quick to realize this older man with the gentle soul had immediately taken to her. He pushed the slice of lime down the neck of the bottle and took a thirst-quenching gulp. It was hot and humid and there was a crush of people at the bar. Beads of perspiration had started to gather across his face.

Someone pushed in front of him to ask for a whisky and soda and a Jack Daniels and coke. "Diet?" she asked, not looking at the customer but continuing to look at Daniel instead, giving him the warmest of smiles normally reserved for dreams. "My name's Brianna, by the way." She smiled again, and her deep brown eyes sparkled. "Just call my name if you want another." And then she was gone attending to the other orders. He wandered slowly around the pool, nodding at some he recognized but did not know to speak to. Later, he had a lengthy chat with his boss and old friend, Richard Crossly, about the kerbing of the new road.

The machine they had brought over from Florida was not doing the job properly and so they were going to have to do it all manually.

There was only a handful of stragglers by the time Daniel and Richard Crossly decided to call it a night. Daniel made a slight detour after telling his boss he wanted to say goodnight to someone he had met earlier. He was disappointed when he discovered the Jamaican girl had already left and the small bar was shuttered for the night.

No fool like an old fool, he lamented in memory of his long-departed youth. He had recently celebrated his sixty-second birthday, and like a lot of men his age, he was starting to regret life's missed opportunities, whether real or imaginary. He still loved Pia in his own way. But they had really never shared the romance and thrill of living. These were feelings and emotions he had seldom even experienced. He had always been faithful, had not been with another woman since before their marriage. The last had been a brief yet passionate relationship with an English girl he'd met on the beach in Negril when he was only in his twenties and was working at Kaiser Bauxite in Jamaica. He recalled how he had been pleasantly mortified one afternoon when she lay beside him on the beach after taking off her bikini top.

Now he could see old age beckon on the horizon, and he missed the excitement of being a young man. Tonight, Brianna had brought it all back, yet it had as quickly slipped away, like any fleeting memory shrouded in the mist of the past.

The place was deserted now and on the spur of the moment Daniel decided to walk to the car park the long way, around the front of Tara to see if he could perhaps take a peek inside. If the stories were only half true, he was certain the premier would be upstairs by now entertaining his harem of girlfriends in his sumptuous master bedroom. If someone saw him, Daniel thought, he could always tell them he was simply interested in seeing the quality of the workmanship – because he was the new engineer for the company that had constructed the house. Lord Elm, who had a financial stake in Richard Crossly's construction company had donated the land to the premier, free of charge, no doubt anticipating future concessions and favours from the government.

The grass was still wet from the sprinklers using recycled water from the septic treatment system. He continued walking, holding his fourth Corona of the evening by the neck of the bottle and swinging it by his side, attempting to avoid the spray from the sprinklers whilst peering in various rooms on the ground floor.

The first thing he saw was the two-storey, oak-panelled library rumoured to have cost one million dollars. The spiral staircase alone was an additional hundred thousand or so. This winding, ornate wooden structure set in the centre of the room was cleverly carved with flamingos and osprey and other birds of the islands. At the top of the staircase, he could just make out a coloured carving of the coat of arms of the islands. Just below that was an official photograph of the great man himself posed like an American president in portraits on display at ports of entry to the United States. Daniel simply smiled at the absurdity of a man with an electorate of less than 10,000 attempting to emulate the US President. The official salary he had quietly awarded himself was even larger than President Obama's.

Ambling further around the next corner he was suddenly aware of men's laughter, followed by what sounded like muffled cries for help. Then there was a loud crash of something metal and the sound of glass breaking.

Daniel dropped his beer to the grass and hurriedly went towards the commotion. Later he wished that he had not, because it would irrevocably change his life.

Brianna was standing there looking horrified. Shards of glass were scattered by her feet from the broken glasses she had been collecting from around the gardens, tidying up before she took a jitney home. There was a metal tray lying upside down on one of the stone flags of the patio. She was staring through a transparent mist of condensation laminating the glass French doors of the premier's indoor pool. She did not immediately hear Daniel approaching.

He saw enough to realize the immediate danger, and without uttering a word, quickly yanked her from the line of sight of those inside. In the shadows outside the house, the premier's driver and bodyguard saw them both as they hurried off around the next corner to the car park. He recognized the girl but not the man.

By then standing upright, the premier had also seen Daniel Hannaford, whom he had spoken to briefly earlier in the evening about the progress of the new road.

CHAPTER 3

NIGHTMARES – Lucaya

December 2015

He lay completely naked on the thin mattress. The moon's light, sneaking between open louvres of the window by his bedside, tracked brightly over his body, illuminating glistening beads of sweat. It was not the mosquitos' repeated attacks to draw blood that was preventing him from sleeping. Disturbing thoughts continued to swirl inside his head, horrified as he was by events that evening when he had witnessed the brutal spectacle of man's utter depravity. Even the random police killing of an old Rasta he had witnessed years before in Jamaica did not have such an immediate and profound effect.

Daniel had been on the Caribbean island for close to six months, engaged as the chief engineer on the construction of a new paved highway. It was a thirty-million-dollar government contract to upgrade what had been nothing more than a sandstone track. This east to west primary artery, connecting the port and airport to the tourist resorts, was littered with potholes and jagged rock that had been carved by the effects of weather over time and the addition of many more vehicles to the road. The almost constant traction of dangerously overloaded trucks hauling building materials caused the original sandstone surface to deteriorate until the road became unsafe to travel. These supplies catered to a recent building boom and were critical for the development of the island's economy; they were shipped every five days from Port Everglades to

Lucaya and then towed in containers on barges by tugs that navigated the shallow waters through perilous coral reefs.

At the beginning, Daniel had found his job quite challenging, despite his qualifications in both mining and civil engineering. Most of his adult life had been spent working as a mining engineer, just as his father had been in Kalgoorlie, following in the footsteps of generations of Hannafords who had first emigrated from Cornwall seventy years after Captain Cook anchored in Botany Bay. For the lack of anything else he wanted to do, he had taken the path of least resistance after school by submitting to his father's wishes to continue two hundred and fifty years of Cornish family mining tradition. Now, working as a civil engineer so late in his career, he realized it was something he should have done from the start. It had been difficult to adapt at first, but he found this new work far more satisfying.

Commanding a dark and brooding presence, Daniel's father, Peter, was not someone to be opposed when championing his ideas. They were governed solely by the egocentric laws of what he believed was best for his family. He was a domineering man with, at times, an uncontrollable rage that had pooled within him since his return from war in Europe in 1945. Daniel's mother, Rosalind née Jessen, who had been born in Norway, had died in 1960, or at least was presumed dead after she mysteriously went missing from the family home. There was speculation at the time that Peter had done away with her and had disposed of the body down one of the many old mine shafts scattered across Western Australia. A body was never discovered, but this vicious rumour, among others, had nonetheless added to the torment that shattered the lives of the family during that awful period. It was always hanging over them, as in the surreal stillness the second before the guillotine blade dispatches yet another soul to an eternity of darkness. None of their lives would ever be the same again.

Daniel's sister, Jane, who was fifteen years older than he, had escaped to live in Tasmania; Daniel had been shipped off to his grandfather's old school in England because there was no one else to care for him. By then, Peter Hannaford was drinking heavily and incapable of looking after a seven-year-old boy, a responsibility he had always abrogated to his wife.

Other than being so far from Australia and Pia, Daniel enjoyed his life on Lucaya. There were approximately eight thousand inhabitants, roughly two thousand of whom came from other countries, mostly from Haiti and Jamaica. Fewer than five hundred combined came from Canada and the UK. The majority of the expats had work permits, and only a handful were permanent residents.

Most of the citizens of the territory were descended from the human cargo on two European slave ships that had run aground on the coral in the island's turquoise waters on route to Jamaica. The locals, Daniel soon determined, were unlike other Caribbean people he had encountered who, for the most part, were extremely friendly towards strangers and demonstrated a certain dignity, including many in dire poverty. Lucayans were quite different, often unfriendly and resentful of strangers, even towards people of colour who came to their shores, including the impoverished Haitian refugees who endured perilous sea crossings to find the better life to which every human is entitled.

For reasons Daniel was unable to fathom, Jamaicans were the most disliked group on Lucaya, more so even than the Englishman who had first stolen their ancestors from Africa yet still controlled their destiny as an Overseas Dependent Territory hundreds of years later. Daniel suspected the Lucayans simply envied the Jamaican culture because they had never developed a distinct one of their own. The vast majority of Lucayans were poorly educated; through necessity they had flocked illegally to the United States for decades to find work in Miami or New York. Once there they had adopted the very worst of American influences, which their descendants would later bring home to Lucaya in more affluent times, suffocating any emergent local culture.

A loud, urgent knocking at the front door woke Daniel in panic from a collection of disturbing dreams, vignettes of terror and violent debauchery plaited together. He pulled on his shorts and stumbled from the bedroom and through the living room. It was dark now, as the moon was hidden behind clouds. He navigated his way only from a single moving beam of light that appeared to be surveying the inside of his house. On either side of the front door were two rectangular louvred windows with mosquito screens. Through one of them Daniel could make out a patent leather black boot and one black trouser leg imprinted with a long vertical red stripe. He knew immediately that it was the police.

CHAPTER 4

THE THREATS – *Lucaya*
December 2015

H e returned to bed and slept an hour or so after the police had gone. Thankfully, his earlier nightmare was followed by a collection of less disturbing dreams from a slightly happier time in his life, when he had first discovered Jamaica at the age of twenty-five. There had certainly been little joy growing up in a dusty mining town five hundred miles east of Perth on the edge of the desert, a place stifling hot in summer and bone-chillingly cold on winter nights. Any happiness he might have experienced in his early life was wiped from his memory the day his mother disappeared when he was seven.

JAMAICA, 1978

Daniel had immediately taken to Jamaica. He loved the total chaos of the place, the unfamiliar fragrances of Jamaican food and the crowded bars pumping with Reggae music and the air dense with the musty, overly sweet smell of Ganja. The first time he smoked it he was nauseated. It was here, at a bar in Negril, that he first met the topless English sunbather who taught him how to inhale and enjoy it, and who also explored and shared with him the sublime delights of her carnal experiences. She was older than he was, and he had wanted to follow her back to London. He never did, nor did he ever hear from her again once they had briefly kissed goodbye at the airport in Montego Bay and she had flown off to resume her life in London.

He quickly became addicted to the spicy Jamaican food, nearly always washed down with a quenching bottle of Red Stripe beer or two. Salt-fish, beans and rice with Akai was his favourite dish. Goat was too bony for his taste. He was fascinated, though, by how locals could crunch, then swallow and digest fish and goat bones that would choke most foreigners– or at least threaten to slice their intestinal track beyond surgical repair.

It was a dangerous time in Jamaica. Even Bob Marley had fled for London after being shot and wounded in his home on Hope Street in Kingston. But these dangers only heightened the excitement and romantic flavour of the country for Daniel. He spent many of his days off exploring the threads of the ragtag towns of St Ann's parish, stretching along the coast from Ocho Rios to Discovery Bay, or venturing to Montego Bay.

Oracabessa Bay and the Goldeneye Estate, where Ian Fleming wrote his Bond novels, was midway from Runaway Bay. There Daniel would hail the jitney to Port Antonio, once home to another Australian, the swashbuckling movie actor, Errol Flynn. Weaving in out of the traffic on their journeys, the often-unlicensed minibuses would make dangerous dashes to overtake vehicles – and occasionally ended up a scatter of twist-ed metal and mangled bodies.

He lived alone in a rented, concrete block house with protruding rebars waiting for a second floor. It was close to Browns Town, a bustling market community with a distinctive flavour and an atmosphere of Africa: electric with life, confusing, colourful and noisy with the cheerful chat-ter of the local patois first spoken by slaves to confuse their often-brutal European masters. The town had more churches than any other of its size in Jamaica, thanks mostly to a Scotsman called Dr James Johnson who based his Jamaican Evangelical and Medical Mission in Browns Towns in the late 1800s. His legacy was that abundance of churches, but there was little evidence of God those days in a society where, instead, gunmen preached their deadly gospels.

Often after gorging himself on spicy Jamaican patties for lunch, Daniel would wander between the market stalls in the congested town centre, chatting to vendors only too happy to explain for a sale that an odd-looking vegetable was an okra, or encouraging him to feel the bread-fruit, which was introduced to Jamaica by Captain Bligh, the infamous captain of HMS Bounty.

One day walking past the Bank of Nova Scotia on the High Street, he saw an old man with filthy dreadlocks and bare feet being gunned down on the street and left in the gutter to die like a dog. The perpetrators were helmeted police on patrol after earlier breaking up a violent political brawl between supporters of the two rival parties, the JLP and the PNP. Daniel was too shocked to move; the police brushed by, knocking him against a church wall, and continued up the road to the Dry Harbour Mountains plateau. A few miles further along the road was Nine Mile, the small ham-let where Bob Marley was born, and where thirty-six years later he would be buried in a brightly painted red, yellow and green mausoleum along with his favourite guitar.

It was daylight and now someone else was gently knocking at Daniel's front door. "I'll be there in a minute," he called. He quickly dressed in a pair of white cargo shorts and a navy-blue t-shirt.

The houses in the small estate had been built packed together to maximize the permitted density per acre. The louvred windows allowed residents to hear practically every sound coming from their neighbours.

Someone next door to Daniel's house was busy clearing his throat and nasal passages. Then there was a disgusting guttural sound, after which the man spat and immediately flushed the toilet in his bathroom. It was a morning ritual that sickened Daniel and he swore to himself he would have to move elsewhere on the island as soon as he had the chance.

"Can I come in?" the voice asked.

Brianna was standing there alone. Gone was her cheery disposi-tion of the previous evening when he first saw her serving drinks at the pop-up bar. Now she appeared anxious and scared. She was wearing a pair of old jeans and a cheap white blouse. Her grubby running shoes were scuffed and she had no socks on.

"I am sorry to trouble you, Mr. Hannaford." The words had come tumbling from her mouth. "I was threatened last night after you saw me home!"

Her eyes were darting from side to side as she fidgeted with her long slender fingers. Daniel noticed her elaborately painted fingernails, each with an intricate miniature design with a tiny embedded artificial diamond. "Someone must have seen me!"

"But who threatened you, Brianna,?" Daniel asked in alarm.

"It was a man I had never seen before who came to my house this morning once everyone else had gone to work."

"But what did he say?"

"If I ever told anyone what I had seen last night I might never see Jamaica again!"

Daniel gestured for her to sit down by the small wicker dining room table. She was frowning as she sat and did not look at Daniel directly. He was silent as he decided whether to tell her he had a visit in the night from the police. Would it be better not to mention it in case it worried her even more? In the end he decided he ought to tell her, and perhaps then she might not feel quite so alone. "Yes, they saw me too."

"And they threatened you as well?" she exclaimed, now clearly alarmed.

"Only indirectly. But, yes, I believe they were delivering a message I was not supposed to ignore," he explained. "They informed me they had received a report of someone screaming at the premier's house, and for security reasons they needed to determine what had been going on. Someone had given them my name and had suggested the incident merely involved party guests enjoying themselves in the premier's indoor pool."

"So, they didn't actually threaten you, then?"

"Well, no, not exactly," Daniel replied, "unless you consider that the only people who could have seen us were the premier and Lord Elm's son. Or perhaps there was a security guard about who we didn't notice." He paused, reflecting for a moment as it started to dawn him.

"It was a risk for them to take, but they probably had no alternative. The narrative they provided the police was intended for me, I believe. In other words, I should shut up if I know what's good for me and confirm their story. There was no other good reason to give the police my name. "Of course," he continued, "they must have seen me dragging you away and would have known I would only do that if I thought you were at risk, that you and possibly the pair of us must have seen them raping that poor young woman."

Now Brianna looked simply terrified. "You didn't tell them anything, did you?"

"No," Daniel assured her, "just as we agreed last night – to keep it to ourselves for now."

As soon as he had said it, he began to worry whether he had made the right decision. Perhaps keeping quiet made them complicit; then again who would listen to two expats on work permits? Only if the girl who was assaulted reported the vicious crime could they come forward and corroborate her story. Until then, their very lives might well be at risk. They were not just dealing with a tinpot leader of some tiny British colony in the middle of nowhere. Daniel's real concern was Geoffrey Elm, one of the wealthiest men in Britain. He might go to any lengths to protect his son – and undoubtedly succeed without suffering any consequences.

CHAPTER 5

THE MOVE – Lucaya

December 2015

They were sitting apart on either end of a worn 'L' shaped sofa. It had several scattered cushions strewn over it covered in bright, rainforest-patterned fabric. In the corner was a Sony TV. On the left side of the open-plan area there was a small yet fully functional kitchen. Directly behind where Daniel was sitting were two bedrooms with en-suite bathrooms. It was not a large house, barely twelve hundred square feet, but in dramatic compensation for its size there was a stunning panoramic view beyond the terracotta tiled deck. Bougainvillea trailed from brightly coloured Mexican ceramic pots and wove along the wooden railings and between the balustrades. He was as comfortable here as he had ever been, including his large Queenslander in New South Wales. The only problem was the close proximity to other houses in the small estate.

Daniel sometimes had time to come home from work for lunch and sit outside eating a hurriedly prepared sandwich or salad, never ceasing to be captivated by the sea's shifting shades of blue and the breakers thundering in explosions of white froth on the coral reef. Pia would have been enthralled by the sheer dramatic beauty, just as she was with the stunning views from their house in Eden. Despite his urgings, she had decided not to share this chapter of his life with him, preferring instead to remain at home in Australia. At her age, Pia lacked Daniel's urge to travel, plus she was terrified of flying.

Brianna was still quite agitated, perhaps more than when she had arrived fifteen minutes earlier. She sat looking over his shoulder at a large, framed print hanging on the far wall. It depicted a small boat moored to an old wooden jetty with a row of palm trees behind.

"Tell me again, Brianna," he urged, "who threatened you and how?" She looked at him with large, terrified brown eyes; she was a different person from the previous evening when she had first noticed him at the bar. Then, she had barely been aware of the captivating smile she had given him, reacting instinctively to what she saw beyond his strikingly handsome mask – someone unable to disguise his gentle spirit. She could read it from his eyes and his self-conscious manner and from the sincerest smile any man had ever shown to her. She had immediately become aware that this man was unlike any other she had met.

"Who was it, Brianna?" he repeated.

Inexplicably, Daniel had started feeling a growing sense of unease in Brianna's company. It was nothing he could fully explain. It was as if he were on the cusp of some unknown and momentous event, a portentous warning that his life was about to change forever. He tried to shake loose from these thoughts to focus on the moment.

Brianna began to reply, clasping her hands and entwining her slender fingers as she took deep breaths at the end of each sentence. Tears had started to well in her eyes yet did not fall to her dark cheeks. Jamaican women were far too resolute, too defiant from often harsh lives, to allow tears to flow in public. To do so would have left her vulnerable in a world of men ready to take advantage of the slightest display of weakness.

She was looking at Daniel directly now and appeared slightly less terrified. "He was a large man, like a boxer," she began, speaking slowly. "I have seen him about before when Harrison hung out at the bar at the hotel with his girls and his government dogs. I think he might have been the premier's driver or something."

Daniel smiled at her description of 'dogs' in reference to Harrison's cabinet members, who often congregated at the airport bar swapping suggestions about how to make themselves even richer at the expense of the electorate.

"Yes, I think I know who you mean, Brianna. If it's the man I think, he sounds very much like Harrison's driver, as you suggest."

Lloyd Bailey had been Walter Harrison's driver for more than three years when the government ministers decided to purchase a fleet of brand-new SUVs worthy of any US presidential entourage. They were the largest vehicles of the type on the market, all black with fixed pennants on either side displaying two identical national flags. It was all quite ludicrous, really, for an island that was barely sixteen miles long and five miles wide. Harrison's driver cruised the short distances along Lucaya's main road at seventy or eighty miles an hour where the speed limit was only forty. The flashing blue lights and blaring sirens served as a warning to vehicles ahead to pull over.

Suddenly, Brianna allowed one single tear to fall, fascinating Daniel as it slowly channelled a single damp path down her cheek. She was horrified by this sudden crack in her façade.

Daniel had only driven this road late the night before when he had taken Brianna home after the premier's party. It all seemed quite different now in the daylight. Her house, if it could be described as such, was no more than a shack at the end of a dusty road leading to the water's edge adjacent to a tangle of mangroves. It seemed to have been built as a hodgepodge over a number of years with illegal extensions of old plywood, often stolen from building sites and painted in different colours. Outside by the entrance there was a shabby brown sofa with tufts of dirty white padding protruding in places. There was a young, almost emaciated woman sitting on it breastfeeding her baby.

There were also two other women sitting on the steps to the side of the sofa eyeing Daniel's car, anxious in case it was Immigration checking for work permits. Payments in cash or kind would be demanded from many of the women who failed to produce the necessary documentation. If they had no money or were unwilling to barter sexual favours instead, they would be subjected to immediate deportation to a home where life was even harsher.

On the other side of the road, a jerry-rigged cable connected illegally to the power company pole trailed high over the road to the shack, providing free electricity.

Daniel sat there with the engine running, his hands on the steering wheel. He noticed two scrawny dogs scavenging through a pile of rotting garbage where a small boy was urinating in the dirt. It was all far beyond Daniel's comprehension and experience of life. This island was, per capita, one of the wealthiest in the Caribbean, second only to Grand Cayman.

Just across the water, about two miles away as the crow flies, stood some of the most expensive homes in the western hemisphere. The mangroves conveniently hid this poverty, so as not to create an eyesore for the wealthy. One of those great houses was worth in excess of one hundred million dollars; it boasted, among other things, a wooden drawbridge over a narrow moat allowing access to the property. Inside there was a huge dining hall with a minstrel gallery above lined with thousands of books, including many rare first editions. Daniel had heard that the dining hall could accommodate two hundred dinner guests.

"How many are living here, Brianna?" Daniel asked still clasping the steering wheel.

"I am not sure, perhaps as many as twenty-five of us, all women of course. Mostly Jamaicans but there are a few from the Dominican Republic and two older women from Haiti."

"And they are all legal?"

"Some of the Jamaicans are but most of the others are not. The ones from the DR and Haiti nearly all arrived illegally by boat."

"And so how come Immigration doesn't pick them up and deport them back home."

Brianna laughed and started to open the door to get out. A blast of hot air blew into the car as though a furnace had opened without warning. "Use your imagination, Mr. Hannaford," she said holding on to the door. "They have to pay off the immigration officers somehow."

It was precisely at this moment that Daniel made the first major decision in his life without considering the consequences. He had been thinking about it on the drive from his house and now his mind was made up.

"Go and pack your suitcases, Brianna," he said firmly, almost as a command. "No way you can remain here after what has happened. And don't worry, I am old enough to be your father and you can trust my intentions are completely honourable."

Brianna was quite shocked by Daniel's sudden proposal, but at the same time she was thrilled someone should actually care about her. There was no need for him to tell her he was a good man. She had realized that when she first saw him at the bar. Clarifying the situation further, he explained, "and there's a second bedroom with its own bathroom and so you will have all the privacy you want. I can take you and pick you up from work every day. Harrison's 'dog' won't bother you again when they see you with me."

Brianna smiled. She went and quickly packed her two cases in the room she shared with two other Jamaicans. No one was curious about why she was leaving. They assumed she had simply found a white man to look after her for a while. They all did from time to time.

Waiting in the car with the air conditioning on the highest setting and blowing directly in his face, Daniel stared mindlessly at the two dogs fighting over a chicken carcass and without realising he was shaking his head, horrified with what he had witnessed here this afternoon; the stark reality of a world he had never seen before.

CHAPTER 6

WINDWARD PASSAGE

December 2015

It was a full moon, and the one hundred-and-sixty-four-foot motor yacht caught in its beams reflected shimmering colours as it cruised slowly in bright calm waters through the Windward Passage. In the distance, the lights of small towns were visible on both shores. On the starboard side they were sailing past Guantanamo province in Cuba with the US base at its southern tip. To port there were fewer lights on the poverty-stricken half of the island of Hispaniola, where many in Haiti struggled daily to survive, a never-ending battle to stave off starvation. The crew and passengers of the *El Gordo* were oblivious to the woeful poverty of the poorest country in the western hemisphere, so close to them yet separated by a chasm of wealth that would be eternally too far to bridge. The billionaire and his guests gorged on small Caribbean lobster, caught illegally by fishermen from the Dominican Republic in the shallow waters of the Turks and Caicos Islands, and drank wines from France and California. Two hundred and nine Haitians to the south of them remained adrift at sea with a smashed rudder, no food and little water. They were the pariahs of humankind, unwelcome wherever their leaky craft might be fortunate enough to touch land.

These small, colourful wooden hulks often sank during the perilous sea voyage to a better life. Emaciated and terrified, adults were cramped together with young children and tiny infants. Nearly all were unable to swim; if the violent actions of the waves capsized the boat, it would leave a trail of bloated corpses to drift in the currents.

But on the *El Gordo* the wine flowed as they waited for their serving of panna cotta aromatized with coffee.

Later in the evening after several of the guests had retired for the night, Lord Elm and his equally arrogant yet improvident son, Michael, were drinking Remy Martin from Waterford cognac glasses. Now that dinner had been consumed, they were lounging on either side of the U-shaped sofa with room to seat twenty people comfortably. Dimmed pot lights from above bathed the lower aft deck in warm yellow lighting as the engines hummed in the background, driving the aptly named *El Gordo* ('the big one') through the night, east of Guantanamo Bay. They still had twenty-six hours until they docked in George Town to top up with diesel before continuing to Belize, their ultimate destination.

Richard Crossly sat alone on the elbow side of the sofa wearing complimentary, eight-hundred-dollar *Loro Piana* deck shoes provided by the peer to prevent scuffing to his precious teak decking. His gin and tonic sat on a silver coaster on the large custom designed and weather-proofed oak cocktail table. He was not smoking a Havana as the other two men were. He loathed both of them and displayed deference only because they ultimately paid his salary. Fortunately, he would be departing the yacht alone for Lucaya on Lord Elm's private jet as soon as they arrived in Cayman.

Geoffrey Elm slowly swirled the cognac in his glass, staring with beady and bespectacled close-set eyes at his polished deck as if deep in thought. In fact, the peer was desperately attempting to contain himself from throwing the crystal glass at his stupid son. His pent-up fury was at the point of exploding and he knew he could never allow that to happen. There was far too much at stake and a level head had to prevail.

Geoffrey Elm had a reputation for being prone to extreme fits of anger when things were not going his way. He was also shrewd enough to have recognized it early on in his career, turning this character flaw to his full advantage. He used it like a nuclear weapon in business negotiations. In the mid-seventies he purchased his first company; it manufactured one of the earliest mobile telephones long before they became widely accessible to the masses. He screamed and bullied the directors, whom he had discovered had huge personal debts and homes heavily mortgaged, always threatening to pull out of negotiations whenever he was not getting his way. He knew how desperate they were for money.

Ultimately, the two directors succumbed to the relentless pressure from his intimidation tactics and accepted an offer for half a million pounds. Geoffrey had managed to obtain the purchase money over a number of years engaging in illegal stock market transactions from information provided by a friendly stockbroker. This particular broker had attended the same third-rate university as Geoffrey and was desperate for cash, having developed a penchant for the better things of life working in the City.

Ten years later, Geoffrey Elm sold the company for just under two hundred million pounds, and his legend was born.

A sudden warm breeze scurried across the aft of the boat and briefly uncurled the red ensign of the Cayman Islands. "So, you haven't spoken to your engineer yet, Dick?" Lord Elm asked, still not looking up from the floor.

"And why would I?" Richard Crossly replied with a hint of impatience. He revealed a harsh Yorkshire accent acquired growing up in Quarry Hill Flats, built in Leeds in the 1930s as a workingman's rehousing scheme. "If he was witness to the episode there's nothing that can be done. He either reports the matter or he bloody doesn't."

"Well, it's your job to make sure he bloody doesn't," Michael Elm warned angrily, swinging himself upright on the sofa and staring at Richard Crossly with cold blue eyes. Now it was Richard's turn to want to throw something at this obnoxious fool. Unfortunately, Michael Elm was his father's favourite and heir apparent, despite his elder brother, Matthew, being far more capable. Both sons had different mothers; Lord Elm still had an amicable relationship with his second wife, but the divorce from his first had been particularly acrimonious. He partially blamed Matthew for the unhappy situation, merely by association.

With some effort Richard Crossly retained his composure, "I am not quite sure what you are suggesting I should do, Michael, unless you want me to arrange to have him thrown down one of those sinkholes?" His sarcasm escaped Michael but not his father, who smiled at the reference to the problem they were encountering building the new highway. The island was made up mostly of soft sandstone, porous like honeycomb, and construction had been bogged down with huge sinkholes opening up, often overnight.

"Well, you know what's at fucking stake if he did witness everything and then blabs to the police!"

"Yes, I am fully aware, Michael! There could be a sensational trial, and if you are both found guilty, you'll end up in prison for decades. Hopefully, for your sake, you would be returned to the UK and not have to serve time on Lucaya, or indeed in Jamaica, where white boys are a sweet delicacy for the black prison population!" Richard knew as soon as he said it that he had overstepped the mark. He could detect that Geoffrey Elm was about to have one of his explosive tantrums.

"I have sufficient money to buy my son out of this mess, may I fucking remind you! You and that fat yob of a premier will be the ones who will lose the most!"

"Why me? Why would you suggest that, Geoffrey?"

"Lord Elm to you!" he spat, warning him in no uncertain terms, "because I can cancel your fucking contract whenever I choose, for anything I fucking well wish! And, yes, I am fully aware my bank virtually owns you and could pull the plug at a moment's notice." Geoffrey Elm let his threat sink in for a moment before continuing, "and the premier will undoubtedly end up in jail where he belongs for twenty years to life, incarcerated at Her Majesty's pleasure over in the UK where black boys are a white boy's 'sweet' delicacy," he sneered.

Richard contemplated his dilemma in full realization that he should have heeded the warning of others. Never get involved with Geoffrey

Elm. He was a crook like any other, albeit a very rich one, with an accumulated wealth of just over five billion British pounds. He could buy absolutely anything, and anyone.

Michael Elm laughed rudely as Richard, ignoring the remark, capitulated and hurriedly assured them both he would do all that he could. On a more positive note, he told them, Daniel Hannaford had been interviewed by the police two nights before at his home and had claimed he knew nothing about the incident.

"But you do not know that for certain," Geoffrey suggested aggressively.

"Correct, Lord Elm!" Richard replied, with disguised contempt. "But the Jamaican woman will never say a word after Harrison's 'man' persuaded her. She obviously saw what was going on and is sufficiently street smart to know the possible consequences. On the other hand, we are only assuming Daniel 'may' have seen something as well. Perhaps he was telling the truth when he denied all knowledge to the police."

"I'm off to bed then!" Lord Elm suddenly announced, standing without warning, seemingly bored with the conversation. "Just sort out this fucking mess the pair of you!" He headed up the spiral glass-tread staircase running his hand along the laser-cut aluminium balustrade. At the top, he turned to his luxurious cabin suite, where the wife of the former premier of Lucaya was waiting patiently curled in his bed.

Richard Crossly had no intention of 'sorting out' something none of his making. Instead, after finishing off his gin and tonic and saying an abrupt good night to the loathsome Michael, he headed off to bed in one of the guest cabins on the deck below the billionaire's luxury accommodation.

Michael Elm completely ignored Richard as he left. He sat, finishing off his Remy Martin and thinking. He was not concerned. Why should he be? Nothing money and a little intimidation could not resolve. The American woman had already, and very wisely, withdrawn her allegations for a significant amount of money, coupled with threats to her wellbeing if she ever came back for more. Doesn't money corrupt everyone?

No, Michael Elm was not in the least bit concerned. The police did not have a prima facie case against him or the premier for rape unless they could provide a reliable witness to the events. The American woman was no longer a threat, and he had already been assured that the Jamaican woman would never pursue it on her own. Apparently, she had far too much to lose; she was supporting a mother and three siblings back home in Jamaica. The only problem he could see now was the engineer. If he had seen something and was subpoenaed as a witness, then things could become very difficult indeed. Nonetheless, they still had enough time to find a solution without resorting to any extreme measures, he thought.

Walter Harrison and eight of his political cronies had been indicted for corruption. Because of the number of defendants and the volume of charges brought, the earliest the corruption trial could begin would be late 2016, if not the following summer. Despite some optimistic predictions of it being a short trial, it was widely believed within the legal fraternity on the island that it might take as long as a year to reach a verdict, perhaps longer.

The CPS would surely wait to lay criminal charges related to that night inside the indoor pool at Tara. Not waiting might be interpreted as an attempt to influence the outcome of the current corruption trial. Assuming Daniel Hannaford had seen something, Michael Elm calculated that they had at least two years to ensure the engineer was never called as a witness at a possible trial for rape. Hopefully this could be accomplished without having to silence him permanently. It would be the very last course of action his father would wish to pursue when he had his eyes firmly set on No. 10. Killing the man was not an option at the moment.

Back in his cabin, Richard Crossly lay on his bed considering whether he should mention something to Daniel. He knew exactly what Geoffrey and Michael Elm were capable of, particularly if they thought their empire was being threatened. It was a perpetual conundrum for Richard: to protect his integrity or weigh it against what would be lost should he reveal what he knew about Lord Elm's business transactions.

The police had questioned him several times in connection with the land transfer and subsequent construction of the premier's house, Tara. He had no substantive proof, but he'd overheard sufficient conversations between father and son to confirm that some sort of sweetheart deal had been made with Walter Harrison. One of the earliest indications was a sudden decision by the local planning board to increase the occupancy density of a new hotel Geoffrey Elm was about to develop on Coral Bay. It was closely followed by an announcement from the local government that the contract for the new highway had been awarded to a little-known holding company with a forty-five per cent stake in Richard's own construction company. Had anyone gone to the time and effort they would have determined that several directors of this Panamanian-registered company were also directors of Elm's bank on Lucaya. Additional investigations might have shown that the island bank had provided a huge loan to Richard's company – a loan he was having problems servicing.

Doing the right thing would cost him his livelihood; he understood that only too well. But declaring to the police that he had information concerning the rape of the American woman at Tara, obtained from conversations with Geoffrey and Michael Elm, might very well cost him his life. He had already been drawn into the conspiracy when he first approached the American woman with a financial offer over in Florida. It was too late to back away from it now.

Just before he drifted off to sleep, Richard accepted that he should remain silent and say nothing to Daniel when he arrived back on the island.

CHAPTER 7

SAN FRANCISCO

October 1850

*T*he population of San Francisco had swollen from around one thousand souls in 1848 to almost fifty thousand by 1850. The California gold fields were the incandescent lure for the hopes and imaginations of thousands who became enveloped, as if by the silk of giant spider webs spun from every corner of the globe.

They were amateur prospectors whose dreams of great wealth turned to despair after a few months with nothing to show for their back-breaking labour. Yet they still clung in the futile hope of striking it rich one day. There was nothing else for them to do. And the thieves, conmen, vagabonds and beggars would cling like parasites to their hosts, sucking them dry before moving to feed elsewhere. And then there were the men who, having found wealth and success, still searched for something lost, something forever beyond their reach.

There were more than one hundred masted ships moored at the Port of San Francisco. It was not unusual for them to have to remain at anchor out in the bay waiting for a berth to allow people to disembark and the cargoes to be off-loaded.

The streets were a heaving cauldron of humanity: coolies from China mingling with fashionably dressed men from New York and Boston, prospectors down on the luck looking for their next drink, pickpockets and sailors. Prostitutes did a roaring trade, whether rolling in the mud under

35

the wharf or standing up against a whitewashed brick wall. The brothels with the expensive and cleaner girls were packed all hours of the day in a city where there were few wives to accommodate their men.

San Francisco was a free-for-all, a jumbled, noisy Tower of Babel. Those from London could barely comprehend their compatriots from the colony of New South Wales, let alone the men from almost every country throughout the civilized world – and the not-so civilized.

Benjamin Boyd and his brother Mark were sitting at a rough-hewn bench on three-legged stools in a raucously overcrowded room serving as a tavern at the Niantic Hotel. One year earlier, it had been the interior of a whaling ship built in Connecticut in 1832. In 1849, it had brought a complement of passengers from Panama to San Francisco and was abandoned when the passengers, crew and most of the officers headed to the goldfields to seek their fortune. The ship was sold for desperately needed accommodation as the growing city extended beyond even the edge of the bay. Many of these water lots were later filled with sand excavated from the nearby sandhills by steam-driven excavators. Unaware of the rapid conversion of water lots to dry land, Benjamin and Mark Boyd were puzzled about how this ship had become perched in the middle of a busy street some distance from the water and was now a hotel. Another ship, the Apollo, was a smaller hotel two-doors down.

They were drinking ale from stoneware bottles brewed by the Adam Shuppert Brewery, the first to start brewing commercially in San Francisco two years before. Benjamin Boyd glared at a half-intoxicated man who knocked his elbow as he was taking a swig from his bottle. Two men at one of the corner benches were arguing over a game of Five Stones. It would end in a fistfight, with one man being knocked out cold to lie in a heap of straw on the ground, along with three of his teeth.

Mark Boyd, Benjamin's younger brother by three years, had arrived two weeks earlier from Sydney aboard the Wanderer's *tender, the* Ariel. *They were discussing Benjamin's options for extricating himself from being jailed for fraud if he returned to Australia or went back to England.*

The directors of the Royal Bank of Australia had built a very strong case that he had misled them since arriving in Australia to establish the bank. He had procrastinated for years over providing detailed accounts of the bank's real assets and expenditures. The extent of the fraud was only discovered when it was far too late. Boyd had been using bank funds as his personal source of financing, without any accountability to the directors and investors back home in England.

It was becoming much noisier now, with some of the boisterous tavern patrons drinking to excess; they slammed their stoneware bottles hard on the tables to gain the attention of a barmaid whose breasts almost came free from her loose white bodice. She laughed as she slapped one of the men with the back of her hand; he'd been attempting to reach up her skirt. Her slap delighted all the patrons, except the Boyds, who were too engrossed in conversation to have noticed.

The barmaid banged two more bottles on their table and then left with her arms firmly by her sides to avoid any more wandering hands searching for her husband's joy!

Mark was telling Benjamin that the situation was slipping perilously out of control now that the London directors had replaced their cousin, William Sprott Boyd, as manager of the Royal Bank of Australia and had begun the process of closing it down permanently. Besides trying to apprehend Benjamin, the directors were attempting to drive Mark into bankruptcy, and they would eventually succeed.

It had been eight years since Benjamin Boyd had first landed in Australia at Port Philip after his circuitous pleasure cruise from Plymouth. Accompanying him aboard the Wanderer *had been his brother, James, and Oswald Walters Brierly, who later became the marine artist to Queen Victoria. Others included two men who would become captains in Boyd's whaling fleet. Although Benjamin had put on significant weight since leaving Sydney, no one could ever accuse him of indolence, Mark thought. He had accomplished in seven years what most men would not achieve in a lifetime. Benjamin was one of the largest landowners and graziers in the colony, with over two hundred and fifty thousand acres and one hundred and sixty thousand sheep.*

He had owned a fleet of steamers and whaling vessels and a whaling station in Twofold Bay. He had been building his own port town, with a hotel, houses and a church. His intention had been to ship the wool from his sheep from Boydtown to Neutral Bay in Sydney to be prepared and cleaned before being shipped for England – along with tallow from his whaling industry, to provide lighting for her cities and homes. He had even briefly been a leading politician after being elected to the New South Wales Legislative Council for the electoral district of Port Philip, better known as Melbourne.

Matters started to go awry for Boyd as early as 1845, three years after his arrival in the colony. His first setback was losing a costly legal battle involving an insurance issue resulting from damage to one of his steamers, the Seahorse. A year later, he was accused of misrepresenting accounts of the Royal Bank to the directors back in England. It resulted in his ouster in 1847 in favour of his brother.

His time in the colonies slowly revealed Boyd's true nature to all those closest to him. It was obvious that he was driven to succeed at all cost, with no mind to what was right or wrong. Had he built his empire on solid foundations guided by the inherent goodness in most men, his colonial adventures might never have foundered. His legacy might have been heralded and preserved for centuries. But Boyd chose a different path, as so many men do, forgetting their lives are not eternal. Striving at any cost to enrich themselves, they forget that the price is one's soul. It inevitably transpired that many of those flocking to California in the 1800s willingly traded a commodity of far more intrinsic value than any fleeting happiness wrought by material possession.

The final straw for many of Benjamin Boyd's former supporters and investors was his attempt to introduce blackbirding to New South Wales. The price of sheep in the colony had suddenly fallen quite sharply, and he was finding it difficult to retain labour after becoming delinquent in paying wages. His personal funds were drying up, as were the reserves at the Royal Bank of Australia.

The government of New South Wales had balked at Boyd's suggestion of using convict labour, contending that it was not dissimilar to slavery, which had been abolished fifteen years earlier within all the territories of the British Empire. It was too sensitive a matter to be agreed to by the Legislative Council and so Boyd later turned to blackbirding. His captains scoured the Pacific islands, primarily the New Hebrides, and recruited native people by enticing them with promises of great wealth if they signed contracts to work in Australia. Many were easily persuaded unaware they were signing up to become indentured workers living in the harshest of conditions. Rarely, if ever, did they receive any compensation for their labours; after the cost of their food, accommodation and transportation had been deducted from any money they may have earned, nothing was left.

Once Boyd had departed for California, these half-naked and starving island people began looking for passage back home to the islands. But with so few ships sailing in that direction most of the islanders were abandoned, eventually to die in squalor in the backstreets of Sydney.

After several more ales, Benjamin and Mark finally hammered out a feasible plan that would allow Benjamin to start life anew. He had some of the money he had siphoned from the bank by way of wages he had withheld in Australia and from the sale of several properties he had acquired privately in Matthew's name. When he had first set out on his journey to the South Seas, meandering from port to port, he'd had the forethought to use some of the Royal Bank of Australia's one million pounds to invest in foreign property. He'd always registered it in the name of his ten-year-old cabin boy, with Boyd's signature and Matthew Stevens' power of attorney issued in London. Mark had been diligent in his brother's affairs and, armed with Matthew's current power of attorney issued in Sydney, had sold everything over the past two years.

They left the tavern and walked to the quay where Matthew was waiting with a small boat to row Mark to the Ariel and himself and Benjamin Boyd to the Wanderer, moored side by side out in San Francisco Bay. The brothers would not meet again until Guadalcanal.

CHAPTER 8

MIAMI INTERNATIONAL AIRPORT – Florida

8 November 2016

They shook hands briefly at the airport before he went through to Departures pulling his small carry-on and his computer bag hanging from his shoulder. He was taking the early morning flight from Lucaya to Miami, a journey of less than ninety minutes. Turning, he gave a final cheery wave before passing through the departure doors, leaving Richard Crossly already walking to the terminal exit, eager to start his day. In recent weeks, Daniel had been tempted to stay on in Lucaya.

Then common sense prevailed and he made his decision to leave. Richard had asked him to stay to oversee the construction of yet another concrete monstrosity, directly contradicting the tourist board's 'Beautiful by Nature' advertising campaign – intended to entice tourists to what had indeed been the closest place to a paradise on earth. Now it was starting to attract less-favourable reviews; one of the Sunday newspapers in Britain had published an editorial about the island entitled *Paradise Lost.*

Money and development had changed everything in the brief span of twenty years. Long afternoon shadows cast by international hotels and unsightly condominiums shaded the rows of deck loungers competing for space on a receding strip of beach congested with North Americans and a smattering of Brits. Obese sun-worshippers tried to avoid the more energetic few engaging in raucous and often downright annoying beach activities. Expensive speed boats roared by, skimming the tranquil waters of an area once designated a national park to protect the natural offshore reef.

The coral was dying now, not only from global warming but from the wilful damage of out-of-season lobster fishing. Local fishermen hurled sticks of explosive or poured bleach onto the coral in order to dislodge the lobster from their habitats and catch them in improvised pole nets. The illegal catch was sold to the hotels and restaurants before being advertised on their menus as frozen seafood from the previous season.

The American Boeing 737 flew low over the length of the island as it started gaining altitude before banking to the northwest towards Miami. From his seat, Daniel had a spectacular view of the thirteen-mile stretch of the recently completed highway below, traversing the island like a skeletal spine. He was immensely proud of his part in its construction, particularly after the difficulties they had encountered, many of which he had managed to resolve using only his initiative and ingenuity. It was a very satisfying end to his long career.

Daniel had realized early on that he would have to leave before the start of the corruption trial. Otherwise, he would be placing himself in an untenable situation; whatever his decision might be, he could never serve his conscience and his peace of mind at the same time. He understood what his conscience was telling him to do, yet to agree to possibly testify against the premier of the island and the son of one of the wealthiest men in England in a second and far more serious trial for rape could well compromise his own and Brianna's safety.

Just ten days earlier Richard had asked Daniel to renew his contract for a further two years. He had tried to appease his own conscience by explaining to Daniel, without being too explicit, what Lord Elm and his son were perhaps capable of doing. The Elms would stop at nothing to protect themselves and their financial empire.

To prove his point, Richard recounted a fascinating story that occurred in the eighties, long before Elm's odious son had left Westminster school in London. Concerning the lord's business ethics, it had been circulating for years. Most people took it with a pinch of salt, but it was all true:

For some reason or other, Lord Elm had arranged for a local man to be dragged forcibly from his home on a quiet street on Lucaya. The story never indicated why, or what this unfortunate man had done to provoke someone to inject him with a mild sedative and throw him inside an unoccupied wooden casket. A selection of small holes had been drilled around its base beforehand, to supply the occupant with just sufficient air not to suffocate on his long sea voyage to Florida.

It was a three-day trip aboard an old barge towed by a rusting tug. Piled six high on the barge, a hundred or more empty ship containers rattled and groaned on their return journey to the US mainland to be re-used. The casket had been locked inside one at the very top of the stacked cargo. Surprisingly, the terrified man was still alive when the tug finally docked in Port Everglades, but barely! He had been fully conscious once the sedative had worn off, lying in abject terror and completely isolated inside his casket. There was no one to hear his screams and he had only three small bottles of water to quench a ravenous thirst. In all likelihood, he would have remained inside the container until it was too late had a passing DEA dog patrol at Port Everglades not picked up his scent once the container had been offloaded.

The man was never quite the same again; he spent close to a year locked up in a psychiatric facility for his own protection in Fort Lauderdale. No one ever determined what this man had done to elicit such wrath from one of the richest men in the United Kingdom.

It was the Eighth of November, and at the airport in Miami everyone was glued to suspended TV monitors showing CNN and the election predictions running continuously along the bottom of the screen. Once he had cleared US Immigration and collected his checked luggage,

Daniel headed towards the Miami Airport International Hotel in the main terminal.

He had made a reservation online and so it only took a few minutes to check in and then go to his room on the fourth floor.

An hour later, after a shower, he was sitting in the Top of the Port Restaurant in the lounge area on the seventh floor with panoramic views of the extensive airport apron. Planes belonging to various international and domestic airlines sat at departure gates or taxied to one of the runways. It was a beautiful day outside. The restaurant was almost deserted; a little early for lunch, just two tables were occupied with people finishing late breakfasts.

At noon, the policeman saw Daniel and came over and sat down. "Thought you might be glued to the TV, Daniel," Inspector Sage said sardonically.

"Lord no, Roger! Australian politics are bad enough. And this one is a forgone conclusion. Hilary will win for sure."

"I have no doubt at all. No one except the 'deplorables' would ever vote for such an utterly despicable and reprehensible human being like Trump, supposing he even qualifies as human of course. Vile man!" Roger Sage placed his briefcase on the coffee table, clicked it open and took out a file.

Daniel and Roger had arranged to meet in Miami because Roger had been back in London for a couple of weeks and Daniel was on his way home for good to Australia. Daniel had agreed to leave two days later to coincide with Roger's stopover in Miami on his way back to the island.

A waiter, clad in a white jacket, interrupted and asked them if they wanted a drink in a thick Latin American accent. They both ordered coffee and confirmed that they would be having lunch later in the main dining room. Roger opened the file and passed several sheets of paper to Daniel. "I understand why you are not prepared to sign this document, Daniel, for all the same reasons we always discussed back on the island. However, I would like you to reconsider after you have read it through again and had time to think more about it. I believe every single word you told me."

Daniel would never have found himself in this position had Sage not received an anonymous tip a year ago suggesting Daniel had some information pertaining to the case. He suspected it was Richard Crossley who had said something to the inspector. He was the only person Daniel had told that he had been a witness to the crime, but only in the strictest of confidence. Richard denied it of course but Daniel was convinced it was him.

Ever since, Sage had phoned him once or twice a week urging him to sign a statement based on what little Daniel had revealed in Sage's initial conversation with him; this was something Daniel had so far refused to do. He would not even officially admit he had been a witness.

Richard Crossley had also revealed Brianna's name to Sage after Daniel had mentioned she had been with him that night. Sage had not pressed Brianna to testify, because at the time she had been far too frightened. Now, when he wanted to talk to her again, he found that she had already left the island and was somewhere back in Jamaica.

"But it has to stand up in court, Daniel, now even more so" Roger Sage said in a renewed attempt to convince Daniel to sign the statement. "

The victim has suddenly clammed up since making the original accusations and wants to withdraw her statement."

"What on earth?" Daniel interrupted, shocked by this new information.

"Probably for the same reason your Jamaican lady wouldn't say anything. They have either been offered money to keep quiet or physically threatened."

"Well, Brianna certainly wasn't offered any money, I can vouch for that," Daniel stated firmly. He began drumming his fingers on the coffee table, thinking carefully before he continued, "Brianna would never have remained on the island for as long as she did. She was scared witless but desperately needed the money to send back to her mum in Jamaica."

"But she has left the island now, right? That really doesn't add up, Daniel. Why would she leave after just a few months? She was probably only getting fifteen dollars an hour, if that, certainly not enough to retire to Jamaica to look after her mum. You're sure she wasn't paid off?"

"That's not possible, I would have known!"

Roger Sage noticed Daniel's barely perceptible smile.

"Ah, I see," he said, "and so the rumours are true?" Not anticipating an answer to that particular question, he followed it with another, "And I don't suppose you will tell me how to reach her in Jamaica, will you?"

"No," Daniel responded flatly.

The two sat in silence for a moment as the waiter fussed about arranging their coffee cups on small paper coasters before pouring. "The thing is, Daniel," Sage continued, "once they are all put away you and your family will be perfectly safe."

The waiter wished them both a wonderful day in broken English and departed to clear the last breakfast table and prepare it for lunch.

"But you cannot guarantee that!" Daniel countered sharply.

"That man and his son have the protection of the Foreign Office."

"That's nonsense!" Roger retorted.

"I really don't think so," Daniel responded shaking his head. "Then you really are too young to recall the Profumo scandal?" he said, without anticipating a reply. "Even back in those days, particularly those living overseas not subject to British censorship laws, were all fully aware of the FCO and Home Office cover-ups, and the involvement of certain members of the royal family."

"Meaning Philip, I assume?"

"He was one of them, yes, but it never amounted to anything in Britain other than speculation and rumour." Daniel took a mouthful of coffee and went on, "Listen, Roger, I know your intentions are good, but I can guarantee neither Lord Elm nor his useless son will ever be charged. That family has far too much money and influence." Then, emphatically, he added, "and we all know the Foreign Secretary is up to his neck in all of this! He was even there at the premier's party that night, remember? He flies around the world in their jets, stays at their homes and hotels and cruises on their luxury yachts. Do you seriously think that all comes without a price, Roger?"

Roger Sage was unable to argue with Daniel, although he tried to diminish the seriousness of the accusations by chuckling that Daniel was perhaps a conspiracy theorist. But previously veiled warnings from the Met in London (he had been seconded from the Met to investigate the corruption mess on Lucaya) had confirmed to him that Daniel's accusations were quite possibly correct. Proving it, however, was a different matter entirely. This was why Daniel's statement was utterly crucial.

Daniel was a respected engineer and highly credible. He claimed he had seen the rape with his own eyes; his testimony alone could put them both away for years. Roger Sage realized only too well that if Daniel refused to sign the statement, the rape case could fall apart before it ever reached court. He also knew there was still time to try and change his mind, as no additional charges would be laid against Walter Harrison until the corruption trial was over, which might not be until sometime in 2017 the way things were going. Perhaps he should try searching for the girl again in Jamaica? Sage appreciated that it was a long shot at best. He really needed Daniel to sign that damn statement!

After they had eaten lunch, Daniel saw the policeman off at his gate to catch the late afternoon flight to Lucaya. They had shaken hands warmly, but Inspector Roger Sage remained unconvinced that his stopover in Miami had been worth it. Though he liked him, he could detect that Daniel was procrastinating, was unable to make a decision, one way or the other. Roger had decided that tomorrow morning he would make a call to someone he knew in Kingston in the Jamaica Constabulary Force, better known as the JCF, to see if they could run another check on the whereabouts of the girl.

Daniel never mentioned to Sage that he was not returning to Australia immediately. It was none of his damn business, of course, but he wanted no one to know. Several hours later, Daniel called for room service. He ordered a salad and a bottle of wine and then watched the election coverage on CNN for a while, soon becoming bored with the predictability of it all. Who cared anyway? It certainly wasn't going to affect his life in any way if a woman became leader of the free world! He went off to sleep quickly.

He was woken shortly after two am from the flickering light of the TV he'd forgotten to turn off. The sound was down, but the crawl along the bottom of the screen was forecasting CNN's prediction that Donald J Trump would win the presidential election. Utterly insane, he thought, switching off the TV. Looking forward to tomorrow, he rolled over in the bed and went back to sleep.

CHAPTER 9

THE ATLANTIS – Nassau, Bahamas

November 9, 2016

Two of her three half-brothers were taxi drivers in the city affectionately known as Mo' Bay to the locals. He was one of them. The battered Hyundai belched blue exhaust smoke and rattled as it wove in and out of the chaotic stream of traffic towards Sangster International Airport. It was not yet eight am, but the heat of the day was already making the driver and his passenger sweat profusely.

"Mon, you need to get the air conditioning fixed," she yelled over the noise of the traffic, waving her hand in futility at the stench of pollution drifting through the taxi's open windows. She was used to the heat, but the fumes from outside were causing her eyes to sting. Worst of all, she thought, she would still be stinking of Montego Bay's traffic by the time she reached Nassau in five hours.

Beanie, as he was called, simply laughed as the car drew alongside the curb at Departures, scraping his one remaining hubcap in the process. He had to lean across to thump her passenger door open to allow her to get out with her one backpack, containing sufficient items for the two nights she would be away.

"I'll call you when I get back on Friday," she shouted over her shoulder, "An nuh kill anyone mi day crazy piece of shit!"

Beanie laughed hard and then drove off, rolling a spliff with one hand; his other was on the wheel navigating his way back to the city. Peter Tosh was blaring from the radio.

With the two-hour stopover in Kingston, it took slightly under five hours for her flight to finally land at Lynden Pindling Airport in the Bahamas. She had no checked luggage and quickly cleared Immigration. Once outside the arrivals building, she found an air-conditioned taxi to whisk her off in relative comfort to the Atlantis Paradise Island Resort that dominated the skyline of Nassau.

Facing northwest with an expansive view of the Atlantic and a seascape of Caribbean turquoise, the Atlantis appeared to be rising from the deep, a terracotta monolith comprising a variety of accommodations built around Aquaventure, a one hundred and fifty-four-acre waterscape featuring water activities for all ages. The resort also boasted one of the largest casinos in the Caribbean. Technically, the Bahamas were in the Atlantic, delineating, along with the islands of Cuba and Hispaniola, the northern reaches of the Caribbean Sea.

Brianna had seen the Atlantis from a distance when she worked in the Bahamas for about six months before moving to Lucaya. Nonetheless, she wasn't prepared for the breathtaking size of the place once the taxi had dropped her at the entrance to the lobby. Inside, she had to take a minute to stand and survey the overwhelming mix of colours and the outrageous size of everything she viewed.

Beyond reception there was a cupola as large as St Peter's in Rome. Eight ornate columns reached to a canopy of yellow scallop shells within a circular frame of several brightly coloured terrazzo panels depicting real and mythical marine life and sixteenth-century Caribbean adventurers. There were two circular stairways to the right of this cavernous reception area leading down to an amazing concave glass-screen aquarium containing a vast array of sea life, all co-existing in plain sight: half a dozen types of sharks, barracudas, manta rays, and myriads of smaller fish flashing in silver, red, yellow or blue, and schooling together in perfect choreography.

An hour later, Daniel arrived and took the elevator to the twenty-fourth floor, where he had booked a deluxe, one-bedroom suite at the Royal at Atlantis. He had fleetingly wondered about a bridge suite but recoiled in horror at the twenty-five-thousand-dollars-a-night-charge. He opted instead for a deluxe at seventeen hundred dollars a night. It was four times the cost of anywhere he had stayed before.

The flight over from Miami had taken less than an hour. He had one checked suitcase to collect, which he then deposited at the Travel & Luggage Centre, paying two days in advance before he wheeled his carry-on and computer to the curb outside to wait for a taxi. He had spent the hour on the plane carefully considering his situation and the dilemma he now found himself.

He was utterly torn as to what to do. If he signed the statement, as Sage had urged the previous afternoon, he knew he would be endangering others as well as himself. Both Inspector Sage and Richard Crossly had made it quite clear that Lord Elm and his son would stop at nothing if they felt threatened in any way. Even murder? With five billion pounds at his disposal, Geoffrey Elm could organize a massacre without a whiff of suspicion ever drifting in his direction.

On the other hand, Daniel thought, debating with himself as always whenever he had to make a difficult decision, what sort of a world would it be if people like Geoffrey Elm were allowed to behave as they wished with total impunity?

Daniel understood that if he did not sign the statement and agree to be a witness, not only would he be indirectly facilitating future abhorrent behaviour by the perpetrators; the knowledge that he had stood idly by and done nothing would torment him for the remainder of his life. He would always bitterly regret that he had only ever participated in life as an observer, never someone who had spontaneously done the right thing, someone who had made a difference without fear of consequence. It was this selfish streak and lack of commitment that had

50

created the divide between himself and Pia. She loved him, that he had always known, but he knew she would probably never really forgive him for not giving her children.

And now, he thought, he had made an impossible situation far worse by sharing himself with another. Yet he was unwilling to make a clean break by way of sincere contrition. He was most disturbed discovering that he was really no different from all those he despised, people driving their lives with relentless self-gratification. Or perhaps the real problem was that he simply loved both women equally and was terrified of hurting either.

CHAPTER 10

SOME SECRETS ARE BEST KEPT – Nassau, Bahamas

November 9, 2016

It was a huge Californian king size bed. Even so, they lay together as they had the first time on that bright sunny day three weeks after she had moved into his house from her shared shack close to the mangroves. They would have had plenty of room even in a single bed. They lay passionately embraced by the edge with a single white sheet covering them both. She was wide awake whilst he was sleeping peacefully. She could feel the steady rise and fall of his breathing.

It was comforting to have him curled beside her. So often she had slept alone and the occasions she did not she rarely recalled as being particularly pleasant. Most of the men had served only their own pleasure without the slightest consideration to her. She was merely an object of their selfish indulgences, once satiated to be cast aside like a rag doll. There was one young man she had known when she was not even eighteen who was different. He was Swedish and kind and gentle. He was a tourist from Gothenburg and a guest at a small hotel she was working at in Negril. He proclaimed his love every night for two weeks as she did to him in return. It was the first time in her life she experienced genuine feelings for someone – until at the end of his holiday he caught a plane home to Sweden and she never heard from him again.

Daniel turned and lay on his back and she followed him from the edge and placed an arm across him. She allowed her fingers to brush through the soft tangle of hair on his chest and she pulled closer and placed her head on his shoulder. She was finding it very difficult to sleep although the room was silent apart from the soft rustle of the sheer curtains disturbed by the quiet flow of centralized air conditioning. The moon illuminated the large room.

Since meeting Daniel, it had been the very best time of her life, except for one thing. Ever since she had returned to Jamaica, she had been tormenting herself always asking the same question, over and over again; should she be keeping secrets from someone she loved so much? Some Jamaican men were known to beat their wives or girlfriends once they discovered such secrets. In her own mind, though, it was perfectly natural to share love freely without the constraints imposed by society or religion. But what would Daniel think, she wondered? Would he turn his back on her and she would never hear from him again like the Swedish boy? It would all simply be too much for her to bear.

Eventually she drifted off to sleep still holding him close still undecided whether to mention Rosa. What good would it do after all, she wondered, before she began dreaming about the gentle man by her side. They were walking somewhere she did not recognize, through green fields overlooking an emerald ocean. Far below was a small fishing village with colourful boats nodding in the sunshine on the water.

The next day Brianna and Daniel were as happy as any two people could ever deserve to be. They were sitting at a small table eating breakfast in the sitting room, bathed in bright colours from the sun's reflections skipping off the deep blues of the Atlantic. There were a few palms in the foreground by the shore's edge but nothing else. They had the sliding door wide open, a gentle breeze rustling the sheer curtains. Brianna had never been this happy in her life, despite the struggle of her concerns in the night.

Daniel allowed her to finish her bowl of tropical fruits before he started to speak of things that needed saying. He could have waited until their last evening together, or had the conversation tomorrow morning. Speaking to her now, however, at least he would have all day and all night to answer her questions and to reassure her that he would not abandon her.

There was an envelope on the table; he slid it across to her. She looked at him, puzzled seeming reluctant to touch it. "Open it, Brianna," he urged as he refilled their coffee cups. She took out the slip of paper from the envelope and stared at it for a while in disbelief.

"What's this?" she asked, almost accusingly. "Is this your way of telling me I'll never see you again after tomorrow?"

Daniel could tell she was about to cry and quickly intervened to prevent her misplaced sadness. "No, not at all, Brianna! I promised you I should be back sometime next year. You know I have to return to Australia first, though. I have been away far too long, and I must see my wife." He picked up her slender hand from the table and squeezed it gently. "You must know you have turned an old man's world upside down. I have really thought of no one else since you left the island six months ago," he said, looking into her beautiful dark eyes glistening from tears yet to fall. "But now we need to talk about other matters."

The brief moment of joy when she heard he would see her next year quickly dissolved. Instead, she was becoming agitated over what he might say now. He seemed so serious. She imagined it could only portend something bad.

CHAPTER 11

A NEW LIFE
November 20, 2016

Brianna had been born in Montego Bay the same day Bob Marley had been shot in Kingston in 1976. Political violence within the country was commonplace in those days, and the two main political parties had established paramilitary groups that roamed the streets in the country's two largest cities. There had already been over one hundred people murdered in the violence Michael Manley and Edward Seaga escalated in their battle for power during the 1976 election campaign. Manley eventually won a second term as leader of the PNP.

Two days after she was born, a marauding group armed with semi-automatic rifles fired randomly at innocent people walking the streets in Montego Bay; they killed Brianna's father as he was crossing the road on his way to register his daughter's birth with the Local District Registrar. It was the responsibility of parents to register children born at home, such as Brianna. She had turned four before her mother realized her daughter's birth had not been registered with the parish, and she was naturally concerned about being fined for not following the law. Disobeying authority was a national pastime in Jamaica; it was the money she might have to pay as a fine that concerned her most. Like so many Jamaicans, she could barely feed her three children, each having different fathers who were either dead, like Brianna's, or who had quickly disappeared on learning their 'woman' was pregnant!

Brianna's mother had eventually explained her difficulty to a friend of hers next door who was also a local JP. The woman said she would take care of it and certified a Late Registration Application on January 6, 1981 indicating Brianna had been born in 1980, not in 1976. In error, she entered the four-year old's middle name on the document, omitting her first name altogether, and so Brianna was legally registered as Abigay Williams, born in Montego Bay in the Parish of St James on March 28, 1980.

She saw her own reflection in the window of the airport limousine and smiled. Her transformation was startling. She was returning to Montego Bay a sophisticated woman in a pair of suede high-heel shoes and a tailored pale blue suit, a handmade Italian handbag hanging from her shoulder. She was wheeling a partially empty Octolite red suitcase.

Not quite three days ago, Brianna had departed Jamaica wearing a pair of old jeans and a scuffed old backpack on her shoulder. Now she had on a brand-new auburn wig that even Beyoncé would be proud to wear to complement her new wardrobe. The driver saw her coming and got out quickly, taking her suitcase as he opened the back door to let her get in. Inside it smelled of new leather; the air-conditioning hummed and gentle music played from six small speakers surrounding the rear passenger seats. *Man, nuttin' like Beanie's crazy piece of shit*, she was thinking as she settled into the welcoming comfort of real leather, crossing her legs as she imagined herself as the singer Rhianna might have been when first exposed to enormous wealth. Now Brianna's own mother would have not recognised her had she been sitting beside her.

"*Weh yuh wa fi guh lady*?" The driver asked, immediately regretting speaking in dialect to such a respectable and obviously educated lady.

"Mandeville. The Victoria Bed and Breakfast Hotel, please."

She settled in for the two-hour trip to Mandeville via Sav-la-mar, where she had built her one-storey home, a raw concrete two-bedroom house on government land for which she was paying a peppercorn rent for ten years. Then the land would be deeded to her in her own name. The driver had no instructions to stop in Sav-la-mar, and so they drove on past the entrance to the housing estate in the tiny suburb of Old Bridge.

Brianna had sent a text to Beanie to tell him she had found a job in Nassau for a few months and would not be back for a while. Could he please tell her mum, and added that she would call her on Sunday? The comfort of the car and the music was making her sleepy, but she continued to think about her time with Daniel, as she had from the moment they parted in Nassau. It was hard to believe he was still in Miami waiting for his flight to Dallas Fort Worth.

She envied the ease with which Daniel could catch a flight to just about any place in the world he wanted to go. She had always wanted to visit London and Paris, but being Jamaican unless you could prove you had a substantial amount in the bank and a good job, it was extremely difficult to obtain travel visas except to obscure, third world counties like Panama or the Dominican Republic.

It was the same travelling to most other wealthy countries; they discriminated against people of the Caribbean and Central and South America to keep them from entering and working illegally. What was considered a God-given right in the EU or North America or Australia, to travel freely, was not something God had sanctioned for those living in the poorer regions of the world.

Her plan now was to find a place to live in Mandeville where no one would think of looking for her. It was not somewhere a hotel worker from Savanna-la-Mar would ever dream of living, a town in the hills accommodating mostly white folk and wealthy, retired Jamaicans or middle-class professional people working in Montego Bay with the luxury of owning a reliable car to get to and from work in comfort.

The business centre of Mandeville was a good forty-minute walk from the hotel, an easy one in jeans and sneakers, but not in the outfit she was planning to wear today for her business meeting at the bank – the same she had worn the day before. The front desk called her a taxi and she waited outside for less than five minutes before one arrived. The Victoria Bed & Breakfast Hotel was a far cry from the luxury she had experienced in Nassau at the Atlantis, but she had nonetheless been impressed when she arrived late Friday afternoon.

The taxi dropped her outside the First Caribbean Bank on Main Street. A receptionist inside asked her to sit and wait and someone would see her shortly. Five minutes later the new accounts manager introduced herself as Miss Jennie and escorted her to a small office at the back. Brianna introduced herself as Abigay Williams. She explained that she had been living in the Bahamas for the past few years until her Bahamian husband had died suddenly, six months before. He had been a lawyer with his own practice. Now she wanted to return home to Jamaica and had decided on living in Mandeville.

Taking her passport and nodding now and again as she completed the application form for a new account, Miss Jennie welcomed her to Mandeville and told her she had made an excellent choice. Port Antonio was the only other town in Jamaica she would have recommended.

Miss Jennie explained that Brianna would have to obtain a reference from her bank in Nassau to complete the account application. Brianna had anticipated this in conversation with Daniel, and he said he would deal with it if it became a problem. For now, though, it could wait and more than likely the bank would never follow up on the request. The final step in the application process was a deposit to open the account. It was then that Brianna handed Miss Jennie the twenty-five-thousand-dollar banker's draft made out in her name that Daniel had given her at the hotel in Nassau. The next day he had given her an additional two thousand dollars in cash for the new clothes they had shopped for together at the boutiques in the hotel, as well as for incidental expenses she might incur before she arrived in Mandeville.

CHAPTER 12

BACK TO EDEN
November 23, 2016

The fifty-five seat Saab was buffeted in strong crosswinds. The pilots were maintaining vigilance in the last minutes of the plane's final approach, slowly making its descent from the south to Merimbula Airport. It landed at 15:36, only six minutes later than scheduled, to the relief and applause of four American tourists who had been anxiously gripping their armrests since taking off from Sydney.

Daniel was exhausted. He had no idea how long he had been in the air, but it had seemed interminable, even discounting the lengthy stopovers in Miami and Sydney. Fortunately, he had flown business class most of the way using his Qantas points from Texas to Australia on the double-decker A380-800. Still, he had managed to sleep less than two hours on the long-haul flight.

The non-stop American Airlines flight from Nassau to Dallas had been just over three hours. Because the passengers had cleared US Customs in Nassau, there was no need to shuffle in line at Immigration in Dallas waiting to be interrogated by a surly Homeland Security official clad in a black uniform reminiscent of an official in Nazi Germany. Daniel made his connecting Qantas flight with over an hour and a half to spare.

In Merimbula, he collected his suitcase directly from the aircraft as it was off-loaded, and then he wheeled it along with his cabin bag inside the claustrophobic, arrivals terminal. It had the appearance of a large shed from the outside, with sixties décor inside. The four Americans were grumbling about having to carry their own luggage and were now engaged with one another criticizing the dated appearance of the building and the obvious lack of facilities normally available in regional airports back home.

"Worse than a bunch of whingeing Poms," Daniel muttered under his breath overhearing them.

Pia was waiting outside on the opposite side of the road under the shade of a large wattle; she immediately noticed that Daniel had lost some weight and seemed ten years younger. He looked extremely handsome, she thought, with his golden Caribbean tan.

The road was quiet, so he crossed with his luggage. They kissed and patted each other affectionately, both genuinely happy to be reunited after a nine-month separation since his last trip home. Daniel opened the back of the SUV and threw his bags in and then sat in the front next to Pia, who drove.

The following day they decided to have lunch at the Seahorse Inn. It was beautiful outside, not too hot, with a gentle breeze from the northeast. They ordered two salads and Daniel then brought a glass of merlot and a schooner of pale ale from the bar inside. They were sitting at a trestle table on the grass under the shade of a large umbrella. Further out in the bay, the grey hull of the HMAS Canberra light aircraft carrier loomed incongruously large at anchor waiting to dock at the ammunitioning facility on the south shore. There was an Anzac-Class frigate currently occupying the space, taking on missiles for the ship's MK57 system.

Pia peered at him over the rim of her wine glass as she took her first sip. He seemed quite different, she thought. Not only did he look ten years younger; he was also more youthful in manner. He was still reticent and preoccupied, as always, yet something had changed. He seemed more relaxed and less troubled; he wore the fleeting expressions of someone relieved of a heavy burden.

It was as if for the first time in their married life she could see another person rising beneath the surface of his permanent anxieties. He was undoubtedly still bothered about something, but every so often she detected sparks of what almost seemed close to genuine contentment, a singularity she had never witnessed before in a lifetime of living together.

Or was it perhaps in her imagination, and he was just simply happy to be home again?

"Are you OK, Daniel? You seem quiet."

He took a long thirsty gulp of the Pale Ale and reflected for a moment. "I am absolutely fine, Pia," he assured. "Still jet-lagged even after twelve hours of sleep. That's all," he explained. "It was an unbearably long flight. Next time I will definitely stop off someplace for the night rather than flying direct."

"You are not going back, are you?" she asked, expressing surprise. "Two years was too long to be here on my own, Daniel. I have my job at the surgery in town, yet the evenings and weekends were often very lonely. It's hard to make real friends in a place like Eden," she said, stating fact without complaint.

"The people are nice enough but rather insular; a bit like you, Daniel," she added with a wry smile. "I suppose here must suit you, or perhaps not so much now after your hectic life in the exotic Caribbean!"

Daniel nodded, reflecting for a moment. A gust of wind blew his beer coaster off the table and he bent down to pick it up from the grass. A dog off its leash suddenly came bounding to the table and started worrying Pia, nuzzling the side of her leg and trying to place its front paws in her lap. "Oh, I wish it would go away," she said, shifting her chair sideways to encourage the dog to leave. "I really don't like dogs! Their wretched owners shouldn't let them roam free at a hotel where people are eating."

Daniel expressed a look of annoyance as the dog's owner came rushing over to their table to retrieve the animal, offering a less than sincere apology.

"Apology accepted, but you should try and remember not everyone likes dogs," Daniel quietly admonished. The owner ignored the remark, and with nothing further to say, he returned to his table raising his eyebrows at his much younger Asian wife, as much as to say, "How on earth can people not like dogs?"

"I'm so sorry, my love," Daniel began to respond to her earlier question, "but I may have to fly over to England next year at some point. I should have mentioned, Richard asked me to testify as a witness at the trial involving those priests at our old school."

Pia seemed genuinely shocked. "You can't be serious, Daniel! Why on earth would you want to get involved with all that? Leave it alone! Keep it buried where it belongs, in the past!" They remained quiet as a pleasant young girl who had served them on other occasions placed their salads in front of them on the table.

"Anything else you need?" she asked, smiling.

"I'd like another beer," Daniel said, but Pia shook her head when she was asked if she wanted another wine. "No thank you, Sue."

"You promised me you weren't going to get involved with that nasty business, Daniel, and indeed why would you?" she asked when they were alone again, becoming a little agitated. "Why drag all that up again, pursuing something that has been chasing all of you since you were so young, and destroying lives in the process? Try to enjoy your retirement and forget about those creatures. Those still alive are all destined for hell along with all the other perverts." Expressing her frustration further, she said, "And please try and explain to me exactly why you would all want to spend your old age revisiting nightmares from your youth? Makes no sense, Daniel!"

In order not to concern her, he had made no mention of what he had witnessed almost a year before at the premier's party. To justify another trip overseas had required a different reason to get away for a while – to do what he had finally accepted he must in order to live with his conscience. He never had any intention of becoming involved with the legal action brought against priests at his school in England.

For once in his life, he had to do the right thing and yet at the same time, he knew he was still being less than honest; Brianna was the other reason he had not said anything to Pia, and he was having a hard time justifying it to himself.

He had finally decided to sign the witness statement, though it was not absolutely necessary to fly halfway around the world to do so. On the other hand, Inspector Sage had advised that it would be better if it were witnessed in Lucaya rather than by a JP in Australia, in case the defence team challenged the document's validity to exclude it from evidence at trial. Sage had also promised that Daniel would be reimbursed for any out-of-pocket expenses, such as his flight to the island including accommodation. And there was a strong possibility, if she agreed, that Brianna would be asked to fly over to the island as well!

They both fell silent for a while. Pia pushed her plate of half-eaten salad to one side and Daniel escaped briefly, closing his eyes to imagine he was sitting in the sun twelve thousand miles away in the Caribbean. He should never have taken that job; he realized that now. The situation was becoming untenable, and whatever decision he made would inevitably affect people who loved him. He could choose to ignore it all, yet he could never hide from the hypocrisy of accepting evil over what was the right thing to do.

He had been grappling with the dichotomy of this dilemma for over a year and it was tearing him apart. His only relief came from those moments of genuine happiness with Brianna. They were the very antithesis of the recurrent waves of terror and confusion that had accompanied him throughout most of his life, walking his fears through a Flanders Field of unexploded ordinance.

CHAPTER 13

SANTIAGO – Dominican Republic

December 2016

Oh, Jesus, effing Christ! he thought.

Michael Elm could barely contain the sudden urge to laugh out loud. He was walking up the stairs from reception when he noticed Walter Harrison. The former premier, who seemed to have put on considerable weight, was leaning over a large display case similar to those in museums stuffed with artefacts, his chubby fingers splayed on top of its protective glass.

From that distance, the idiot ex-premier, as he referred to him, seemed to be emulating some general directing his forces from an underground bunker in London or Washington. Then again, perhaps he was not such an idiot after all, Michael decided. Harrison *had* managed to secure a salary during his time in office equal to the one the president of the United States received and far exceeding the British prime minister's miserable stipend. When asked by a *Guardian* reporter once why he was paid so much, Walter Harrison replied in all seriousness that he was more deserving because he worked harder!

Striding over towards him, Michael Elm was contemplating what an ugly little bastard the former premier of the island truly was. He was still furious about having to make the long journey to meet the man in the first place. It was not the distance, but rather the time it took to fly from Belize via Miami to Santiago, the second-largest city in the Dominican Republic. He had conveniently forgotten that the trip would have been unnecessary had it not been for his egregious behaviour in the first place! Though it was true that he'd encouraged Michael, the premier had not actually participated in the heinous crime. Nevertheless, Harrison was just as responsible in the eyes of the law.

Stringent travel restrictions had been imposed on the former premier after he had fled to Brazil when he and the eight others were charged with corruption. He was convinced as any guilty man might be that he would be convicted for his crimes. The prospect of receiving a sentence of twenty years or more in some grim Victorian jail in England seemed highly probable.

Eventually, Harrison was brought back from Brazil in handcuffs under an extradition warrant issued by the British. It had taken a year of legal wrangling before he was released from Rio's notorious Ary Franco prison only to be re-arrested and charged formally by British police. Though he would never admit it to anyone, he was secretly relieved to be back in the custody of the British. Though handcuffed by the very colonial slavers he'd condemned since his initial arrest on the island, he found it a day to celebrate. Hardened criminals were often terrified at the prospect of being jailed in Ary Franco prison where so many were brutally murdered or raped by fellow prisoners. Walter Harrison had lived in fear that he would never leave the prison alive.

He arrived home in Lucaya several days later. The plane had briefly stopped in Florida where he was questioned by the FBI regarding money-laundering issues the Americans were investigating him for. In Lucaya, he was greeted by hundreds of local islanders, chanting and holding placards high comparing him to Gandhi or Mandela. One curiously suggested that he was another Martin Luther King. He was their hero, their 'Bro', and nothing like the common crook his British colonial slave masters had made him out to be.

To avoid the symbolism of slavery, the British had removed his handcuffs before the ex-premier descended the four steps from the Royal Air Force executive jet. Reminiscent of Richard Nixon's defiant final departure from the White House, he saluted his crowd of supporters with both arms raised high in the air. Then, in a theatrical gesture worthy of an African dictator, he fell to his knees on the ground and kissed the tarmac. There were thunderous cheers and applause from 'his' people, who would continue to support him even if he were to gun down the British governor in cold blood at one of the resort hotels.

Shortly after his return, the High Court ordered Walter Harrison to remain on Lucaya for the duration of the corruption trial. The one exception to the Chief Justice's ruling was the occasional trip to the Dominican Republic, a mere half-hour away by plane, where Harrison's newest wife was living. These trips, made under the escort of a burly British police officer, were essentially conjugal visits. The FCO in London and the judge were concerned about a backlash by the local populace, who still maintained that Walter Harrison was some sort of a hero.

Despite the extent of the suggested corruption, the thinking in London was to treat the nine accused with an additional element of dignity to help prevent the possibility of violence by their supporters during the lead up to the trial. The Lucayan government had already made tentative preparations in case of any disturbances.

Walter's fourth wife, Mariella, was the daughter of Francesco Salazar, President of the Dominican Republic. The President had given his guarantee to the British embassy in Santo Domingo that he would accompany ex-premier Harrison and his police escort to and from the plane, personally ensuring the conditions invoked by the court were met. It was the very least the president could do for his daughter unless he wanted to risk losing her altogether. He had already forbidden her to move to Lucaya, or to even visit her husband there. He feared his son-in-law could be planning another 'Great Escape', this time with Mariella, possibly to a country unwilling to extradite her husband to the custody of the British.

Walter Harrison saw Michael Elm coming from the corner of his eye and stood back from the display case to give him a big man-hug. Michael Elm recoiled at this public display of affection, normally the preserve of ebullient Latin men and teary-eyed Americans who seemed incapable of the emotional self-control the English had cultivated over hundreds of years.

Naturally, Michael was thinking, tin-pot politicians from the Caribbean have a habit of emulating their effervescent African American counterparts with hugs and high fives and a penchant for the theatrical. Good God, he thought, this fat goon is going to crush me to death!

"Walter, great to see you again," he said freeing himself from Walter's embrace and feigning interest in the content of the display case. It looked like a crude relief map of some WWII battle with plastic soldiers and Corgi toy military jeeps and tanks and a building in the foreground appearing to have cardboard flames leaping from the cardboard windows and roof. There were small signs pinned in various spots to the papier–mâché battleground. They'd been typed in Spanish by an ancient ribbon typewriter, and they demarked various combatants and various stages of battle and the time of day of each attack of the Hotel Matum in Santiago on December 19, 1965. That event had happened fifty-two years ago, exactly to the day.

"What's all this about, then?" Michael asked even though he could clearly understand the fading explanations.

"I believe it was one of the final battles in the two-year civil war, right here on this very spot," Walter explained authoritatively, as if he had knowledge of the incident for more than the five minutes or so that he actually had. "It was fought with the support of the US 82nd Airborne, because the Americans were shitting bricks, petrified the DR would end up another Cuba."

"I don't really know much about the history of the Dominican Republic," Michael responded with no sign of interest to continue the topic. "I do know the DR has the best-looking girls in the western hemisphere though," he added, chuckling at his own joke. "Listen, I'll just drop this off in my room and have a quick pee and be right back. I need to eat, I'm starving," he said and chased nature's call, rolling his small suitcase behind him.

They had purposely chosen the Matum, an undeserving three-star hotel in the centre of the city, because there was little chance either of the men would be recognized by anyone who mattered. The Matum was mostly frequented by tourists, but its faux fourteenth-century bedrooms also served as discreet rendezvous spots for married men and their young mistresses. There was a disco and casino at the hotel for the single men who returned from one of the many surrounding nightclubs alone, a last chance to find a warm body and sleep in the arms of a beautiful Latina.

The atmosphere was electric with anticipation of the coming Christmas festivities. It was ten-thirty pm and the restaurants and bars were lively and noisy, as was to be expected in a country where people often eat late in the evening. People of all ages were dancing to a pleasant cacophony of assorted music. They danced in congested bars or squeezed one another tightly to romantic favourites, shuffling in step between small wooden tables in restaurants. Others chose the pavement outside to move to the beat of the Merengue – young adults and middle-aged couples, happy and excited children, all born in a country with rhythm in its soul.

Michael Elm and Walter Harrison sat inside the Ahi Bar and Grill, an open-air restaurant favoured for having some of the best food in Santiago de los Caballeros. The customers were utterly absorbed by the intoxicating and jubilant Christmas holiday atmosphere.

Across the street was a park surrounding a small hill where people were ambling the steep steps to the Monumento a los Heroes de la Restauracion. It was a white edifice reaching to the night sky like an elaborate wedding cake ornament, built by the dictator Trujillo in 1944, ostensibly as a monument to peace and not a celebration of his own glory. A petite and extremely pretty black girl wearing a white halter and red miniskirt, a pink hibiscus in her short, jet-black hair, brought their meals, along with two ice-cold El Presidente beers and two frosted glasses. Michael had ordered fish with a selection of vegetables; the premier tucked into a greasy tripled-stacked hamburger and French fries.

They were sitting toward the back of the restaurant, talking quietly. Had they been overheard no one could possibly have understood that their cryptic conversation was about disposing of a man on the other side of the world.

Michael Elm and Walter Harrison were the unlikeliest pair of conspirators. One had enjoyed a privileged existence satiated with all the material things life had to offer. The other had been aggressively determined to achieve the lifestyle of the white men, whilst publicly deriding them for it in order to win the votes of his mostly ill-educated black supporters. It was his way to latch on to their inbred racism, exactly as Donald Trump had gained support in the recent presidential elections by tapping into the bias of the group Hilary Clinton had aptly named the 'deplorables'. Neither man liked the other. They had zero in common, yet each one's futures rested solely in the hands of the other; they were attached at the hip like conjoined twins.

Michael asked whether any trial date had been set. Walter looked pensive, for a moment exposing the insecurity that lay beneath his public persona. He felt like he was that small boy again running about in bare feet, always fearful of an abusive father who would beat him with anything that came to hand, even the flat of a rusty machete.

"My lawyer thinks it could start in June and possibly continue through early 2018."

"Not so good for your corruption trial but certainly good for 'us'," Elm commented. "It provides us breathing space to decide how to proceed with the previous problem we were just discussing – the engineer." Rosa De La Cruz had recognized the two men as soon as she saw them sitting at one of her assigned tables. After she had served them, she lingered to clear a table close by. She scrunched up the old paper tablecloth and replaced it with a new one that had the same map of Santiago with points of interest for tourists.

Rosa understood English perfectly. She had first picked it up working at the hotels in Puerto Plata. Then she'd moved to Lucaya for five years, first working in one of the seedy bars where local men had more than just a beer and a plate of fried conch on their minds. Two years later, she found a job at the new Ritz Carlton, where she cleaned rooms until she was promoted to cocktail waitress at one of the beach bars. This job lasted until she was unable to renew her work permit after declining to provide sexual favours to an obese local politician.

For a second time she heard Michael Elm refer to an engineer and the Jamaican, though neither by name. They also spoke of the American woman at Harrison's pool that night. Rosa was unaware exactly of what had happened but was concerned for her friend. She had never provided details of what had occurred but Rosa was aware it was something that seemed to worry her friend a great deal.

Brianna had pleaded Rosa's case unsuccessfully with Immigration at great risk to herself. Brianna could very well have ended up in precisely the same situation as she had for her efforts and been deported home to Jamaica. Rosa had never had a friend like her before.

When she arrived home after work, she called Brianna in Jamaica from her smartphone. Brianna was just drifting off to sleep until she heard the familiar ring of Messenger on her computer.

The next day Brianna took a taxi into town to send a brief email message from an internet café at one of the bars in Mandeville. The town was originally a nineteenth-century British hill station located two thousand feet above sea level. Later, it became a haven for English gentlefolk who deemed it the closest thing to home in Jamaica. It had not changed a great deal since then, except most of the English had left at the time of independence in 1963. These days the town continued to be gentrified, now instead by wealthy Jamaicans.

She ordered a coffee after she had sent the email using the special account Daniel had set up for her, *PleaseReleaseMe@yahoo.com.uk*. The message would not be traceable to her from an internet café using a computer with a different IP address. She did not quite understand this, but she did as Daniel had instructed.

CHAPTER 14

MANDEVILLE – Parish of Manchester, Jamaica

March 2017

She had rented a two-bedroom apartment on the top floor close to the Northern Caribbean University just south of Mandeville. The two identical whitewashed buildings with terracotta barrel roof tiles were two years old. They were located on a quiet street more reminiscent of a small town in Spain than Jamaica. She had remained at the Victoria B&B Hotel until just after Christmas, when a local real estate agency had informed her about the vacancy. As soon as she saw the apartment she knew it was exactly what she was looking for.

It was situated in a nice area a short walk from the town centre and it was relatively cheap for Mandeville at JA$45,000 per month. There was a good view from the third floor, looking north over Mandeville to the hills of the Manchester Plateau. Above all, it offered her complete privacy. The landlord and other tenants, whom she seldom met, assumed she was a university student known as Abigay Williams, a young woman recently widowed whose husband had been a fairly wealthy lawyer in the Bahamas. In conversation she had merely only alluded to the real estate agent that she was thinking of enrolling at the university. Jamaicans thrive on gossip, particularly if the subject is a glamorous and apparently wealthy widow, and so it was not long before the agent had convinced himself and the other occupants of the building that she was already a graduate student.

Brianna was playing her new role to perfection, some days even believing her fictional biography. The few who knew her in Mandeville would never have imagined she had come from an impoverished neighbourhood in Montego Bay and had never completed high school.

She had possessed the intelligence to continue her education, but her mother lacked the money to pay her school fees. And she had been needed at home to help raise her siblings and start bringing in money to support them all.

First, she worked with her mother as a seamstress, undertaking small sewing jobs for neighbours who could afford to pay them. There were times when they had no money at all and Brianna had to go to the markets to beg for spoiled fruit and vegetables to supplement the little they grew at home, some yam and ackee from the tree outside the window of the bedroom she shared with her younger sisters.

The children's three separate fathers had all disappeared, each one when they discovered their mother was pregnant. Jamaican men often left their families with no financial support and their children with no father. It was a never-ending cycle of abandonment in a society where young boys had little positive male influence in their lives.

As was the lot in life of so many Jamaican women, Brianna and her mother had had to feed and clothe everyone in the family. Eventually the financial situation became so dire that Brianna was forced to leave Jamaica to find work, first in the Bahamas and then in Lucaya. She had religiously sent half of her earnings home to her mother via Money-Gram each week, retaining just enough to pay her rent and cover her basic needs. Brianna was now able to send her mother four times as much each week, by direct transfer from the First Caribbean Bank in town to her mother's account in Montego Bay. Her mother never checked her statements and so never noticed the payments had been made from Mandeville.

Daniel had given Brianna a substantial amount of money, but her only other major expense was the purchase of a brand-new Apple Mac Air. She had never owned a computer before, but it was easy to get the hang of once she realized it operated much the same way as her iPhone, which was an older model and now unreliable.

Daniel had suggested she would need a computer to exchange emails with him, and perhaps keep her occupied if she was not working. It allowed Brianna to travel as far away as Australia and visit the town where he lived. She had Googled his address and was able to see his house from a satellite, miles above the earth. She could even make out someone at the back of the house and wondered if it was his wife. She thought she would like to meet his wife one day. Daniel never spoke ill of her and she admired him for that, but not nearly as much as she loved him.

When Rosa had called a few weeks before Christmas, concerning the conversation she had overheard between Michael Elm and Walter Harrison, Brianna's immediate reaction had been one of terror. She had remained in her room at the hotel for much of the following two weeks, until she moved into her new apartment on January 2, only venturing outdoors occasionally to go to the shops and check out places to rent.

She exchanged email messages with Daniel, who was horrified to read that the men had, indirectly, actually alluded to getting rid of them both. He did not express his concern to Brianna; he had always considered it a possibility and had implied as much to her when they were on the island. But now Rosa's telephone call had made it all too real, and yet he knew he had to remain calm for Brianna's sake. She was alone with no one to turn to except someone twelve thousand miles away. She had only just started to venture out more frequently after she moved from the hotel and he did not want to alarm her unduly: locked in her apartment and terrified was not an option.

At first, she couldn't imagine how her new computer could also be a source of income, but soon she would spend hours browsing in the local market for things to buy and resell on eBay. As Daniel had noticed, she possessed a brilliant fashion sense. She was capable of coordinating styles and colours in a way that would have propelled her into a totally different world had she ever been encouraged.

Had she ever had the opportunities, Daniel had told her, she might very well have been a fashion model or be working for a designer scouting the latest fashion trends in Paris or New York. Lacking the innate self-confidence of someone with experience and education beyond the mind-numbing daily routine of working in a bar or cleaning hotel rooms, Brianna was not so certain. If this was what Daniel truly believed, however, then she would try hard to believe it as well, for she trusted him as no other.

She loved what she was doing and was excited to watch her little online business start to grow. Most days she walked to the post office with one or two packages to mail to the United States, England and even as far away as New Zealand. As the days passed, she thought less and less of what had occurred on the island and began to feel confident again, without looking over her shoulder for someone who might never appear. Every Sunday she would phone her mother in Montego Bay from her computer using Express VPN to disguise her location, as Daniel had advised. She did not think this entirely necessary and occasionally forgot. She would chat for hours with her mother and her sisters, but she never once mentioned that she was living less than a hundred miles away in the same country. They all thought she was working at the Atlantis in the Bahamas.

Back in December, she had been frightened by Rosa's call. By March, nothing bad had happened, and she was positive that it never would. Life had never been better for her, especially today, after receiving an email from Daniel saying he hoped to see her again soon on his way over to London in August.

CHAPTER 15

GROSVENOR HOUSE HOTEL – London
February 2017

Guests invited to the birthday banquet had to struggle to squeeze through the scrum to enter the hotel. This unruly mob of paparazzi was jostling for advantage in their usual way, shoving and elbowing each other whenever another luxury car drew up to the front entrance, regardless of who was inside. Each was desperate to get the photo to make the front pages of the following day's editions around the world.

A haggard Mick Jagger, clinging to some dark-skinned, glamorous woman in a stunning Stella McCartney original, had arrived ten minutes earlier in a Bentley. Sir Mick was followed by the Foreign Secretary in a black chauffeured BMW, beaming idiotically, as if he had no idea that he was one of Britain's least popular politicians. A black Range Rover drove almost sedately into the hotel through the open wrought-iron gates. Only inches behind it was an armour-plated Jaguar XJ Sentinel. A second black Range Rover was almost touching the rear bumper of the Jaguar.

Two ex-army RaSP security officers exited the first Range Rover and walked slowly by the side of the Jaguar as it drew up to the entrance of the hotel. Then two more emerged from the one behind and bullied their way through the maelstrom of photojournalists, pushing them back to leave a clear path for the prime minister to enter unimpeded. As she exited the car, additional security personnel linked arms with the PM, leaving their other hand free ready to draw a firearm concealed beneath their jacket at a second's notice. Inside the hotel a band of the Coldstream Guards in full military dress struck up a brassy rendition of *Happy Birthday to You,* in practice for the pending arrival of the guest of honour, Lord Elm, just as the prime minister strode through the main lobby doors with her bodyguards.

The vast majority of guests were entering the Banquet Great Room from the entrance on Park Lane, with the main lobby entrance now cordoned off to the public for the arrival of the PM. Prince Harry, whose mother, Princess Diana, had been a friend of Lord Elm's, was due to arrive a quarter of an hour later. The Rolling Stones' lead singer had been ushered in the same entrance. He was, a few years short of eighty, perhaps considered almost royalty these days. Back in the sixties he would have been dragged out by a team of burly police officers had he come within a mile of such an event.

Geoffrey Elm was sitting with his son Michael, one on each of the two sofas in a Premium Executive Suite. A log fire danced in a hearth framed by marble. There was a white mantle with an antique clock warning that they only had half an hour before the Foreign Secretary would announce his arrival and Michael Bublé, accompanied by a small orchestra, would start singing Sinatra's, *My Way* to the applause of the five hundred guests. They were all there to celebrate the billionaire's seventy-fifth birthday. Many in the Great Room beneath the massive chandeliers privately wished it would be his last!

"Simply because the Foreign Secretary believes the trial will drag on well into next year, changes absolutely nothing, Michael!" Geoffrey Elm scowled at his son, exasperated by his lackadaisical attitude. Michael was seemingly unable to grasp the nuances of a situation that could result in financial ruin for the family, with the real possibility that one or both of them would spend time at the discretion of Her Majesty in one of her Victorian facilities. It wouldn't be Brixton or Wormworth Scrubs at least – not unless other secrets were to emerge. Nevertheless, five years or so in an open prison would be the end of his business empire and political aspirations. Lord Archer had survived his ordeal and made money from his years in prison. Sadly, for him, Lord Elm did not have the advantage of being much of a writer.

On the other hand, Michael might spend the better part of his life in a real prison, not at some country club retreat where they would send his father!

"All the money in the world will not save you from this if it all falls apart!" Geoffrey Elm warned him. "And at the moment there are too many possibilities that it might!"

Lord Elm was deeply troubled. Despite the delays in the corruption trial, sooner or later the press would catch wind of a possible criminal indictment against his son and the former premier of Lucaya. Yes, there had been bribes and money laundering; he had been through all this nonsense before. Threats of lawsuits and cash payments to keep people quiet had always worked in the past. But they wouldn't if criminal charges were brought against Michael. A voracious media would keep digging for dirt, magnifying each revelation within the public domain, subjecting every aspect of his personal and business life over the past forty years to the full scrutiny of the law. He would lose everything, including his peerage.

"Sometimes, Michael, I feel I made a huge mistake anointing you as my successor rather than Matthew. For once in my life, I allowed my emotions to override common sense because of my dislike for his mother!"

"What the fuck do you mean, Dad, what the fuck do you mean?" Michael was furious with his father for suggesting his older brother would have been better at his job. "What does he know about anything, grovelling at everyone's feet just to be liked. He doesn't understand anything about business, the little jerk!"

"Perhaps he doesn't, Michael, but I know he would never have created this untenable situation we find ourselves, thanks to you and that black bastard!"

Michael was taken aback for a moment surprised by his father's racial slur. "Now, shut up for once in your life," his less than doting father commanded. "Listen carefully and perhaps the gravity of 'our' situation might just sink into that dim-witted brain of yours." Then Lord Elm began explaining to his son that the so-called 'black bastard', Walter Harrison, posed far more of a threat than the Australian engineer.

"Before you had the insane idea of meeting up with Harrison in the Dominican Republic, I was reliably informed by my contact at the Met that Daniel Hannaford is ready to sign a statement incriminating both you and Harrison in a very serious crime, punishable under island law by a minimum of ten years in jail."

"But Dad.....!"

"Don't you fucking interrupt me when I am speaking!" Michael had had quite enough; he stood to leave.

"SIT DOWN, you little shit!"

Michael did exactly as he was told, acutely aware of his father's wrath when pushed too far. Geoffrey continued: "If Walter Harrison and his merry gang are convicted, which they almost certainly will be, Harrison will try for a plea deal prior to sentencing. He'll give them everything he has, which is plenty. He'll not only turn on you, suggesting you were the primary instigator, which you were; he'll dump everything else he's been hoarding about me, the Foreign Secretary and other Tory MPs who have jumped aboard my bandwagon over the years. Eventually it will bring down the government and leave the Tories out of office for a decade, or even longer." He paused for a moment, looking directly into his son's eyes. "Walter Harrison is a much bigger threat to us than Daniel Hannaford. Yes, Hannaford can cause us problems down the road too, but first things first. Anyway, all we have to do is intimidate his wife and family. He'll never testify and can always recant his statement."

"Your Royal Highness, Prime Minister, distinguished guests, ladies and gentlemen," the Foreign Secretary announced, now standing next to the assembled band of the Coldstream Guards at the top of the stairs. A bugle blast had shocked everyone into silence with several bars of the

Reveille. "I give you our guest of honour, the First Earl of Holt, the Rt Honourable Lord Geoffrey Elm KBE."

Right on cue, the band began playing the happy birthday song, as Lord Geoffrey Elm slowly descended the imperial staircase into the grand ballroom, waving to the crowd of well-wishers. Five hundred celebrity guests at fifty circular banquet tables stood to applaud someone who had done very little to help his fellow man, rather than bask in the adoration of people who respected only his money.

He was ushered to his chair at the centre of an oblong table placed on a dais facing his guests. There was a microphone directly in front of him. He stood there smiling and waving as the other distinguished guests filed in from both sides of the table, including Prince Harry, the British Prime Minister, the British Foreign Secretary and the US Ambassador, all crucial to his political aspirations once he had successfully contested a safe seat in the next by-election.

Michael Bublé came to the dais, shook Lord Elm's hand and wished him a happy birthday; then he took the microphone and began singing several selected verses of the song 'My Way'.

I've lived a life that's full
I've travelled each and every highway
And more, much more than this
I did it my way

"Damn you, I'll show you, Father," Michael thought, as he departed the ballroom. The crooner continued to the second verse and Lord Elm's eyes glistened with emotion. "Now I will start to do things, *my way!*"

His father was too caught up in his celebrations to notice the empty seat at the end of the table. Michael Elm had left the hotel and was on his way to the Palm Beach Casino in Mayfair. There was someone there who just might be able to help.

CHAPTER 16

RED LION TAVERN – London

February 2017

Turning up the collar of his old parka, Inspector Roger Sage walked briskly along the Embankment opposite Westminster Pier. It was a slate grey day with the temperature hovering slightly above freezing as an icy wind gusted over the muddy flow of the Thames. He turned right up Derby Gate and walked to Parliament Street and the Red Lion. It was built on the site of a medieval tavern called the Hopping Hall, which had stood there almost six hundred years before. In the summertime, baskets of flowers and Union flags would hang outside, adding an array of cheerful colours above the gold embossed name of the pub. The flowers were all absent now.

Sage would have remained on Lucaya given half the chance. Unfortunately, a wife and two young children living in Highgate had precluded that idea, especially as he had been unable to return for Christmas due to the pressures of the impending trial. So, instead of enjoying long walks on Caribbean beaches he'd found himself back in London, marooned on a sofa with twin pre-schoolers, a boy and a girl, both noisily competing for his attention. Perhaps his harassed wife would be in the kitchen, frantically attempting to avoid burning her usual English stodge while he remained longing for tender island lobster or the fresh grouper that he was accustomed to on Lucaya.

Inspector Sage found immediate relief from the cold as he stepped inside the pub that had served Charles Dickens and had seen many prime ministers at the bar until the 1970s. By that time, the public had begun to frown on the excessive drinking habits of their politicians.

It was three-thirty and the bar was almost deserted, apart from some regulars who worked at the Ministry of Defence located just beyond New Scotland Yard. He passed photos and portraits of politicians adorning the walls. A bust of Churchill in RAF uniform sat on a plinth in a corner recess. In a back room he noticed the man from the Foreign Office sitting at a table for two beneath a large glass mirror with Fuller, Smith and Turner digitally printed on it. He had met him on one previous occasion on the island.

"Thanks for coming, Roger," Bryce said without standing or shaking Roger's hand. "Something has come up, I'm afraid!" Roger sat down and noticed there was a glass of what looked like whisky in front of him. "I thought you might like that to warm yourself up a little before we get started. Do hope a single malt will do the trick?" Roger nodded and thanked him.

They declined menus but ordered two more whiskies, after which Bryce took out a folded sheet of newspaper from one of the pockets of his Barbour Corbridge jacket. Overweight and in his early sixties, Bryce looked ridiculous in a fitted jacket intended for a fashionable and much younger man.

On the table he lay flat the front page of the late morning edition of the *Evening Standard*; on it was a photo of two men. Roger recognized Michael Elm and Richard Wagner, the latter with a look of surprise on his face, as though realizing his photo had just been taken. Michael Elm appeared intoxicated. His arm lolled over the shoulders of a topless girl sitting in some nightclub, and two empty bottles of champagne sat on the table.

"Taken in the Platinum Gentlemen's Club in the wee hours this morning," Bryce explained. "Given the Foreign Secretary's close relationship with his father, we are concerned why Michael Elm would be keeping company with someone well known to the police."

Bryce explained that there had been a seventy-fifth birthday bash the previous evening for Lord Elm at the Grosvenor. Michael Elm had left abruptly as his father was making a speech to his guests, including Prince Harry and a host of celebrities. Bryce mentioned that Mick Jagger later performed 'Sympathy for the Devil', although the irony of the words of the song was completely lost on the peer. Two of his lordship's security men had followed Michael, first to Mayfair to the Palm Beach Casino, where he apparently had remained in conversation with Mr. Wagner for a couple of hours before the pair moved on to the Soho strip club.

"You see, Roger, we all know Michael is an impulsive young man and how his father dotes on him. What we need is for someone to have a quiet word and rein him in. The last thing the prime minister needs right now is yet another scandal before the Brexit negotiations start next month."

Roger smiled to himself. The prime minister could probably not care less about Lord Elm and his son; most likely she had nothing to do with instigating this meeting. And there was no way he intended to have a 'quiet word and reign him' as Bryce was suggesting. It would compromise everything!

The animosity the PM and Lord Elm had shared towards one another over the years was legendary, and Roger was convinced the PM would be at the forefront of those cheering to bring Elm down for good and all. It was an open secret that Geoffrey Elm was considering running for the vacant seat of the Harrogate and Knaresborough constituency in North Yorkshire. If he won, he would likely challenge the PM for the leadership of the Tory Party.

Roger was guessing Elm had been on the phone first thing this morning to the Foreign Secretary to discuss the impact of the photo. Wagner had long been suspected of being involved in the murder of a celebrity journalist in 2013 in broad daylight on the steps of her own home. It remained unsolved almost four years later. Though nothing could be proven, the police were convinced she had been silenced because of stories she had been reporting about the flow of illegal drugs into Britain.

Roger nevertheless assured Bryce he would look into the matter after the latter mentioned he had discussed it over the telephone with the commissioner herself a few hours earlier. Roger, he explained, had been recommended because of his background knowledge of the Elm family and his investigations into Geoffrey Elm's involvement in the corruption scandal on Lucaya.

It was snowing as he walked back to New Scotland Yard, and Roger was busily digesting the task given to him by the man from the FCO. Yes, he would make some very discreet inquiries. Depending on what he unearthed, he would have to tread extremely carefully as the last thing he wanted was to prejudice the corruption trial in any way.

He seriously doubted anyone other than a few senior police officers on Lucaya, himself included, knew anything about the incident involving Michael Elm and former premier Walter Harrison. It had been purposely kept quiet because of the possibility it might derail the corruption trial. Far too much money and effort had been spent bringing it to court to allow that to happen. Only he and the chief prosecutor on the island were aware that criminal charges would eventually be levelled against Michael Elm and Walter Harrison – but only if Daniel Hannaford signed a statement. If not, they had to either find the Jamaican girl or persuade the victim to change her mind. Otherwise, the CPS would have no substantiating evidence to take to trial.

He finally decided to phone the commissioner once he returned to the office to recommend the police ignore what essentially was a political matter instigated by the Foreign Secretary. The police focus should only be on the criminal activities involving the father and son. Nothing, not even the Foreign Secretary and the FCO should compromise that.

Roger would have given anything to be walking Coral Bay beach right now rather than watching the snow swirl outside his office, dreading the journey home in the cold to Highgate on the underground later that evening. Hopefully they would all be in bed by then and he could enjoy a whisky on his own while catching up on the BBC News.

CHAPTER 17

UNCHARTERED ISLAND
September 1851

*O*n setting sail from San Francisco, the Wanderer took the direct south-
erly route for the Solomon Islands; the slower Ariel had departed al
most a month earlier, sailing due west. The Ariel was a one-hundred and
twenty-ton schooner purchased in San Francisco that served as a tender
for the Wanderer. She had on board a large stock of goods, including toma-
hawks, pocketknives, mirrors, paste jewellery, fancy necklets and a number
of other items worthy of bartering with the uncivilized South Sea island
natives. It was the intention of the English sailors to exchange these trinkets
for such supplies as wild pigs, fruit, cocoa and a wide variety of other foods
to sustain the crews of the two ships as they established the first settlements.

It was Boyd's ambitious plan to develop a South Seas Republic of the
fertile group of islands, appointing himself as president.

Captain Bradley of the Ariel took a course well north of the Solomons,
for he had been instructed to rendezvous with an American brigantine at
a deserted and unchartered atoll in the mid-Pacific. It would officially be
discovered in 1856 as the Midway Atoll and claimed by the United States.
In 1851 the atoll was known only from a handful of unreported chance
discoveries by ships of commerce that had anchored there to replenish water supplies and look for fresh food to supplement the usual meagre diet of
hardtack biscuits, often infested with weevil maggots. The coral reef surrounding the atoll produced an abundance of marine life, with over two

hundred species of fish and sea turtles. There were millions of wild birds, including albatrosses. Those who dismissed suspicions generated by Coleridge's poem of the Ancient Mariner soon discovered the large birds made an extremely tasty stew. Captain Bradley was under orders to investigate stories of an abundance of guano on the island. If they turned out to be correct, he was then to determine if there were sufficient quantities to mine for export to the Solomon Islands for use as agricultural fertilizer. It would take the Ariel about eight weeks to reach Midway from San Francisco and possibly another seven to then sail south to the Solomons, weather conditions permitting. Allowing for the extra month, the Ariel and the Wanderer could conceivably arrive at Guadalcanal within days of each other.

Mark Boyd had remained in seclusion ever since he'd secretly boarded the Ariel in San Francisco. Only Bradley and one trusted crew member, Aaron, knew that one of the owners was on board. Aaron brought Boyd food and drink and supplied him each day with soap and water. Aaron had previously been in the employ of the Boyd estate in Scotland and was considered almost family. Mark Boyd had his own private toilet in his cabin with a view down it to the ocean below.

He had passed the hours poring over reams of barely decipherable notes and columns of meaningless figures in his brother's hand in an attempt to understand where all the money had gone. The more he tried to untangle the weave of Benjamin's financial history from the time he had set forth from Portsmouth ten years before, the more he realized that his brother would most certainly be committed for trial for fraud. It was impossible to calculate exactly how much of the money he had used for his personal financial ventures, but it was significant. As much as two hundred thousand pounds of expenditures, by way of personal bank loans to himself as managing director of the Royal Bank of Australia, had not been reported to the bank's directors back in London.

Among other things, Benjamin had used the money to develop Boyd-town, becoming the largest shipowner in Australia in the process. He also became the largest landowner and grazier in New South Wales, with over two hundred thousand head of sheep. All this had been accomplished in *the first four years after his arrival in the colony. Mark knew with abso-lute certainty that his brother could never have achieved any of it without the bank as his well of fortune. No one would ever know that Benjamin had purchased several properties on his meandering voyage to Australia, spending over sixty thousand pounds. The handsome profit he made af-ter selling these properties, the equivalent of ten thousand pounds, he had deposited, along with the principal, at an extremely favourable rate in the Massachusetts Bank in Boston, the second oldest in the country. Its origi-nal charter had been signed by none other than John Hancock, and Mark knew the money would be safe there and readily accessible when required.*

Mark was woken early in the morning by the rattle of the anchor chain. He knew they were in shallow water because the anchor took no time at all to settle on the ocean bed. It was soon holding the schooner in position, yet not quite motionless, as the ship creaked, slowly turning with the drift of the currents. He peeked through the small porthole that had been his only window to the outside world for the past two months, other than the view from the 'head' to the sea below when he was urinating.

The sun was just rising, casting an orange glow across two or three small islands. They appeared to be quite flat, with just a handful of tropi-cal palms scattered randomly in a lunarscape of low-growing vegetation. Almost immediately, deafening trills overloaded his sense of hearing, until he had to place his hands over his ears. Even this did not block out the cacophony of noise made by millions of birds nesting on land or circling above the sheltered islands protected in the coral shallows. Then he began to see the shape of a coral reef, as small waves outlined it like a pearl neck-lace strung around a slender turquoise neck.

He had seen albatrosses now and then at sea, including a pair that perched in the upper riggings of a ship, resting in mid-ocean until their massive wings would carry them on the remainder of their flight. But nev-er before had he witnessed – nor indeed had he ever imagined – the sheer numbers of birds gathered in such a small area. There were over two mil-lion albatrosses, either swirling effortlessly above the island and the Ariel or protecting a million nests on shore. Three million birds of different species added to the tumultuous cascade of birdcalls emanating from every direction of the compass. Mark was unaware that many of the larger birds were already roosting in the ship's riggings, cursed by the crew splattered by their droppings. Captain Bradley had no real need to go ashore to know there would be sufficient guano to export to the Solomons, if not to England itself!

He could see the two-masted American brigantine with sails furled on the other side of the atoll. There were no flags flying to indicate her nationality, and the crew of the mystery ship had draped part of an old sail over the stern to ensure that no one on the British ship would ever know its name. Only Captain Bradley and Mark Boyd knew it was the Pacific Pearl. The crew above-deck was too busy avoiding the bird droppings to give much attention to the larger ship at anchor. One sailor on the Ariel warned it could be pirates, who still roamed the oceans in the 1850s, but the idea was quickly dismissed and the presence of the ship forgotten.

Leaving Aaron on watch late that night as the rest of the crew slept, Mark Boyd and Captain Bradley descended quietly down the Jacob's ladder to the wooden dinghy that Bradley had ordered lowered from its davits shortly after they'd arrived at the atoll. The dinghy was spattered with bird droppings, but the birds' chorus was silent for the night. Some roosted on their nests, asleep with one eye open, alert for any indication of danger. Millions of other birds roosted on the ground or in the shallows protected by the reef. Earlier that evening Aaron had loaded the dingy with two saddlebags, one containing some of Benjamin Boyd's accounts and five hundred dollars in cash.

It took them a little over an hour to row over to the Pacific Pearl on the outer edge of the reef. It was just after one am when the dingy finally nudged alongside the brigantine.

"Captain Bradley?" an American with a southern drawl called out above. "Careful climbing up! Don't want to lose either of you!"

CHAPTER 18

BOYDTOWN BEACH

May 2017

She looked down at the sand and saw a decaying blue bottle jellyfish that was caught in a tangle of seaweed swarming with kelp flies. She hurried by, keeping her mouth firmly closed, batting in futility at the buzzing cloud with both hands as they attempted invasions of her eyes, ears and nostrils.

Scurrying by almost blindly, she left them behind except for a few momentary followers and continued untroubled, splashing through the water in bare feet towards her 'thinking' spot.

Pia sat down on her special flat rock. For a while she looked over at a fisherman in his small boat. He was checking the mussel ropes attached to a row of buoys that bobbed in an increasing swell fifty metres offshore. Beyond them, a dark gathering of clouds was forming to the north, hopefully bringing some relief to the long drought in this region of New South Wales.

She loved this end of Boydtown Beach. It was sacred to the local Aboriginal people, a place in their history of thousands of years where the relationship between the orca and man was born. The beach was a seven-kilometre stretch of powdery white sand that rivalled any in tropical Queensland or the Caribbean. Not being in the tropics, the colour and temperature of the water were different. Apart from the surrounding shallows and the Nullaca river estuary, the waters of Twofold Bay were quite cold year-round and had a hue of silver grey.

She could just make out the white corrugated roof of their house halfway up a steep hillside on the opposite shore of the bay, slightly west of the town of Eden. The view from their Queenslander home to the opposite shore, where she was sitting now, would have changed little since Benjamin Boyd arrived in the region in 1842. The one notable exception was the addition of the Seahorse Inn built in 1843 and named after one of the steamers that had sailed with him from Portsmouth.

She began thinking about Daniel. He was by nature a quiet man and often preoccupied with some worry or other. It had been the same since they had met, even the torment he seemed to go through deciding whether to get married. It was understandable, she supposed. They were both in their early twenties then. Now, in hindsight, she thought he was perhaps too young at the time, having experienced very little of life. Later in their marriage, however, she came to realize how difficult it really was for him to express his true feelings, possibly influenced by a terrible childhood he rarely spoke about. Slowly, over the years, she began to accept the idea that he loved her in a different sort of way. He was a kind and gentle man, attributes perhaps many women would happily accept as crucial concepts for love. Even so, nothing could ever compensate her or temper her secret sadness for what was missing from her own life. She could not help thinking of how he had changed since he returned from the island late the previous year. These days he was more attentive and far more thoughtful, at least when his mind was not elsewhere.

Her thoughts started drifting and she began reflecting on the story of the scoundrel Benjamin Boyd, entertaining in her imagination how things might have been in this place almost two centuries ago. There were of course many more houses now on the opposite side of the bay. The town of Eden had grown from a mere two hundred inhabitants in 1843 to close to four thousand by 2017. Not such a huge increase in population, she supposed.

From the town of Eden across the bay it was possible to see the caravan and trailer park further north from the Seahorse Inn, which she considered an ugly blot on the landscape. It was situated on private land that had been part of the original Boyd landholdings. Had money exchanged hands for council permission to create such an obvious assault within a scenic national park? Pia didn't realize that no such approval was ever needed. It had been this way since Boyd began development of the area almost two centuries ago, when he had to provide shelter for the labourers and their families. The only difference was that the past's ragged tents had become expensive camper vans.

It had begun sprinkling with rain from the approaching dark clouds and she decided to head back to the car parked at the inn. Mount Imlay was already shrouded by the storm. The tide was out and the sand was firm, allowing her to walk quickly. Hopefully she would reach the car before she was drenched.

Suddenly, Pia was violently knocked forward from behind! She landed on the hard sand face down, and then something began pounding on her back.

The slow and menacing growl and the steamy hot breath on her neck suddenly registered in her brain. A state of terror and panic took hold and her heart raced to bursting. She could literally taste the bile of fear. She covered her head instinctively to protect herself from a vicious dog. Pia had no idea that it was a pit-bull terrier, seemingly ravenous to tear her throat into bloody shreds.

The man came from the bush and walked slowly towards her and then motioned to the dog as if it had been anticipating the signal. "You should be more careful, Mrs. Hannaford," were the only words the Englishman spoke before he turned and headed back towards the bush skirting the beach. The snarling dog seemed reluctant to leave Pia, until it finally scrambled off, following the man close at his heels.

CHAPTER 19

BOYDTOWN DREAM – Sapphire Coast NSW

May 2017

*P*ia was sitting with her legs stretched flat on the sand and her back supported against a log that had drifted ashore from across the bay. A large swath of trees was being felled on the other side of the bay for building material now the official survey had been completed. At long last, the government of New South Wales was auctioning off various plots of land to establish the township of Eden where ships already docked in safety in its deep-water harbour.

Named less than ten years earlier after Lord Eden, the British Secretary for the colonies, the settlement had consisted of just one dwelling. It was only forty-four years since Lieutenant Matthew Flinders of the Royal Navy had made his first encounter in 1798 with a group of Kooris, or 'people' in the indigenous languages of New South Wales and Victoria.

He had first come across several women and children who quickly ran off in fear on first sight of this Gubba, or white man, accompanied by five other white men carrying long sticks they had seen firing white smoke. It was at least an hour before a single male from the same tribe, the Katungal or 'Sea Coast People', cautiously appeared from the bush as if from nowhere, garbed only in a loincloth and holding a long spear.

It was a friendly enough first meeting, marred only by the unusually tall Koori spitting out a piece of whale meat in disgust, and then again when he attempted to eat a hardtack biscuit. This food from the ship's crew *had been intended as peaceful offerings. Much to the relief of Flinders, no hostility ensued after the Koori found the Gubba's food so unpalatable.*

It was odd, Pia recalled thinking. Flinders' ship, the HMS Norfolk, had suddenly vanished, and she found herself decades later with the Wanderer lying offshore at anchor with furled sails and the crew busily swabbing the decks. Benjamin Boyd stood aft watching the longboat as it was lowered into the water along with four oarsmen standing with their oars pointed towards the sky. Then a group of as many as forty very dark-skinned men, almost naked and shivering uncontrollably from the cold wind from the south, were being urged angrily by the crew to clamber down rope ladders to the longboat in the water below.

It was winter, and sluggish dark clouds were preparing to scatter hail like lead shot over the grey slate of Twofold Bay. Two of the Micronesian natives fell into the frigid water. One drowned and was taken on the outgoing tide with little concern from the white crew. The other was pulled aboard the longboat and died from exposure an hour after reaching shore. It took time to enforce the Slavery Abolition Act passed in the British parliament in 1833. Yet nearly fifteen years later, there remained unscrupulous Englishmen and adventurers like Benjamin Boyd attempting to circumvent the law, a practice called blackbirding, and one very much frowned upon by most people in the colony.

Not that the Pacific islanders had been snatched from tropical islands against their will. They were at first eager to go, enticed with promises of good money to support their families as wealthy men on returning home. On the contrary, many of these island people setting sail for the big land far to the south never saw their families again, nor their tropical paradise set in a turquoise sea. They were cursed and threatened by their employer and barely clothed in the freezing cold winters as they built Boydtown, the larger of the two communities facing each other on the twin shores of Twofold Bay. Boydtown was being purpose-built to support the whalers and whaling stations. It would be supplied by vessels carrying materials from Sydney and England that docked in the safe deep-water harbour of Eden. Later they would return to their home ports packed to the gunwales with bales of wool and barrels of whale tallow …

Pia sat up with a start in her bed. For a moment she was back on the beach where she had lain for what seemed like an eternity, too terrified to move. It was five-thirty am and still dark outside. She found herself pondering the same question that had kept her awake last night: how could a man she'd never seen before know her name? He'd called his dog and given that warning as he stood over her, "You should be more careful, Mrs. Hannaford."

The brief snatches of sleep she had managed last night were disturbing, vignettes of the past she did not understand, sitting in the same spot where less than twelve hours before she thought she was going to die in such a horrific manner. Even now in the quiet of her bed, the terror of it all still consumed her.

She had called Daniel on her mobile from the car parked outside the hotel. Unable to comprehend her screaming bursts of distress, he hung up and ran down the stairs as fast as any sixty-four-year-old possibly could, attempting as he went to quell a rising tide of panic. He couldn't make out what exactly had happened. He only knew that it had to be something unimaginably dreadful to have ignited such terror in his wife. He slammed on the brakes at the end of the gravel drive, narrowly avoiding flying into a gully on the other side of the narrow concrete road. He speeded up a steep hill towards the Princes Highway. Driving far in excess of the speed limit, Daniel navigated the country's main highway and a particularly dangerous section of road snaking through Boydtown National Park in less than ten minutes.

When he reached the car park of the Seahorse Inn, he drew alongside Pia's slate blue Mini Countryman. He could see her inside with her head bowed as another deluge of rain began drumming on the roof of his SUV. Paying it no heed, he scrambled to open the passenger door of the Mini and found Pia trembling and soaked to the skin. Her face was wet with tears and rainwater still slowly coursed down her cheeks in rivulets from her wet hair.

She never said a word on the way home in the Countryman. She was simply too distraught. Daniel was too distressed to say much either. What he could gather from her ramblings convinced him that their lives were in peril, something he had feared might happen. They were coming and they wanted him to know!

Daniel failed to notice the man and his dog standing by a tree immediately past the entrance to the hotel. He was wearing a large-brimmed Akubra to protect him from the lashing downpour. Smiling to himself, the man tugged sharply on the dog's lead and continued walking, taking a shortcut over the hill where the ruin of Boyd's church was still standing amongst the trees. No one saw them as they headed down the other side of the hill to the campsite adjacent to the hotel. It was still raining heavily, and the wind had picked up and it was getting colder. It was midweek; the season was coming to an end and the campsite was almost deserted.

The day before he had set up a *snugpak,* an all-weather tent equipped with a special-forces sleeping bag. There was sufficient room for himself and his canine travelling companion, which had cost him a small fortune on arrival in Sydney. It had been well trained as a guard dog, and the man quickly confirmed that it was an extremely loyal and obedient animal. The man opened the rear of his SUV and the dog jumped in and started becoming agitated, pawing on the lid of a plastic tub that was locked by its handles. Several small holes had been drilled into its lid, and inside was a layer of sawdust, a small water bowl and a terracotta pot tipped on its side.

"Out you get, boy," he commanded, and the dog immediately jumped out. It was still clearly agitated, padding back and forth, now and again giving a little yelp as it looked up into the back of the vehicle. The man dragged the container closer and peered through the lid. The Eastern Brown Snake flicked its tongue and immediately tried to strike him. It would have sunk its fatal venom into the man's arm if not for the thin cover of plastic between them.

It would be fine as it was, the man was thinking. It would not require food for a long time, and he could refill its water using a thin tube he had inserted through one of the air holes. His military training back in the eighties in the jungles of Belize had taught the man how to catch snakes safely, and even to cook and eat them if necessary.

Louis MacPherson had caught this snake the day before, halfway up Mt Imlay.

CHAPTER 20

FLINDERS ISLAND – Bass Strait, Tasmania

June 2017

It had taken Daniel less than an hour with the assistance of Google to locate his sister, whom he had not seen nor spoken to since he had been shipped off to boarding school by his father. He was only six or seven at the time and Jane must have been around twenty-two. That would now make her around seventy-nine or eighty, he thought. He was driving to Merimbula to catch the eight-forty am flight to Melbourne.

It was a wonder she was alive, Pia had said when he had told her he had found an address for Jane on Flinders Island in the Bass Strait. Using information provided by the Tasmanian Archive & Heritage Office in Hobart, he had tracked her as far as Flinders from records of her first marriage to a man called Henry McArthur. She had taken his surname but had not changed it when she remarried for the second and third times. As much as he could determine, she was always known as Jane McArthur even when she finally took up with an Aboriginal man she never married and who had died four years previously. She was living in a two-bedroom bungalow overlooking the sea in a place called Leeka.

The flight from Merimbula to Melbourne took an hour and twenty minutes, arriving too late to catch the only flight to Flinders from the Essendon regional airport, twenty minutes or so from Melbourne's international airport. He took the shuttle bus to Essendon and then checked in at the Hyatt Place Hotel for one night.

He rang Pia from his room to say he had got as far as Essendon and then made a Skype call to Brianna in Jamaica where it was eight am the same day. He had not spoken to her in a while and wanted to find out if she was still managing living on her own in a new town. More than that, Daniel wanted to hear her voice again. They mostly chatted about her business, and of course how much they missed one another. In order not to worry her, he never mentioned the incident about Pia being attacked by a dog. In any case, it was still uncertain that it had been intentional. Perhaps the man had known her from working at the doctor's surgery in Eden. At least this was the explanation he had wanted to believe.

After about an hour Brianna said she had to go as she had arranged to call her mum on Skype. "Call me again soon," she pleaded. "You know how much I love you, Daniel!"

He did not sleep very well that night. He tossed and turned in bed, his thoughts and emotions in conflict, struggling with this moral dilemma he was facing. He knew that whatever he decided, if ever he did, he would irretrievably hurt one if not both of the two people he cared for most in the world.

The next day he was up early to catch the nineteen-seat, twin-turboprop to the Flinders Island Airport, a short flight of thirty-five minutes. It took him another hour to drive north along the coast in his rental car and locate Jane's house from a Google map he had printed back in Eden. It was not terribly detailed, and so the house was difficult to find. Eventually he recognized it on the beach side of the road, as pictured on the Domain website.

His heart started racing as he walked up the narrow concrete path boarded on both sides by long rows of unruly bingo plants, their flowers of summer long gone. Two mature Frangipanis were leaning on either corner of the house and a large lawn with dry patches from the sea air and lack of watering. Attached to the house was a green PVC water tank designed to collect rain from the roof. Beyond it all was a deep blue expanse of ocean curving the full extent of the horizon with a small island resting in the haze of the day in the distance.

Daniel continued to the front door slowly, almost in trepidation. What, he wondered, would be his sister's reaction to being confronted by a brother she chose to ignore for more than sixty years? Would she be angry he had tracked her down? Would the shock kill her? She was after all eighty or thereabouts. He was almost tempted to turn and head back to the car. This could all be a huge mistake, he feared.

It was winter but today it was moderately warm and the main door to the house was wide open; a screen door kept out mosquitoes and flies. He noticed that the interior was immaculate in every aspect. The small kitchen was modern, and he could see part of a polished dining table and two dining chairs upholstered in candy cane stripes of red and cream such as you might find in the great homes of Europe. There was a sideboard behind the table with an art deco figurine of a scantily clad woman holding aloft an ornate pendulum clock, pivoted on a fragile hand as it swung gently maintaining time. The view through the sliding glass doors beyond was astonishing, as if the house were a cruise ship breaking through white-crested seahorse waves.

From somewhere inside he could hear one of Leonard Cohen's husky laments playing on a radio, something about a sister of mercy. He rattled the screen door gently and then knocked on the side of the mesh frame.

After a short while he could hear the light tread of feet coming from the direction of the music, and then Jane appeared.

She was not at all as he had imagined her. He had thoughts of some doddering old lady with unkempt hair and bad skin, dressed perhaps in clothes that would be tossed out by the Red Cross as unsuitable to reuse. How wrong he was! Jane walked swiftly to the door, eyeing the stranger with a certain apprehension. People seldom came to the house these days and those who did she always knew. This man she had never seen before.

She had grey hair flecked with a few strands of the light brown of her youth and trimmed short. She carried herself like someone thirty years younger. She was quite petite and slim, dressed fashionably, like a businesswoman from the city, in a white cotton shirt with a pair of black slacks and leather slip-on sandals. She also had on a necklace of linked beads of green jade accenting the pale skin of her neck. She had a small gold watch on her wrist.

"Can I help you?" she inquired, standing behind the screen door just in case he was some crazed man come to rob her. Daniel spoke slowly and with purpose.

"Your name is Jane McArthur?"

"Yes," she replied, starting to feel quite uneasy about this man on her doorstep. There was just something about him, something familiar.

"Née, Hannaford?"

"OH, MY GOD!" she screamed and teetered forward having to support herself on the door's screening mesh.

CHAPTER 21

TERROR – Eden, NSW

June 2017

There was no reasonable explanation as to why Daniel would suddenly take off for Tasmania to locate the sister, he had not seen in almost sixty years. Rarely had he spoken about her in all the years they had been married. Now, almost without warning, he rushes off to meet this sister who had ignored him for so long. It made no sense to Pia.

For years they had planned to go to Tasmania together one day, so why had he not taken her with him now? Had she not been left alone long enough whilst he was away in Lucaya? Now he goes off galivanting again on his own! It was so unfair and insensitive of him. Worst of all, it revealed how selfish he could be. It was a side of him that had never been apparent before.

It had all been so unexpected. One day he had discovered his sister was living on some island in the Bass Strait; ten days later he was leaving on a trip he had informed Pia he wanted to make alone. Yet since he had returned home to Australia in November, he had seemed far more attentive and considerate towards her than at any time since they were married. She was becoming convinced it would be a long-overdue and permanent change in him.

Despite the loneliness of the past two years, she was almost glad now that he had gone to Lucaya; something about it had made him at long last comfortable in his own skin. Maybe it was the freedom of living on his own. Or perhaps it was just living in the Caribbean again, which she knew had had a profound effect on him when he worked in Jamaica as a young man. He was certainly no longer so preoccupied and lost in his thoughts. There were even times when he seemed genuinely happy.

But his wandering off to Tasmania on his own left her thinking that nothing had changed after all. Perhaps he was the same old Daniel lost in his troubled world.

The sound of a series of sharp cracks woke her with a start! She sat bolt upright in bed, her heart pounding in her chest as her brain attempted to comprehend the incomprehensible. Then it occurred again: first, a violent crash followed by what she thought was the shattering of glass beneath her on the ground floor. It happened a third time, the dreadful din vibrating throughout the house and rattling the windows upstairs.

It went silent for a moment before it resumed, more loud crashes emanating, it seemed, from every corner of the house. This thunderous attack came closer, then moved on as the person or persons responsible ambled, as if at leisure, around the outside deck downstairs, inflicting as much damage as possible.

Pia remained there in bed too paralysed by fear to move, terrified she might be having a heart attack. Then she recalled that she had a torch in the drawer of her bedside table. Her hands were shaking, but she was able to rake through the contents to find it in the midst of the clutter. She switched it on beneath the bedspread to avoid the beam being seen and continued sitting there in bed, barely breathing. For a while there were no further sounds and the house was bathed in absolute silence. She was desperately praying that whoever it was had finally gone.

Very slowly, sliding her body from between the sheets, she started to inch herself out of the bed as quietly as possible.

At almost the same moment there was another huge crash, followed by a loud bang from downstairs, then the sound of something skidding across one of the hardwood floors and careening into a piece of furniture. Ornaments on top of the bookcase smashed to the floor, including the treasured, miniature statue of the Virgin Mary her mother had brought from Italy when she came to Australia.

Pia continued sitting on the bed for over ten minutes, listening for additional movement from below and trying to quell her rising anxiety, which was almost at the point of panic. She thought she heard something, perhaps footsteps on the stairs, but quickly realized with a wave of relief that it was the sound of ice clattering into the plastic container inside the door of the freezer in the kitchen.

At times holding her breath, she remained as quiet as possible, barely moving in case someone was behind the door. Two minutes, then three and then five minutes went by in complete silence.

After ten minutes she threw aside the blanket and sheets and cautiously got out of bed, pointing the torch shakily down at the floor.

She had a sudden urge to pee but put it out of her mind, treading as softly as she could towards the bedroom door. Opening it slowly she saw no one on the other side and went into the living room. She switched off the torch because she could see the stairs and the kitchen from the nightlight in the kitchen. The dim light bathed the large open plan area in an eerie white glow that cast strange shadows on the walls and ceiling. All was quiet apart from a dog barking in the distance.

Gingerly feeling her way along the kitchen counter, she continued towards the stairs, fearing at any moment someone would suddenly rush from the shadows and knock her off her feet. There was still no one and so she continued silently sliding her bare feet along the shiny surface of the hardwood floor. By the time she reached the top step she was gaining confidence. The house remained deathly quiet and only the hum from the fridge was barely discernible. The kitchen tap was dripping into a saucepan she had used to cook herself a plate of pasta earlier. One by one she very carefully descended the hardwood stairs. She knew which ones creaked and she tried her best to avoid them.

At the bottom of the stairs, Pia gasped at the extent of the carnage she surveyed with her small torch. The house had a number of large windows, upstairs and down, and as far as she could tell all the ones on the ground floor were smashed or broken, with large shards of glass still hanging from several of the window frames. Broken panes littered the wooden floor, with deadly fragments and tiny splinters scattered everywhere. Without her slippers it was impossible to walk further.

Despite the chaotic scene of destruction, she saw something that should not have been there. It was a clear plastic container lying on its side without a lid. Oddly, there was a plant pot inside it and a layer of sawdust, some of which had spilled out on the floor.

Then in the light from her torch she saw it! It was there beneath a bookcase, staring straight at her. It was uncurling its lower half from around two of the legs of the bookcase and had begun moving directly towards her. Her heart started racing.

Feeling slightly sick and a little faint, she managed to keep the torch beam focused on what was quite clearly a brown snake slithering towards her, already beginning to arch in preparation for a strike. She had seen a number of less-lethal Western Brown snakes when she was living in Nhulunby. But this was an Eastern Brown and she knew it could easily kill her. Without turning, she started moving almost imperceptibly backwards as the snake persistently weaved its way along the floor towards her.

CHAPTER 22

JANE – Bass Strait, Tasmania
June 2017

He had never witnessed anyone quite this upset in his relatively long life. For a full five minutes she just stood by the open door, her head resting against the chest of his jacket. Embracing her with both arms, he could feel her quivering as she gasped, still sobbing in shock; it elicited a contrast in him, a mixture of joy and sadness. She clung to him tightly, rocking him back and forth like a mother suddenly finding a son she believed was dead.

Daniel was utterly dumbfounded, completely at a loss as to what he should do or say. The best he had hoped was that she would remember who he was and perhaps be glad to see him after a separation of over sixty years. Had she slammed the door in his face or started screaming he would have understood it, but not this overwhelming, emotional display by an elderly woman he could barely even remember.

Slowly she began to regain control. She pushed back a little from him and looked up into his face. There she could still see that young boy with a shock of blond hair, now shaded grey. Despite the passage of time, it was really not so difficult to see her loving little brother with the kindest of eyes. Even today he looked a little lost in a world where he had never seemed quite comfortable. She placed her hands on both sides of his cheek and drew him close again to kiss him.

"Daniel, my dearest Daniel." She kissed him once more and then slipped her hand in his and began tugging him towards the living room. As he sat down on a mustard-coloured sofa, she raised her hand and softly brushed the tears from his face. He had not realized until then that they were his own.

She sat staring at him for a long while without saying a word, intoxicated by the gush of memories rising to the surface like hundreds of joyous tiny bubbles. Daniel was the first family she had seen since she had given him a quick hug goodbye before walking into town with her one suitcase to begin the first of several long and uncomfortable bus rides leading eventually to a boat to Tasmania. It was a tortuous and physically numbing journey of over two thousand miles.

Jane said that she had been selfish and thoughtless to leave, but she was only twenty-two at the time and desperate to get away from their father and the clouds of suspicion that swirled about town. One of the many rumours accused her of assisting her father to dispose of their mother's body down a mine shaft.

Jane believed it had all become too much for their mother and on that sunny morning she had simply left the house, taking nothing with her, no money, no clothes, and possibly walking for miles in a pair of old sandals until she discovered a place where she knew her remains would never be found. Jane was convinced her mother had killed herself to escape the man she no longer recognized since his return from war. She was in no doubt that had she remained and not stepped aboard the bus that day, she would eventually have followed in the lonely footsteps of her mother.

"I was selfish to leave, Daniel, I know that now," she whispered, "but you have to remember I wasn't very old myself at the time and all I could think about was to get as far away from him as possible." She paused and looked at him again in disbelief. "I did love you, Daniel, and I thought about you a lot. I tried looking for you years later, after Dad must have died, but no one knew where you were. I even contacted your old school in England where Dad said he'd sent you after I had left for Tasmania, but it seemed you never stayed in touch and so I had no idea where you were living, nor whether you were in Australia."

"Thank you, Jane." He reached for her hand and held it gently. "That you even tried to find me means such a lot. I thought you didn't care about me."

Crying again, Jane kissed his hand. "My biggest regret was thinking I would depart this life without ever seeing you again, or even knowing what had happened to you. Thank you for making an old lady so happy." She asked how their father had died and he told her it had been from liver disease two or three years after he had finished school in England. Daniel was at university in Perth then. "It was not entirely his fault he became the man he did," she explained. "There were many men who returned damaged from the war who were never quite the same again. Many of them slowly poisoned everything good in their lives, including those they once loved so much and would have gone to the ends of the world to protect."

After a while Daniel told her, "he would often speak about you, you know, and he did his best to stay in touch with you in Tasmania."

"Yes, I know he did," she replied, telling him that he used to send her money from time to time when she was struggling to survive from one husband to the next. "I am uncertain what would have become of me had he not provided some support," she said patting him on the knee. "Anyway, perhaps you're right, Daniel, perhaps he was not quite the hateful man I remember. It's just so very hard for me to forget how he treated our mother."

"How do you mean?" he asked, apparently surprised by her remark. "One night he came home late from drinking at the pub and punched her in the face. Broke her nose! He then kicked the side of her head and only stopped after I ran downstairs and began screaming. That happened before you were born, when I was only about eight or nine, a couple of years after he returned from Europe."

They sat chatting like the two children they once were until mid-afternoon, swapping decades of family history from their own perspectives, a brother and sister from different generations whose lives had been dictated by circumstance and fate.

Eventually Jane went to make them both a cup of tea and Daniel was left staring out over the ocean towards the island in the distance, finally clear of the early morning haze. Now he was aware of the truth, or part of it at least, he bitterly regretted not having tried to find Jane sooner. He was beginning to really appreciate, possibly for the first time, just how much that one cataclysmic event had damaged them all – just as so many other families had been damaged at the time. His father was merely the first victim, devoured and digested by the dogs of war. His mother, Jane and he were the collateral damage. There was no villain at which to point an accusing finger. They had all suffered in their separate ways, unaware that it would have all been so different had they been able to communicate their pain with each other rather than endure it alone.

After she returned with the tea, Jane told him about her two husbands and about the only man she ever truly loved, an Aboriginal man who had befriended her after her second husband had committed suicide with a shotgun whilst sitting in his red MG in their garage. His name was Kalti; he had been passing by their house when he heard the blast and was the first to witness what had happened. He had seen her running panic-stricken from the house but had caught her just in time to prevent her from seeing what little remained of her husband's head.

Kalti had moved into her current house a year later. It was several miles from her previous home and the scene of the tragedy. She could never forgive her husband for that, killing himself in such a violent manner when he must have known, disturbed as he might have been, that she would be the one to discover him only minutes after he had pulled the trigger. Kalti rescued her from all of that!

Daniel gave her a brief summary of his own life, with only a passing reference to his dysfunctional years at school in England. He said that he had been lonely there and hated the miserable climate, but little else.

Jane was not surprised that he had ended up as a mining engineer given the domineering influence of his father. She was very envious of his year in Jamaica. She had never travelled outside of Australia, but Jamaica would have been on her list of ten top countries to visit. She was one of the original 'hippies' and would have been rolling joints all day with the Jamaican Rasta's.

Daniel laughed at that and spoke about Pia at some length, telling Jane their lives together had been happy ones but uneventful. He hoped one day soon she could meet Pia and they could get to know one another. "I would like that very much, Daniel, but don't wait too long. I am eighty next month and may not be around much longer."

That was the last thing Jane said before his phone started vibrating inside his pocket.

CHAPTER 23

THE BEACH CLUB – Naples Florida

5 June 2017

Richard Wagner sat on one of the bar stools at the Beach Club next to a woman wearing a skimpy one-piece bathing suit. He enjoyed women's company but made no effort to strike up a conversation with this particular woman, despite her quite obvious attempts to catch his interest by rubbing her leg several times against his and then placing her hand on his to ask for a light for her cigarette. Wagner gave her a light then moved to the next seat down.

The barman came over and asked if he wanted another beer and winked at him nodding towards the old woman, he had been sitting next to in the skimpy bathing costume revealing way too much sagging flesh from her neck on down. Her skin was smooth, though tightly stretched like white parchment over her face, advertising yet another botched plastic surgery by one of the outrageously overpriced plastic surgeons in the wealthiest city per capita in the United States.

On the other side of the horseshoe-shaped bar was another woman, somewhat older, with a blonde wig, blowfish lips and two soccer-ball-sized breasts. She was being courted by a man in his early eighties, her very own toy boy who had paid for her plastic surgery.

Wagner had been in Naples for less than six hours, after three days driving across the continent from Vancouver in British Columbia. He could have entered the States via Toronto, which would have been far quicker, but it was not as safe as in BC where there were still unmanned border crossings on some of the back roads. With just a little caution taken, it was relatively easy to slip into the US by car.

He had first surveyed the crossing on foot, leaving the car a hundred yards back down the road; he had laughed to himself when he found a crude handwritten sign stuck on the outside of the small shed instructing people crossing the border to check-in at the local police station in the next town, sixteen miles inside the United States. What a joke, he thought as he lifted up the barrier and drove his rental into fortress USA! So much for homeland bloody security!

He had arranged to depart the country aboard a merchant ship from Miami the following week. It had a couple of cabins for paying passengers wanting a leisurely cruise at a very affordable price, stopping often at unscheduled exotic ports of call. But then he was only going as far as Haiti, the ship's first stop; from Port-au-Prince he'd fly to Paris on Air Caraibes using one of the five passports he always carried with him on jobs like this.

He forgot the old woman he had been sitting next to and casually gazed over at a group of five black women sitting at a table towards the small stage. Every Sunday the Beach Bar had a live band. The women were all itching to get on the makeshift dance floor as the band began to warm up. He turned on his barstool to see the crowds of people walking the beach; the sea was flat calm. He would have to put up with this for several more hours, at least until the band stopped playing at around ten pm, when most of the elderly patrons began ambling to their beds, with or without a new Sunday companion.

He ordered his third beer and then walked around the bar dangling the bottle by his side and moving closer to the table with the five women. He was only interested in the thin one who looked like a model, and who had no indication of any plastic surgery scarring her beautiful face.

The five left the Beach Bar sooner than he had anticipated, just before nine. It was dark outside now, but the streets were well lit and there were still people walking on both sides of Gulf Shore Boulevard. It was soon apparent that the girls were not heading home to go to bed any time soon. From the sound of their laughter coupled with their terrible attempts singing 'House of the Rising Sun', Richard Wagner soon realized they wanted to party.

He followed them at a distance for about half an hour until they turned left on 5th Avenue. This was the main artery leading to the ritzy centre of Naples with chic boutiques, art galleries and expensive restaurants and trendy bars. A few blocks further down they stopped and went inside Paddy Murphy's Irish Pub. Sixties music was blasting from inside. Paddy's was in a different class, perhaps the only affordable establishment on the street. It was crowded inside and the dance floor was packed. Even on Sundays it remained open until two am.

This would be perfect, he thought, fingering the short syringe in his jacket pocket that had a small red cap over the needle. It contained enough pure heroin to kill several people.

CHAPTER 24

SHELL-SHOCKED – Boydtown

NSW, June 2017

What he was watching on the overhead monitor defied any logical explanation; it exploded into a jumble of inner turmoil in his consciousness. Once there he tumbled headlong into an abstract universe, divorced from the physical and submerged in perceptual isolation. He had been propelled into this new reality without warning. The peripheral was discarded and only one focus remained. All else had evaporated around him. He walked closer to the monitor with no recollection of where he was or why. There was only one thing that mattered, and that was the *Breaking News* alert on the television screen above.

He was standing at his departure gate in Melbourne Airport where he had been waiting for half an hour for his flight to Merimbula. He could not quite grasp why everyone around him remained unconcerned and was sitting quietly for their flights or ambling along the concourse.

He had barely acknowledged Jane as he fled from her house, promising only that he would call as soon as he arrived home. His neighbour had provided few details in their brief telephone conversation, only that something had happened at his house involving Pia. She was with them, he told Daniel. She was unhurt but quite shaken. Infuriatingly, the neighbour had provided little else before the call dropped and Daniel was left standing in Jane's living room, shell-shocked by this seismic news from Eden.

Jane had tried to convince him to remain the night, explaining that it was too late to catch a flight to the mainland, but Daniel ignored her good advice. When he arrived at the small island airport, he discovered that she had been quite correct; there were no flights until the next morning, with the first departure to Launceston at six-forty am. Rather than return to his sister's and worry her unduly without knowing himself what was going on, he instead found a small hotel in the hamlet of Whitemark, a town of only one hundred and seventy, yet the largest settlement on the island. The airport was five kilometres away. He had been enjoying his reunion with Jane, but now was not the time to be reminiscing with his sister.

He tried calling the neighbour from his hotel but again there was no reply. His calls to Pia kept going through to her voicemail. Despite additional attempts calling them both until midnight, leaving several more messages, both phones answered with busy signals, possibly indicating a problem with mobile coverage in the area. It was only when he reached Melbourne the next day that he found out what had happened, on national television.

There was an aerial shot of their house before the picture panned to a female reporter speaking into a handheld microphone. A yellow caution tape was loosely draped behind her across the steps leading to his front door! Two men were busy boarding up an empty window frame when a dishevelled looking man accompanied by a policeman came from inside the house holding a black bag with red grabs on two of the corners. A news ticker at the bottom of the picture explained that the man was a local snake catcher and had caught a large brown snake measuring over six feet inside the house. It was, the reporter announced dramatically, one of the deadliest snakes in Australia.

Daniel was acutely anxious after the hour-and-twenty-minute flight from Melbourne. He tried calling his neighbour and Pia from the car, but the neighbour's phone was busy again and went directly to voicemail.

A man eventually answered Pia's mobile. "Mr. Hannaford?" the man asked.

"Where's my wife? Put her on," Daniel demanded, petrified that something awful had happened.

"She's OK, perfectly fine," the voice assured.

The man explained that he was with the Australian Federal Police's counter-terrorism division. He was based in Canberra, he said, and had driven down earlier in the day after the report that Daniel's house had been vandalized and a large brown snake had been discovered slithering around inside the house.

"You perhaps didn't get all the details on the news," the policeman suggested and explained that every single pane of glass on the lower level of his house had been shattered and a large brown snake, and possibly more than one, had been tossed inside. They were still checking the premises right now, downstairs, upstairs and beneath the house as well. "Your wife is perfectly safe, Mr. Hannaford. We have secured a room for you both at the Seahorse Inn. She is there now, resting."

This was all becoming far too surreal for Daniel. What the bloody hell had terrorism to do with it, and who had even suggested it? The neighbour? How could they possibly link a few broken windows and a brown snake to terrorism! Perhaps it was because he was exhausted and was not thinking clearly, but it took a while before it dawned on him that the incident could be connected to Elm and his son. But surely not! They would never risk drawing this much attention to themselves.

Superintendent Chase of the Australian Federal Police was waiting for him in the car park when he finally arrived at the Seahorse Inn. He was anxious to see Pia and so was a little impatient having to deal with the policeman first. Daniel remained convinced that Lord Elm had nothing to do with it. It was nothing more than a random act of violence, he said, trying to convince himself. Then Superintendent Chase began updating him on recent events – without, on advice from London, referring once to the woman who had been murdered in Florida.

"In case you are wondering Mr. Hannaford, we were contacted by the Metropolitan Police in London last January by someone suggesting your life might be in danger."

"Was that an Inspector Sage?" Daniel asked, walking along the short pathway with the policeman before they entered the hotel through the main doors. Inside there was no one about apart from a man sitting on a chair by the circular staircase. He appeared to be reading a magazine but looked up quickly as he heard the door pushed open.

"He's one of ours," Chase said, nodding towards the man. Then he returned to Daniel's question. "No, it was their top man," Chase said, "or rather woman," he quickly clarified, "Commissioner Cressida Dick. Obviously, we took the matter extremely seriously, seeing as we've never had a warning like this one before from such a high-ranking officer. We have only been informed of a few details, but normally in matters such as this it would have been left to a lower-ranking officer to liaise with us. You must be of great importance to them, Mr. Hannaford!"

He sat with her until she fell asleep, then made himself a cup of instant coffee from a pencil-shaped sachet of Robert Timms. He was careful not to make a noise as he opened the French window that led outside to a small balcony. Sitting down on a freezing metal chair, he placed the mug of coffee on the table before him and took out an unopened packet of Benson and Hedges from his jacket pocket. He had purchased it at a Caltex petrol station driving through Eden. He stared at it for a long while. He knew that once he opened the packet, the battle would be lost and he would light up his first cigarette in over thirty years.

He could see a few faint lights shimmering on the other side of the bay. He shivered in the cold wind gusting from the south and scurrying between the balconies on the second floor of the hotel. He pulled the hood of the heavy parka he was wearing over his head. He would have gone in where it was warm to finish his coffee but he was enjoying his cigarette too much. He hoped the plainclothes officers wandering the property and the two others in the car were warmer than he was.

He was wishing he was with Brianna. To help him stop thinking about how much he missed her, he dialled Jane to let her know he was back safely. He made mention of nothing else, not about the snake and certainly nothing about his conversation with the federal policeman. He said he would call again tomorrow or the day after. Pia was awake when he went back inside. He went over and sat beside her on the bed.

"You have been smoking, Daniel! Why?"

He shrugged, looking guilty, but did not answer her. Instead, he said, "Unless you want to go back to sleep there are some things you need to know, Pia."

CHAPTER 25

THE FOLLOWING MORNING – Boydtown, NSW

June 2017

Pia had been too tired the night before to talk and so Daniel told her it could wait until morning. They had both had a distressing day and were exhausted. Much better if they got a good night's sleep instead.

For a while they lay there in silence in the dark, side by side on the queen bed, listening to the sounds of the waves pounding the beach at high tide. Pia went to sleep first. Daniel reached for her hand and held it and kissed her gently on the cheek. He was feeling guilty and ashamed for missing Brianna so much.

There was something significant about today's date that he could not recall and the harder he tried to remember the further it eluded him. He eventually gave up and fell into a deep sleep free from the dreams that normally chased him at night.

The significance of the date dawned on him in the early hours of the morning whilst Pia was still sleeping quietly beside him. Yesterday would have been his mother's one-hundredth birthday! She had been forty-two at the time she disappeared, when he was barely seven. That was nearly sixty years ago, yet he could still clearly remember her on that last morning, just before he went to school. She'd given him a longer hug than usual; then she pecked him on the cheek and went upstairs, never looking back.

His last memory of her.

To this day he still felt responsible. Perhaps if he had only held her longer or followed her up the stairs to give her another hug to show how much he loved her she might never have vanished from his life as she had.

Superintendent Chase joined them for a coffee in the dining room the next morning. They had eaten breakfast by that time; two Spanish omelettes made from eggs laid by the hotel's own chickens that wandered free outside. The two were notably anxious for additional news about the house.

"Not much, I'm afraid. They didn't find any more snakes." Chase said. He went quiet for a moment and looked at Daniel before continuing. "But there has been a development concerning someone on the island." Daniel suddenly thumped the table! He stood up abruptly and asked the superintendent not to be worrying his wife any further. All she wanted was to get back in her house.

Pia was astonished at Daniel's behaviour, which was so out of character for him. She tried to say something, but Daniel immediately cut her off and asked to speak to the policeman alone outside. What on earth is the matter with him, she thought? Could it be he really was starting to suffer from dementia? Perhaps this would explain his sudden display of anger? Never before had she witnessed him making a spectacle of himself in public. Several other guests in the dining room were staring at them. One of the waitresses had been so surprised by the outburst that she spilled coffee over the back of a guest's hand pouring him a refill.

Daniel followed the superintendent to the foyer by the front desk. He noticed what he assumed was a different plainclothes detective sitting in the same chair as the one from the previous evening. "Superintendent, please, I really must apologize for being so damn rude in there!" "There's absolutely no need, Mr. Hannaford. It was entirely my fault.

I think I understand," he said pausing a few moments. "Your wife doesn't know anything of what happened on that island, does she?"

"No, she doesn't," Daniel, admitted. "And I really don't want to overwhelm her with any more bad news. What happened to her yesterday would have been a significant shock for anyone," he said. "I'll tell her some things when we go for a walk later on the beach, but nothing that might frighten her." Changing the subject, he asked, "So, what is the news you had to tell me?"

Someone came through the front doors of the hotel and the man by the stairs looked up to see who it was.

"This situation is far more serious than you might realize. I was informed earlier this morning that the police in London are quite certain now that both you and your wife are potential targets, as well as a Jamaican woman you apparently met the evening it all happened."

"What!" Daniel exclaimed.

"I am afraid so, sir, and from now on we will be providing you with police protection. Even this morning when you go for your walk someone will be following you, at a discreet distance of course!" Chase went on to tell Daniel the harrowing news that the woman who had made the accusation against the premier of Lucaya was now dead. She had been murdered from an injection of a massive dose of pure heroin. It had happened in an Irish pub a few nights ago in Naples, Florida.

The police on Lucaya had apparently received an anonymous tip several days before the murder that the woman was being targeted. Someone with a rough English accent apparently. Unfortunately, no specific details had been provided, just a name. Not when, where or how! Subsequently, it took far too long for the Florida state police to locate this woman with the scant information the Royal Lucayan Police had been able to provide on her whereabouts.

CHAPTER 26

GUADALCANAL – South Pacific

October 15, 1851

*U*sing his machete Stevens began slashing a passage through the tangled undergrowth of the rainforest thriving alongside the beaches the full length of the coast. Like a quilt blanket of numerous shades of green, it covered almost the entire island, stretching some fifty miles to the south and more than ninety miles from east to west.

In the centre of the island this living cover, teeming with over thirty million species of plants and animals, climbed a rugged mountain range dominated by a peak almost nine thousand feet high. Beyond, raging torrents caused by the tropical rainfall on that side of the island had cut deep valleys to the southern shore. The rushing waters carrying silt from the mountains eventually collided with the pounding waves along the south coast to create beaches of black sand.

His sharp blade would have no effect at all if they attempted to penetrate deeper into the jungle further south. The tangled forest there was too dense to cut through. Only ten minutes after leaving the beach Stevens was already drenched in sweat. He had taken off his shirt and his skin glistened from the rays of sunlight that would periodically lance through the canopy of trees above.

Benjamin Boyd was labouring his way behind, also sweating profusely and gasping for each breath from the effort of carrying the leather portmanteau with the two, short-barrel rifles inside. He had already discarded his woollen cap and was now considering taking off his thick woollen purple shirt. He had always been embarrassed displaying his corpulent body in front of Stevens and had never done so in daylight. Now he could only pro-long the inevitable until necessity would finally overcome his reluctance.

Several more minutes passed before the humidity and the heat forced him to strip bare from the waist up, exposing a porcelain white torso that justified the crew's cruel comments comparing him to a pregnant woman carrying twins. He slung his water flask back across his shoulder and continued trudging on.

Boyd was beginning to worry that they had not brought sufficient water for their journey. It did not concern him whether they had enough food because there was evidence in abundance that the region was teeming with life. He'd heard hundreds of strange birdcalls, and the staccato screeches from tropical animals in the verdant canopy above were like exotic melodies.

Two megapodes as big as small turkeys startled them suddenly crashing through the undergrowth, before being swallowed again just as quickly. Stevens noticed a large poisonous centipede as they continued on their way and crushed it with his boot.

The Wanderer had moored in a sheltered, crescent-shaped bay northwest of the island. The beach formed a white sandy edge following the bay until it disappeared around the two short headlands. Benjamin and Mark Boyd had managed to acquire a copy of the only Admiralty chart of the island available in San Francisco. They had determined that there was a similar bay roughly ten miles further along the coast; this is where Benjamin Boyd and Stevens were now headed.

To enable them to cut across the headland they would first have to hack a way through the dense undergrowth a few yards inland from the beach. Once they reached the other side they would no longer be in view from the Wanderer, allowing him the possibility of walking the remainder of the journey along the shore.

Two hours later they were well out of sight of the Wanderer, *now far out in the bay on the other side of the headland. Stevens wanted to forge a path directly towards the beach, but Boyd needed to stop a while, he said, to recover from the exertion of the morning. He sat down on a fallen tree in a small clearing and took some food from the portmanteau without offering any to Stevens. To conserve their water supply they drank sparingly from the flasks each carried hung by leather straps across their shoulders. Stevens inquired whether Boyd was up to continuing the remainder of the journey, another seven miles or so, or whether he wanted to camp on the beach for the night. Boyd said he would be fine after a few more minutes of rest.*

The next stage of the plan Benjamin Boyd purposely failed to discuss with his brother. Mark would never have countenanced the idea. Benjamin was a little surprised at his own feeling of reluctance at first, perhaps because he had grown rather fond of Stevens these past ten years since they first set sail on their meandering adventure to Australia – which had ended in such abysmal failure.

It had been only after reaching Sydney at the age of eleven that Stevens began sharing the Captain's cabin whenever the Wanderer *put to sea. Stevens was an orphan and Benjamin Boyd was the only person ever to demonstrate any form of kindness towards him. The captain had been his only family.*

They began their trek again once Boyd was fully rested. Stevens continued as before, chopping at the smaller branches heading in the direction of the ocean, with glimpses of the turquoise water now visible just ahead. Boyd was not far behind.

On the Wanderer *they heard the explosion of a gun onshore. It disturbed hundreds of colourful parrots that flew from their perches. All onboard cheered, already salivating at the thought of fresh fowl they would be roasting on the beach later that evening. They had already been promised an extra portion of rum by the chief mate. One of the petty officers had bought a contraption called a concertina in San Francisco and had become quite adept playing various sea shanties and broadside ballads.*

Excited about what lay in store, the crew went about their duties with an exuberance they had not displayed since leaving San Francisco weeks before.

Benjamin Boyd shot Stevens in the back of his head at close range with his Colt pistol. He had not hesitated, nor did he ever experience any sense of remorse from that day forth.

Stevens crashed heavily to the ground, already dead. Blood briefly pooled from his head wound before running slowly in red rivulets, seeping through the sand. Over the next five minutes or so Boyd fired several more shots from the Colt into the air. Then he fired both of the flintlocks in the same direction. He picked up the machete, rolled Stevens over with one of his Monticello booties and began slashing the young man's face and upper body with the machete before finally plunging it deep into his chest.

He took the portmanteau and scattered the contents and discarded the bag. Then he took off his bootees and black socks and smeared them with blood from Stevens' body and threw them back along the track. After soaking his purple shirt in blood, he threw it over an epiphyte growing on the side of a tall tree. Before filling his water bottle from Stevens', he took off his own trouser belt and dropped it on the ground close to the former cabin boy; then he placed the Colt beneath his body.

Picking up the other two discharged guns he carried them towards the ocean. His feet sank into sand so soft as to leave no footprints as he walked, half-naked and splattered with blood, to the shore and then paddled through the shallow water along the beach. It was close to two hours later when he caught first caught sight of the Pacific Pearl and began waving his arms. He threw the two hunting rifles out over the turquoise shallows into the darker blue ocean where they would never be found.

They had built a small bonfire on the beach shortly before dusk. Twelve of the crew stood in a semi-circle as the second mate walked along pouring the golden elixir into the tin cups each man was holding. The other two, including the first mate, remained aboard the Wanderer on watch. They had already been given their portions of rum and so were quite content to remain behind. Having inched along the bowsprit, they sat with their tin cups watching the fire grow brighter as the night approached.

The fire eventually started to subside and it became too dark to gather more wood. There was no moon; the jungle shadows were encroaching and the men wanted to return to the ship before the fire went out completely. Most of the crew on shore were deeply superstitious; some had already begun suggesting their captain and Stevens were dead and boiling in some cannibal's pot or had perhaps been devoured by some unknown slimy creature crawling along the floor of the rainforest. Too much strong rum also drove their fears, and as the flickers from the dying fire cast dancing shadows on the aerial mangrove roots, they illuminated what seemed a terrifying army of small creatures heading slowly towards them. The crew returned to the Wanderer without their captain.

The next morning, they woke to see a small group of natives on shore throwing stones and hurling what looked like spears in the Wanderer's direction. It was obviously a futile exercise, as the ship was moored a good distance from the shore. The first mate decided to take three men ashore in one of the jolly boats to investigate. He would not have endangered himself and the crew if the Captain and Stevens had not gone missing. Questions would be asked and reports written to establish what had happened once they arrived back in England. He would have to show that he had done all that was expected of him.

As soon as the boat neared shore the natives, wearing only small loin cloths, began wading towards the boat. The first mate ordered one of the men to fire a warning shot but they kept on wading closer, continuing to hurl stones and shouting curses in a language none of the Englishmen understood.

The first mate then took his own pistol from his belt and fired a shot just over the head of the leader of the angry group. He continued ploughing through the water towards them until a second shot hit him in the chest. The others immediately turned in the water and fled, leaving their chief face down and staining the turquoise water crimson red.

Having landed, the four sailors stopped a while when they reached the edge of the beach and the rainforest. The first mate had decided they must find Boyd and Stevens; it was looking more likely that they had come to harm. They soon found the track Stevens had carved from the jungle and began following it, alert now to every rustle or sound of breaking twigs.

It took them half an hour before they finally came upon Stephen's body. Already, in less than twelve hours, the corpse was covered in maggots and carrion flies. Something else, a larger animal or several king rats, had been tearing chunks of flesh from his chest. One of the sailors vomited and the other suggested they leave immediately and head back to the ship before becoming carrion for the rats themselves.

Before they left, they collected Stevens' and Boyd's few belongings and placed them inside the empty portmanteau. They found the Colt beneath Stevens' body but no sign of the other guns they knew Boyd had taken with him to shoot birds. One of them remembered that at least one of the gunshots they had heard from the Wanderer was from a flintlock, a quite different sound from the Colt. It seemed apparent that the natives had attacked them and Stevens had been using the Colt to fend them off.

Boyd's body was never discovered and it was assumed the natives had carried him away as a trophy, perhaps later to boil and eat. They buried Stevens in a shallow grave in the sand using their bare hands to dig. The four crew then retreated to the safety of the ship as expeditiously as they could – in case the remaining natives, infuriated by the death of their leader, swam out to the Wanderer and attempted to board her.

CHAPTER 27

OVER THE ATLANTIC

30 June 2017

Though he was well aware of the truth, Geoffrey Elm feigned ignorance. "I'm sorry, Michael, I simply cannot believe you weren't somehow involved!" he said, accusing his son indirectly of lying. He was moving his neck from side to side and oscillating his shoulder blades, trying to find some relief.

He had suffered from a bad back for years and was currently in a great deal of pain. He adjusted the upright on his power recliner to allow additional support. The chair was one of a kind, having been custom designed for his executive jet, a Dassault Falcon. Michael Elm was sitting across the narrow aisle in a drab grey seat. It was not as comfortable as his father's but certainly preferable to a first-class seat on a commercial carrier.

The interior of the craft was also grey, apart from a single white stripe along both sides, delineating two rows of cabin windows. There was nothing else to distinguish the cabin as the jet cruised at an altitude of forty-one thousand feet, higher than a commercial airliner. The main cabin could very well have been a cheap office in a featureless concrete building in any of a number of British cities. It was basic, functional and nothing more. Certainly not worthy of a billionaire, Michael was thinking, carefully considering how to reply. He would of course admit nothing, knowing his father would throw him under the bus as quickly as anyone else if he felt threatened.

"Fucking coincidence that black bint from the premier's shindig should end up dead, then, pumped full of heroin in some fucking Irish pub," his father sneered with heavy sarcasm. He turned, looking directly into his son's face. "You might just as well have advertised it on BBC World!" Geoffrey Elm was ridiculing his son not for what he had been planning, but for his being photographed drunk with an unsavory character like Richard Wagner.

"How incredibly stupid you were getting drunk with that thug in Soho back in February! You should have allowed the police a little more credit, Michael. They are not quite as dumb as you seem to believe."

Michael had already decided not to respond and instead simply shook his head, reproaching his father with silence for even suggesting he was involved. A steward brought Michael a single-malt whisky and a small bowl of mixed nuts as he continued sulking in silence and staring out of the window. Meanwhile, Geoffrey Elm had pushed his pile of paperwork aside and was dozing as the plane cruised steadily at 915 km/h with Belize City as their ultimate destination.

As his father snored quietly, his son concerned himself with the latest developments; the original plan had been fairly simple, involving only himself and Richard Wagner. But once that photo had been published in the Evening Standard, Michael had called it all off. It was too risky. Yet several days after the evening at the strip club, Wagner started working on a plan himself. Michael only found about this weeks later when he received a curious, encrypted text message from an unknown number in the United States:'The composer has played the first venue'. The pair had initially agreed at the strip club to establish a special code to communicate. Wagner would be the 'composer' and the 'venue' the target. Michael would be the 'conductor'.

Michael had exploded on reading the text and never responded, not that it would have been possible anyway. Wagner would have used a 'burner' phone that was probably already buried in some landfill in

Florida. For days later Michael was beside himself, not knowing what he should do. He dared not bring it up with his father, nor did he have any idea how to contact the fucking idiot who had taken matters into his own hands.

Why would he do that, Michael kept asking himself. It simply made no sense whatsoever!

He had been sleeping for over an hour when his father shook him. He sat up still half asleep, wiping some spittle from the corner of his mouth. "Christ, father, what the fuck? Something wrong with the plane?" He started getting out of his seat and knocked the half-empty glass of whisky off the table.

"Don't be a complete moron, Michael!" Lord Elm said. He sat down again slowly in his seat grimacing from the effort. "Read this!" he ordered, passing his iPhone over to Michael who read the message and groaned. Martin, their attorney on Lucaya had emailed that the trial was reaching a conclusion, months earlier than anticipated. That very afternoon the prosecution had made its final rebuttal after the closing arguments of the defence, and the matter was now in the hands of the presiding judge. It was a bench trial without a jury. Guilt or innocence was entirely the purview of the judge, a man now well into his eighties. If he found them guilty, he would also determine their sentences.

Weighing the volumes of evidence, Martin seemed to think it could take as long as three months before the judge announced his verdict. It might take another month or so to impose sentences if that verdict was 'Guilty', in all likelihood jailing the defendants for years.

"I had a quick word with Martin on the phone before I woke you," his father said. "He believes it a foregone conclusion they'll all be put away. There will be an appeal, of course, which could take years, but there's no chance they will allow Walter out on bail, particularly when they had to drag the little bastard back from Brazil the last time. He'll be done for if he's found guilty. Martin believes he could get twenty years or even longer."

Geoffrey went quiet for a few minutes. Eventually he started to say something, hesitated briefly and then said, "Listen, Michael, time we both started telling each other the truth."

Michael had never been so angry as when his father revealed that he had known of Michael's plans from the start, ever since that night he had been spotted by the press in Soho fondling a half-naked woman in the company of an ex-convict. Geoffrey Elm calmed him down, convincing him how dangerous it would have been for him to have any further association with Richard Wagner.

He made no mention to Michael that he had decided to reach out himself to Richard Wagner via a third party the day the photo had been splashed all over the *Evening Standard*. All the while Wagner believed Michael continued as his employer and had simply distanced himself by engaging an intermediary to deliver instructions. Payments for his efforts would continue to be made to his account in Gibraltar. Until recently the man who had contacted Richard Wanger the next morning as the intermediary had been a valued member of the crew employed on Geoffrey's yacht, *El Gordo*, the same Falklands War vet Geoffrey could depend upon above all others to resolve an unpleasant situation.

One such matter had involved an underage girl. She had been seen drinking with him on deck of his yacht as it was moored on the Essequibo river off the port of Bartica, sixty miles upstream from Georgetown, Guyana. A reporter from the *Guyana News* was dispatched from the newspaper's office in Bartica to find out more on the story. Subsequently, the reporter went missing and was presumed drowned. A week or so later his small boat was found adrift in mangrove swamps not too far from where the *El Gordo* had been anchored.

The permanently traumatised young girl was returned to her village south of Georgetown the next morning, oblivious to who the lord was, or to the fact she was the victim of a serious crime. Her parents were concerned only that they were paid.

On the flight to Belize, Geoffrey Elm failed to get more sleep. His mind would not allow that luxury of escape as he agonized, calculating the permutations of all the things that could destroy what he had achieved or still hoped to achieve; his political ambitions, his yachts, jets and homes, his considerable fortune and the respect that only money can secure. They would all disappear in a puff of smoke, along with his handcrafted legacy.

Time was of the essence now. They only had a month or two before their world might come crashing down on their heads. His son might end up in jail, branded forever as a criminal. But far worse and too horrific to contemplate was the very real prospect of finding *himself* incarcerated, possibly for life in the United States, if they ever discovered the extent of his nefarious activities. Unlike Michael, Geoffrey understood that Walter Harrison's only option to avoid jail would be to strike a deal with the British government, trading him and Michael for his freedom or a reduced sentence. To achieve this, Harrison would require corroborating evidence from any of the remaining witnesses.

Geoffrey's plan now had to be accelerated at all cost!

CHAPTER 28

HALF-TRUTHS – Boydtown, NSW

18 June 2017

A federal policeman followed them at a discreet distance. It was a perfectly clear day with fewer than half a dozen lazy wisps of cloud about. It was much warmer than the previous night, with the temperature at a very pleasant seventeen degrees centigrade. With no breeze blowing, it was difficult to remember it was even winter.

Exposed at low tide and baked like asphalt by the morning sun, the sand was firm underfoot as they walked towards her favourite place on the beach, her 'thinking spot'. Over breakfast Pia had displayed a degree of exasperation with him for not explaining his behaviour; she finally demanded to know what was going on. "You were so rude," she exclaimed. "What on earth was wrong with you?"

She bent down and picked up two shells from the sand to add to her collection at home, at least whenever the police deemed it safe to return. It was going to take some time to replace the glass and repair most of the custom-made window frames. She enjoyed making things from the seashells she found. Once, years ago, she had made a small jewellery box from shells she had collected on beach walks in Western Australia when they were living there. The box now held pride of place on her dressing table. One of the things she kept inside it was an old photograph of her parents taken on the ship departing for Australia. There was a view of Vesuvius in the background puffing an idle plume of ash dust from a landslide within the crater. The last real eruption had taken place shortly before the end of the war in 1944.

"And where are you taking us?" he asked, ignoring her question for the time being. "Not sure our companion is used to all this exercise and fresh air," he said looking over his shoulder. The federal officer appeared to be falling further behind.

"I think he's just giving us some space, Daniel, that's all. He looks like someone who works out at the gym and so I wouldn't worry about him too much. I am sure you wouldn't survive more than two minutes with him in a boxing ring!" They both laughed and continued walking further towards the end of the beach where there had been a small avalanche of rocks from the cliff face.

Daniel started speaking about his time with Jane on Flinders and how genuinely happy she had seemed meeting him. "I was so surprised," he said. "She sobbed her heart out as soon as it dawned on her who was standing at her front door."

"You'll have to invite her up to Eden for a few weeks once all this other business is over. She sounds lovely. It would be nice to have some female company for a change."

They were approaching the end of the beach by then and Daniel could see it would be impossible to continue without clambering over the fallen rocks blocking their way or paddling through slimy green rock pools of seaweed skirting the shore. This was as far as Pia had ever come, always afraid to go further by herself in case she slipped and fell and there was no one around to help her.

"Here, Daniel, come and sit next to me," she said patting a place next to her on the rock. It was so flat it almost seemed nature had intended it as a bench. Daniel rubbed his hand along it, amazed by how smooth it was. "Welcome to my 'thinking spot'," she said, smiling.

So as not to alarm her he did not refer to the dog attack. The federal police were convinced it had been a first warning, something Daniel had briefly suspected but later discounted. He even found it hard to believe the Elms had any involvement in the incident at the house two days ago.

Surely, they would not be so brazen. But once he learned about the woman's murder in Florida, he quickly changed his mind about everything; the dog on the beach had to be intentional and the smashed windows and the deadly Eastern Brown had to be a second warning! They were blatant indications of just how far Geoffrey Elm and his son were prepared to go to protect themselves. The news of the murder of the girl he had seen forcibly held down on the wet tiles of the premier's pool placed an entirely different perspective on things. Now it was becoming all too real!

Chase had mentioned the girl's name, Vanessa Hall, but there was no need to remind Daniel she was the twenty-two-year-old model from Fort Myers who had been savagely raped. How could he ever forget the brutality of that night, which had haunted his dreams for weeks afterwards? He often thought about the girl and the effect it must have had on her and her family. Now she was dead.

Vanessa Hall had been on a week's break to Lucaya back in 2015 accompanied by a gay photographer she had contracted to take some shots for her portfolio. The premier had noticed her sitting alone drinking cocktails one evening at one of the Coral Bay bars and had struck up a conversation with her. Vanessa was suitably impressed when he casually mentioned who he was after a few drinks, and she eagerly accepted an invitation to attend the party he was holding at his lavish residence two days later.

If the Elms had been responsible for murdering the poor unfortunate woman in Naples, Daniel thought, becoming increasingly alarmed, surely, they might consider killing Brianna. And himself as well! It was something he had only considered a remote possibility when he urged Brianna to move to his villa on Lucaya. Intending it purely as a precaution, he had no deep-seated belief that a British peer and the premier of a Caribbean island would actually collude to kill someone. Yes, they might threaten her work permit, or even have someone slap her about a bit. But murder? No, he never imagined they would go to those extremes.

They knew where he was living, something he had never made an effort to hide. Unlike Brianna, however, he was not as vulnerable, especially now that the police were involved. They were already setting up a mobile command at the house and would be providing him and Pia twenty-four-hour protection until it was no longer necessary. No one as yet had any idea how long that might be.

Brianna had no protection at all. She would be at risk if they discovered her whereabouts.

In the coming days he would try to fill in some of the gaps in his account to Pia, details he had either intentionally left out or had forgotten. She deserved to know the entire story eventually, especially considering everything she had been put through. For now, though, she had quite enough to process. Without having spent time on the island, Pia would be unable fully to comprehend why he had not gone to the police in the first place two years ago. He was unsure that even he had the answer. Had he once again simply exposed his inability to make a real decision? It was his lifelong curse, the recurring struggle, tearing him apart from the inside when faced with a moral dilemma and the irreconcilability of different outcomes.

Daniel had his hand on the flat rock when Pia took it with both of hers, squeezed it with affection and placed it gently on her lap. One of the first things she had noticed about him when they first met in Perth were his hands, with the long delicate fingers of a pianist and skin smoother than her own.

He resumed telling her more about the island; how different it was from Australia, and the blatant corruption that was endemic throughout the territory. The expats were no different from the locals and were often worse, in particular the expat lawyers. They all seemed to exude an arrogance well in excess of their abilities or position, as if they truly believed they were more deserving than the rest of the rabble, both the ignorant local blacks, as they perceived them, and the equally ignorant whites. This last group often came to the island to enjoy a lifestyle, rather than to make money by fleecing everyone else, something lawyers could at least understand and respect.

"And this is why you didn't go and make a statement to the police?" she asked. "Because you couldn't trust anyone?"

"Partly," Daniel replied, "but I also knew enough about Lord Elm to realize he was not someone to tangle with. People like him with billions in the bank believe they can get away with anything, and more often than not they do," he said. "Richard Crossly warned me to be extremely careful dealing with either of them when I first started working on the island. He said the father and son would stop at nothing to protect themselves or their businesses."

Pia was not quite as concerned as Daniel had imagined she would be. Granted, she did not know yet that someone had been murdered, but nothing he was saying seemed to faze her that much. She was more complaisant than he would have imagined. She also hadn't criticized him or blamed him once for bringing this nightmare halfway around the world to their home. He knew she had never wanted him to take the job on the island in the first place. They lived in one of the most beautiful spots in the world and were financially very comfortable. Then again, it was his life and she respected him for taking on a new job at an age when other men had celebrated their retirement before turning sixty, and later downsizing as they described it. Pia could never imagine Daniel doing that, settling down and downsizing, simply waiting for his final journey to the cemetery!

CHAPTER 29

MORGAN'S CAY – Lucaya

July 2017

There was no guarantee he would make it ashore safely without drowning. Every sailing to the island was perilous, fraught with unimaginable dangers. A sudden tropical storm accompanied by violent winds could blow them off course, possibly overturning the wooden sloops, tipping their human cargo overboard. Once in the water a hellish frenzy would ensue as those still living would grab on to anyone, flailing in desperation to remain afloat. Struggling in terror before being swallowed by the chilly North Atlantic, occasionally they dragged one another down with them. Far from land and the shipping routes, their bodies were seldom recovered for a decent burial unless they washed up in some distant mangrove swamp or a foreign beach far from home.

The sloop could also remain adrift for days in the currents unless the captain of the barely seaworthy vessels had some basic navigational skills, in which case they could bypass the island completely. If becalmed in the Antilles Current drifting north, their only hope was to be picked up by a Bahamian or US Coast Guard vessel or find landfall on one of the outer islands of the Bahamas. The distance to the US mainland was over six hundred miles. Many Cuban refugees had never made it is as far as Florida, which was a mere ninety miles from Havana. There was little chance a small Haitian sloop would make it all the way from Port-au-Prince or Delmas.

More than twenty men, women and children were huddled on board with insufficient food and water; it was possible that many would die on leaving Cape Haitian, perhaps all of them. But it was a chance they were all prepared to take to escape the wretched poverty and violence that had been their history since Haiti had proudly proclaimed independence from the French to become the very first black republic.

Assuming the journey was without mishap or delay, it would take at least thirty hours to sail the one hundred and twenty nautical miles to Lucaya before these desperate refugees would see the low flat outline of their destination on the horizon. Still more dangers might face them. On occasion over the years, local inhabitants had discovered bloated bodies decomposing along the remote beaches of Northwest Point, trapped between iron-shore rocks and undulating obscenely in the lapping waters.

Sometimes these poor souls were forced at gunpoint by avaricious and heartless captains to abandon ship half a mile or even further away from the island, to swim for a shore only a few would ever reach alive.

Flight number TX558, Air Caraibes, was called over the intercom and Richard Wagner stood up to wait in line. He showed his passport, a South African one this time, handed the woman his boarding pass to scan and then walked through the doors to the waiting A356. He found it rather a nuisance that no sooner had they taken off from Port-au-Prince than they were preparing to land in Santo Domingo, just a short flight down the coast of the island of Hispaniola.

Joseph Pierre Toussaint was in his early thirties, well-nourished and a strong swimmer. He saw two people drown, an infant and a teenage girl, as he swam almost effortlessly towards the shore. He had tied a small waterproof bag to his waist containing a pair of sandals, a t-shirt and shorts. He was still wearing his waterproof watch but otherwise had no other form of ID or any other personalized item that might identify him if he were picked up by the local authorities.

Joseph had studied a basic map of Lucaya before leaving Haiti and so had a fairly good idea he was heading for the western and remotest part.

As he neared the shore, he could see no visible lights or any sign of a welcoming committee such as the police. The nameless man on the phone, who Joseph thought was English, had told him that the new radar was highly unreliable in detecting smaller craft and this is why he finally chose the sloop over a larger motorized boat.

A week after the initial phone call with Monsieur 'English', a man came to Joseph's larger-than-average shack, with a real tin roof instead of tarpaulin, and gave him a manila envelope containing two thousand dollars. He would be paid the balance of three thousand dollars once there was confirmation that his mission had been successful. The owner of the boat was a distant relative; Joseph had paid him a little extra to keep the cargo of illegals to a minimum to avoid the sloop being destabilized by overcrowding. It was not unusual for these small boats to cram on as many as seventy-five desperate people.

It took him almost three hours to walk to the small beach community called Morgan's Cay where many of the Haitian expats congregated at the bars and brothels seeking news from home or word about the latest illegal landings. Locals were also drawn to perhaps the liveliest nightspot on Lucaya, where sex and drugs were cheap and guns readily available for purchase. Expat Englishmen and Canadians, including lawyers and judges who lived in luxurious condos or multi-million dollars homes on the beaches, went to Morgan's Cay to satiate their carnal lusts with women much younger than their wives at home.

No one paid him any heed when he walked into the bar and bought a Prestige beer and sat at one of the tables outside. Within five minutes one of a dozen or so Dominican girls who worked this bar and several others in Morgan's Cay wandered over and sat beside him. He bought her a beer and then half an hour later followed her to one of the rooms at the rear of the bar. Inside was a single bed, a chair, a washbasin and a toilet behind a partition. He paid her for the night and shortly afterwards he fell asleep leaving the pretty *Dominicana* free to continue to ply her trade using a friend's room close by.

Joseph slept soundly for the next nine hours.

CHAPTER 30

NEW BUSINESS – *Parish of Manchester*
Jamaica, July 2017

She finished taping up the twelfth and final box of the morning and then made herself a coffee and sat down for a break. She was thinking how quickly Daniel had recognized her creative talents, attributes she was aware of but had lacked the self-confidence to pursue until he urged her to seriously consider starting a little business of her own.

It was hard not to notice her gift for fashion and design even from the time he had first caught sight of her at the premier's party. It was the way she could distinguish in her mind's eye the sublime from the unexceptional that he found so intriguing, clothes which she uniquely fashioned by coordinating colours and inexpensive materials that never failed to highlight her best qualities, or indeed those of any woman's. Not only could she envisage the intricacies of beauty in how an article of clothing was worn, according to the complexion, size and age of the wearer; it was quite clear to him that she also possessed the natural acumen to become a successful businesswoman. All she lacked was a little self-confidence. All it took to create that was for someone who cared to point her in the right direction. Until now, working for herself had never really entered her head. That she had always thought was a dream belonging to someone else.

Brianna, or Abigay as she called herself these days, also possessed the knack to rummage for hours through the market stalls and discount shops, never failing to find quality clothing in the most beautiful materials and colours, always at the lowest prices. She took full advantage of her personality, always smiling and often laughing with the stall owners, who quickly succumbed to her infectious charms. They called out to her as she weaved through the market crowds, picking up garments that caught her eye. She would haggle over the price, giggling with owners when they feigned exasperation, only to concede five minutes later by accepting her offer.

No one genuinely resented her ability to drive a hard bargain. Some would pretend to shoo her away, urging her to move on to the next stall and take advantage of their neighbour instead. No sooner would she start moving on than they would laugh, pleading for her to come back. They all loved Abigay and she made each one of them feel very special. So, what if they rarely made a profit from her? She brought something to their lives worth more than money.

She was already making more than she had ever made working for someone else. It was not even like real work, because she enjoyed it so much. Each morning it was the same. She would be up before dawn and rush to town as soon as the market had been restocked from Kingston. It was open twenty-four hours a day, and nearly always she discovered something unique to purchase. After the shopping she would carry everything back to her apartment, where she'd photograph it using her iPhone before posting it on eBay. Some items ended up selling for twice as much to customers in cities she had never heard of in England and the United States; there was even one order from Alice Springs in Australia. She found it all terribly exciting and always looked forward to the following day, even on weekends.

She started thinking beyond eBay shortly after becoming friendly with one of her neighbours, an IT teacher at the university less than half a mile from the apartment. One weekend they had started talking when the woman, whose name was Jevon, invited Abigay over for a drink in her apartment on the third floor. They shared a half bottle of Appleton's rum and Abigay told Jevon what she was doing, only later revealing her story about being a widow recently returned from the Bahamas. Jevon suggested she should develop her own website to promote her fashions. In exchange for a few well-chosen items from the market, Jevon agreed to build a website for Abigay. They called it Caribbean Fashions & Accessories. On the website it was advertised as CaribFash.

Jevon also offered to promote the website on social media if Abigay would help coordinate her wardrobe. There were other people at the university she could introduce Abigay to who would pay good money for someone with such terrific fashion sense to shop for them. These were predominantly middle-class Jamaicans; they had money, but most of them worked long hours and had neither the time nor the fashion sense Abigay possessed.

Brianna was receiving so many orders after just a few weeks that she was unable to take them all to the post office in a single trip. To overcome this problem, she arranged for a local taxi company to pick her up each morning, and with Jevon's assistance she would fill the taxi with as many packages as it would carry. At the post office the driver would help her carry the parcels inside. Once she had finished filling out the various custom declarations and DHL Fast Track documents, she would walk home. Brianna paid fifty per cent of the shipping costs and the customer paid the balance.

One evening when she was taping up the last package for the day, she started thinking about Daniel. She had not heard from him since he told her he would be going to see his sister in some place called Flinders and would call her on Skype when he got back. That was over ten days ago now and she had started to worry. He was usually so punctual and reliable. She prayed he was OK because he was her whole life now, the only man she wanted to be with. 'Love is only a four-letter word' – she had previously believed the lyrics from the Joan Baez song. She had understood how wrong she had been ever since that fateful night under a canopy of stars brushed by the warm trade winds.

She knew he felt exactly as she had when they first looked at one another that night on Lucaya. It had been an abrupt and intimate connection of two like minds in an undefined moment, full of the promise and magic of unconditional love that neither fully understood nor could quantify at the time. It had been the strangest of feelings, like two halves colliding and finally becoming whole again.

Brianna accepted that Daniel remained in love with his wife, just as she understood that she could only ever borrow him. But wasn't this the case in any relationship, when nothing in life is permanent? It was a condition few women would dream of accepting, at least not without the promise of a long-term future together, when happiness might be discarded for the lure of financial security. Brianna was a Jamaican woman, both resilient and realistic. It was better, she believed, to have a man who truly cared for her, even if she saw him only rarely. Demanding more than he could ever give, possibly destroying other lives in a selfish quest for her own happiness – that would never be an option. She knew she would only lose him that way.

There were good Jamaican men, but she had yet to meet one. Most of them wanted the same thing, after which their women were disposable, and certainly if they became pregnant. There was no chance of her ever falling into that trap! Spending time, no matter how long, with someone she truly loved and who loved her in return was infinitely preferable to living a life on the edge of poverty with several children and no man to support her, as her mother had endured for so many years.

Some days she forgot entirely why she had moved to Mandeville in the first place. That she could still be in grave danger no longer really concerned her, nor often occurred to her. The more she became immersed in her business, the less she thought about what had happened on Lucaya, or the conversation her friend had overheard in the Dominican Republic between the premier and the peer's son. None of it seemed real to her anymore, except the love she had for Daniel and the excitement she derived from her business.

But today she was feeling anxious again. Daniel should have called her by now or at least have sent her an email. Once she had completed all her morning chores and had been to the post office and the market, she returned home and sat on her sofa until it started growing dark, imagining the very worst. In three hours, she only got up once to use the bathroom and make herself a cup of tea. What would she do, she wondered, if something awful had happened?

She jumped when there was a sudden knock on her door. It was Jevon wanting to share another bottle of Appleton's. Brianna laughed and let her in and forgot her worries for a while. Around nine, after Jevon had returned to her own apartment, singing and blowing kisses to her friend Abigay, Brianna decided to have a chat with her mum, using her Skype-to-phone plan, to check whether she had enough money for the week. Jevon and the rum had cheered Brianna considerably by then.

The first thing her mother said was that someone had come to the house looking for her, a white man wearing a suit. She thought he was an Englishman.

CHAPTER 31

THE CURTIS BUILDING – London
July 2017

Roger Sage received the call from the commissioner's office as he was working on several urgent emails at a hot-desking bar on the second floor. The verdict in the corruption trial was anticipated in the next few weeks, possibly before the end of September, and he was busy corresponding with his island colleagues on a secure line. They were all in the process of developing and coordinating an emergency action plan should the verdict create social unrest.

Although he was confident there were enough police on the island to take control of any situation, he supported having additional police on standby who could be flown in from the UK at short notice. The idea of a military rapid-reaction tactical team, supported by factions within the FCO, he considered political suicide. The local population, he warned, would immediately begin screaming blue bloody murder. They would describe it as an invasion by the racist British, their 'colonial masters', which might create a chain reaction of upheaval in other British Dependent Territories. Certainly, it would generate anti-British sentiment worldwide. With Brexit looming ever closer, the country desperately needed to avoid problems from one of its overseas dependent territories, especially one that had expressed a desire for independence (which Britain quietly supported simply to be rid of the irritation).

The Commissioner of Police of the Metropolis had assumed her position less than six months before, the first female ever appointed to the rank. She was sitting at one of a number of otherwise vacant tables on the penthouse level of the recently renovated Curtis Building. The building had been part of a complex comprising the original Scotland Yard until the headquarters required larger accommodation back in the sixties. Now, due to the promotion of a more agile working environment and the introduction of the latest architectural innovations, the Met could operate from its riverside Curtis location once again. With its spanking new neo-classical façade and five hundred and fifty workstations, rather than the more than three thousand in the purpose-built building on Broadway designed for a far different era, it was ideally suited to meet the requirements of a modern-day British police force.

As Roger Sage approached the table, the man he knew only as Bryce stood up. They had first met in February at the Red Lion Tavern around the corner. Roger doubted Bryce realized how idiotic he looked with the halo of the London Eye on the other side of the Thames revolving around the back of his head.

Bryce introduced the commissioner, who Roger Sage had not yet met, and they all sat down. A male constable brought over a tray with three cups and saucers and a pot of tea. There was also a small plate of digestive biscuits. Bryce hosted the event and played mother.

"Inspector," the commissioner began, "you appreciate the potential volatility of the situation on Lucaya, perhaps more than anyone else."

Sage nodded in acknowledgement.

"You are involved in drawing up contingency plans with the Royal Island Police, am I correct?"

"Yes, Ma'am," he said, taking the cup of tea Bryce handed him.

"Well, I didn't ask you to come here today to discuss the implications resulting from the verdict," she stated firmly. "That's a political matter and we can leave that up to the politicians down the road." She tilted her head sideways towards Parliament less than half a mile along the Embankment. "We are here today to discuss if you have made any headway on the other matter."

"Meaning, Lord Elm and son?"

"Exactly," she said. "It's for good reason the CPS on Lucaya did not want to bring formal charges against the former premier and Michael Elm until the judge in the corruption trial had announced the verdicts."

"That decision was made on our advice, Commissioner," Roger explained, realizing that she was so new to the job that she would need further briefing on all aspects of the case. "From the onset," he continued, "we had to separate the two issues, because the defence attorneys in the corruption trial would have jumped at any opportunity, no matter how frivolous, to demand the judge declare a mistrial. Prevailing thinking at the time doubted a retrial would ever happen because much of the evidence could be compromised by linking the former premier with the son of one of the UK's wealthiest individuals."

"You made the correct decision, of course, but I wanted you here today to discuss what's happening on the ground right now, including the murder of one potential witness and the intimidation of another!"

Interrupting Sage, claiming to speak on behalf of the prime minister and the Foreign Office, Bryce began to detail the possible political fallout if the police or the government were perceived as having turned a blind eye and done nothing. The prime minister, he said, was concerned that it would undermine British democracy if a corrupt billionaire could manipulate the system to protect his son. "Strictly between us sitting here in this room," Bryce said, "it is conceivable that even my own boss, the Foreign Secretary, has been bought off, as well as others in the FCO and almost certainly others within the police."

The commissioner then interrupted Bryce at this point. "As you well know, inspector, Michael Elm or his father, or indeed both of them, is making a concerted effort to intimidate or dispose of witnesses in this matter involving Michael and the premier. If they prove successful, the presiding judge will likely throw out any statement made by those witnesses without at least one willing to testify in person before a jury."

Roger Sage agreed, as did Bryce.

"Daniel Hannaford is our only viable witness at the moment, ma'am," Roger said, "but he hasn't signed a statement as yet. Understandably, he's concerned about his wife and I don't blame him for procrastinating. I know he wants to sign, yet he feels caught between a rock and a hard place. Unusual for this day and age, he appears to have scruples and has indicated to me personally that he thinks Elm's son should be prosecuted for such a heinous crime.

"On the other hand," Sage continued, "he doesn't want to endanger his wife either, a veritable Catch-22 situation for Mr. Hannaford."

The commissioner told them that she had telephoned the federal police in Canberra several months back asking them for their assistance should it be required. They had agreed to contact the police in Eden, a small coastal town close to the Victorian border, who would try to keep an eye on the Hannafords. "Only problem with that," she said, "is that the Eden station is short on manpower and too limited by budgetary constraints to be very effective." Commissioner Dick was encouraged, though, by the way the Australian feds had cooperated when the situation merited an immediate response. Canberra could not have been more helpful since the attack on the Hannaford house.

Roger interjected and told them that he was currently liaising with Canberra to devise ways to protect the husband and wife. Also, Daniel Hannaford had indicated that he was finally willing to fly over to the UK to sign and have his statement witnessed. He knew that he and his wife would remain at risk whether or not he signed a statement.

"We are watching Geoffrey Elm very closely these days," the commissioner mentioned towards the end of their meeting. "We believe he was directly implicated in the woman's murder in Florida." Sage and Bryce had not heard this story yet, but the commissioner was unwilling to elaborate until she had something more substantive. Sage and Bryce both guessed that this new information would likely have emanated from MI6.

"Well, gentlemen, thank you both for coming. Obviously, this is all to be kept confidential for the time being, strictly on a need-to-know basis during the course of your investigations."

"One last thing, ma'am," Roger Sage said as they all stood to leave. "I am interviewing a young woman this afternoon from Lucaya. She is married to a British lawyer there, though they are currently separated. Anyway, the lawyer works for a firm on the island that handles some of Geoffrey Elm's legal work, one of several law firms he engages from time to time. They say he contracts many of the best firms and lawyers on the island purposely to create conflicts of interest should someone who has a problem with Elm need a good lawyer. He wins by default. No one is going to sue him and win if they can't find a half-decent brief."

"Smart," Bryce commented.

"I don't have much more time, Inspector, what about this woman?"

"Sorry, ma'am, but the woman indicates she wants to make a formal complaint about Michael Elm who apparently tried to rape her when he was last on the island."

"Oh, my God!" the commissioner exclaimed. "When was this?"

"Last year, ma'am. She wasn't going to mention it to anyone, but she has been in fear of her life since Michael Elm's driver and bodyguard threatened her. She's terrified, too afraid to talk to the authorities on the island in case it gets back to Geoffrey or Michael. That's why she is here to talk to us in private. She's also scared for her two children!"

"You don't think they might do anything to harm her children?" the commissioner queried.

"Indirectly they already have, ma'am. Her estranged husband is threatening to sue for custody of the pair. He's a real lowlife who went off to have an affair with the daughter of another influential lawyer on the island. By the sounds of things, to advance his career," he added.

"At his family's expense. Nice man! She is very brave for talking to you, Inspector. She could lose everything." The commissioner paused to finish her tea, and then said, "We must work diligently to bring a successful prosecution against them both. People like that are cancerous and require to be surgically removed to protect society, as quickly as possible."

The commissioner began walking towards the elevator then quickly turned. "And what about the other witness, the one in Jamaica, I believe? Any word on her yet?"

'No, ma'am," Roger answered, "the Jamaican police are still looking for her but are stretched to the limit with their own domestic problems. Interestingly, however, someone passing through Jamaican Immigration a few days ago was red-flagged, someone who used to work on Elm's yacht, a Falkland War vet."

"OK, well, monitor that and see where it leads, if anywhere. Could be just a man on a holiday. Anyway, I have to dash. Have a meeting with Catherine de Bolle from EUROPOL in fifteen minutes."

CHAPTER 32

LEEWARD ISLAND BANK – Lucaya

August 2017

Ex-premier Walter Harrison no longer had access to the government Range Rover provided him when he was in office, though he had retained Lloyd Bailey as his driver and bodyguard. The Foreign and Commonwealth Office in London had insisted that, in addition to absorbing the cost of the lengthy corruption trial, the Lucayan government cover the cost of their former premier's security detail, consisting of Lloyd Bailey and a British police sergeant from London who doubled as a second bodyguard and relief driver.

The latter's duties also included monitoring Harrison's activities, where he went and with whom he met. And he had to ensure the former premier maintained the ten pm to seven am curfew imposed by the court. During curfew Harrison was confined to a luxury beach penthouse condominium paid for directly by London. The FCO were determined his detention on Lucaya would be perceived by the public as more befitting a former head of state than his incarceration had been in Rio de Janeiro.

Lloyd Bailey parked Walter Harrison's personal Suburban Premier SUV in the no parking zone in front of the bank. Even now few were brave enough to ask the disgraced premier to move his car. He still had many supporters on the island, many of whom claimed he was being used as a scapegoat by the British to cover up the parts the FCO and

Lord Elm and his son had played in the decade of corruption. Others even suggested it was a diabolical plot to re-establish colonialism.

Geoffrey Elm's thoughts on the matter were quite different from the current thinking of the British government. Because of the massive amount of money he had invested in real estate there, he needed Lucaya to remain British. His bank was the island's largest mortgage provider. Via loopholes in local laws, the Leeward Bank had also taken full advantage of the territory's convenience as a tax haven for the mega-wealthy. It was rumoured to be a money-laundering facility for criminals and citizens of pariah states in Africa and the former Soviet bloc. Half of the bank's money was said to come from Russia. The Leeward Bank was private and the majority of shares was owned by Lord Geoffrey Elm, who had a vested interest in retaining the political status quo. Bailey opened the rear door to the SUV and Walter Harrison stepped out and walked to the front entrance of the building. No one was there to let him in as they had when he was premier. He had pressed the security door buzzer yet was left standing there for several minutes feeling annoyed and slightly foolish. He pressed the buzzer again and eventually someone he had never met before came to open the door. The man was a recent expat employee from Belize; he had no idea who Walter Harrison was nor, as it turned out, had anyone else in the bank been informed he was coming that afternoon.

This was outrageous, Harrison thought. How dare they treat him like this after he had supported the bank for six years? Especially when his government had been instrumental in establishing its charter in the first place. From the corner of his eye, he saw that someone was talking to his driver, a conversation that seemed to be escalating into an argument of some sort. He was about to go back outside when the bank manager stepped from around the corner; he had summoned Harrison to the bank without advising any of his staff. He was a spindly looking man in his early forties wearing rimless glasses. Walter Harrison had always intensely disliked him because of the man's disingenuous attitude towards him, feigning respect only for the office of the premier, not the man.

Walter had been socializing with white people long enough to see through the thin veneer protecting their racist views from public scrutiny. Pretend as much as they liked, given the opportunity, white men such as the bank manager would be one of the first pulling on the rope in the lynching of a black man.

The bank manager had no chance to speak before Walter Harrison suddenly turned and headed for the door to find out what on earth was going on outside. His driver was now banging the hood of the SUV.

"Lloyd, what's going on?"

Lloyd pushed the man before him, but he stood his ground and turned his attention to the former premier a few yards away.

"I was simply telling your driver he had to remove the car and park in the general parking area over there," the man said, pointing to several other cars parked where they were supposed to be. Harrison did not respond but told his driver to get inside the car, lock the door and remain exactly where he was until he had finished inside. He had kept the door to the bank open with one hand and so was able to re-enter the building without the embarrassment of having to press the buzzer again.

He then stormed inside fuming, stopping just inches from the manager who stepped backwards in surprise. The man from Belize who had first opened the door and a receptionist appeared, shocked by Harrison's sudden aggressive behaviour.

"What is the reason for this?" Harrison yelled. "You know exactly who I am and you know my driver has always parked there when I come to the bank! Not only have you disrespected my driver, you are disrespecting me, the man responsible for your fucking charter."

When Stewart Miles failed to comment and instead turned on his heels to head back to his office, Walter Harrison had only two choices: follow him or leave the building! Curiosity, however, got the better of him.

Because he had no idea why the manager had personally called him to the bank in the first place, he decided to follow him to his office. Shortly afterwards he wished he had not.

For the second time in less than ten minutes, the Rt Hon Walter Harrison was enraged. He crashed from the manager's office in fury. He had been subjected to the insults of a man who was only there because he had approved his work visa! How dare this white trash talk to him this way, Walter fumed, someone on a work permit no less!

Walter was determined to call Immigration immediately and have this white fucker's visa revoked and him sent packing back to Canada or England, or whichever shithole he had crawled from. He threw open the car door and got into Suburban before Lloyd had time to get out and open the door for him.

"Take me to Immigration, Lloyd, NOW!" he ordered.

Without any fanfare of prior notification, written or otherwise, Walter Harrison had been put on notice that the bank would take possession of his mansion, known to many as Tara, in exactly one month unless Lord Elm's bank had been paid the eight million dollars it was owed. Two years ago, he could simply have transferred funds over from his bank in Slovakia. However, the British had managed to freeze those funds along with the rest of his money and assets. The British could not touch Tara, of course, because the bank still maintained title on the property and Elm was the principal owner of the bank.

Walter could have arranged to have Elm kicked off the island – except that he was largely responsible for conferring citizenship on the duplicitous bastard a decade ago.

In a month, Walter Harrison would be stripped of his entire fortune and left virtually homeless. Walter Harrison has been well and truly duped by the British lord!

It was on the trip downtown that he revisited the idea of approaching the British government with information concerning Lord Elm's son, something so damaging it would crack his lordship's empire in half and see both father and son incarcerated in a Victorian prison over in that vilest of countries. Walter realized he had nothing to lose. He had already decided this would be his endgame if he and the others were convicted on corruption charges. The Brits and the Americans had been after Elm for years and he had information to trade to avoid jail time.

CHAPTER 33

THE HAITIAN AND THE GUN – Lucaya
August 2017

Richard Crossly was far from being a prude, but he was appalled by what he discovered in the former fishing village of Morgan's Cay. He had been living on Lucaya off and on for several decades and had never remotely imagined something like this would have been permitted to flourish. It was even more striking when you took into account that the island was governed by a population of self-professed, God-fearing believers in the teachings of Jesus Christ.

The Lucayans had encouraged their neighbours to believe they were devout worshippers who regularly attended one of the many new churches that had sprung up around the island over the past twenty years. Catering to every Christian denomination under the sun, Lucaya, it was claimed, had more churches per head of population than any other country in the world.

Congregations filled the large churches to capacity on Sundays, or on Saturdays if they were Seven Day Adventists or Jehovah's Witnesses. There were also many smaller venues of worship, often no more than a shed or a ten-by-ten storage unit down by the docks with less than a dozen or two faithful followers.

Their self-proclaimed preachers would set up ad hoc speakers balanced on old crates for their worshipers standing outside in the heat of the sun. There they could hear the Good Word spoken in Creole by a so-called man of God earning more on one Sunday morning than he might ever have done over in Haiti the entire year.

The women church-goers trudged along the side of dusty roads in their garish finery, perspiring in the sweltering heat and mopping their brow with napkin-size towels. They competed with one another in their large often outrageous hats more suited to Ascot, whilst the men followed behind in suits too big, wearing ties under shirt collars too loose.

Men carried their bibles proudly under their arms, proclaiming to the outside world their devotion and self-importance on the Lord's Day, which the expat or tourist had for the most part discarded. This was the one day of the week when they felt superior to the white man. Blind to their own hypocrisy, they ignored the egregious failings of their pastors, who amassed personal fortunes in offerings from their congregations, or who persuaded underage girls and boys that they had been chosen by God to satiate the earthly needs of His anointed clergy.

Richard had often heard others talk of it, but he had never witnessed himself the dramatic change that had taken place during the six years Walter Harrison had been premier. He was always too busy working, trying to keep the business afloat and pay off outstanding debts. With all his many faults, he had never been one to seek carnal pleasures other than with his wife, and only then two or three times a year, whenever he returned to England.

These days his wife never visited him on the island. She had felt uncomfortable on the few occasions she had been obliged to associate with the British faux gentry, people subtly adept in denigrating one another in the nicest of possible ways. Many expats perfected this skill once they escaped the limitations of their social class back home. Here on the island, they could enjoy a level of social recognition beyond their dull, middle-class lives in suburban Britain. On Lucaya they could be anyone they chose.

Ten years before, there had been a few houses in Morgan's Cay and two small shops selling essentials (to save a jitney ride to the island's large supermarket whose prices were designed for the expat's wallet). Back then, the community had banded together in an initiative to buy a portion of the local daily fish catch at a reasonable price instead of it all going to the tourist hotels and the expensive Coral Bay supermarket. The community then paid a little more during the summer months, after the tourists had gone, to compensate the fishermen for their marginal losses during high season.

They also made arrangements with the captain of a brightly painted, wooden yawl that sailed twice a week from Lucaya to the Dominican Republic to take advantage of the lower prices on that half of the island of Hispaniola. It returned fully loaded with fruit and vegetables, canned goods and cases of El Presidente beer, soap, toothpaste and even contraceptives. Cartons of cigarettes were smuggled within the cargo to avoid local duties, as well as the Dominican cigars the residents of Morgan's Cay sold to American and Canadian tourists. They brought over supplies of every conceivable style and colour of wigs, hygiene products and cheap make-up for the women who otherwise would pay three times as much in stores catering to the special needs of black women in Miami or Fort Lauderdale.

Guns and drugs were smuggled to the island as currency for survival by desperate refugees on the Haitian sloops. The captain of the brightly painted yawl was earning sufficient money without jeopardizing everything for such illegal goods.

But there was no longer any regular day-to-day commerce in Morgan's Cay, at least none that Richard noticed. Money changed hands only in the bars emitting an ear-pounding scramble of rap and Latin rhythm virtually twenty-four hours a day. Morgan's Cay was only a hamlet by day. At night it became a busy town as men from all walks of life on the island began to drift there to relax from their day's toil. It was a brief respite from their otherwise dull lives.

Sweating profusely and grinning foolishly the men lumbered from one bar to the next checking out the girls like cattle in a market. The locals born on the island controlled the politics of this British Dependent

Territory, including the issuance of work permits, and confident no policeman would ever arrest them for breaking the law by contributing to prostitution.

Even local island paedophiles received no more than a slap on the wrist, whilst many children remained cloaked beneath dark family secrets hiding the endemic island scourge of incest, seldom reported to the police. The expat constables seconded from Barbados and St Lucia were all too familiar with the problem on their own islands. All were too afraid of losing their jobs and being shipped back home if, God forbid, they ever upset a Lucayan and charged them with molesting a son or daughter, no matter the pleadings of a mother or a relative.

The next in the power hierarchy were the professional, mostly white men, the lawyers, the bankers and the British government officials. As long as they did not step over recognized boundaries and commit an egregious crime, they could get away with practically anything they wanted. But the voyeurs who hugged the shadows and avoided eye contact were the illegals or the poor who still had the same human urges as any man; they could only look and not touch the scantily clad Latinas plying their trade.

Their employers, who forced the girls to work if they ever wanted to retrieve their passports, paid very little if anything at all. Nearly all were illegals, brought over by boat with promises of mucho dinero only to discover they had been entrapped in the world of sex slavery on an island where they'd been assured it did not exist. The British would never permit it, they were told, although the British civil servants, many of the police and almost all of the British and expat lawyers often partook in the delights of Morgan's Cay.

Richard found the bar he had been told to go to and sat down at one of the tables. Almost immediately an extremely pretty Dominican girl, quite possibly a year or two under age, came and sat on his lap and clasped her arms around his neck. She was wearing a tight-fitting blue halter top with a pair of equally tight-fitting red shorts that revealed every aspect of her form. He was overwhelmed by the pungent and almost sickly-sweet perfume she was wearing.

He pushed her off and said he was meeting someone. He said he only wanted a drink, whereupon she disappeared for a couple of minutes and returned with two beers, one for him and one for herself. She then asked him to give her one hundred dollars to pay for the two drinks, which even at one of the luxury hotels would not have cost more than ten dollars each. At any regular bar on the beach, they would have only been six dollars.

He had already taken a gulp of the El Presidente, and so it was too late to complain, and in any case, he did not wish to cause a scene. He just wanted to get the whole thing over and then find a jitney and go home to the wealthier, expat end of the island.

Once the girl realized her time with him was not a good investment, she left, after giving Richard a parting flourish of her hips to make sure he understood what he was missing. The owner glared at him in disapproval from across the bar for daring to take a table with no mind to be entertained by one of his girls.

It made no sense whatsoever making Richard the errand boy – other than the fact that he owed the bank close to two million dollars in various loans accumulated over a decade. His interest payments alone were over twenty thousand a month. The moment they insisted he start paying down some of the principal as well as interest, he knew he might as well pack his bags and head back to England. It would leave him destitute, although eligible next year for a British state pension that would do nothing at all to resolve his state of insolvency. The Elms could count on his full co-operation because they controlled his future. Even so, despite the possibility of imprisonment once he did this – under duress as he would later assert – he would own theirs.

Lord Elm and his son were not thinking long-term as he was. Handing the package over would compromise him and maintain his silence, or so they thought, but his silence could cost them the loan. It was well worth the risk, he had considered, once they understood the police might receive a complete file of all their activities during the time he had known them. He had the means to pressure the father and son. The problem he was facing now was whether he had the courage.

He sat there for half an hour watching men of all colours as they passed his table on the prowl. He saw two lawyers he knew, one from Canada and the other from Ireland. He even noticed a diminutive QC from Liverpool whose Australian wife had recently had a baby. He was busy drooling over a Haitian woman several inches taller. Then the former premier of the island walked by with two women clinging to him on either side.

Why on earth would he come here, Richard wondered. He had access to a beach apartment and sufficient money to pay for half a dozen women.

Perhaps it was the seedy atmosphere that attracted him to the place. Or was Walter Harrison escaping from his luxury confinement – a life he was not born to – to revisit a past he was more comfortable with before his life changed forever in some prison overseas?

Yet he seemed to have no cares in the world, Richard thought. He didn't know that Harrison was actually out celebrating his deal with the British government. London had finally agreed to no jail time for information that would lead to the convictions of Geoffrey and Michael Elm. The Dominican girl had insisted Richard have another beer and brought it to his table suggesting he could have a young man if he was not interested in girls. Richard shook his head wearily and she went off pouting, wriggling her behind suggestively. Ten minutes later, a tall and remarkably healthy-looking Haitian man sat next to him at his table. "My name is Joseph Pierre Toussant," was all he said. Richard took out a package from inside the small shoulder bag he had been carrying and placed it on the table directly in front of the man and then stood up and left without saying a word.

Joseph picked up the package and also left the bar, following in the same direction as Richard. He had recognized Crossly from a photo he had been shown by the other white man in Haiti.

CHAPTER 34

SOLOMONS TO SAN FRANCISCO

December 1851

*C*aptain Bradley of the Ariel and many of the crew knew Mark Boyd
by sight, yet only Bradley was privy to certain aspects of their secret
voyage to the South Seas.

From the onset, he was purposely led to believe the need for secrecy
was a condition of the British admiralty, which had a non-commercial
interest in the voyage. This was what Mark Boyd had told Bradley months
before in San Francisco. No one apart from the two brothers had any idea
the real purpose was to assist Benjamin to disappear forever. Certainly,
Captain Edward Blyth of the Pacific Pearl had no advance knowledge,
and Captain Bradley was told only that Mark Boyd was sailing secretly to
Midway to confirm there were substantial commercial quantities of guano
on the island to be harvested.

Prior to leaving San Francisco, Bradley had met privately with
the Captain of the Pacific Pearl and had paid him a hefty advance to take
Mark Boyd to Midway. He promised that the remainder would be payable
on their return to San Francisco, the city on the bay the British had seriously considered annexing from Mexico only a decade earlier.

Bradley had introduced Mark Boyd to Captain Blyth as Aiken
Taverner, an agricultural specialist under instruction from the Admiralty.
As far as anyone was aware, apart from Bradley, his purview to export
guano from Midway to the Solomon Islands was intended as an initial

study into the feasibility of future intensive farming projects in other developing countries of the empire. More importantly, he was told, the Admiralty also had an interest in guano because of its high explosive content.

Once Bradley and the Ariel were well over the horizon and on their way to Cape Town, 'Aiken Taverner', or Mark Boyd, instructed the captain of the Pacific Pearl to set a different course for the return voyage from Midway to San Francisco. They would go via the Solomon Islands, adding over five thousand nautical miles to the voyage, to collect two English botanists who had been exploring the islands. The captain saw the bag of gold coins Aiken was prepared to pay for the inconvenience and immediately agreed, asking no questions. The captain was also aware that Aiken would be handing him a sight draft for the original balance due once they arrived back in San Francisco.

They anchored five days later in a separate bay from the Wanderer a few miles further up the coast. The crew were happy to have the time off; they relaxed in hammocks above decks in the warm sunshine with plenty of grog. There was not much to do except wait. They were not allowed ashore in case contact was established inadvertently with crew from the Wanderer – or there was a chance encounter with the natives who were considered dangerous. Expeditions ashore for food or water were also not permitted.

The Pacific Pearl already had plenty of fresh water aboard to drink, but it was rationed for personal hygiene, limited to one bucket each, twice a week. Those who could swim jumped from the deck to refresh themselves in the cool, clear water below.

Mark Boyd and the crew had heard the gunshots a few hours earlier and Mark was becoming concerned. His brother and Stevens should have shown up three days ago. Like many of the others he was starting to believe 'the botanists' were already dead, and he was almost convinced of it when they heard the guns firing a few miles up the coast. Mark suggested sending a search party ashore, but the idea was quickly dismissed by the captain who was reluctant to risk the lives of his men.

He told Mark Boyd they would wait one more day before setting sail. In all likelihood the botanists were dead, boiled and digested by this time!

Benjamin Boyd sat waiting in the shade under a slender bowed palm that seemed to be genuflecting towards the brigantine moored offshore. He could just make out two men clambering into the small boat knocking gently against the hull of the Pacific Pearl. He had no doubt that one was his brother. There were a dozen or so other men on deck, all staring out over the turquoise blue in his direction.

The small craft finally came ashore and he saw his brother get out and walk towards him over the sand. The sailor who'd rowed them both remained with the boat. Even from that distance Mark could tell there was something seriously wrong. Benjamin was half-naked and he had what looked like blood covering his face and torso; he had been burnt raw from the sun.

"Heaven help us, what transpired for you to arrive in this condition, dear brother?" Mark took off his jacket and draped it over his brother's shoulders to protect him from the hot sun. "Where is Stevens?" he asked.

Benjamin had to dissuade his brother from organizing a search party to recover Stevens' remains. He told him how his former cabin boy had been butchered by at least six or seven Micronesians, most likely cannibals, but that was not before he had put up tremendous resistance, permitting Benjamin to escape. Later, as he ran for the beach towards the ocean, Benjamin told Mark, he had turned briefly to see Stevens fall. The natives began slashing at his body with their machetes.

Luckily, they did not come after him, he told his brother. Stevens' misfortune allowed Benjamin time to wade out into the sea, splashing through the shallow water in a frantic escape.

"The crew from the Wanderer will no doubt find his remains at first light on the morrow, brother, once they realize we are missing after dark. God willing, they will provide him with a decent burial and read passages from the Holy Scriptures over him. He was well-loved by us all."

Benjamin paused and whispered, "And may the good Lord bring him eternal peace."

"Amen," said Mark.

It took the schooner over three weeks to return to San Francisco from Guadalcanal. During the long voyage, Benjamin remained in his cabin alone until nightfall, or occasionally Mark would come to see him during the day to speak on various matters. They had agreed that Benjamin should remain out of sight for the duration of the voyage, allowing him time to recover from his severe sunburn, but primarily to avoid any possibility of recognition. Only late at night would he venture from his cabin to stretch his legs, when there was little chance of him being noticed.

All the crew had seen of the botanist was when they had helped him aboard with the assistance of Mark. The coat covering his shoulders partly obscured his face when he stepped onto the deck of the Pacific Pearl. Not that it would have mattered had anyone seen his face, because by the time the ship docked out in San Francisco Bay no one would have recognized him.

Mark had cropped his brother's hair short, and over several weeks Benjamin washed it in a strong soap called lye made from ashes and goat fat. His hair became much lighter and tinged with red, a process discovered in olden times when the Vikings purposely made themselves look fiercer with their long, flowing red hair and beards.

Benjamin had also shaved off his muttonchops and had started wearing a corset to enable him to dress in a fashionable suit appropriate for his profession. A Chinese tailor in San Francisco had made it for him months before he had departed for the South Seas on the Wanderer. Mark had brought it with him on the Ariel along with some shirts and other accessories for his brother to wear. Benjamin at long last was starting to relax; he slept soundly each night on the voyage over to California. Never once had he thought about Stevens since departing Guadalcanal.

The Pacific Pearl found a mooring in San Francisco Bay on 2 March 1852. It was cold and blustery out on the water as they were rowed to shore. Rain clouds scurried low overhead and sea spray from the gusting *wind drenched them both. For the first time Benjamin thought back to Guadalcanal and the devoted cabin boy who had taken care of him for over ten years. But he soon erased the errant thought from his mind and wiped away only the rain from his face with the back of his sleeve.*

California would not be admitted to the Union until three years later, in 1855, and it remained quite isolated from the rest of the country for over a decade after that. The railroads had not yet been built and Benjamin Boyd's destination precluded him from reaching it by boat. Travelling overland by horse was his only choice, which would take him several weeks. Not only was the journey over rugged terrain, it was dangerous. Encounters with the Comanches remained a threat despite the treaty the tribe had signed assuring the safety of white settlers.

There were other hostile tribes looking to scalp the white man as well, angry with the US government for so many broken treaties. Outlaws and every other charlatan, quack and vagabond also roamed the West; they would be merciless if they happened on such easy prey as the Boyd brothers, especially if the brothers had attempted their journey alone.

Mark and Benjamin had ridden as far as Los Angeles with two trusted scouts they had contracted in San Francisco, one a Pawnee from Oregon and the other a French scout who had drifted down from Canada and tried unsuccessfully to pan for gold. The four then picked up the Old Spanish Trail to Santa Fe in New Mexico, which had been maintained as a US provisional territory since being ceded to the US by Mexico with the end of the US-Mexican war three years before.

Other than a mummified body they found hanging from a tree, possibly a rustler (they cut it down and quickly buried it), their journey to Santa Fe was unremarkable. They arrived at their destination safely but longing for soft beds and warm baths.

The brothers then parted company in Santa Fe; Benjamin continued riding southeast with the French scout while Mark headed north with the Pawnee to New York. From there Mark hoped to find quick passage home to Liverpool.

CHAPTER 35

LUCAYA AIRPORT

August 2017

The distinctions between the premier and his former cabinet were as nuanced as the blue shades of the Caribbean Sea. Walter Harrison was a thoroughly *arrogant* man, contemptuous of everyone, including even his childhood friends standing alongside him drinking at the small bar/restaurant. Located inside the airport terminal, it was, like the rest of the building, badly in need of a refurbish.

His four vulgar cronies, by contrast, and based on unfounded measure, were all incredibly *conceited*. Their self-perception allowed them all to cope with their numerous shortcomings, each holding himself in the highest esteem. They were smarter and more capable than any of their peers with the sole exception, perhaps, of their 'dear leader', the former premier! There were, however, already two or three among them considering exchanging information on their 'dear leader' for a more lenient sentence should they be found guilty in the ongoing corruption trial. A man standing over the other side of the bar listened to their banter and identified them all as ignorant fools.

"We should have dragged that fucking faggot out of his house kicking and screaming and thrown him on a fucking plane back to that cesspit of a country," Harrison suggested bravely, speaking about the previous British governor. He was already well on his way to getting

169

drunk, purposely speaking loudly so the tourists sitting at the tables behind them and the Canadian lawyer drinking at the bar could hear. They heard every word but avoided looking in his direction in case he targeted them personally.

"Give me another rum, Chicken-man!" Harrison shouted at the bartender. "Well, we are about to get rid of one of them!" he exhorted to the entire room, banging his fist down hard on top of the bar, which resulted in loud cheers and raucous laughter from four of his former Cabinet. The expat across the bar folded his paper and stood up shaking his head, appalled at the behaviour; he walked out with his small carry-on and headed over to the departure gate for a flight to the Bahamas. Many of the tourists inside the restaurant also began leaving, some without finishing their food or drink. These local people at the bar were making them all feel uncomfortable, as if a group of children with ADHD disorders were about to run riot.

"Fuck off, honkeys," they chorused as the tourists hastily departed leaving dollar bills with their invoices on the bar, in most cases far in excess of the amounts they had been billed, without hesitating to wait for change. Certainly, this group of tourists would never return to this island. The atmosphere was not unlike what they imagined existed in West Englewood in Chicago or Vinegar Hill in Brooklyn, although none of them had ever ventured into such violent neighbourhoods in their lives. This situation in fact was by no means dangerous, but those scattering to board their planes were unaware of that; they were only conscious of an unpredictable situation developing in a country far from home.

"There's the motherfucker," the former Deputy Premier suddenly yelled. He was a short man who resembled the American comedian, Eddie Murphy. Normally self-effacing and polite, he would never have dreamt of screaming such obscenities in public. Times had changed, however, and he was no longer the respected politician he once was. These days pressures were mounting on him and his family, as it was for all those awaiting the verdict in their corruption trial. Like the others he was also becoming quite drunk.

The five men rushed out of the airport restaurant, each of them clutching as many paper cups and beer and coke cans as they could find on the bar counter. The former Minister of Immigration had two Corona bottles by his side as they moved quickly towards the departure gate and immigration control. At the same time, the automatic doors to the terminal opened and two policemen entered escorting a tanned white man. He was not handcuffed to them. There was no need. There was nothing more the man wanted than to leave this hateful island. Indeed, he would have pleaded to be thrown on the plane, any plane, had they suddenly had a change of heart and allowed him to remain in the country.

Stewart Miles, until a week ago the manager of Lord Elm's island bank, was also gay. He had been living in one of the most homophobic yet hypocritical societies in the western world. Island men said one thing in public yet behaved differently in private. Pastors, politicians and police from the island had all been spotted at times enjoying forbidden pleasures in the gay clubs and bars of Miami's South Beach.

The former Minister of Immigration lobbed a Corona bottle at Miles that narrowly missed his head. This prompted the others to follow suit, tossing plastic cups and empty beer cans whilst the two policemen struggled to push the former manager through the line of passengers waiting to have their carry-on items processed through the only baggage scanner at the airport. There was a minor uproar as some of the projectiles missed their target and bounced off passengers who had been forced to leave the bar. They recognized the local group of thugs without realizing they had not too long ago been the leading politicians of the island.

"Someone call security," one obese American tourist yelled; he was wearing a pair of obscenely tight shorts detailing every curvature of his backside and private parts. His belly sagged over his belt in several rolls of white flesh exposed by a t-shirt several sizes too small.

Walter Harrison and his quartet had run out of projectiles, but they continued hurling homophobic abuse and a torrent of obscenities until

Miles had disappeared from sight to wait in the departure lounge. None of the airport staff had attempted to intercede. Lloyd Bailey, meanwhile, had sauntered in from the taxi and hotel shuttle bus area, where he was parked illegally; he whispered in Walter's ear that it was time to leave.

CHAPTER 36

AUTORIDAD DEL CANAL PANAMA

August 2017

The *El Gordo* had been moored in Limon Bay for three days waiting for a scheduled transit time for the eighty-kilometre passage through the Panama Canal. Normally it took over eleven hours to navigate. The necessary fees had all been prepaid by bank draft at Citibank located close to the Cristobal Pier in Colon. All that was missing now was the owner, Lord Geoffrey Elm, and his guest, who were currently on route from the Enrique Adolfo Jimenez International Airport.

It had taken the Dassault Falcon a little over three hours to fly the pair down from Opa Locka City in Florida. Louis had flown in earlier on a BA flight from London. Geoffrey's chauffeur had driven him from his estate in West Palm Beach to Arrivals at MIA to meet Louis and had then driven fifteen miles north again to the Opa Locka Executive Airport where the Dassault was kept ready.

"Do you ever miss the days when you were working on the *Gordo*, Louis?"

They were sitting next to one another at the back of a small tender ferrying them through choppy waters from the pier to the yacht. A big man, Louis McPherson was feeling a little constricted on the narrow bench, but he did not let it concern him. He was a former sergeant in the 2nd Para Regiment who had seen fierce, hand-to-hand fighting in the Falklands and two tours in Northern Ireland during the IRA insurgency.

"Fuck, yes," he replied, "the best fucking days of my life, sir!"

Geoffrey Elm smiled and asked why then had he resigned when he still had some good years left ahead of him.

"My wife wanted me home," he explained. "Couldn't argue with that," he said, "the poor cow had waited years. She'd had enough." He went on to say she had wanted him home after the Falklands campaign. "Going off to sea afterwards when I was supposed to be retiring was more than she could really take at the time. She even considered leaving me at one point and perhaps would have done if she hadn't loved me so much, and still does," he said, shrugging, wondering why. "When I saw your ad in the paper looking for a security officer with military training to crew your new boat, I couldn't resist. And I have never regretted it since, not for a single moment."

It was ten years later when realization dawned on him that Flo deserved more from life than just waiting for him from one overseas posting or one port to the next. He had been gallivanting all over the world, mostly without her, for most of their married life, except for a stint in the Balkans when she had joined him on leave twice and they had explored Italy and Spain together. He had provided well for her over the years, and they owned a lovely mortgage-free semi in Colchester. But then she had always missed him when he was away, not that she really complained.

Then one day he woke up and accepted the fact that she was a wonderful wife and he had been an utterly selfish pig of a husband. Right then and there, still lying in his bed, he decided to call it a day and finally retire.

"However, I don't think she minded me coming on this trip too much, sir, or my other excursion," he said with a wink, referring to his recent trip to Australia. "Said she needed a break. I think my being home every day was becoming too much of a good thing!"

The tender nudged alongside the *Gordo* and the two men were assisted aboard. The captain met them on deck and informed his boss they would be moving into the canal in about four hours along with a superyacht owned by a Russian oligarch, reputed to be a cousin of Vladimir Putin.

"Hah, that gangster," Elm snorted. "How dumb the West was back in those days! We had the bastards by the short and curlies. We should never have helped the fuckers back on their feet."

Louis nodded in agreement. He had always greatly admired Lord Elm. Not so much Michael, though, whom he considered a spoiled and petulant, chinless wonder, like so many sons of self-made men. Louis was thirteen years younger than Lord Elm. Over the decade he had worked for him they had got to know one another fairly well. There were both psychopaths, completely lacking in empathy except in consideration of those they loved, at least in the case of Louis. Geoffrey's wives and lovers would all argue that he was incapable of loving anyone or even displaying any true affection. His children from his first marriage loathed him. He was estranged from his daughter, after the way he had treated her mother at the time of their divorce, whereas his son, Matthew, barely tolerated him and then only because his father paid his wages. Michael, Geoffrey's son from his second marriage, was, like his father, devoid of normal human feelings. He hated his two siblings. Money and what it could buy was his only driving force.

Louis had been responsible for all aspects of security on the yacht, including the life of his employer, whom he would often sit relaxing with at the end of a long day. One of the stewards would pour them each a large brandy as they reclined on loungers on the top deck by the helicopter pad. Sipping their Remy's, smoking Cuban cigars and discussing events of the day, they would remain there until dinnertime, well after the sun had set.

Michael Elm had always considered it inappropriate for his father to consort with the riffraff, but Geoffrey ignored his son because he was fascinated by the many stories Louis had to relate about his life in the army, particularly the battle for Goose Green. On one occasion several years before, they had returned to drinking their cognacs and smoking cigars by the helicopter pad after dinner. It was then that Louis admitted he had 'executed' two Argies at Goose Green. He never regretted admitting this to Geoffrey and was in fact proud of the fact. For his part, Geoffrey Elm was not shocked at all. He was fascinated by the story and admired Louis for telling him.

On higher terrain west of the town, closer to the settlement of Darwin, the Argentinian 12th Infantry Regiment had already officially surrendered. An hour or so earlier, however, whilst the battle had still been raging, pockets of Argentinian soldiers began waving white flags in mock surrender. It soon revealed itself to be a deadly ruse providing the Argies a few vital seconds advantage to swiftly raise their automatic rifles and fire on **las madres cabronas ingles***.*

Still high on an adrenalin rush after the official surrender, Louis never thought twice when he shot two young Argentinian prisoners in the face. They were kneeling in front of him with their hands bound behind their backs, pleading for their lives. Sixteen paras had been killed at Goose Green, his brave comrades whose sacrifices had been a turning point in the war. His commanding officer had witnessed the killing but had never said anything apart from giving him a thumbs-up.

Nor did Louis hesitate when he killed the reporter who had stolen aboard the Gordo on the Essequibo River in Guyana to take pictures of Lord Elm with an underage girl. When Louis had discovered him on board, he utilized his military training, swiftly twisting the reporter's neck and snapping it with a crack. Then he heaved him overboard to be consumed by red-bellied piranhas within minutes. He released the line attaching the reporter's small outboard to the Gordo; it was soon caught in the fast-flowing river current, eventually ending up half-submerged in a mangrove swamp close to shore.

The oligarch's boat was twice the size of the *El Gordo*, but each vessel still required two electric mules on either side of the canal running on rail tracks to guide them through the Gatun locks, the first of three that raise and lower ships a total of eighty-five feet from the Atlantic to the

Pacific before they reach Panama City. An ACP agent and four line-handlers would guide the smaller boats, the latter usually volunteers with little experience seeking passage through the canal. Drifters, sailors and young holidaymakers would hang about in Colon to catch a free ride. If these smaller boats had sufficient crew they would undertake the job on their own, without line handlers; they had better experience navigating the canal and took more care with their boats than some drifter exploring the world.

Geoffrey and Louis had traversed the canal many times and were quite nonchalant concerning the activities happening on either side required to haul the boats through the locks. They were standing at the bow looking at the stern of the *ARKHANGELSK*, the huge Russian super-yacht that dwarfed the *El Gordo*.

"She was only recently launched in Germany, about a year and a half ago," Geoffrey commented. "Apparently it cost over half a billion to construct and several million a year to operate. They say the Russian owner even has his own art gallery inside, hung with masterpieces, including one called the *Salvator Mundi*."

"The what?" Louis asked.

"Oh, it is supposed to be a work of Leonardo da Vinci. Not confirmed, but he paid $450m for what could quite possibly be a fake. If it is not, and they prove it a genuine Leonardo, then our Russian oligarch friend could quite possibly triple or quadruple his money."

"You want me to get aboard tonight and borrow it permanently, sir?"

Geoffrey Elm chuckled and patted Louis on the back. "You think you could with your arthritis!" he joked.

"You misunderstand, sir. I had anticipated you would be tagging along!"

Louis detected pent-up fury in Lord Elm's voice as he told him about the latest disturbing revelation concerning Michael. They were sitting in their usual space on the top deck as the *Gordo* motored slowly past the former US administration buildings in the canal zone district of Gamboa, heading in the direction of the Pedro Miguel locks that would lower them the first thirty-one feet.

The *ARKHANGELSK* was over half a mile ahead and they could easily make out the full sleek outline of the white craft as it turned in the bend of the canal. It had the most unique bow Geoffrey Elm had ever seen. From this distance it appeared to resemble a huge dolphin gracefully gliding through the water. A group of colourful squawking parrots suddenly startled him as they flew overhead before disappearing into the rainforest.

"So, the girl has made no official complaint, signed a statement or something?" Louis asked. He was referring to the Lucayan lawyer's wife.

"I believe so. Problem now is that she has vanished! Left the island, her husband and three kids, and no one has heard a dickey-bird since – if we can find out where she is, we can try terrifying her as we did with the wife of the engineer in Australia," Louis suggested.

"That appears to have had little or no effect, I'm afraid, Louis. Unfortunately, as I learned the other day through a source in London, the engineer has agreed to sign a statement. It seems our plan had the opposite effect from the one we hoped, and he is now determined to see Michael and the premier prosecuted."

"And you have absolutely no idea where she is now?" Louis asked, returning to the lawyer's wife.

"She's been talking to the police in London and so my guess she is over there."

"Do you believe it's true?"

Geoffrey paused for a while unsure how to answer the question. "You mean the attempted rape? Well, yes, I am afraid I do, Louis," he responded, speaking quite openly about his son to someone else for the first time in his life. "The girl would otherwise never have abandoned her children like that, almost guaranteeing custody to the father. I met him a couple of times at the bank on the island. Nasty piece of work!"

Shaking his head slowly from side to side, Louis asked what he could do to help.

"Regarding my son, nothing much at the moment, I'm afraid. When you get back though perhaps you could make some discreet inquiries and find out where she might be."

"And if I find her, what then?"

"I haven't decided yet. It may be too late, as the police will be all over this like Trump to junk food! At some point I may have to cut Michael loose to fend for himself. Anyway," he continued, "after considerable thought I have finally decided to appoint his older brother, Matthew, as my successor. God knows why I didn't from the start. Matthew is by far the smarter one. He's obviously better suited to run the various companies once I depart the scene."

Geoffrey had believed Michael was more ruthless than Matthew. This was perfectly true, but Lord Elm's original decision was based entirely on his hatred of Matthew's mother and not the ability of his son. He is not ruthless, perhaps, Geoffrey thought, but Matthew made up for that by having the inner fortitude and resilience to succeed through hard work, something his half-brother completely lacked.

"Right now, Michael is a problem for another day, Louis. He is still my son and I need to try and protect him for as long as I can. If he goes down so might the company," he warned, before adding, "and, so might I!"

During their private dinner later that evening, Lord Geoffrey Elm explained why he had arranged to have Louis join him on the yacht.

"Being constantly in the public eye is not easy, Louis, particularly at the moment, with the tabloids linking me to the corruption scandal. It'll only get much worse once the verdict of the trial is announced."

"Why so, sir? Unsubstantiated rumours were all that ever connected you."

"Very true," Geoffrey responded. "Except I have it on impeccable authority from the FCO that the ex-premier has already done a deal with the British government to escape jail time in exchange for information involving me and my son." He made no reference to the fact that the information had come directly from the Foreign Secretary. "As you might know, Harrison has sufficient evidence to put Michael away for years, possibly even me!"

"But what about the other incident at his party? He was also involved. Harrison is as likely to go to jail as Michael."

Geoffrey explained that Harrison had been there but there was no real evidence that he was directly involved. His lawyers could argue he was trying to stop Michael. "However, I have also heard he reached an agreement on that with the British government, too. I'm informed he won't even be charged, that they consider him small potatoes when their real focus is to bring me down. I am the one in their crosshairs, not Michael."

By the time they finished dinner they had entered the Miraflores locks where ships were lowered fifty-four feet in two stages to sea level. Later, coffee and cognacs were served on the top deck. Geoffrey asked Louis to contact Richard Wagner to give him the green light to execute the final part of the plan. It was imperative that the engineer was silenced, also the girl in Jamaica, if she could be located.

"But that still leaves the ex-premier and this other girl in London."
"We'll throw some money at the lawyer's wife. It's not as serious as the other matter in any case. There were two witnesses at the premier's party, and one is highly credible."

"What if the engineer can't be silenced in time?" Louis wondered.

Geoffrey Elm thought for a moment as he lit up a thick Havana cigar.

"That would be very unfortunate. In such a case, I may have to ask you to return to Australia and deal with it, Louis. It would have to be a permanent solution, both the engineer and his wife."

"And the ex-premier?" Louis asked, understanding that if Harrison ever testified against the father and son, it could be the end of the dynasty.

"That's being taken care of separately, Louis."

The *El Gordo* dropped anchor for an hour just inside the Pacific entrance to the canal off Balboa. Before them the Bridge of the Americas, linking the two halves of a country split by the Panama Canal, stood illuminated in the dark, reflected from end to end in the water below. With a sudden roar a helicopter landed on the upper deck pad and Louis took hold of his one small bag and prepared to leave.

"I made a reservation for you at the Bristol for a week, but remain longer if you wish. Everything will be charged to the Panamanian company account," Geoffrey shouted over the noise of the helicopter. "And you'll find a recent $500,000 deposit to your numbered account on Balboa Avenue."

The two friends shook hands before Louis clambered inside the helicopter that began to take off almost immediately. Geoffrey turned and went back inside realizing he would probably never see his Falkland soldier friend again.

Half an hour later the *Gordo* was headed out into the Pacific, setting a course for the Cook Islands almost ten thousand kilometres away, where Lord Elm was building himself a luxury beachfront home. He needed time to spend on his own. He had much to think about. He sat down at the desk in his cabin to make a call to a cellular number on Lucaya just to ensure there were no loose ends. There was no reply, only Richard Crossley's voicemail.

Ten minutes later he strolled outside smoking a fresh cigar. He stood at the stern for a while wondering how things could have gone so terribly wrong. It was seeming highly likely he would not escape from this situation unscathed. He watched the pinprick twinkles of the lights of Panama City slowly fade in the night. A gust of wind smacked at the maritime flag of the Cayman Islands and brought to mind the last moments of his friend Robert Maxwell, staring down at the dark water of the Mediterranean from the aft deck of the Lady Ghislaine. Was it the swirling wake that had hypnotized him to take that final plunge to eternity?

Geoffrey shivered, threw his unfinished cigar overboard and went back inside to his cabin.

CHAPTER 37

THE BISTRO RESTAURANT – Lucaya

August 2017

The Bistro Bar Restaurant on Coral Beach had started life as the island's first beach watering hole. It was where the few expats living on the island at the time could relax among their own kind, sitting around a horseshoe-shaped bar where only basic food was ever served: hamburgers, fries and conch salad. Local islanders rarely frequented the place in those days. Unofficially, everyone understood the beach was reserved solely for foreigners, better known as 'white people'. Additionally, as was the case on most other Caribbean islands, few of those born on Lucaya could actually swim.

Two gay Austrians had built and operated the restaurant until they had fled the island due to an outbreak of homophobia. They were the very first to proudly raise the rainbow flag on Lucaya over their modest villa on the south side of the island. It had remained there for less than twenty-four hours before it was torn down and large rocks were hurled through the back windows of their cars. Moments before, all their tires had been slashed.

Inspector Roger Sage had returned to the island the previous week and was met on arrival by two constables. They bypassed Immigration through a gate in the airport's perimeter fence and were joined in the parking area by one of the twenty Royal Marines who had been flown in by the RAF two weeks earlier. The thinking in London was that the local population would not consider twenty British soldiers an invasion. They were there specifically to protect British government personal in the lead up to the verdict in the corruption trial, anticipated in the next week or two. Along with the governor and the chief justice, Inspector Sage was viewed as having a significant enough profile to be provided with a military escort. Only the governor was given two marines.

Each of the marines had been issued with the new Glock 17 sidearm and a Canadian C8 Colt short barrel carbine. They had orders not to intervene in any local skirmishes unless the life of a British official was at risk. They were not permitted to use deadly force, only their batons; in extreme circumstances they were allowed to engage using rubber bullets. At all cost they had to avoid the perception of an occupying force interfering in local politics. Nevertheless, disgruntled islanders very much resented their presence, a fact the US news media were quick to headline during the slow news cycle of late summer.

In the opinion of London and most of the officials on Lucaya, including the police, the situation would probably never escalate into violence. Many of the educated locals would be only too glad to see their former premier carted off in handcuffs to spend the next twenty or thirty years in a British jail. They were sick to death of him and the discredit he had brought on the island. Locked up in the UK he would be a complete unknown, just another prisoner forgotten in time, even, eventually, by his ardent supporters back on Lucaya.

Half a dozen or so of the tables on the covered deck had reserved signs, allowing a ring of privacy for the two solitary tables tucked in a corner adjacent to the wooden railings and the beach. These tables were laid out with white tablecloths and silverware. The British had reserved this entire section of the bistro solely for their personnel, not only for their privacy but for their safety. A marine with a loaded carbine was crouched on one knee in the shadows below as a precaution. Roger had been largely responsible for gathering evidence for the trial and so was considered a high-risk target.

"Hello, you old bugger," Harry said as he sauntered up to the table. "I come bearing gifts." He placed two three-hundred-dollar bottles of Veuve Clicquot on the table. "Tonight, we are drinking only the best in celebration of your return to paradise."

"You are obviously still quite insane," Roger commented, standing and greeting the lawyer with a bear hug. In the ten years he'd worked investigating the corruption allegations of several of the country's former politicians, Roger had considered Harry to be a true friend.

"Now, now, Roger, I have a reputation to maintain," Harry Charlesworth said breaking free from Roger's embrace. "Doesn't look good being hugged by a Brit. Everybody knows you're all queer."

"Your reputation precedes you, Harry, and I can assure you nothing I can do or say can ever change that," Roger chuckled as they both sat down.

Harry Charlesworth was one of several Canadian lawyers on the island. Unlike many within the legal fraternity he was well-liked among the expat community. All the pretty girls in Morgan's Cay absolutely adored him, if not for his resemblance to an ageing yet leaner version of Colonel Sanders of Kentucky Fried Chicken fame, certainly for his incredible generosity. He had the unique ability to make anyone feel very special. Harry had a high-octane personality and a cavalier approach to life. He was just as relaxed with billionaire clients trying to hide their money offshore as he was with the young women he paid to come home with him from the bars in Morgan's Cay. Home was a penthouse suite in one of the most expensive condominium developments along the Coral Bay strip, where he would party with as many as three girls all night.

By comparison, Roger Sage was a serious man who rarely relaxed. He used to be able to unwind with his young family back in London, but even this was becoming increasingly difficult. He was finding it hard to transition from his idyllic Caribbean island life, where he lived alone, to the humdrum existence of working at the Met whilst juggling his responsibilities as a husband and a father. He was not looking forward to leaving the island for good once the trial was over. He would surely miss the wonderful cuisine and his drinking buddy and good friend, Harry.

Harry was a good deal older than Roger, almost seventy-five. He should have retired years ago. Harry's youthful attitude was infectious. Once exposed to Harry's eternal and exuberant optimism, Roger always experienced a sense of release from his everyday cares. Of course, it helped that their infrequent meetings were always accompanied by several glasses of Pinot Grigio, a bottle of champagne or two, and several shots of Baileys as a nightcap before they each headed home.

Harry's Bar, as Roger liked to call the Bistro Restaurant, was situated directly on the beach and from their table they could just make out the gentle waves lapping the shore from the lights of the restaurant. They were both surprised when a horse suddenly rode up with a rider looking like an ageing Marlboro man wearing a cowboy hat, jeans and cowboy boots.

"That's Jack," Harry said. "One of the first expat residents on the island, now recently retired from one of the most utterly boring occupations on the planet."

"And that was?" Roger asked after Harry failed to elaborate. "An accountant, of course! Really, Roger, everyone knows that!"

Jack was just about to dismount and loop the reigns around the wooden railings when he must have noticed the marine crouching in the darkness. Deciding a British soldier with a carbine less than ten feet away was not conducive to an evening of relaxation, Jack decided to remount and ride on elsewhere. Many people would not have cared, but Jack was originally from Northern Ireland and had seen enough British troops for one lifetime.

"Quite a character, our Jack. He will sit at the bar for hours drinking rum and cokes until he's completely pissed. Then he staggers to his horse, releases the reigns and slaps the horse on its backside, and away it goes back home. Jack has a sort of sixth sense, a built-in homing device and manages to find home and stable his horse for the night no matter how drunk he gets."

Roger was discreet with his official questions, and Harry even more so with his replies. Lord Geoffrey Elm was an occasional client and Harry was prohibited from saying too much to Roger, a British policeman. "We are simply trying to determine exactly where he is," Roger explained. "Lord Elm, that is. Michael is currently in Florida, we know that much, but the dad seems to have disappeared. We just want to talk to him, that's all."

"Last thing I heard he was sailing through the Panama Canal but after that, who knows. I'll try and find out for you," Harry promised, which was more than Roger had expected. Now their business was out of the way, Harry and Roger both ordered the island lobster and then opened one of the bottles of champagne that had been chilling in an ice bucket by the side of the table. They talked about the never-ending corruption trial shortly coming to an end and Harry mentioned another Dominican girl he wanted to marry. He had already been married six times in his life and had six children scattered from Canada to Colombia. The remainder of their evening was whiled away feeding titbits of island gossip to one another and becoming ever more drunk.

The Royal Marine was relieved when the two finally decided to call it a night and drove home each in their own cars. Drinking and driving was almost a prerequisite on the island, unlike the rest of the world!

CHAPTER 38

MANDEVILLE – Jamaica

September 2017

It was all so amazing that she still found it too difficult to fully comprehend. The person she had been not too long ago was now quite different, was someone she barely recognized. In less than three years she had become a sophisticated and confident woman, thanks in no small part to her dearest Daniel. She was no longer that rather shy young woman struggling each day to survive with little formal education in a male-dominated society. Moreover, she was also now a successful businesswoman.

A year ago, the world had little to offer her apart from some menial job in hospitality or working from home as a seamstress like her mother. She had tried cleaning homes and offices and perhaps would have been good at it had she developed the confidence back then to hire staff and manage her own company. Finding a husband or a man to live with was often the best option for women living in Jamaica, resulting in the inevitable production of children that few fathers even wanted. Instead of the care and protection women needed, Jamaican male chauvinism committed young mothers to a life far worse – one of gruelling hardship driven by their maternal and innate capacity to protect and love the children they could never abandon.

Jamaican society is brutally misogynistic. Sooner or later most of the men move on, abandoning those they once proclaimed to love to an uncertain future, often locked in poverty with only the love of their children to sustain them. Brianna had grasped this once-in-a-lifetime opportunity that her man had proposed. She had grasped it almost greedily with both hands, never imagining she could become so successful, and certainly never so quickly.

An it did yuh mi beutiful Daniel who mek dis all possible, she thought, lying naked on the new king size bed that had only been delivered on Friday. It was Saturday. Despite promising herself she would sleep in for a change, she had not been able to contain her excitement and was already wide-awake by six am. She remained in bed for another hour after making a coffee, scrolling through her website on her new iPad and the one hundred and sixty-three new orders she had received since the previous evening.

It was astonishing. She was making so much money now she had to open a business account at the First Caribbean Bank. Her account manager had been equally surprised and had brought it to the attention of the bank's manager, who readily admitted that she had rarely come across a customer who had achieved almost overnight success. It was the manager who proceeded to provide Brianna with all sorts of financial advice, including opening the business account.

Deposits in her business account already exceeded the amount Daniel had given her in Nassau. And this was after she had repaid close to eight thousand dollars to her personal account that she had spent on rent and general costs associated with her business, plus the money she had been sending to her mother. Brianna now had over thirty thousand of her own money in the business account with Daniel's twenty-five thousand safely secured in her savings account waiting to return to him. At this rate, she speculated without being too serious, she would have to engage an accountant early the following year.

Jevon, who still knew Brianna as the widow Abigay recently returned from the Bahamas, continued to help her as often as she could when she was not at work at the university. She updated the *Caribbean Fashions and Accessories* website almost every day, listing the continual flow of items Brianna was discovering at various shops in Mandeville as well as smaller towns in the parishes of Manchester, St Elizabeth and Clarendon.

After her mother had told Brianna about the white man asking questions about her, she'd been too nervous to venture further to Negril, Montego Bay or Kingston. In these cities she was convinced she would find a treasure trove of exciting new clothes and accessories; handbags, shoes, belts and cheap make-up she could mark up two or three times at least. Her selection of wigs sold out almost as soon as they appeared in her online catalogue, mostly to middle-class African Americans in New York and Los Angeles. Expat Jamaicans in London had started buying from her website as well, not only wigs but any item of clothing in startling colours or unusual styles not found in south London, otherwise known as Little Jamaica.

When Brianna decided she needed somewhere else to pack her shipments, Jevon helped her find a two thousand square foot vacant warehouse not too far from the university. They employed two first-year students who packed in the evenings and arranged for two courier companies to pick up the following morning when either Jevon or Brianna was sure to be there to supervise. Brianna eventually insisted she start paying Jevon a salary. Without her help she knew she would never have been able to achieve what she had in such a short space of time. It would all be legit, Brianna had told Jevon; she registered her TRN number as a part-time employee. Unlike most Jamaicans, Brianna wanted to do this all by the book. The university actively encouraged staff like Jevon to find additional work because the wages were so poor, as they were for most Jamaicans.

Brianna had spoken to Daniel over Skype about the white man who had knocked at her mother's door. He was concerned, but he told her to remain exactly where she was in Mandeville. Even her own mother, he reminded her, still thought she was overseas. The only way he could imagine them finding Brianna was if someone recognised her, and there was little chance of that these days, the way she now dressed and carried herself. Daniel had promised he would see her before Christmas when they would have plenty of time to talk. From then on, Brianna had put the mysterious white man out of her mind.

CHAPTER 39

THE PALMS ESTATE – Lucaya
September 2017

The bare-footed pair kicked up the soft white sand along the beach to Walter Harrison's mother's house. She had a four thousand square foot home in the Palms Estate where half a dozen expensive villas had been built exclusively for wealthy islanders. Lloyd Bailey had previously declined to join them for dinner despite Anesia Harrison's earlier invitation; he was sensitive to Walter's preference to spend the time alone with his mother on his infrequent visits.

Lloyd had brought along a six-pack of Corona Lights and would happily drink them outside on the deck for a couple of hours until his boss was ready to return home. He also had his iPhone with him and was thinking of making a call to his own mother on WhatsApp. She had been living in the suburb of Scarborough, Ontario for the past year with his younger sister who was studying for a hospitality management degree at Centennial College.

Anesia Harrison was a stout woman with large breasts, who stood less than five feet high. Beaming as usual from ear to ear she had greeted her son with a huge hug, squeezing him so tightly it almost made his eyes water. "Come, come," she urged, pulling him with her chubby hand towards her kitchen, which was large by any standard, as was the remainder of the five-bedroom house. Walter had bought it for her when he had been a successful real estate agent, several years before he had entered politics. It was therefore not subject to any form of legal scrutiny in the corruption scandal.

She had moved there after her third husband had died when they were living in the Fort Lauderdale area. Walter's father was the second husband of four, and he had died in a boating accident. "See what I have got for you tonight," she said to her favourite child. "Your very favourites: grits, grouper, corn and fresh beans." She sat him down at the kitchen table and placed a large plastic tumbler of rum and coke in front of him that she had poured just moments before he arrived. Her dearest boy was always so punctual. She had four sons by three different husbands and Walter's only full-brother, Tom, was a real estate agent, as Walter had been.

Still beaming, she pinched his cheeks as if he were a five-year-old. "So, you said you have some good news for me, son? You know I have been so worried for you and this court business," she said referring to the trial that had in her mind been dragging on forever. It was not even a legal trial, she continually proclaimed to her friends whenever she had the chance. Whoever heard of a trial with no jury! It was all a big sham because the British scum wanted to shut up her son and prevent him from declaring unilateral independence, setting their people free once and for all. Her son had done nothing wrong, she would tell her friends more times than they cared to listen – most of them knew the real truth.

She understood that he had a considerable fortune – over two hundred million US dollars was mentioned at the trial – but it never once led her to question how he had amassed so much in such a short space of time. Corruption was endemic throughout Lucaya, and even if she were to be convinced of his guilt, in her mind he would still have done nothing wrong. It was just the way things were done on the island.

The pair of them preferred to eat in the kitchen rather than the formal dining room and living room, which were gaudily furnished and could well have been the waiting area at some bordello in the French Quarter of New Orleans. Local islanders nonetheless thought it was high class. They had known little else, until just over twenty years ago, than the ramshackle wooden shacks where most of them had grown up virtually in poverty.

"Well, come on, son, you have kept your old ma waiting long enough," she said once they had both almost finished eating. "What's this good news all about?" she asked as she stuffed the last mouthful of grits into a mouth missing half of its teeth.

"The good news, Ma, is that I will remain a free man. The British have signed an agreement with my lawyer not to send me to jail if that corrupt judge finds me guilty." He explained that in return for information about Lord Elm and his son, the Brits would allow him to continue living in his beach apartment and permit him to retain five million dollars from the total of two hundred and twelve million he had in scattered accounts around the world, which had been frozen by court order. Also, he told her, after five years his criminal record would be expunged so he would be free to travel again without restrictions.

"But that's criminal, my son! They can't steal two hundred million from you like that. How can you live on just five million dollars in that pokey penthouse?"

Walter smiled at his mother's remark, remembering that it was not that long ago when she could ill afford new shoes for her children. He reached across the kitchen table and held her hand. "It's all right, Ma, better than rotting in an English jail for twenty years. I'll manage, and there's nothing stopping me getting back into politics at some point and leading the country towards self-determination."

Later in the evening Anesia suddenly had a thought. "And what about the others, did you get them the same deal, dear?" She was in the process of clearing away the dirty dishes and washing them all by hand. She had never quite worked out how the new and largely unused dishwasher worked.

"No, Ma, I did not, he replied. They were not prepared to discuss the others."

Anesia went quiet for a long while as she wiped the dishes. She had been thinking and she was giving her son a worried look. "But they will all hate you, Walter. They'll never forgive you!"

Walter had been so absorbed over the smart deal he thought he had made with the Brits that he had never really considered the implications of leaving his friends behind in jail. When he thought of them at all, it was to console himself that at least none of them would be handed down a long sentence. Perhaps they would get ten at most, far less than the twenty-five years the scumbag judge was apparently prepared to award him.

But now that his mother had stated what should have been so obvious to him, a different thought came to his mind. His chances of being re-elected had evaporated with his decision to abandon the friends who had always supported him. He had exposed the dark underbelly of his character. He was singularly obsessed with himself at the expense of his friends. Was his own mother now thinking the same thoughts? She was certainly no longer beaming at him.

"Ma, don't worry, I'll sort this out," he lied, trying to regain her respect. It was something, he understood now, he might never be able to do again.

Half an hour later he departed, upset and somewhat ashamed, explaining to his 'ma' that he had some meetings early in the morning. Inwardly he was praying to his selfish god that Lloyd Bailey had heard none of this conversation as he sat outside on the deck drinking his Coronas.

CHAPTER 40

COLCHESTER CASTLE – England

September 2017

Louis McPherson remained just two nights at the Bristol Hotel in Panama City. The helicopter that had picked him up from the *El Gordo* landed on a helipad on the roof of a thirty-story office building across the street from the hotel. It was as he was sitting inside the rattling frame of the old Bell Huey left behind from the 1989 invasion, almost deafened by the roar of the rotors as the helicopter flew low over the city, that he decided he wanted to head home to Flo sooner than later. He was already missing her after less than a week since flying out of Heathrow to Miami.

In the old days he would have gone on the prowl all night, especially in a place like Panama City, boozing until the early morning hours, always in the company of some dark-skinned young woman. Nothing back then would have enticed him to return home until he was ready to collapse from exhaustion. Once, in an outrageously expensive hotel in Cape Town at the time of apartheid, he had woken up in one of the rooms, suffering from the worst hangover of his life, to discover he had managed to completely trash the place. Entangled in the bed were four naked black girls. It was back in the early days of Aids and he had worried himself sick for months afterwards. The management had asked him politely to leave, but not before maxing out his credit card to pay for the damage.

Sadly, the nights of wild parties for Louis were long over, and all he wanted these days was to sleep peacefully in his bed beside Flo in their cosy little semi in Colchester. He was also anxious to complete Geoffrey's assignment as soon as possible. He had the foreboding feeling that his friend's world was unravelling and he wanted no part of the resulting chaos.

The day after he had checked into the Bristol, he took a taxi to the Banco G&T Continental on Via Espana where he maintained an offshore company account in the name of the F&L Trading Co SA Ltd. He had named the company using his and Flo's initials and had registered it in Panama back when he was still working for Geoffrey Elm. Geoffrey had paid him handsomely, and over the first five years Louis had managed to accumulate over a quarter of a million dollars, excluding the three thousand pounds a month he had been sending home to his local Barclays in Colchester. When Geoffrey mentioned that he had deposited the unimaginable sum of five hundred thousand dollars into his F&L account, he realized that he would probably never meet his billionaire friend again. The deposit was far more than he was owed, which was less than one hundred thousand. He understood that the additional money was the peer's generous donation to guarantee his future silence.

The medieval castle at Colchester, the largest Norman castle in Europe, was built on the Roman Temple of Claudius, constructed between AD 49 and 60. The castle's foremost architect, William the Conqueror, had died during the construction, leaving the monk, Gundolf of Rochester, to complete it by AD 1100. Colchester was the first capital of Britain and the first city to be built by the Romans on an ancient site predating their arrival in 55 BC. As it did to the Romans before them, the city offered the Normans proximity to the sea and easy access to quarry stone to build their castle. A large park established in the first half of the 20th century now surrounds what remains of the castle. The chapel is the most unique venue in Colchester to be married; beneath it a prison was maintained until the mid-19th century.

Richard Wagner was sitting on a wooden bench directly facing the castle. It was September and warm and the gardens remained ablaze with an array of colourful summer flowers. Green lawns now carpeted almost two thousand years of history and the fragrance of freshly mown grass pervaded the air shimmering with drifting pollen in the late afternoon sunshine. It was a quintessential English summer's day.

He checked his watch and then noticed a man in his sixties walking towards him with a camera hung over his shoulder like any other tourist. Richard guessed that he was the one who'd left the brief voicemail a few days before. He had recognized the voice as belonging to the person who'd contacted him months earlier concerning an envelope he would find tucked behind a particular back-row seat at the Odeon Cinema in Leicester Square. The envelope had contained photographs of two black women, one living in Florida and the other thought to be in the Bahamas or Jamaica.

Louis recognized Richard Wagner from the newspaper photo taken at a nightclub with Michael Elm earlier in the year. The memorial bench was painted jet black and there was a sign nearby indicating it was a *talking bench* donated by the National Lottery. Richard had no idea what a *talking bench* was until he noticed two buttons; when pressed they played nostalgic memories recorded by visitors about the castle and the park. Louis sat down at the far end of the bench with a heavy sigh. It was far too hot to be wearing clothes intended for a chilly autumn day, which had been his understanding after listening to the weather report the previous evening on Channel 4.

"Just remain staring ahead and don't look in my direction," Louis instructed Richard. He then slid a manila envelope towards him. "Inside the envelope you'll find a picture of a man and woman," Louis explained. "We believe one or both of them will be flying to England from Australia before the end of the year." He paused for a moment before continuing in a soft almost conspiratorial tone. "You need to take care of the man as you did with the black woman in Naples." He hesitated, allowing his instructions to fully register, and then added, "Once we know they are in the country we'll text you again. You'll probably not get much warning. Best be well prepared because they may not be in the UK too long."

"And what about my payment?" Richard asked.

"Half a million US dollars has already been deposited to your numbered account in the Turks & Caicos Islands and an additional one million will be deposited in the same account once the job has been completed."

Richard was curious about why Louis had made direct contact rather than keep his identity unknown. True, he did not know the man's name but now he had seen his face.

Louis thought for a while before continuing with what he came to say. Has was startled briefly when a football kicked by a teenage boy hit the back of the talking bench and activated it. The recorded voice of an older man, possibly a former gardener, began relating the story of Charles Grey, the 18th-century politician who had been a previous owner of the castle and the man largely responsible for the development of the gardens and the park. Richard Wagner turned and glared at the boy. Richard had a thin almost emaciated face dominated by a nose like an eagle's beak highlighted by deep-set and piercingly cold eyes. His appearance was quite intimidating. The boy hurried away without giving him his usual reply, a two-finger salute.

"Our employer wanted me to convey an important message, one that had to be delivered by hand, as it were." Louis turned, and for the first time looked directly at Richard Wagner. "Should anything go wrong, anything at all and for whatever reason, we are forewarning you of the severest of consequences if you implicate our employer or his son to try and save your own skin."

Richard Wagner smirked and started pushing back the envelope to Louis. "I don't take to threats from anyone. Go and tell your master to ram his money where the sun doesn't shine!" He was smiling because the man threatening him had finally confirmed his suspicions that Lord Elm was also directly involved. It was not only the son acting alone!

Louis McPherson said nothing in response. He had anticipated Wagner's reaction and was fully prepared. "Take it!" Louis ordered. "Unless you want to attend your daughter's funeral rather than her fifth birthday next month! You remember your daughter, don't you, the one whose mum looks after her in that apartment you purchased in Barcelona?"

Richard was horrified. He would have killed Louis there and then had he felt confident this man was the only person who knew his entire life centred on his daughter, Hilda, and his German wife, Elske. Other people would surely know, but how could they have possibly found out? No one in the world knew apart from him. Even his wife and daughter knew him by a different name.

Louis noticed that Richard was perceptibly paler than before. The side of his mouth twitched as he clenched his jaw. Give it a go, boyo, Louis was thinking, anticipating that the man was about to punch him in the face. I may be sixty-two but I could still snap your bloody neck within seconds. No barrow boy from the East End like you could ever hope to take me on and win.

Louis gave him a pleasant smile and stood up. "We understand one another then?" Without waiting for a reply, turned and walked away, but he stopped for a second as if an afterthought had suddenly struck him. "I passed your wife and daughter once coming down the stairs from their apartment in Barcelona. Nice family!" he said.

Richard remained sitting on the bench for over ten minutes, grappling to control his fury. He knew there was nothing he could do unless he was prepared to lose the only two people that had ever mattered in his life. He stood up and kicked the bench hard in anger. It started talking and he kicked it again and walked off.

Louis McPherson walked the two miles back to his house confident that he was not being followed. He was not quite as confident with the result of his meeting with Wagner. He was thinking that he might have to contact Elm one last time using the satellite phone. He might have to revisit Australia if the business plan did not work out in the UK.

CHAPTER 41

THE SUPREME COURT BUILDING – Lucaya
September 2017

Lucaya had never witnessed such a gathering of the international news media; CNN, Fox News and the BBC were all streaming live over the Internet. Reporters from the *Miami Herald, USA Today*, the *New York Times* and the *Guardian* were battling for access to the currently empty podium standing at the bottom of the steps to the Supreme Court Building. Announcers with the CBS syndicated show, *ET Live*, had flown all the way from California, given the ex-premier's international playboy status. Local police appeared ubiquitous in their short-sleeve, blue pinstriped shirts. All were wearing distinctive peaked caps, red cummerbunds, red-striped black trousers and patent leather boots. They were struggling, unsuccessfully for the most part, to maintain order. The young policemen kept turning to look beyond the barbed-wire enclosure of the forecourt, as if seeking help, to where six armed Royal Marines patrolled across the road. The balance of the small contingent of marines had been posted at various government buildings about the town; four more were at the airport and a similar number at the local port. They were all under orders to maintain a very low profile with the world's news media there in witness. The poorly trained Royal Island Police would have to handle any eventuality, unless the lives of the British governor or other senior British officials, including the presiding judge in the corruption trial, were at risk.

A brief scuffle broke out between a local television reporter and one of the crew from the Italian national network, RAI. An Italian cameraman had inadvertently knocked the side of the head of the local reporter with his shoulder camera. Luckily the female reporter, who had been speaking directly into the camera at the time, was thoroughly professional about it all and immediately apologized, quickly diffusing the situation. Her facial expressions and body language conveyed the sincerest regret. Only another Italian could detect that it was not quite as sincere as a foreigner might realize.

The doors to the courthouse suddenly opened wide and three of the nine defendants exited accompanied by their expat lawyers. Amidst cheers of support from Lucayans standing beyond the rolls of barbed wire, the former premier, deputy premier and one ex-minister were swamped by a tangle of outstretched arms holding microphones advertising their station logos. As if orchestrated, they shouted in unison demanding to know the verdict.

The only woman in the trio of defendants present was standing slightly apart sobbing unashamedly. This was the former Minister of Immigration. She was grossly overweight and well known even by her own people to be an extremely unpleasant person. She had enjoyed intimidating expats on work permits to secure free meals at the best restaurants on the island, or tickets from the local agent of American Airlines to go shopping in Miami. In the three years since she'd been charged with corruption, she had become a Baptist minister, preaching for all her life to convey that she had found Jesus and was truly repentant.

Walter Harrison's lawyer strode to the temporary podium and fixed the two adjustable microphones closer to his mouth. He was heavyset and tall, well over six feet. He was wearing a navy-blue pin-stripe suit and sporting a yellow bow tie with red polka dots. He was Irish and his demeanour was pompous and aggressive, believing himself to be on a higher plane than mere mortals. Two years before, another judge had even suggested this to him during his own trial – for assisting a client to avoid government stamp duty on a two hundred-million-dollar home on the island. The jury later exonerated him of all charges, whether because he had bribed someone on the jury or because most local people thought there was nothing wrong in defrauding the government, no one would ever know for certain.

The lawyer looked at his watch and began speaking as the crowd slowly fell silent. "Good afternoon, ladies and gentlemen. This will be a very brief statement," he announced. "Neither of my three clients nor I will be taking any questions and therefore I would be extremely grateful once I have finished to be allowed to leave unimpeded. The two lawyers representing the six other defendants will also provide a brief statement once I am finished."

Pausing, the lawyer looked over at the Royal Marines who were crossing the road to move behind the crowds who had started sing ing the civil rights movement song, 'We Shall Overcome'. Some in the crowd were holding aloft banners and placards saying, **BRITS OUT!** and **INDEPENDENCE NOW!**

"Quiet down. Please allow me to speak," Michael Reilly pleaded. He paused until the commotion had stopped and then began speaking again.

"I very much regret to announce that my three clients were all declared guilty a short while ago by just one man, an eighty-one-year-old with all the indications of early dementia." The crowd began booing and jeering and someone threw a large rock over the gates at the courthouse; it landed far short of the target, at the feet of the former premier.

Michael Reilly motioned with his hands for everyone to settle down. "No judge of his calibre should have ever been permitted to single-handedly decide the fate of any of those on trial without a jury. Not only was he totally unfit due to his age, but he should have been disqualified months ago for demonstrating personal bias throughout a bench trial that has lasted over two years and cost millions of dollars."

An uproar ensued and several of the defendant's supporters attempted to remove the crush barriers directly in front of the gates, which were not obstructed by the razor-sharp wire surrounding the remainder of the perimeter of the building.

"Please, remain calm," he pleaded, secretly wishing for an incident involving the Royal Marines. Heaven forbid they would shoot someone, he was imagining. That would create political upheaval back in Westminster resulting in the Brits tripping all over themselves to exit the island. If such an occurrence were to happen, and the British withdrew, there was a strong possibility his clients would never see the inside of a jail cell. More likely they would all be returned to office in the next election, after which they could quickly steer through legislation demanding independence. The Legislative Assembly would have no problems at all if the British were seen around the world as murdering imperialists ready to kill unarmed civilians.

"Sentencing may take several weeks, again at the sole discretion of just one man!" he added. The crowd was growing larger; it now spread across the road stopping the flow of traffic in both directions. The marines were looking concerned. They could see they were becoming sandwiched between the group of islanders in front and the one growing behind them. The sergeant in command gave the order by arm and hand signals for his men to move slowly to each side and take up positions alongside the swelling crowd without being trapped in the middle of what could quickly turn into an angry mob.

"Before we leave here today, we are demanding that all the defendants should remain free until the appeal we shall be lodging has been decided by the Supreme Court."

Michael Reilly quickly moved aside and ushered Walter Harrison to the podium. It was a spur of the moment decision; one he would come to regret. It had been decided earlier that none of the defendants would make a statement until after sentencing in case they said something that might negatively impact an appeal application.

At first there was complete silence as Walter Harrison stood reviewing them all without saying a single word. After a full minute, Michael Reilly started to become nervous, knowing Walter would follow his statement by denouncing the judge in the harshest rhetoric possible. After all, this was their future plan, demolish the judge's character and credibility to the point that the Court of Appeal would be forced to overturn the verdict as unsafe. Considering the cost of the recent trial and the lack of support in any quarter for a retrial, there was little doubt that all charges would be dropped against the nine defendants.

Walter Harrison continued to remain silent for a while longer until, without warning, he lifted his clenched fist high and screamed aloud,

"INDEPENDENCE!" over and over until the crowd joined in the chant. The Royal Marines moved further back so their proximity would not antagonize what was very quickly becoming an angry mob of anti-British demonstrators. The police looked bewildered, not knowing how to react as the screams for independence grew louder. They backed towards the doors of the courthouse. Some of the reporters were beginning to look concerned, even the veterans who had filed stories from war zones and were conditioned to violence.

One of the marines closest to the gate suddenly collapsed. Believing he had simply tripped, none of the other marines was concerned at first. Then someone screamed and the crowd stepped away from the twenty-four-year-old corporal lying on his back; his upper torso was on the road and his legs were splayed out on the pavement. He was gasping, holding the side of his neck where someone had sliced him with a sharp blade of some kind. Blood from the wound was spurting onto the asphalt.

There were more screams when people realized what had happened. Then panic set in as they started to flee the scene. The five remaining marines took immediate stock of the situation, surrounded their dying comrade to avoid him being trampled; then the sergeant fired a single plastic bullet into the air and then tried in vain to staunch the flow of blood pulsing from the marine's neck.

The rush to get away became a stampede and within minutes only the soldiers remained outside the courthouse barrier.

Inside, the world's media aimed their lenses at the marine whose life was ebbing away just the other side of the gate. The sergeant continued making a futile effort at quelling the flow of blood from the neck of his fallen comrade.

The three defendants literally ran towards the courthouse, as it appeared the police inside were about to close the doors. Michael Reilly moved away from the podium but did not attempt to follow the others. The crowd had disappeared, and the other Royal Marines had taken up defensive positions around their comrade who now lay dead. The situation was contained as only the British military could have done.

There was no chance of any appeal succeeding now, Reilly realized, with pictures of a British Royal Marine so brutally murdered and already streaming live across the globe. The Brits had displayed complete restraint and no one could fault them, not even their enemies.

Richard Crossly drove past in his SUV minutes after they had removed the marine's body. Blood was still pooled on the road and the reporters were milling about waiting for transport, some still finding it all difficult to comprehend. The story they had all anticipated had now become something quite different with repercussions as yet unknown. One thing was for certain, however, within seconds British standing on the island had become stronger than it had been in many years because of the death of one twenty-four-year-old.

Richard decided to stop off at one of the beach bars where he knew some of his Australian crew enjoyed drinking, particularly on Friday afternoons when they finished work early. He saw a lady he knew sitting on her own in the corner. She looked quite burnt from the sun after having walked the entire four miles of what was touted as one of the best beaches in the world. Richard saw she was drinking an El Presidente and ordered two more from the bar and then went over and pulled out a chair and sat beside her.

CHAPTER 42

THE THINKING SPOT – Boydtown Beach, NSW
October 2017

It was several weeks before they were able to return to the house. Many of the window sashes had been ripped away as each of the heavy double-glazing sections had crashed to the floor. The police were convinced a sledgehammer had been used. Large pieces of glass had exploded from the custom-made frames on impact and had thundered on the parquet panelling beneath the windows. Some of the larger shards fell intact as others shattered, scattering thousands of tiny fragments in every direction throughout the lower half of the house. It took well over three weeks just to replace all the wooden frames before new glass could be installed. In the meantime sheets of plywood covered the windows.

When Pia and Daniel had returned home from the hotel in July, the federal police initially maintained a mobile command unit at the rear of the property. It was manned twenty-four hours a day with one federal policeman and one local officer from Eden. These would be relieved by another two officers every few days. It was an expensive exercise for the Australian Federal Police. Had it been solely an Australian affair they would probably have remained no longer than a week to ten days. This was an unusual situation, however, because politicians in Canberra were under immense pressure from the AFP to go out of their way to support the Met in London. After all, London had guaranteed they would underwrite much of the cost.

September had already drawn to a close, almost twelve weeks since the attack on the house and the police presence was gradually reduced to just one patrol car. The AFP command vehicle was sent back to Canberra. It was replaced by police cruisers on regular duty making unscheduled visits to the house, day or night, providing Pia and Daniel with a modicum of assurance they still had police protection.

As soon as she told him, Daniel insisted he would accompany her to the beach. He suggested it would do both of them good to stretch their legs for a couple of hours. Pia did not exactly want him tagging along. She sought solitude to make notes for the final chapters of the novel she had started writing about Benjamin Boyd, but she relented.

It would have done her good to get away from him for a while. He had started getting on her nerves a little, moping about the house and complaining that they should never have moved to the east coast in the first place. He would forget to mention it had largely been his idea! Pia would have been happy to have moved to Perth rather than bury herself in a small rural town where there was not a single decent restaurant or even a bookshop. They might just as well have remained in Nhulumby.

The Eden locals were pleasant enough, as she had discovered working at the doctor's surgery. They were quite reserved, though, and often reluctant to reveal too much about themselves – not that it ever prevented them from trying to find out as much as possible about the new arrivals. As Pia had soon discovered, there was an almost unwritten code suggesting it would take two or three decades for anyone to be accepted as a true local. She and Daniel were now both in their sixties and no longer actively engaged in community life; that would always preclude them from being truly accepted.

He's the one who suggested we move here and yet he continually whines, she thought. It was always about the cold and damp or about how it reminded him of England! There were times she was convinced he must have had lessons on how to become a 'whinging Pom', no doubt part of the regular curriculum for foreign students at his dysfunctional school. She imagined his unhappiness was due to the stress of everything that had been happening in their lives recently, particularly the incident with the dog and the house being vandalized. There was also the shocking murder of that poor woman in Florida.

Chase had flown over from Canberra especially to give them the news about the events in Naples, which had been relayed to him by Roger Sage. The police patrols to the house were immediately doubled. The pair were panicked by the news until Inspector Sage had phoned from England assuring them everything was under control, whatever that may have meant, and they should not be overly concerned.

Easy enough for him, Pia and Daniel had commented to each another! Sage also informed them the Met believed they had identified the man responsible for the girl's death in the Irish pub but had insufficient evidence to charge him at that time. However, they had no leads as to who the man with the dog was or who had smashed all their windows. They were still working on this with the local police. It was difficult at the moment for anyone to fully understand how the two incidents in New South Wales could even be connected. If indeed they were, someone had gone to a great deal of trouble to determine the daily movements of the two retirees.

There was the optimistic view in London, which Inspector Sage conveyed to the Hannafords, suggesting Elm and his son would be more concerned with problems closer to home than Daniel half a world away. Furthermore, it was the general belief that Michael Elm would be charged immediately after the corruption trial verdict, whilst Lord Elm could very well end up in the dock for money laundering and possibly even conspiracy to commit murder. The consensus was the Elms would soon forget what Daniel and Brianna had witnessed on Lucaya and would have far bigger problems to face.

Roger, however, held the opposing view, believing Daniel's testimony would be all the more relevant because the rape and conspiracy charges were directly related. Roger was far more circumspect and was convinced Lord Elm would be even more determined to try and dispose of all the witnesses.

Nonetheless, during their conversation, Sage asked Daniel once again if he would be prepared to sign a statement testifying to the events back in 2015. He almost dropped the phone when Daniel finally committed to his original promise and said that he would as soon as possible.Due to the status of those involved – a Peer of the Realm and possibly the Foreign Secretary – Roger reconfirmed it would have to be signed in London in the presence of witnesses from the Foreign Office. They also wanted to question him and Brianna and have the interview recorded at the Met.

But then Daniel continued to procrastinate further by putting off making his flight reservations. Pia kept urging him to go as soon as possible and finally get it all over and done with. It had been hanging over them far too long already, she complained. He wanted her to go with him but she flatly refused. Nothing on earth could persuade her. She hated flying at the best of times. Flying to London only held the promise of an excruciating journey cramped inside a metal tube suffering from what she had self-diagnosed as fibromyalgia, a condition causing her legs to ache if she sat for too long. Daniel said they could fly first class giving her more room to stretch her legs out. The police would be paying for everything, including the hotel and food and drinks, but Pia remained adamant.

When they arrived at her 'thinking spot', Daniel clambered higher up on some rocks and sat where he could see her below. He had brought along a couple of newspapers to catch up with world events, one being the previous week's London *Sunday Times*, which he had got into the habit of reading on Lucaya. He still much preferred printed news to listening to the opinions of often ill-informed TV announcers with their plastic smiles, displaying rows of perfect white implants of pot teeth. He could also do the *Times* crossword if Pia wanted to remain longer scribbling down her thoughts. At least it was a beautiful spring day, the first really warm day since mid-April.

A few yards away Pia was already busy writing in her notebook. She had become devoted to her fictional account of Benjamin Boyd, the Scottish adventurer who had such an enormous impact on Australia in the half dozen years he had lived there before fleeing the law. He was so unlike Daniel, she was thinking. Benjamin Boyd let nothing or no one deter him from his goals in life, with never the slightest thought of the cost to others. He was self-centred, greedy and morally bankrupt. He could be charming when it was to his advantage yet crush anyone who stood in his way in his single-minded obsession of becoming exceedingly wealthy. If there was an excuse for his behaviour, it had to be his relentless drive to escape the family's shame after his father's bankruptcy. Daniel was Boyd's polar opposite, someone always tormented in making the 'right' decision when there was really no 'wrong' decision other than a simple question of choice. Boyd could murder without any qualms, as long as it suited his purposes, something Daniel could never possibly conceive of. He was no saint, she knew, but he had always tried to be a good man while battling the demons of his childhood. In one way, she realized, Daniel was extremely fortunate.

The awful events he had experienced as a child might just as easily have shaped him into someone like Benjamin Boyd.

He seemed to be gazing down at Pia now, but his mind was elsewhere, thousands of miles away. He was back on Lucaya in the Caribbean walking along a white sandy beach with Brianna. She had her head covered with a cotton scarf, like a woman from the middle east, protecting herself from becoming even darker than she already was, which was a huge concern to many Caribbean women who strove to be as pale as possible. These days this was more to do with social standing within the black community, much for the same reasons white people will bake in the sun for hours to achieve the perfect tan!

The harsh reality of his situation now began to torment him and he was wishing he had never gone to Lucaya in the first place. What in God's name was he thinking? He lived in a beautiful home and had a wonderful wife he loved and who loved him. Albeit a bit too late, now he was beginning to understand how utterly selfish it had been to leave Pia in 2014 simply because he felt he was not ready for retirement. He should never have left Australia.

Had it all been about wanting to prove to himself he was still a young man when he had galloped off in pursuit of something that had always eluded him? In that he had been more successful than he ever imagined; for the first time he had broken free from his past and had come face to face with the reality of life as he imagined it was for most people. Throwing caution aside, he had allowed the inner equilibrium he'd maintained all of his life to be carried away in the Caribbean trade winds in that one single moment, that evening on the island when he fully embraced life for the very first time.

Yet guilt consumed him once more as he grappled with the complex consequences of that decision. He felt he was being pulled deeper into a web of deceit from which he might never escape, entangled and irrevocably lost, the true happiness he had only recently experienced once again eluding him.

Pia suddenly looked up and saw her husband's worried frown. She had heard him gasping and could see he was scrolling through something on his iPhone. "What is it, Daniel?" she asked sounding a little alarmed.

He looked at her and she noticed the frown had been replaced with a look of disbelief.

"We have to get home immediately. Something has happened! Chase is on his way here from Canberra!"

CHAPTER 43

THE DEAL

*W*alter Harrison's concerns regarding his deal with the British were *unfounded. Without his knowledge the Queen had already granted Her Royal Prerogative of Mercy on the advice of the British Governor of Lucaya in consultation with the Foreign and Commonwealth Office. This would include all nine defendants and would become effective shortly after sentencing – once the former premier had provided credible evidence implicating Lord Elm in the decade-long corruption scandal. He would also have to agree to be a prosecution witness if Michael Elm were to be charged with the brutal attack of the woman at the premier's mansion in 2015.*

The convictions of the nine accused would still stand, and even though they would be spared jail, certain restrictions on their freedoms would remain. Each of the defendants would have to report to the Royal Island Police once a week for five years and none would be eligible to vote or be involved with politics for the same period. Furthermore, they could not travel overseas for a minimum of five years, longer to countries where visas are denied to convicted criminals for as much as ten years, including the United States.

For the sake of transparency, the governor would make an official announcement, composed by the FCO, stating that a period of incarceration for the defendants would not be in the best interests of Lucaya and would only serve to perpetuate the divisive effects of the trial, possibly setting its people against each other for years to come. By no means, however, was the royal prerogative to be misinterpreted as an exoneration of the criminal actions of the defendants, the governor would say. Each of the defendants would remain a convicted criminal in perpetuity. They would forever be branded as such, whilst the consequences of their crimes would inevitably follow them in one way or another for the remainder of their days.

The British decision to pursue justice would be viewed as a magnanimous gesture by the majority of the islanders. Bringing criminal charges against the British peer and his son, whom Lucayans largely held responsible for dragging their country into disrepute, could only serve to diffuse the unrest and anti-British sentiment that had simmered for years.

Despite the sympathy over the death of the British soldier and the reaction of support by the general population to the way the troops had handled the situation outside the courthouse two weeks earlier, there were elements within the British establishment itself that realized Britain was just as culpable for the years of corruption. The governor at the time was well aware the island's leaders had been helping themselves and emptying the treasury. Instead of calling the island government to account he had turned a blind eye, just as his superiors had back at the Foreign Office. After all, the British Foreign Secretary was only too willing to do the bidding of Lord Elm. Greed is a companion that has no soul.

From the experience of its long colonial past, the United Kingdom understood that no problems could ever be resolved where resentment festered. Now their commitment was to move forward as true partners; the Overseas Territory of Lucaya could either remain a dependent territory as long as its people wished, or it could seek independence with the full support and assistance of London. The latter was the favoured option in Whitehall, given Britain's often rocky relationship with its petulant territory.

More importantly from the British perspective was the need to regain international respect in its judiciary and system of government, for centuries touted as the best in the world. This would be possible only once the decay of corruption, which had infected British politics like a cancer for more than two decades, had been rooted out.

The trials of Geoffrey and Michael Elm would go a long way to ensuring just that.

PART 2

CHAPTER 44

BOARDING SCHOOL – *England*

Winter 1963

*H*e was not quite ten and he was terrified. He lay perfectly still, barely breathing at all. The only sound he could hear apart from the blood pumping in his ears was the rustle of bedclothes as one of the sleeping boys turned in his dormitory bed.

Then he was startled by the sudden hoot of an owl in the woods before all went quiet again. It was winter and it was cold outside, with a fresh dusting of snow on the ground. It was only a degree or so warmer inside, although beneath the several layers of blankets he was warm enough.

He and fifty other boys were forced to trudge each evening after dark from the early 19th-century faux-Tudor buildings. They snaked across the sprawling playing fields to pick up a track through the woods. It was blanketed in beds of bluebells in early spring, the air still thick with the aroma of wild garlic. Eventually they would reach an old cottage nestled amongst the trees. It was painted white and it served as temporary sleeping accommodation. It would be another year yet before the new addition had been completed to the main school building, including several new dormitories and a refectory.

Each child held a small torch to see the way, and a former boxer, pugnacious and brutal in appearance, with red hair and pale-blue, piercing eyes, marched alongside like any RSM ensuring his troop kept together and did not speak on their one-mile walk. If they should speak, they would surely be beaten later that evening. The boxer from Cardiff was now a priest, a convenient calling in those days for the sons of poor Irish immigrants living in Wales. It was a respectable career path when the only other alternative was working in the coal mines.

He squinted through partially closed eyelids only to see that the dark figure at the end of his bed was still standing there, looming like the butcher in the poem Daniel read years later, "with blade in hand", and Daniel was the "Spectre Pig".

The butcher was moving ever so slowly now towards the top of his bed. Dread consumed Daniel entirely. He shut his eyes even tighter, but the butcher was now touching him, shaking him slightly by the shoulder.

"Put on your dressing gown and follow me to my room, Hannaford!"

Daniel immediately did as he was told, fumbling in haste to tie the cord of his dressing-gown and failing to notice he had his slippers on the wrong feet. The stairs were narrow and each one creaked as he climbed them, one by one, winding upwards to the attic. Slowly and reluctantly, he followed the red-haired brute of a boxer in the black cassock. Daniel was shaking when he entered the priest's small, overheated bedroom. There was an electric radiator with two elements blazing a red glow too close to an old armchair that had seen far better days. The boxer sat down arranging the skirt of his black cassock. It had a stale, musty smell.

"Sit here on the floor, Hannaford." He indicated a spot in front of the radiator where Daniel was to sit with his back to him, almost between his legs, had it not been for the cassock. Daniel tried to move further back from the intense heat of the two-bar radiator, but the priest's legs prevented him. "Now, Hannaford," began the boxer, "what's this I hear about these filthy jokes you and other boys have been sharing on the playground during lunchtime?"

The interrogation went for half an hour or longer in the late evening hours when children should be safe in their slumber. The perverted priest demanded every detail of every joke, curious to know whether he or any of the other boys touched themselves at night in bed.

"I am not sure what you mean," stammered Daniel truthfully. He was after all only very young. It was at this point that the boxer became agitated, displaying an anger that belied the earlier tone he'd previously assumed – of someone almost caring in his gentle demands and urgings for answers.

"Get up, Hannaford, NOW," he ordered. His voice sounded odd. Daniel immediately did as he was instructed. "Now, take off your gown and your pyjama bottoms and then lay over the bed," the priest commanded. "I am going to thrash you for your sinful behaviour," he spat in feigned disgust.

Daniel did what he was told and lay there shaking in fear, looking at a wall with a photograph of some old Italian clergyman who was apparently the founder of the school's religious order. He noticed the boxer's breviary open on the bedside table next to an ashtray brimming over with cigarette butts and ash. And then he winced in pain once the hand began viciously slapping him, over and over again on his bare behind.

Daniel was never the same again after the night of the Inquisition, as he always referred to it in his private thoughts. He became detached, anxious and indecisive, and for the remainder of that term he started failing in class, the small Australian boy who had until then always shown such academic promise. The pugnacious priest had introduced real fear into Daniel's life, a coerced attribute that would remain an integral part of his personality until the day he died. Other boys had their lives shattered, essentially broken by men of God who had been commanded to protect and nurture, not abuse the innocents in their care.

CHAPTER 45

BLOOD IN THE SAND – *Lucaya*

2 October 2017 (EST)

Jimmy the Jamaican barman was performing his usual party trick for two white female American tourists sitting on high stools at one end of the bar. In their mid-twenties, working on their master's degrees, they had flown down to the island on the AA flight from New York for a few days. Already slightly intoxicated, they giggled as Jimmy brought their fourth round of piña coladas, one at a time, balanced on top of his head. Bending his knees, he slowly lowered himself so the prettier of the two girls could take the first drink off his head. The other girl clapped and laughed as Jimmy went back for the second piña colada.

At the other end of the bar Walter Harrison and Lloyd Bailey sat discussing the eight other defendants whose sentences would be announced by the judge before the end of the week. Still unaware that the British government was about to extend the same deal to all of them, Walter was attempting to justify his decision to sign the agreement without considering the other ex-ministers, most of whom were childhood friends.

"Your ma was right, Walter, they will never forgive you! Man, they'll turn on you like a pack of crazy island dogs."

"I had no choice, Lloyd. The Brits have me by the balls and they'll keep on squeezing until I cooperate. Otherwise, I'll be left to rot in some stinking British jail."

Lloyd was not an educated man, but then neither was Walter who had been fast-tracked through a virtually unknown British university established for potential leaders of third-world countries. During term breaks Walter continued to work at the real estate agent on the island.

The pair looked up as a Royal Marine walked in with an automatic weapon straddled across his chest. Walter simply shrugged and said nothing, accepting the fact that without the British presence he might very well be strung from a lamppost once the news was known that he would remain a free man after making a deal with the British without ensuring the same one for his co-defendants.

By now the American students had been joined by two local men and they were all laughing about nothing in particular. All were well on their way to getting merrily drunk.

Having given the place a cursory inspection, just as they did every other night, the Royal Marine eventually walked out to re-join the other crouched on one knee, before they both continued their patrol further up the strip towards the next condo development. Both were looking forward to heading back home to the UK in a couple of weeks. The island was making them soft and there was nothing much for them to do. The fracas down at the courthouse was the closest they could ever expect to see any real action.

Walter asked Jimmy for another Scotch and Lloyd had his usual Corona Lite. "I understand you had no choice, mon," Lloyd said shoving a section of lime down the neck of the bottle. "Problem is I am not sure anyone else will. You already mentioned your ma is even not too happy about it."

After finishing their last drink, they waved to Jimmy and headed out to walk back to Walter's condo building a few hundred yards down the beach. The two girls had already left ten minutes earlier, laughing and lolling against their two companions who had a Jeep parked in the car park. They had decided to move on to one of the local clubs to have a couple more drinks and a game of pool, not that the girls had any chance of winning or even hitting a ball with a cue in their condition.

The restaurant had closed almost an hour before and now Jimmy began shutting down the bar for the night before heading home.

"I'll hope you'll remain as my driver, Lloyd, once this is all over," Walter said, appreciating Lloyd's company when he was an anathema to most everyone else these days.

"Sure, I will boss," were the very last words Lloyd would ever speak.

A loud crack from behind exploded the front of his head, spattering brain tissue over Walter walking beside him. Joseph Pierre Toussant then turned the gun on Walter, who instinctively ducked and took off like a startled gazelle, heading directly towards the ocean. It was a decision that proved to prolong his life. Had he fled towards a beach exit to one of the condominium resorts, the powdery soft sand would have slowed him down, making him an easy target.

The Haitian fired off two more shots, one of which grazed Walter's shoulder as he ran, crouching low and zigzagging towards the water. He plunged in headlong, kicking off his sandshoes in the water. Then he pulled himself beneath the surface of the incoming waves with two or three powerful strokes. Wearing a polo shirt and shorts, he had little difficulty remaining under; Walter swam further out and then turned parallel to the beach. He realized he would have to surface sooner or later. Perhaps whoever was trying to kill him would not see him immediately, allowing him precious seconds to catch his breath before diving below the water again.

Joseph Toussant was a professional not prone to panic when something went wrong. He should have shot his primary target first, but instead of dwelling on that, he put himself in the mind of the fleeing man and considered his target's options. He could not stay under forever, that Toussant knew. To swim out too far would mean exhausting himself; he might drown or, if he did make it back to shore, he would be in no fit state after the waves finally washed him up on the beach. There was a full moon, and then Joseph would easily spot him and be able to finish him off.

Be patient, Joseph was thinking. The sound of the waves would have muffled the gunshots. In any case no tourist or privileged white condo owner would venture out at night to discover the source of gunshots.

Yes, they might call the police but by the time the indolent island constabulary arrived, dawn would have broken and Joseph would be safe on the other side of the island. He was guessing the former premier would turn and swim north, parallel to the shore. There were more hotels and condo developments at that end and more people around who might help, even at this relatively late hour.

Walter Harrison bobbed his head up several times out of the water. He could not see his assailant but that did not mean he was not there; he could be lying low on the beach waiting for him to come out of the sea.

Treading water, Walter scanned the beach for any sign of life. Then he saw a lone figure riding his horse along the sand. Thank God, he thought. His arm where the bullet had grazed him had started to throb. Perhaps it was worse than he had imagined and he required a doctor, or some help at least. It was the crazy cowboy guy heading home. Walter was slightly relieved to see the Marlboro man riding his horse rather than crawling back home drunk to find his mount dutifully waiting for him.

Splashing through the waves towards the beach, Walter began waving his arms to draw the horseman's attention. The rider saw him and pulled on the reigns slowing the horse to a trot. Almost at the same instant Joseph Toussant raised himself from the shallows where he had been lying with one arm outstretched on the sand to keep his gun out of the water. He took careful aim, first at Walter Harrison; then he swung round and shot the Marlboro Man in the centre of his chest knocking him off the moving horse. Walter Harrison had been shot in the side of the head before he had a chance to dive back under the water. Both Walter and Jack the Marlboro Man were dead.

The horse was already galloping home where he would be found several days later, kicking at the small paddock gate, trying to reach its feed. The sound of the distressed animal would eventually alert a distant neighbour, long after the Royal Marines had removed the three bodies from the beach.

By that time, Joseph Pierre Toussant was sailing towards home aboard a vessel on its way to the Dominican Republic to pick up yet another shipment of supplies of fresh vegetables for the residents of Morgan's Cay.

CHAPTER 46

NAGOYA HILTON – Nagoya, Japan
7 October 2017(JST)

He put his classic leather Valextra down on the massive Californian king bed. Feeling for his wallet in his inside jacket pocket, he took out a brand new one-hundred-dollar bill and gave it to the concierge who had placed his small valise inside on a long wooden bench against the bedroom wall. The man took the money, performed a small bow together with the obligatory *arigato* and quietly left the room.

Rarotonga to Nagoya is more than nine thousand kilometres, and the Falcon jet had made the flight in just over ten hours. It was the first time since the *El Gordo* had arrived in the Cook Islands, not quite two months ago, that Geoffrey Elm had left the seclusion of his tropical paradise. He'd come to attend the Formula One race at the Suzuka Circuit, which was located about an hour's drive from Nagoya.

It was something he had been planning to do since the US race in Austin the previous October. He had been an avid Formula One fan for years and counted himself a good friend of Louis Hamilton, who had attended several of his parties in London, including his seventy-fifth birthday bash at the Grosvenor in February. Geoffrey was counting on having dinner with him after the race tomorrow unless the Formula One driver was still high on an adrenalin rush and preferred to party instead.

Geoffrey was glad of the break from overseeing the final details of the construction of his new house. There was no one else who could have done it, at least not to his satisfaction, when labour and much of everything else was in such short supply throughout the Cook Islands. The total population was less than eighteen thousand, inhabiting fifteen small islands spread over more than two thousand kilometres of the Pacific Ocean. It was a huge area to service with limited qualified trades-people available.

He had made a reservation for two nights at the Nagoya Hilton in one of the King Executive Suites at a cost of more than four thousand dollars per night. He had arranged for a chauffeured limousine to collect him late the next morning and take him to the track. The race was scheduled to start at two pm, and so he would have plenty of time.

He had to make a call to Louis in England to determine if there had been any complications in the shooting of Walter Harrison. After the call, he would be meeting up with Michael in the Executive lounge on Level 26 of the hotel for a couple of drinks, followed by dinner at a small restaurant where they served the very best Japanese food he had ever eaten. He was hoping their delicious Nagoya Meshi was still on the menu.

Geoffrey called using his Intactphone, one of the best-encrypted mobile devices available. He entered the special code when prompted and then dialled the number in the UK. It started ringing at the other end. He knew that if Louis was there, he would be keying in the same code on his Intactphone in order to unlock both handsets simultaneously. Once connected, no security agency in the world was able to intercept the call. Any data transmitted from one encrypted and locked phone to the other could not be traced.

"Hello, sir," Louis answered, sitting in his small upstairs office. It had just gone eleven am and he was alone in the house. Flo was out having a coffee with one of her friends at the Lion Walk shopping centre in the heart of Colchester.

"Good to hear your voice again, Louis."

The reception at both ends of the line was excellent. Geoffrey continued, "So, why the urgency?"

"Nothing to be alarmed about, sir!"

"Please," Geoffrey interjected, "we have known one another far too long for all that 'sir' bullshit."

"Yes, of course," Louis chuckled. "Well, Geoffrey," he went on to say, "I am rather concerned about Richard Wagner, especially after my meeting with him a few days ago."

"Why is that, Louis? What's the problem?"

"He did not take very kindly to the fact we now know he is playing happy families in Argentina after moving his wife and daughter from Barcelona. He seemed genuinely shocked and furious that we had been keeping an eye on his family in Spain".

Louis went on to suggest perhaps there were too many loose ends and everything could easily start unravelling if they did not pay more attention to detail. Their immediate priority, he warned, was the engineer and possibly his wife, both of whom were still in Australia.

"Given there's no guarantee they will ever fly to England, no matter what our source suggests, I am thinking I should take another flight Downunder … but God knows why," he said with a pained expression. "My fucking haemorrhoids end up killing me whenever I fly to the butt side of the globe."

Smiling at Louis' analogy, Geoffrey Elm agreed with him, emphasizing that they had come too far now, that it was necessary to bring an end to it all. He instructed Louis to fly to Australia as soon as possible and deal with the engineer and his wife. However, if by chance they did show up in the UK in the meantime, Wagner was their next best chance of neutralizing the threat. Geoffrey and Louis realized they didn't have any better option, nor did Richard Wagner for that matter.

Louis went on to provide the latest update on the assassination of the former premier of Lucaya, which had been in virtual lockdown since it happened. At the same time, London had immediately imposed direct rule and suspended various civil liberties; all flights to and from the country were cancelled and the local newspapers and radio stations were prohibited from publishing or discussing on-air anything about Walter Harrison, whether related to his death or what might happen next to the remaining eight defendants in the corruption trial.

Fanning the flames of outrage was the last thing the British wanted until all the facts were known. It was imperative to find out first who was responsible for the killing of Harrison and his security detail. Once a thorough investigation had been undertaken by a contingent of five detectives flown over especially by commercial aircraft from London, civil liberties would hopefully be restored and life for the local citizens would return to as near normal as possible.

In the meantime, an RAF Airbus Voyageur airlifted from Brize Norton an entire company of Royal Marines consisting of one hundred and fifty fully equipped men. It was followed several days later by an A400M Atlas carrying sufficient supplies to sustain the troops for up to two months. These were in addition to the nineteen marines already in situ on the island. Onboard the Atlas there were six Land Rover Wolfs, all of which could be armed with 12.7mm heavy-duty machine guns. But for this mission, viewed strictly as a policing exercise, the guns had been left in the UK.

The troops would still have access to live ammunition for their small arms. The company also had as part of their kit four Black Hornet miniature drones weighing less than sixteen grams and just four inches long. These had proved extremely useful in Afghanistan when troops had to advance on a building with unknown numbers of defenders; they were also used for surveillance of a general disturbance in congested areas.

"So, nothing about who the shooter was or why?" Geoffrey asked.

"No, nothing at all. We have absolutely nothing to be concerned about."

"Let's hope so," Geoffrey replied.

"Of course, that leaves the question of the Jamaican girl," Louis mentioned. "No luck there at all, I'm afraid. She has simply vanished."

"Well, keep looking, Louis! We don't want her to turn up out of the blue. Best if she was out of the picture as well," he advised. "But I don't think that other girl on the island poses much of a threat at all. There were no witnesses to that incident, just her word against my son's. Her testimony could have provided credence had the other case ever reached court, but now with two of the participants from the night of the premier's party already dead, that's never going to happen!"

"The engineer is now the main problem," Louis warned again. "With him gone even the Jamaican girl will no longer be such a problem. She's never going to come out of the woodwork once she discovers her white man is dead."

"OK, I have to go now, Louis," Geoffrey said, checking his Omega Seamaster and explaining that his son would probably be waiting for him at the bar two floors below on level 26.

"Have you told him about Matthew yet?" Louis inquired.

"No, but I am about to this evening. Depending on his reaction I may end up eating alone!"

The two men said their goodbyes and hung up, with Louis promising to provide Geoffrey with an update once he reached Australia.

Geoffrey Elm sat on the edge of the bed afterwards with his head buried in his hands. This situation was starting to concern him a great deal and the stress was not helping his ulcer. There were too many moving parts, leaving the possibility of something going dreadfully wrong. All the money in the world would be of no use if that happened!

And how was Michael going to take the news that his brother was going to take over the business empire one day? Not well, he was certain of that! He could have put off the conversation and left Michael in the dark. But he felt a sense of urgency to ensure the business was in capable hands in case everything went completely wrong and both he and Michael ended up in jail. It was a worst-case scenario, but Geoffrey knew he had to be prepared for all eventualities. This is what had made him so successful over the years, never leaving anything to chance, always attending to the smallest detail.

CHAPTER 47

EXECUTIVE LOUNGE – Nagoya Hilton, Japan
7 October 2017 (JST)

Michael was sitting at a table half-hidden by shadows in a corner of the bar. Soft yellow mood lighting provided exactly the right atmosphere to relax with business associates, wives or girlfriends after a long flight or a busy day at work. A dozen or so others were in the executive lounge at tables or standing by the bar. Those engaged in conversation spoke in quiet almost hushed whispers respecting the sheltered peace and comfortable ambience of their surroundings.

Geoffrey Elm strode up to the table, having noticed his son sitting with his head bowed as if looking for something nasty floating in his whiskey.

"Michael, how was your flight from London?"

"How do you think it was, Father, on a commercial flight?" Michael responded sarcastically without looking up. He was slightly slurring his words from the effects of the whiskies he'd had in first class, plus the two he had just consumed waiting for his father in the executive lounge. Michael was too angry to look up and acknowledge his father. He was concerned that as soon as he saw Geoffrey's arrogant features, dominated by his prominent nose, he might lunge at him with the fork he was currently twirling between his fingers and stab him in both eyes.

What his father did not know, and Michael did, was that Richard Crossly had overheard a private phone conversation between Geoffrey, who was in Rarotonga at the time, and his secretary, whom Richard was having a couple of beers with on Lucaya.

Richard, however, had completely misunderstood at the time the gist of the one side of the conversation he could hear that the secretary was having with her boss thousands of miles away. He had understood Matthew would be the new CEO whilst assuming Michael would be Chairman. Yet he could not have been more wrong when, a few days later, he had congratulated Michael who called Richard from his home in England.

From that point on Michael was well aware of exactly what his father was planning weeks before their meeting in Japan.

Geoffrey ignored his son's mood and sat down at the small table. He turned and looked out at the panorama of illuminated skyscrapers, like beacons to a future that was no longer his. It belonged to his sons now, albeit briefly, before theirs too would belong to the following generation. "I won't be coming to the race tomorrow, Father," Michael suddenly announced, finally looking up from his drink and staring coldly at his father.

"You don't want to meet Louis Hamilton then? I was hoping we could all have dinner together tomorrow evening somewhere nice. You'll like Louis!"

"Really!" Michael snorted in disapproval, beginning to laugh. He took another large gulp of whisky and this time emptied his glass. "Why do I care about Louis bloody Hamilton, the ex-go-cart boy? He's still a fucking kid, driving around in circles to become the world champion of absolutely nothing!"

It was slowly dawning on Geoffrey that Michael must somehow have got wind of his plan to promote Matthew. Damn you, Michael, who told you? This was not going to be a very pleasant evening at all. Obviously, they would not be going to the restaurant together, Geoffrey thought, lamenting the possibility he might never again experience one of the best meals he had ever eaten in his life, the Nagoya Meshi. He was in no mood now to eat by himself.

Michael waved to the waiter for another whisky.

"Don't you think you have had enough, Michael? You must be exhausted after your flight and there is plenty we have to talk about tonight." "Go fuck yourself, Dad! What in the world have we got left to discuss?" The waiter balked imperceptibly at hearing the younger man swear and hurried away after placing the whisky on the coaster before Michael.

"No, there is nothing left to say, dearest father, my fucking back-stabbing, dearest, deceitful father!"

So, he did know everything! For once in his life his son was quite correct, there was nothing left to say. Michael would never forgive him and so that was the end of the matter. Nothing would ever resolve it. And yet Michael was entirely to blame for creating the situation in the first place by raping a woman in front of witnesses.

Geoffrey realised now what he should have understood years ago – after Michael had been expelled from Rugby School for pulverizing a much younger boy with his fists and sending him to a hospital emergency – that his son was unfit to take up the reigns of the empire. Michael, much like his far more intelligent father, was a bully. He had been expelled, of course, but Geoffrey had had the foresight to donate fifty thousand pounds to the school to ensure the incident would be expunged from his school record and would not follow him through life.

Geoffrey avoided any further conversation concerning the future control of his business empire. There was no point now. Instead, he warned Michael that the next few weeks could prove perilous to them both if they failed to cooperate with one another in the wake of Walter Harrison's assassination.

"So, this is still all about you, Father! And what might happen to you if the shit hits the fan!"

Geoffrey grabbed and pulled hard on his son's hand. He was furious and his face flushed with anger. "You and you alone own this shit, Michael! Don't you forget it, ever! You are a fucking rapist!"

Michael threw off his father's hands and stood up from the table. "And your hands are covered in blood, Father, don't you ever forget that," he shouted, slamming his glass and walking out of the lounge.

Other guests looked at Geoffrey as his son departed, wondering what he had meant by the comment that everyone had heard. The guests murmured amongst themselves for a while and then continued their previous conversations, finally forgetting the man in the corner a few had recognized but not by name.

You'll come crawling back, my boy, Geoffrey was thinking. You'll need a place to go if the police come after you. You should have been thinking ahead and got yourself a new citizenship and passport. They will never extradite me from Rarotonga, he thought, trying to convince himself of something far from certain. I am their wealthiest citizen and they won't want to lose me. But you, travelling only on a British passport, you'll have no place to hide, unless the North Koreans think you might be useful.

"Best of luck with that," he whispered to himself.

Later, after a few more drinks, Geoffrey Elm had calmed down. His son would be quite different tomorrow, contrite even, no longer suffering from jetlag and no longer brave from the effect of alcohol. There was no way he could stand up to his father when he was not drinking, a fact of which Geoffrey was very well aware.

He cancelled the limousine for tomorrow and told reception he would be leaving at noon for the airport. He doubted he would convince Michael to return with him to the Cook Islands, yet he realized the desperate urgency of discussing with his son the full implications of the situation in case things exploded. They had to be fully prepared for the worst!

CHAPTER 48

SEVENTH-DAY ADVENTIST – Jamaica

8 October 2017(EST)

Brianna and Jevon attended the evening service at the Seventh Day Adventist University campus church. It was Saturday, the Sabbath for Adventists. Neither of the two friends was overly religious and yet both kept abridged copies of the Holy Bible by their bedsides, from which they would occasionally read passages of scripture. Many of their white contemporaries would never be seen dead reading a bible in this day and age, but it was still common in Jamaica and other Christian black communities to refer to the bible. It provided solace for them in a troubled world.

One of Jevon's supervisors had admonished her earlier in the week for not attending religious services often enough. It was after all an Adventist university. Best she made an appearance, Jevon thought, to reassure everyone she was a practising Adventist. So, she asked Brianna to accompany her for support, joking that she may have to rescue her if other Adventists began stoning her as a heretic.

Brianna had been brought up a Baptist and enjoyed taking a jitney to church with her mother and siblings on Sundays when she was growing up. There was always a large crowd of worshippers packed inside the New Testament of God Church. The lively music and singing, the hand-clapping and hallelujahs excited Brianna. She especially looked forward to the good food after the service, spread along trestle tables in the church hall for worshippers to help themselves. Because of the family's circumstances, many times it was the only substantial meal they had all week.

As she grew older Brianna attended church less frequently. She still loosely believed in the word of God but not the hypocrisy of the pastors and their shameless adoration of money and all it could buy. Their sexual appetites were legendary; Brianna had had first-hand experience of this when she was only fifteen.

One Sunday after services a pastor was embracing the parishioners outside in a farewell blessing. When it was her turn, he whispered in her ear that he would enjoy having carnal knowledge of her and could she possibly stop by the church one day in the week. Too shocked and afraid to say anything at the time, she did inform her mother later when they arrived home. Needless to say, that was the last time the family ever attended that particular Baptist church.

Seventh-Day Adventists have an almost cult-like approach to their religion, interpreting certain passages from the bible quite literally to provide a structure of beliefs very different from most other churches, but not entirely unlike the Jehovah's Witnesses, whose dogma is even slightly more bizarre to the orthodox Christian. Fortunately for Brianna, Jevon was not such an ardent follower, so religion was not an obstacle to their growing friendship. They believed in a God, or at least a higher being of some kind, but they were too intelligent to follow their religions blindly, believing without question what they were told to believe by lecherous preachers.

It took less than five minutes listening to the monotonous drone of an assortment of pastors and elders continuously praising God for her mind to wander. The drones were followed by intermittent chants of 'AMEN!' whenever someone in the congregation felt moved; they raised their arms aloft as if they could actually see the gates of heaven above, beckoning through layers of flyspecked green paint peeling from the ceiling.

She thought of Daniel and how fortunate she was to have met him, even under those terrible circumstances. He had been so good to her, always concerned about her safety and wellbeing. She loved her mother and her siblings of course but not nearly as much as she loved her Daniel.

She knew from that very moment they first met at the premier's party. Crazy as it may seem to most people, it really was love at first sight, or at the very least her concept of love between a man and a woman.

And she could tell it was as much for him. It was as if a gossamer thread had somehow magically connected them both with a painless shock of static electricity. It began as a slight tingling sensation at that base of her spine that raced to her neck, then sped upwards to explode in her brain as a single jolt of such pure joy as no writer could ever express in mere words.

Daniel had been a little different when he had last spoken to her. He sounded distracted, slightly remote, and she could sense the stress in his voice. Was there something he was not telling her? It was curious; he barely ever mentioned the circumstances that had brought her to Mandeville in the first place. He had sounded genuinely concerned about the visit of the white man looking for her at her mother's house, but he failed to ask questions about her business after she had told him all about her recent successes. This was not like him at all. He was definitely preoccupied about something or other and this worried her immensely.

It was shortly after midnight when the congregation began leaving the church, some in the direction of the car park and others towards homes nearby. For the two friends it was less than a fifteen-minute walk. They were chatting away, at one point falling into fits of giggles over the outrageous hats some of the women wore in church. Then the conversation became more serious when Brianna began expressing her concerns about Daniel.

"I know he's tearing himself to pieces," she said. "He loves his wife, very much in fact, but I honestly believe him when he tells me I'm the only person he's ever felt really connected to, that we are like two peas in a pod despite our age difference."

"But don't you think that's a real problem, the fact he is so much older than you, sweetie?"

"Age is only a number, Jevi," she explained using her affectionate form of Jevon's name. "It doesn't matter to me at all, although it seems it does to Daniel," she said, "but that's only because he is thinking about us both, his wife Pia and also me." They rounded the corner leading to their apartment block at the top of a fairly steep street. "I don't want to own him, you see. I just want him by my side now and again, to come and visit and to continue loving me as he does. It is a very special relationship, very different perhaps yet far preferable to living with a Jamaican man who like countless others vanishes after a year or two."

"It all sounds very romantic, Abigay, but you may think twice in a few years when you suddenly wake up one morning and find a wrinkled old white man with no teeth lying next to you." They both got the giggles again at the thought.

There were two men standing by her door when they reached the third floor. Both were black men dressed smartly in business suits. Jevon looked at Brianna who suddenly seemed apprehensive and stopped walking towards her door. Jevon made no move to go to her own apartment and remained by Brianna's side.

Why were the two men there waiting for her? What could they possibly want at this very early hour of Sunday morning? Brianna decided there was only one explanation she could think of and that she must make a run for it!

CHAPTER 49

Daniel and Pia sat next to one another in the AFP Bombardier Challenger. It taxied to the far end of the airport and within minutes was roaring down the runway and lifting off, seemingly perilously low above the roofs of Merimbula. Daniel knew Pia hated flying, so he held her hand tightly as the plane climbed upwards, bumping through some low-level clouds to reach its cruising altitude.

Superintendent Chase, in the seat in front, turned around and inquired whether they were OK. "We'll be stopping in Sydney just for half an hour or so to refuel," he shouted over the noise of the aircraft. He spoke to Pia whom he thought looked quite terrified. "After landing, your husband will be leaving us immediately, Mrs. Hannaford, and you and I will remain on board," he told her, giving her a reassuring smile.

Neither Pia nor Daniel spoke very much on the remainder of the flight. Pia was still extremely upset by the new arrangements. Putting aside that they had only recently resettled in their home after all the repairs, she failed to understand why it was necessary now for her to disappear to Tasmania to stay with someone she had never even met. Never mind that she was Daniel's sister; even he had not seen her for over sixty years and did not really know her.

She'd become extremely concerned over Daniel's safety when the superintendent had explained how seriously the British police were

J Michael Bailey

taking the assassination of the former premier of Lucaya. Though they had no tangible proof to substantiate their suspicions, the Met were nonetheless quite certain Lord Elm and his son were somehow behind the killings on Coral Bay Beach. And why, she thought, did Daniel have to fly to England to provide a statement about something that had happened on a small island in the Caribbean three years ago? It simply did not make any sense.

She was unaware of how well-known Lord Elm was in the United Kingdom, a 75-year-old man deluding himself about becoming prime minister one day. The political pundits gave him extremely poor odds and doubted he could even win a seat to Parliament. His age was against him for one thing and he was not popular with the middle classes who despised him for his billionaire lifestyle and total lack of empathy. But like everything else in his life, he firmly believed anything could be bought, for a price!

The British police understood that the only way to connect Geoffrey Elm to the death of Walter Harrison was through Elm's son. This was why Daniel's statement was so important; with it, they hoped to begin to strip away the Teflon layers hiding the truth, protecting one of the richest and one of the most corrupt and influential men in the United Kingdom.

Daniel was quiet for most of the hour-long flight. He continued holding Pia's hand, wishing he could say something truly comforting to console her, rather than what seemed just like hollow words. He was the cause of this terrible disruption in their lives, now two pensioners who should have been enjoying themselves rather than having their lives under threat as if they were criminals in witness protection. He should never have been so selfish as to leave her to go off on his own to the Caribbean. Nor should he have fallen in love with a younger woman!

The worst part of it all was that he still loved his wife. But he now found himself hopelessly trapped in a situation from which he knew there was no escape. Happiness, he realized, would likely elude him forever.

Daniel was not only anxious about leaving Pia behind; he had also not heard from Brianna in days. There had been no emails, no text messages, nothing to assure him she was safe. He would try to call her again when he arrived in London. If he could not reach her, he would have to ask Roger Sage to contact the Jamaican police in Mandeville. It was the last thing he wanted to do because it meant revealing her whereabouts to a third party.

After they had landed at Kingsford Smith Airport in Sydney, Daniel only had time to give Pia a hug and shake hands with Superintendent Chase before he was quickly escorted off the plane by two federal police officers.

He had turned away too abruptly from Pia to notice the tears starting to well in her soft brown eyes.

A police vehicle drove him and the two policemen across the airport apron and over one of the main runways just as it started to rain. They drew alongside a Qantas 747 at one of the international gates; Daniel was taken up some stairs that ended halfway along a jet bridge connecting the terminal to the aircraft. There was no one about; the two officers accompanied him to the entrance of the plane where they were met by one of the flight attendants. He gave Daniel a boarding card and a ticket and then took him up the spiral stairs to the first-class dome and showed him to a single seat just behind the door to the flight deck. His small suitcase was stowed along with the flight crews' so he could avoid the baggage area at Heathrow, allowing him to bypass immigration control along with his security detail. A British police officer would be sitting two seats back from his. Neither of them disembarked on the stopover in Singapore.

Pia never said a word after they had taken off from Sydney. Superintendent Chase could see she was upset and went to sit forward to give her some privacy. It had been a long day and he realized she must also be extremely tired. Left alone with her thoughts, Pia was almost numb to the reality of what was happening to her. Her life had never been so complicated. She had been born to hard-working yet loving parents, and she had worked hard as a nurse, rarely complaining. When she did it was to herself, and always about the most important thing missing from her life.

It was late afternoon when the Bombardier landed in Launceston. From there they were airlifted by Tasmanian Helicopters over to Flinders where a local police car was waiting to take them the remainder of their journey.

CHAPTER 50

PENDOWER COURT – Cornwall, England
14 October 2017 (GMT)

She was his distant cousin, the eldest daughter of a by-then deceased vicar from Exeter in Devon. For some reason he could not explain, this cousin, whom none of the extended family in Australia had ever actually met, had corresponded with his father over a number of years. Perhaps she was merely intrigued to learn more about her relatives in Australia. Daniel preferred to believe that his father had approached her to ask if she would be his son's guardian during his time at school in England. He had never thought to confirm this before his father died, and the subject never came up with Aunt Aggie who was killed in 1971 by a car as she was crossing a road in Truro only a few yards from her antique shop.

He remembered meeting her for the first time shortly after he went to the school in Leicestershire. She had come by bus all the way from Truro. In the early sixties Leicestershire was a long trip from the south-western tip of the country where exceptionally narrow roads were lined by high hedgerows on both sides, obscuring views of the ruggedly beautiful Cornish coastline.

Had Operation Sea Lion ever occurred, the panzer divisions would certainly never have made the rapid advances through Cornwall they had through northern France where the countryside is mostly pancake flat. In Cornwall they had been so well prepared for an invasion that it wasn't until the early sixties that the local councils in the Duchy had changed all their signposts to point the correct way. Until then, there were many strangers to the county who would end up on a cliff edge or drive around in circles for hours on end trying to find a village that had no signpost to it at all.

She asked him to call her Aunt Agatha, though she was not even a second cousin. He liked her all the same, because he had no one else, or at least no one who cared, and so from then he had always called her Aunt Aggie. She was a jolly, rather plump lady with an infectious laugh. Everything seemed so amusing to her, in the nicest of ways. She lived alone in Truro above the small antique shop, catering to the few who came on holiday from other parts of England. In those days Cornwall was often too far to travel even for those who owned a car. For the most part Devon and Cornwall remained rather exotic destinations with palm trees and smugglers' caves and pirates brought to life in the imaginations of readers of Daphne Du Maurier and Winston Graham.

He exited the plane as he had boarded it, escorted this time by two burly British police officers, each armed with a Glock 22 service pistol. They took him on a circuitous route to avoid customs and immigration, down several flights of stairs that led to what seemed to be a loading bay shuttered from the outside. Parked inside was a black BMW with tinted windows. Another car was parked alongside.

"Welcome back to England, Daniel," Inspector Sage said as he got from the car to shake Daniel's hand before ushering him into the back seat. One of the policemen opened the boot and placed Daniel's small suitcase inside. Roger slid in next to Daniel and the two policemen returned to their airport duties. The armed driver of the BMW and a similarly armed policeman in the passenger seat were ex-army, elite RaSP security officers. Given recent events and an assessment by the Home Office of the level of risk, it was decided that additional security was warranted to keep their witness alive and safe.

"We've decided to take you directly to the safe house, Daniel," Roger said, explaining why they would not be driving into central London. "Frank there in the passenger seat will be remaining with you for a day or two because I have to deal with another matter in London and will be unable to join you. When I come down, hopefully the day after tomorrow, we'll take your statement, 'in-camera', and then you'll sign before a judge and two barristers from two separate law firms, all of whom will be travelling down from London a day or two after I return."

"Sounds all a little over the top," Daniel commented. He did not fully appreciate that his signature, witnessed by only one policeman, might not stand up in court if something happened to Daniel beforehand, especially not in a case that would generate global interest. Roger Sage failed to respond, purposely avoiding any explanation that might suggest Daniel's life could be in danger.

In a while Roger said goodbye and got into the other car next to the BMW. Five minutes later speeding back to central London he was scribbling notes in the margin of a document regarding the shooting of a Russian diplomat a couple of hours before in Hyde Park who had loose connections with Walter Harrison. The Russian was still alive but Roger needed to speak to him urgently in case he did not survive.

Daniel was beginning to feel drowsy on the drive south. Only just after ten am in England, it was early evening back home in Australia. It was overcast and raining, just as he always remembered England. Soon he was fast asleep with his head supported against the window with a small pillow.

They would arrive at their destination shortly before three pm, a journey that, sixty years ago, would have taken ten hours or even longer. The BMW was now on the M4 heading for Bristol where it would later pick up the M5 to the southwest.

Daniel was awake. He peered out of the window in absolute astonishment as the black BMW turned off the A3078 from Tregony and started creeping slowly down a lane only wide enough for a single car. On one side of this lane was a bank of bright green, apparently tropical vegetation that none of the passengers apart from Daniel had ever seen before in the British Isles. This was not entirely surprising considering the two policemen in the front seats had not been further south than Dover. Neither was aware that Cornwall was classified as sub-tropical with a climate similar to regions of Mexico and Vietnam.

The car had to slow even more as the road narrowed between several oak trees and a long hydrangea hedge still fully in bloom in mid-October.

Framed like a painting at the very end of the driveway, just coming into view, was the white hotel Daniel remembered, its roof tiled in grey Welsh slate. The backdrop beyond fell steeply to a sea, tinged aqua blue, and the entrance to the English Channel. Brittany lay four hundred miles over on the opposite shore, invisible in the hazy distance. Three hundred miles further along the Channel only twenty miles of sea separated Dover and Calais.

The BMW drove into a parking place behind what had once been the Pendower Hotel, now renamed Pendower Court. Several years before it had been converted into seven privately owned luxury flats overlooking Gerrans Bay, spanning from Nare Head to the fishing village of Portscatho. Apart from the neat parking bays with the numbers of each flat carved on seven wooden plaques set in the grass, nothing had changed. He could have been transported more than sixty years back in time.

The policemen watched Daniel with curiosity as he wandered a few feet from the car and looked around in bewilderment. First, he studied the full length of the rear of the hotel, then he walked to check the view of the ocean from each end of the building. He looked at a bank of flowers alongside the car park bays. Further up a steep rise he could see more of the same luxuriant vegetation that had been growing along the hotel driveway.

He recalled that there was an old garage hidden up there some-where, or it could possibly have been a storage shed, where he and Rich-ard used to play before they had their dinner. Perhaps it was their age and the sudden awareness of life about them that made it all seem so special, so magical; it was permanently etched in his mind.

"Are you all right, Mr. Hannaford?" the policemen called Frank asked.

"Indeed, I am, thanks," he replied and suddenly smiled.

"This is the strangest coincidence I have ever experienced in my life. Not only had I no idea you were bringing me to Cornwall today, I would never for one second have believed I would be standing in this particular place again after over fifty years!"

They listened in quiet surprise as Daniel told them he had stayed here in the early sixties with someone who was his second cousin but who was more like an aunt. She only had a one-bedroom flat in Truro, and she wanted to treat him and his young friend to a week's holiday at a real hotel. It was the first holiday Daniel and Richard Crossly had ever enjoyed, and both would remember it for the remainder of their lives.

Looking back now, it could well have been the first time, at least one he could remember, that he'd ever experienced a genuine act of kind-ness and love, freely given by the short, chubby lady who never stopped laughing and hugging them both.

Aunt Aggie took them everywhere there was a scheduled bus ser-vice: to Portscatho where they had their first Walls ice cream chocolate bar, and to Truro via the King Harry Ferry on the River Fal, where sev-eral merchant ships were moored alongside a handful of rusting naval vessels waiting patiently for a new buyer, or another war. Most of the ships would be dismantled eventually for scrap.

They took busses north to Mevagissey and St Austell where they had wandered about the old china clay mine at Wheal Martyn. The highlight for Daniel was the day trip to Penzance to see the nearby Levant Mine where his ancestors had mined for tin before migrating to Australia in 1840 on one of Benjamin Boyd's flotilla of ships from Portsmouth.

"My goodness, quite a coincidence, sir! Imagine, of all the places in Cornwall, this is the one you stayed in as a child." Frank had Daniel's small suitcase by the handle. "Well, let's show you to your flat."

"My flat!"

"Yes, two bedrooms, living room, kitchen and two bathrooms and a balcony that commands the best view. It's on the ground floor with stairs out to the lawn that slopes to the cliff edge and steep steps down to the beach."

"They only had small hotel bedrooms when I was a boy. I am sure I won't recognize it inside now," Daniel said. "The front lawn and steps to the beach I remember."

Frank informed Daniel he would be remaining in a smaller flat on the same floor and then led him around the side to the front of the building and up several steps to the main door of flat number five.

"This is as far as I go," Frank said. "Just have to have a word with the other officer before he returns to London".

"It's safe for me to go in alone?" Daniel said, only half in jest. "Perhaps you should knock first to make sure," Frank chuckled, then quickly departed walking briskly down the steps and back around the corner to the rear of the hotel where the BMW was waiting.

"Everything all right, Frank?" asked the other policeman, who was waiting there with Frank's carry-all.

"No doubt it soon will be, Eric," Frank replied with a broad smile. They both laughed as Eric got in the car and then drove off. A rental car had been left by the company earlier in the day for Frank's use in case he needed it. The keys were under the mat and Frank took them and put them in his pocket after locking the door.

Daniel placed the key in the lock but hesitated before he turned it. Taking Franks's advice, he decided to knock first. He heard someone suddenly slide the bolt chain free and then the knob handle started to turn. He was in two minds about whether to leap down the steps and follow

Frank to the car. The door opened slowly and Daniel received the shock of his life!

Brianna was standing there, beaming from ear to ear, displaying her rows of pearl-white teeth. Tears of absolute joy were running freely down both of her cheeks.

CHAPTER 51

NOWHERE SAFE – Tasmania
15 October 2017 (AEDT)

Pia found the thirty-five-minute helicopter flight from Launceston to the Finders regional airport utterly terrifying. In addition, she was exhausted, having barely slept the previous night, consumed as she'd been by anxiety over the recent chain of events that appeared to be ruling her life. What made it all so much worse was that it was absolutely no fault of her own. She had done nothing to deserve any of this and yet here she was, a hostage to the machinations of unscrupulous men she did not even know existed until recently.

An unmarked police vehicle from the Lady Barron Police Station had driven across the island on the B85 and was waiting when her helicopter landed at the airport, four kilometres northwest of the hamlet of Whitemark. Superintendent Chase was the first to descend from the helicopter. He took Pia's hand and helped her down as if she were more fragile than she was. The plainclothes constable had the door open for Chase to carefully assist her into the back seat.

It was already becoming dark outside from a thick overcast of cloud and there were few lights to be seen.

"How far is it to my sister-in-law's, Superintendent Chase?" she asked.

"I'm not sure, Mrs. Hannaford. My first time on Flinders Island, just like yourself!"

"Only a couple of minutes, madam," the driver replied; he had lived on Flinders Island his entire life, save for various training courses over on the mainland. Pia continued staring into the darkness and wondering where Daniel would be on his long flight to England. Perhaps he was almost in Singapore by now. True to his word, the driver drew up alongside the low white fence enclosing Jane's house thirteen minutes later.

He remained in the car as Chase escorted Pia slower than necessary up the path lit dimly by a solitary light at the front door. The curtains were closed but Pia could see chinks of light sneaking through. Superintendent Chase had earlier explained that he would be staying in a small, rented bungalow less than a hundred yards over the road from Jane's house. His respect for the Hannafords had grown over the weeks he had known them both; he would have found Pia's resilience and courage amazing in any one of his female subordinates in Canberra half Pia's age. With no end in sight to this ordeal, however, he didn't know whether her protective emotional veneer would be sufficient to sustain her.

Shortly after the sisters-in-law met for the first time, Chase walked back to the car and told the driver he could head home. "You'll need these, sir," the constable said, handing him two bunches of keys, one to the house and the other for the rental car that had been left earlier in the bungalow's carport by Flinders Island Car Rentals in Whitemark.

"Do you want me to drive you there, sir?"

"No, not necessary, I know where it is. I'm hoping they put some food in the fridge for me."

"I believe so, sir, and even a couple of beers."

"I'll be on permanent duty here, Constable. No drinking for me, I'm afraid!"

Superintendent Chase would not be entirely alone. Another unmarked police car was already parked further down on the same side of the road as the McArthur house.

Both of them felt somewhat awkward at first, two total strangers feigning affection. Jane had only recently discovered she had a sister-in-law at all.

Pia was tired, of course, as was Jane, an early-to-bed-early-to-rise type of person her entire life. She no longer had the stamina of a young woman, even someone in her early sixties, like Pia.

Jane had only found out two days ago that Pia would be coming. The reason was not entirely clear to her; Daniel had only said that he had to fly to England urgently. Given the terrible scare Pia had experienced the last time he was away, he needed her to be as far from Eden as possible. Although he would have preferred her to accompany him to the UK, it did provide him with some peace of mind to know she would have Jane's company and not be entirely on her own. Federal and local police would be there to protect her as well. Pia argued she wanted to remain at home but relented when Daniel repeatedly reminded her what had happened when he left her the last time to visit his sister.

Jane had believed every aspect of Daniel's story until the visit from the police yesterday. A male sergeant accompanied by a policewoman knocked on her door to advise her of a police presence on the street for a few days. It was merely a precaution due to the attack on her brother's house a few weeks before. Their lack of direct eye contact and their paltering assurances that everything would be just fine confirmed the contrary to Jane; she still had enough wits about her to suspect something was going on beyond a random home invasion. Daniel had even made light of it to her at the time. Yet now the police suddenly had the time and resources to 'keep an eye' on a middle-aged woman from Eden whose husband had flown off God knows where. None of it made any sense.

She may be in her eighties, she thought, but she was neither stupid nor quite as senile as they might suspect.

Pia had only brought a few items in one small suitcase, assuming she would be staying with Jane for less than a week before Daniel returned. He was after all going to England to provide a statement. How long could that possibly take? Neither was in the mood for much conversation and so after a few sandwiches and a cup of tea they decided to retire. Jane showed Pia to a small guest bedroom with a view of the road.

Jane's room opposite was much larger and had an expansive outlook over the Bass Strait and Prime Seal Island.

Over one thousand miles north, in Sydney, Louis McPherson was fast asleep. He had arrived on the BA flight earlier in the morning and had battled jetlag as long as he could. He had made it until just before nine, when he admitted defeat and threw himself on the bed still fully clothed.

His hotel overlooked Darling Harbour. Since checking in at one pm, he had either watched TV or raided the mini bar, which was poorly stocked with a couple of beers, a small bottle of Beaujolais and two energy snack bars, certainly not sufficient to keep him going until the morning.

He had been wearing the same Akubra hat he had worn on Boydtown beach that day, hoping its low brim would make it difficult for anyone to readily identify him later. Apart from the one girl at check-in, who had not given him a second glance, no one had seen him. He only ventured outside once to go to a nearby IGA X-Press to buy some food when the mini-bar stock was depleted, except for the wine. He also bought a small bottle of Appleton's rum that he liked to drink straight without a mixer.

Just before midnight his encrypted satellite phone began to ring. Disorientated from sleep, it took him a while to remember exactly where he was and where he had put the phone. Eventually he managed to punch in the code to answer the call. It was from someone speaking in a distorted almost robotic voice. It lasted less than thirty seconds and it told him all he had wanted to know. The recorded voice synthesizer informed him that the woman had been flown to stay with a relative on Flinders Island called Jane McArthur; it then provided an address in Tasmania.

Another bloody Scot, Louis thought and disconnected the phone. Five minutes later he was fast asleep again.

CHAPTER 52

MARSHALL – Texas
May 1852

*B*enjamin Boyd and his half-breed Canadian scout, Leon, rode alongside one another down the dusty main street of Marshall in Harrison County, Texas. Like half-empty sacks of grain, they sagged in their saddles from exhaustion. Both horses and men were desperately tired and hungry, with tongues of leather parched from thirst. They were also in need of a hot bath after their arduous and often perilous journey from Santa Fe, where they had parted company with Mark Boyd and his Pawnee scout almost four weeks before.

Marshall had been founded in 1841, the same year Boyd had sailed from Portsmouth to Australia. Eleven years later it was the fourth largest city in Texas, with a bustling population of around one thousand seven hundred.

They left the horses at a livery stable next to the barbershop and then trudged back in the scorching heat to the Marshall Hotel, smacking the dust haphazardly from their clothes along the way. They took two rooms for a week at a cost of seven dollars a day, plus fifty cents for each use of a tin plunge bath. They had a meal of meat and potatoes swilled down with Persimmon beer and shots of bourbon whiskey down in the saloon. Refreshed, yet slightly intoxicated, they stumbled up to the mezzanine level overlooking the saloon, each to a separate small room with views of the main street baking in the heat.

*Across main street Benjamin Boyd could see a row of newly con-
structed wooden coffins standing upright outside a carpenter's shop, waiting for customers, dead or alive hardly mattered. A mangy dog slunk past,
lifted its leg and urinated inside one of the coffins. His room was slightly
larger than Leon's and the walls were so thin it was impossible not to hear
the 'daughters of sin' hard at work three rooms down. Boyd sat on the side
of his bed and admired a young Negro slave who brought up several buck-
ets of hot water from the woodstove down in the kitchen to fill the old tin
tub. He smiled at the young boy who kept his eyes to the ground.*

*Boyd took off his boots and clothes and lowered himself into the
warm water; he luxuriated there for a good hour, the accumulation of a
month's worth of dirt seeping from his pores until he started to feel clean
again. When he was finished, he dried himself off with a small towel, threw
his clothes to soak in the bath and collapsed naked on the bed. He slept for
ten hours straight, oblivious to the fights and commotions and gunshots
beneath his window during the night.*

*It was Mark who had suggested he go to Marshall when they had
met in San Francisco before Benjamin set sail for Guadalcanal almost one
year earlier. Marshall was in the northeast of the state, over two hundred
miles from Galveston. The land in Harrison County was suitable for growing almost anything; cotton was a burgeoning crop, brought by farmers
from Louisiana. Land was only thirty-five cents an acre and folk in the
state still minded their own business, seldom asking questions about their
neighbours. The Caddo Indians of east Texas were largely peaceful people
who had been there to welcome the Spanish. Once the Anglos began arriving in numbers, the Caddo people were slowly pushed from their land to
live on reservations.*

*Feeling refreshed after a good night's sleep in his first real bed since
leaving San Francisco, Boyd ordered a cup of thick black coffee at the bar.
None of the crew of the* Wanderer *would have recognized him had they
been standing next to him. He was clean-shaven and his hair had grown
in curls shaded a light ginger brown. Most notable was all the weight he
had lost since the day he was hoisted down from the* Wanderer *to young*

Stevens waiting in the jolly-boat to row him ashore. He appeared years younger and was no longer stooped like an ageing man carrying a pregnant belly before him, which his crew had found so titillating. They would all have agreed that the twins had been delivered months before!

There was a newspaper on the floor and he bent and picked it up. It was a copy of the Texas Republican dated 13 March 1852, not quite two months old. On the back page there was a 'for sale' notice for a farm comprising one thousand acres with a plain but substantial dwelling, including a blacksmith shop and a gin house. There was an apple and peach orchard; the primary crop was oats, but over two hundred acres were used for cotton. The property came with 'Nine good negroes in number; all good hands and five of them very likely'. An E Fraser had signed the advertisement.

Leon the scout had been checking on the horses over at the livery. He returned to the saloon to order a breakfast of cornbread, stew and boiled eggs, along with a pot of the same thick coffee. The plan was for them to ride south to Galveston in about a week to attend the Galveston Banco de Commercia y Agricultura originally established by the previous Mexican administration. There they would draw an amount of silver and gold coinage on presentation of three promissory notes, each of one thousand dollars, in the name of Samuel Bethel. The notes were issued by the oldest colonial bank in Massachusetts, founded in the 17th century. Most of the money would go on deposit at the same bank, immediately establishing Samuel Bethel as one of its wealthiest clients.

Two years earlier, Mark Boyd had prepared this monetary transaction when the two brothers had hatched a plan for Benjamin to disappear. He'd given the notes to Benjamin in San Francisco when they returned from Guadalcanal. The money could be drawn only from this one chartered bank in Texas. Mark had also handed Benjamin a copy, witnessed by a Presbyterian minister, of the birth records of a deceased parishioner by the name of Samuel Bethel, who had been born in a small village ten miles from Aberdeen in 1801. He would have been a year older than Benjamin and had once worked on his father's estate at Merton Hall. This certified birth entry from the parish register would suffice as sufficient proof of Benjamin's new identity in an age long before passports or national birth certificates.

Boyd's Canadian scout had agreed to ride with him to Galveston and accompany him on his return journey, when he would be carrying sufficient funds to buy the one thousand acres advertised by E Fraser in the Texas Republican newspaper. Leon also agreed to stay on at the plantation for several months once the purchase was complete to help settle the property. By then title to the property would be legally in the name of Samuel Bethel. It was the name by which the scout had known Boyd since they had first met met in San Francisco.

CHAPTER 53

A WALK TO PORTSCATHO – *Cornwall, England*
15 October

A sliver of a new dawn was faintly discernible on the opposite shore of the Channel as he quietly slid from beneath the duvet. He guessed it was not even seven and he did not want to wake her. After almost twenty-four hours trapped on a plane in the air, and two in Singapore, he had decided to go and stretch his legs and clear his head before Brianna woke up.

He dressed quickly and went to the bathroom to relieve himself. Still thirsty after the two bottles of Chianti they had shared the night before, he took two large gulps of cold water from the tap and splashed some of it over his face. Peering in the mirror briefly on his way out, he was astonished to see the old man staring back at him with crinkled, weather-worn features and tousled grey hair.

What the hell could she see in him, he wondered. He still found it difficult to fully understand why a Jamaican or indeed any women for that matter, regardless of nationality, preferred to be with someone more mature. He imagined it was probably a combination of the older man's financial security as well as attention to a woman's emotional needs and the stability seldom offered by younger men, not only in Jamaica but these days in many other countries as well.

An unexpected pang of sadness briefly overwhelmed him; he was not the young man he had almost believed he was a few hours earlier.

Surrendering yesterday to the paradox of a brief eternity when she had opened the door, they had fallen into each another's arms, clinging passionately, almost desperately, once more in their transcendent world where time had no relevance. Each was enveloped by an overpowering rush of joy of an intensity that neither had ever experienced. Brief as it may have been, it would remain the happiest moments of their lives.

She was still asleep when he came out of the bathroom and went through to the spacious living room so elegantly and comfortably furnished in a traditional English fashion. Most of the flat had been decorated by the owner and his Asian wife; they spent most of the year working in the financial sector in Dubai. Daniel unlocked the front door and closed it quietly behind him.

It was all just as he remembered it sixty years before, even the windswept tree in the foreground of a perfectly framed Gerrans Bay, with Nare Head in the distance. It looked like the stunted stone pine they had back home in Australia, he thought, amazed that it still looked exactly as it had when he was eight years old. But that would not be possible, he told himself, not even for a tree, when for sixty years this particular coastline must have been constantly battered by gale-force winds and lashing winter storms.

Instead of the worn dirt path leading down to Pendower Beach, now there were concrete steps with a safety handrail alongside, pinioned by steel clamps drilled into the face of the cliff. The beach at the bottom of the steps, however, had not changed at all, despite global warming and the passage of time. It was predominantly rocky, partly covered in stringy green algae with rock pools recently refreshed from the now ebbing tide. Looking north, a flat stretch of sand led as far as Nare Head several miles in the distance.

He could taste the salt and smell the sea air, absorbing it all and reliving memories from another life when everything was so new and exciting. For a second, he imagined he could see Richard running ahead with Aunt Aggie through the mist of time towards the place they returned to again and again. It was a large rectangular rock pool, almost as big as a small swimming pool, where Richard was learning to swim. Being raised in Australia, Daniel already knew how, but he would always jump into the pool to help his friend keep his head above water, whilst Aunt Aggie sat on the edge cheering them both on. Shoals of small fish would keep them company, swimming together in synchrony, turning and twisting and forming glinting, sweeping shapes in the water.

He clambered over some rocks and discovered the swimming pool carved by the sea. It looked smaller than he remembered it. He took off his deck shoes, rolled up his chinos and dangled both feet in the tepid water. Like anyone else in the twilight of their existence, he understood that happiness was not only fleeting but impossible to capture and bottle, like a prescription to be taken in small doses when life was not so good. For a few days back in the early sixties he had known his first real sense of happiness with his friend Richard, when the world was not quite as bad as others later made him believe. The future was an endless road of joyful tomorrows, stretching before them as if life were eternal.

A single tear ran from the corner of his eye, which he quickly brushed away, annoyed with himself for displaying something he considered a weakness. He was still consumed with this inexplicable sadness at a time when he should have been so happy. The tear was not for himself, rather it was shed for the two he loved most; for Pia and the young Jamaican woman whose love for him was unequivocal. There was no going back now. He understood that the past defined his future, one offering little promise with so little time remaining. True happiness, he knew, could never be achieved at the expense of others. He wanted Brianna more than anything else in the world, yet as with so many other occasions in his life, he was faced with an impossible dilemma. This time it was a decision he could never make without hurting someone else he loved.

They turned the sound on the television higher and then quietly left the flat. The policeman called Frank in Flat #4 never heard them leave, nor was he in the least concerned they might do so after he had heard the squeals of delight from Brianna when she discovered Daniel standing at her door the previous day. Frank had been married for ten years and loved his wife and two children dearly. Nonetheless, he could not help envying the older man having someone so stunningly exotic to love him so late in life.

Wouldn't mind dying in her arms, he chuckled to himself as he was shaving, oblivious that his two charges had already made a run for it!

Daniel's mood had considerably improved from his earlier musings on the beach. At Brianna's urging they had decided to go for a walk to Portscatho to get out of the room for a while without their chaperone. They would make sure he did not get the blame for it when Roger eventually returned from London. It took them a while to find a way up from the beach to the cliff and the Southwest Coastal path that meandered along the edge of the cliff to Portscatho.

"Portscatho is a strange name, Daniel," she said, holding his hand and gently swinging their arms. Daniel was on the cliff-edge side of the path.

"What if I was suddenly to go crazy and push you over the side?" she laughed, pulling him further from the edge as a precaution.

"Then you would never have an answer to your first question," he laughed. He told her the name Portscatho was in fact a Cornish word meaning 'harbour of boats.'

"My Aunt Aggie told me what it meant walking on this very path when the three of us were on our way there, over fifty years ago now."

Brianna pulled up short and made an ugly face and let go of his hand.

"So old," she said in feigned disgust. "Why am I here so far from my home walking along a dangerous cliff with a very old man? No need to push you. You're so old there's no need. You'll just fall over by yourself!" Daniel was unable to maintain the pretense of being angry for more than a few seconds, at which point he succumbed, put an arm around her waist, smiled and kissed her softly.

It took them a little over an hour to reach the fishing village after stopping off briefly at Porthbean beach, where the coastal path drops down before continuing along the cliff again. Daniel pointed out the hamlet of Rosevine as they walked to a small headland and their first picture-perfect view of Portscatho and the harbour.

"It's all so beautiful, Daniel. I never imagined England would look anything like this at all."

"Well, it's not all like this, Brianna. You haven't seen some of the awful cities, such as Birmingham or Bradford. Trench Town in Kingston is a positive paradise by comparison!"

Along the way she told Daniel about the evening two policemen who were waiting at her apartment on her return from church in Mandeville. "I was so scared at first, Daniel," she said. "Never was so scared in my life before. I was convinced the people were working for that crazy British lord, or perhaps his son had finally found me, and within minutes I would be dead after they threw me and Jevon over the balcony down three floors to the road. I was terrified!" she exclaimed, leaving no doubt in Daniel's mind just how brave she must have been.

She told them how they had taken her aside out of earshot of Jevon and explained that one of them was with the British police from London and the other was a policeman from Kingston. After showing her their warrant cards they said she must accompany them because her life was in grave danger.

"I was very hesitant at first", she said, "until they mentioned Inspector Sage and other things that could only have come from you, Daniel".

"But how did they find you? I never told them!".

"They found out where my mum lived in Mo'Bay and she told them a white man had been to see her a few days before. She thought he was an Englishman, about her age but very fit looking. This man had asked her all sorts of questions, and even went to some of the neighbours for information about me".

She paused for a moment and then continued, "Although they did not contact me immediately, once the police found my mum, they began monitoring the iPhone I had bought her and then found me through my IP address on the WhatsApp and Skype calls to her in Montego Bay. Sorry, Daniel, I only ever used VPN on calls to you"!

She finished by telling him how terrified Jevon had seemed to leave her behind as she left with the two policemen. Jevon had no idea what was going on and the police had told Brianna not to say anything. All she did tell her friend was that she would see her at work tomorrow before walking off with her two escorts.

They were silent for a while as they continue on their walk. Then suddenly out of the blue Daniel asked whether she was ashamed of being with someone so much older.

Brianna pulled on his arm and stopped abruptly in her tracks. "*Yuh nutten buh ah crazy assed Englishman*," she sang out, slipping into dialect and giving him one of her beautiful pearl-white smiles. "Age is only a number, Daniel! It means nothing! Our souls are bonded for eternity and neither old age, gender nor death will ever break that. Whether we live apart for the next twenty years, time has no relevance and nothing will be any different than it is today."

"I wish I believed in an eternity or even a God, Brianna. I envy you your faith."

"But you do believe in God, Hun. You just don't realize it," she said, still standing there in front of him on the path and squeezing his hand. Behind him she could see the boats in the harbour. The sun reflecting off the water highlighted the different colours of the vessels bobbing in the current of an outgoing tide. The day was glorious, without a single cloud. Out at sea several ships were navigating the English Channel, starting long voyages or approaching their destination.

She pulled him towards her and pushed aside a grey curl from his forehead. "Daniel, you could never be more than you already are, a truly good person. Don't allow your past to persuade you otherwise." She looked into his eyes. "Be happy for us, my love, for we have something very special. I know you are sometimes tortured inside, but don't be. I know you don't want to be responsible for causing your wife's unhappiness, nor should you."

She went quiet for a moment and looked at him intently. "I have no demands on you, Daniel, except for you to love me. I know you love Pia as well, and that's OK. It's exactly how it should be. It would be a sad world if you could only love one person at a time. That would be crazy!"

Daniel appeared perplexed, so Brianna began to explain.

"I have been very lucky meeting you, darlin'. Not only are you the first person in my life who truly loves me for just being me, you have also helped me establish a new life, allowing me to stand on my own feet for the very first time." As if to emphasize this point, she said, "You have helped me become a wealthy woman by Jamaican standards. Soon I shall be able to return your twenty-five thousand dollars."

She reflected for a moment as Daniel began shaking his head in disagreement in reference to the return of his money. "You are directly responsible for dramatically changing my life without asking for a single thing in return. Wherever we end up living, together or apart, I will always be with you, my dearest Daniel." He took her hand and they continued walking along the path into Portscatho.

Brianna failed to notice him quickly wiping his eyes with the back of his hand.

CHAPTER 54

FALMOUTH – Cornwall

15 October 2017 (GMT)

The schooner *Pickle* was the first to deliver the news of the victory at Trafalgar and the death of Admiral Nelson. Thirty-one years later, in 1836, HMS *Beagle* anchored in the same port after her epic survey voyage around the world. It was no coincidence Falmouth harbour played such a notable part in British history in those days, for not only was it the first major port to the entrance of the English Channel, it was also the deepest in Western Europe.

Nineteen years shy of two centuries after Darwin's triumphant return by stagecoach to Shrewsbury, a ruthless psychopath drove his rental car slowly along Cliff Road overlooking Falmouth Bay. He soon saw the Victorian chateau-style, Falmouth Hotel a little further ahead on the left, the oldest purpose-built hotel in Falmouth. It was a large six-story edifice. Though not quite as big, it resembled the imposing architecture of the Chateau Frontenac in Quebec City, also constructed in the late 19th century.

Planning for all eventualities, he had decided on an Avis Mercedes-Benz 'C' class, something with a little more power than the average rental.

He parked it in the hotel car park and went inside to reception carrying a black duffel bag. The hotel was large enough for him to remain anonymous. The front desk staff were often so busy they could barely remember the check-in once they had issued the key card and pointed the guest in the direction of the lifts.

———•———

If the London Met had not organized Brianna's arrival in the United Kingdom through the Protected Persons Service (UKPPS), no one would have been any the wiser. She had been flown to London from Kingston on a regular BA flight from Montego Bay, accompanied by the same two detectives who had met her that Saturday on her return with Jevon from church. What no one had known was that the woman who organized lodgings for protected witnesses in the UK had been involved in a hit-and-run accident four years previously.

She, in turn, was unaware that the accident had been witnessed by Richard Wagner, who had been turning off a secondary road onto the A169 on his way to Scarborough on the east coast. It had happened near Malton in the middle of nowhere. Switching off his headlights and stopping his car on the grass verge, he had the presence of mind to take a zoom picture on his iPhone of the woman leaning over the body with the license plate of her vehicle clearly visible from the reflection of her car's headlights. She had hit a local drunk stumbling home to his stone cottage on the windswept Yorkshire moors. At the time she's been working for the police in York as a junior analyst and had been heading to Whitby for the weekend.

Once he found out the accident was reported as a hit and run, it took Wagner less than three days through a contact at the DMV in Swansea to find out the woman's address and her name. She was a twenty-eight-year-old single mother called Alice King who lived in Wetherby in the West Riding. She had no previous convictions of any kind, not so much as a parking ticket.

One evening later that summer, someone unknown to her knocked at her front door, introduced himself and then showed her the picture he had taken of her kneeling on a road by the side of a body on the North

Yorkshire moors. From that day on Alice was desperately anxious to please her blackmailer.

She began by feeding Richard Wagner whatever she thought were useful snippets of information, as he had instructed her. She continued doing so even after she had moved down south to London to work for the UKPP, transmitting encrypted messages as often as twice a week using a different email address and a VPN provider. Much of the information she sent had little value to Wagner, but every so often something proved highly useful.

Ten years later, on October 2, 2017, Alice King was instructed by a high-ranking police officer with the London Metropolitan Police to find secure accommodation for a Jamaican female witness who was being flown over from the island the following week. It had to be somewhere fairly remote but no further than five hours from central London by road. The former police analyst took less than three hours to come up with something suitable in Cornwall. It was a flat advertised by an estate agent in Falmouth for short-term rents. It was perfect.

Once her supervisor had given her the go-ahead, she phoned the estate agent and told him she needed to rent the flat for at least a month. He was delighted to take the reservation and even agreed they could extend it with only two days' prior notice. It would be the onset of winter shortly, with the likelihood of strong gales and heavy snowfalls. At that time of year, he would take any rental he could get. Once the details were confirmed, the woman rang Richard Wagner and left a message for him to call back on her private mobile number.

Wagner remained in his room until dark. His route from London had taken him directly past Rocky Lane, which lead to the Pendower Court flats. He slowed down briefly to peer down the lane. There was little he could see apart from a row of trees and the corner of a white building. He accelerated and continued on his way to Falmouth.

He had wanted to familiarize himself with the general terrain before returning later that night. He was pleased to find the location remoter than he had imagined, which should help complete his evening mission without too much trouble. What he did not know was that the Jamaican was not alone. The engineer was in Cornwall, not in Australia as he had been informed.

Otherwise, things had been going well for him over the past few days. His German wife had finally called from Buenos Aires the day before to tell him she and their daughter had arrived safely after leaving Spain, first taking a flight to the UK and spending two nights in London, as he had instructed, before taking another flight over to Paris and then a third flight over the Atlantic to Argentina. Richard Wagner was fairly certain no one would be monitoring their movements but needed to get them to a safer location.

Now the mother and daughter were checked in at the Hotel Club Frances in the Recoleta area of Buenos Aires. As with all the flights, Wagner had made and paid for all the reservations, paying the hotel in full for two weeks in advance. He planned on joining them in a city further north in about ten days, once he had tied up a few loose ends in the UK. Neither the Elms nor the British police would ever track him and his family to Corrientes, close to the *triple borders* of Argentina, Paraguay and Brazil. This would be his last job for his lordship and his snivelling son. At last, he could consider working entirely for himself.

According to the 'thug' he had met in Colchester, the engineer in Australia was now someone else's responsibility. Once the black bitch was dead, there was nothing else to keep him in the UK. He was excited at the thought of seeing his wife and daughter again and setting up an entirely new life. He had decided on Corrientes not only for its remoteness but because smuggling was such a highly lucrative occupation on the Triple Frontier. His life's experience was almost tailor-made for what he hoped would become his new career.

CHAPTER 55

A PURPOSE TO KILL – Tasmania

15 October 2017 (AEDT)

Louis McPherson took a taxi to Braybrook where he was dropped off at a private address after a twenty-five-minute ride from Melbourne Airport. Two young children were playing in the driveway of the house behind a dilapidated '97 VW camper van. They were too busy to notice him as they tried to trample a small lizard to death.

The white van was starting to rust. Holiday decals collected over twenty years from towns and places in Australia had been affixed on some of the windows. On both the passenger's and driver's doors were two large 'ban the bomb' logos, recognized these days as the universal peace sign.

Anticipating his arrival, a man came from inside the house. Louis gave him an envelope containing five thousand dollars; in return he was handed the keys to the van and the necessary paperwork in case Louis intended to register the change of ownership – which he did not.

It had just gone five-thirty pm and traffic was heavy with commuters heading home from work. The drive to the ferry terminal, which should have taken only fifteen minutes took him close to an hour. He was not the least concerned, however, because he would still have two hours or longer to wait before the *Spirit of Tasmania* set sail for Davenport. He had decided to take the overnight ferry to Tasmania to get some sleep before he arrived early the following morning.

The next morning, after an embarrassing delay starting the camper van, with frustrated car passengers bottled up behind him on the car deck, he set off for the two-hour drive to Bridport. Normally passengers have to book four weeks in advance to take the ferry from Bridport to Cape Barren on Flinders, but in October it was possible to make a reservation on the Furneaux Freight ferry with only a few days' notice. He had paid the six hundred and fifty dollars for the nine-hour return trip the day after the late-night telephone call in Sydney from the man with the distorted voice. He had confirmed Hannaford's wife was definitely staying on Flinders with her sister-in-law.

Louis was not intending to use the return portions of either of the ferry tickets he'd purchased with one of several credit cards he possessed in false names, all associated with his numbered account in Panama. With no confirmation of the husband's whereabouts, Louis had decided to remain focused on the wife, who could prove a very valuable witness for the prosecution should anything happen to her husband. No doubt he would have told her everything! She could verify his written statement in court, as well as the veracity of the Jamaican woman's testimony if she suddenly showed up as a witness.

There was only one other car on the old hulk of a ferry as well as five twenty-foot containers as it chugged out into the Bass Strait shortly after two pm, a little over three hours late. It would be close to eleven by the time they arrived at Cape Barren. Louis planned to park the van somewhere quiet once he arrived and kip down in the back in a sleeping bag. He had also brought along some food, water and two semi-automatic pistols together with several boxes of ammunition he had purchased in Sydney from a source he had located on the dark web. Before he went to sleep, he planned to remove the two ban-the-bomb logos from the doors using a couple of spray cans of white paint he had purchased at a Bunnings warehouse, one of the ubiquitous nationwide hardware stores.

It was quite dark by the time he located the campground. The road from Lady Barren was not paved and there had been a heavy downpour earlier in the evening. It was difficult to plough through several inches of mud in a vehicle with balding tires. The Yellow Beach Campground had a toilet and shower and a place to park the VW camper within an easy walk to a beach. It was all he needed. The place was completely deserted by the time he arrived. Before turning into catch some sleep in the back of the van, he switched on the headlights with the engine running and sprayed the two doors with the white paint, careful to do a less than professional job to match the previous re-paint jobs.

The next morning, he could feel the chill in the air when he opened the side door to stretch his legs. An easterly wind with the promise of becoming gale force thrashed through Franklin Sound, agitating the ocean into angry waves of white froth. He drove back to Lady Barren and stopped there to fill up with petrol, purchased a cup of machine-dispensed coffee and a local map of Flinders Island and paid cash. It was only seven-thirty in the morning and he had hours to kill before it started getting dark. He headed back on the B85 in the old van and then took a turning towards Trouser Point Beach. Legend had it the beach was named for a shipwreck survivor who washed ashore without his trousers in the 19th century.

To prolong the journey Louis had decided to make various stops on the route north to do some sightseeing, which would be his cover story if anyone asked. He was just another British tourist who had always dreamed of circumnavigating the Australian continent by car, an almost 16,000-kilometer journey. Being a keen mountaineer from his days in the army, he also wanted to check out Mt Strzelecki. It would help give credence to any story he may have to provide later if things went wrong. He still felt relatively young and was remarkably healthy. He had the time but decided against walking to the top of the 756-metre peak.

He parked the VW in the picnic area at the far end of the beach. There was a spectacular view of the sweep of the beach with Mt Strzelecki looming in the distance. Before getting out he displayed the parks pass on the dash. The girl at the petrol station advised him to buy it when he told her he was heading that way to do some sightseeing. He took several photos on his amble along the beach. Then he returned to the van, ate a couple of granola bars and drank a full bottle of water. He had thrown out the tepid, foul-tasting coffee almost as soon as he had purchased it.

The camping ground was deserted and so he took the opportunity to thoroughly clean the two Browning HI Power semi-automatic pistols he had first become familiar with during the Falkland campaign. Afterwards, he continued heading north on the B85 and stopped to check out two more beaches where he took yet more photographs.

The VW camper eventually pulled up in front of the Flinders Island Interstate Hotel in Whitemark. He got out, strolled to the bar door and went inside. Built in 1911, it looked like many rural hotels throughout Australia. This one was significantly different because the family-owned hotel advertised there were no *pokie* machines inside, much to the relief of many who could ill-afford to throw away money on something rigged in favour of the house.

No one looked at Louis until he ordered a beer and asked to see a bar menu. "Here you go, mate," a middle-aged woman said, handing him a tattered lunch menu that appeared to have been printed the day the pub had opened.

"A bloody Pom?" she asked, smiling and handing him the beer. Some foam was dribbling down the side of the glass. He gave her a ten-dollar note and took a large swig.

"Cheers," he said giving her a broad smile. He chatted with her for a couple of minutes and then took his beer and sat down at a table in front of an old, iron wood-burning stove, unused for years and now missing an exhaust pipe. He sat there a while and went back to the bar ten minutes later, after reading on the menu that they stopped serving lunch in half an hour, at one-thirty. He ordered a plate of locally caught fish with a side of crispy wedges.

CHAPTER 56

LEEKA – Flinders, Tasmania

17 October 2017 (AEDT)

Superintendent Chase of the Australian Federal Police slithered through the soft sand down the narrow path towards the beach. It was partially overgrown with seagrass, indicating how seldom it was used. He continued slipping to the bottom of the gentle rise of sand dunes in a pair of entirely unsuitable leather-soled Oxfords. He was also wearing a suit on an island where men only ever wore them at funerals, in or outside of a casket.

He had been here far too long and felt like he was wasting his time. He had so many other important things to attend to back in Canberra. That was not to suggest he did not like Flinders; part of him was enjoying this break protecting the two pleasant ladies. But he kept thinking of the urgent issues overflowing his in-tray back at the office.

He had been down to the beach as many as ten times each of the two days he had been there. Though he was not convinced the women were in much danger, his instincts told him that any threat would come from the beach side of the house. He was convinced no one would try a direct approach from West End Road. It was too quiet; even a stray dog would be spotted almost immediately by the officers in the patrol car concealed in a driveway of a house further down from the McArthur home.

Ever the professional policeman, regardless of his personal opinion, Chase was still concerned that he had insufficient resources should anything occur. At the end of the day, there was just himself and the one patrol car working in shifts with the only other police vehicle available in the Whitemark region.

It was going to be another beautiful day. The wind was only a whisper and yesterday's white seahorses had ceased dancing the surface of Bass Strait. The crescent beach was quite short, just over a kilometre from Roydon Island due east to Bun Beetons Point in the northwest. He checked that his weapon was still in its holster after his slide down to the beach, before continuing towards the sea where the sand was firmer. He walked to the end in both directions, which took less than twenty minutes. As usual, all was very quiet apart from the occasional screeching gull. Soon he was struggling in the sand, heading back up along the path towards the house. He had seen no one, not even a single footprint on the beach.

———·———

A little way from the turnoff to West Beach Road, on the left-hand side of the road, was a roughhewn track Louis had located on Google Maps. It led towards a small beach on Tanner's Bay, about two kilometres from West End Beach, the other side of Bun Beetons Point. It was no distance at all for him, but he would allow an additional fifteen minutes or so to clamber over the rocks skirting the shoreline from the beach on Tanner's Bay to the one on the other side of the point. It might be a bit tricky even in the moonlight, but nothing by comparison to the long trek in the pouring, bone-chilling rain under enemy fire on the Falklands.

He was encouraged at finding the track in better shape than he had anticipated. He had harboured concerns the terrain might prevent him from a speedy getaway when the time came. It was obviously not used too often, for the ground remained firm despite the overnight rain. The track was covered most of the way by an umbrella of trees. At the end of this tree line to the beach, he managed a four-point turn so the van would be pointing in the direction he had come.

So far, the '97 VW was holding up remarkably well apart from the stall on the ferry, which he discovered later was nothing more than a loose spark plug. Otherwise, mechanically, despite a bit of rust here and there, the vehicle was a tribute to the previous owner. A ubiquitous old camper van would rarely draw much attention in Australia.

He had spent the previous night at a small caravan site on the edge of Whitemark after spending this first day on the island behaving like a regular tourist. It had given him time to reconnoitre and familiarise himself with the lay of the land in case something went wrong and he needed to improvise a quick escape.

A couple was already there when he arrived, parked in a large Parkes-18 caravan. They were from Sydney and comfortably retired. With no particular route in mind, they had set out to explore the country they had ignored most of their lives, preferring to travel overseas when they were not too busy raising three sons. They were happy they did, they told Louis, as the three of them enjoyed a beer under the awning of their caravan.

They complained to him that it was too much effort to fly overseas these days with all the security checks. When they were younger, they always explored places on their own, and were not comfortable standing around gawking at crumbling cathedrals and monuments along with crowds of others, herded like cattle by tourist guides. Most of them would probably have been far better off staying at home in the first place to travel the world on television. At least they would be more comfortable. Their last trip, a cruise to Italy, was a nightmare; Venice was flooded, there was a garbage strike in Rome and the entire country was on high alert after a bomb had gone off at a restaurant on the Isle of Capri killing twenty-five people, nearly all of them foreign tourists.

Louis would have preferred to remain alone, but he decided that being unfriendly when he was supposed to be touring Australia on the holiday of a lifetime would probably only draw more attention to himself.

He sat with them for close to two hours and had three beers. He explained that he was on his own because his wife had died six months earlier from breast cancer. He had promised her he would go away after she died on the trip they had always wanted to take together. Thinking of Flo as he was telling his story, Louis decided he was looking forward to going home soon.

Soon it would just be him and Flo ambling happily in retirement, at least this is what he hoped, failing to understand his past demons would always demand a price far too high to simply walk away unscathed. He had not always been faithful in body but always was in spirit, and he always tried to believe Flo was the only true love of his life.

None of it was true, for he was a man lacking all empathy, a psychopath and a killer.

———

He drove the van several yards further up the track. He pulled over where he had spotted a small natural clearing and turned off the engine. He had five hours to wait before dusk and he could make his way to the other side of the point. It was to be a full moon tonight and he would have no problem returning to the van as long as he kept low, remaining as close as possible to the dunes along West End Beach. After that he would have the cover of the rocks.

He released the hood of the van and then got out to check the plug was still okay and once again he checked the engine oil and water level of the radiator.

CHAPTER 57

THE PLUME OF FEATHERS – Cornwall

15 October 2017 (GMT)

Hand in hand they strolled down the main street that led steeply to the picturesque fishing port. It was close to noon and the village was already busy with tourists, even this late in the year. By order of council their cars now had to park a mile from the village in a designated field overlooking the ocean. Even so, in midsummer it didn't take long before it was full and later arrivals had to park along the narrow road, often a good mile or two from the village. As with many holiday destinations throughout the world, tourism in Cornwall was becoming more of a chore than the relaxing break it was intended to be.

The weather was warm and people were still wearing summer outfits. Children raced ahead, ignoring the commands of stressed parents. They were drawn by the small fishing boats visible below, moored like colour wheels of bobbing corks. The reflections of the brightly painted boats shimmered on the surface of the rippled water.

"What's that?" Briana asked, pointing towards the port as they were walking down the street. Some children and several adults were gathered around what looked like a large red Easter egg squatting in front of the harbour wall.

"I'm not certain, Bri, let's take a look."

He then recalled from his childhood that he had seen it before, possibly when Aunt Aggie had taken him and Richard on one of their walks to this quaint fishing village. She used to buy them ice cream and Tizer at a little café that was no longer there. He remembered as soon as he drew closer that it was an old, defused mine from the Second World War. Brass detonation contacts protruded as if from some gigantic pin cushion. A small wooden box sat screwed to the top of the now harmless mine with a notice asking people to deposit loose change for the local lifeboat station, which was supported entirely by public donation.

Daniel explained to Brianna that the contact points were designed to detonate the mine when it hit a ship or a submarine. "Apparently unexploded ones used to wash ashore all-around Britain for years after the war," he said. "I heard they cordoned off part of Pendower Beach, very close to where we are staying, after a live mine was carried ashore during a storm. The army had to blow it up, right there on the beach."

Brianna had put her arm around his waist and hugged him. "Oh, Daniel, I do love you so much," she said as he began slotting several coins into the lifeboat collection box.

"I love you, too, Miss Jamaica," he replied and kissed her on the side of her cheek.

They strolled halfway back up the high street where they had previously noticed a dirty blue awning hanging from an intricate wrought-iron bracket on the stone wall of a pub. On it were three white ostrich feathers protruding from a gold coronet, with the words ich dien inscribed in gold medieval script. Daniel recognized it as the heraldic badge of the Prince of Wales but considered it rather odd that the inscription was in German. The pub was called the Plume and Feathers and a brass plaque by the door noted it had been established in 1856 when Portscatho was still a thriving port, known especially for pilchard fishing. The lively chatter of conversation came from within. They decided to go in so Brianna could experience a real British pub for her first time.

Despite the warm weather a log fire was burning in the original inglenook stone fireplace. Tables and chairs in different styles and colours were arranged in a haphazard fashion. At the end of the room was a bar with blue wooden panelling on the customer side. Whether left from last year or in preparation for Christmas two months hence, the bar was decorated with a string of seasonal fairy lights from one end to the other. Above, original hand-hewn oak beams stretched the full length of the ceiling. Over in the corner, past the dartboard and the bar, was an archway to a more formal dining room. At least the sign indicated it as such, whereas the plastic chairs and tables inside rather belied the fact it was anything special.

They found a table in the main part of the pub by a bay window looking out to the square. It was comfortable there, despite being near the fire. Without it the one-hundred-and-fifty-year-old pub would be chilly inside even on the warmest days of summer. Leaning close to Daniel, Brianna inquired in a whisper why people were looking at them. "And when we were walking down to see the boats and that old mine," she added. Daniel had been unaware of this and was glancing about the room. He did notice two people quickly turn away.

"You're right, Jamaica," he said, using one of his affectionate names for her.

"Perhaps they don't like black people in England?" she wondered. "No, I don't think that's it," he assured. "Pommies are not really racist, unlike Americans. Jamaicans are the first coloured people to ever settle in the UK in large numbers. Generally speaking, I think they are well-liked and are accepted to be as British as anyone else".

"But they are still staring," she said when she saw one lady looking at them who did not turn away. Instead, she gave Brianna a kind smile.

"See, she likes you, everyone likes you!" he said. "And I love you!" "There has to be something else then, something wrong with my clothes, perhaps?" She'd had little time to pack before she was hustled over to England for her safety with just the clothes she had on, plus a few last-minute personal items they had allowed her to quickly purchase in Mo'Bay and stuff in a new tote bag, including a few clothes. As she was discovering, most of what she had picked out was way too thin for an English autumn.

Today she had on a pretty dress patterned in minute orange and rusty red flowers over white that highlighted her dark complexion.

Perhaps she was displaying too much cleavage? Daniel just laughed at this suggestion. "You're so funny, Brianna! Haven't you seen the half-naked young girls walking around with tattoos on the cheeks of their bums?"

She said she had and they both laughed before Daniel got up to get a pint of beer and a pint of cider flavoured with mango, lime and ginger. Brianna had chosen it from a list of craft ciders sitting on their table in a plastic sleeve.

Daniel was convinced people were staring not only because she was exotically beautiful, but because they were sorry for her hanging about with an old geezer like him!

He returned to the table carrying the two pints and the food menu. Brianna chose the pan-roasted salmon and new potatoes with beetroot truffle. "Sounds nice," she said, as she had not had any fish since she'd arrived in England. Daniel chose the glazed ham, egg and chips before going back to the bar to place the order.

"Excuse us for staring, darling," the woman over at the next table said in a broad Essex accent. "You are such a beautiful girl, and your man is extremely handsome! You are not some famous couple, are you?" Brianna assured her they were not but thanked her for the compliment. The woman had the last word before she continued chatting with her husband, "and we both love your Jamaican accent. It's like music!"

They relished their meals, as they had barely eaten a thing since the previous day, and then only snacks during several hours of sharing their love for one another. After their meals, Brianna had some room left for a sticky toffee pudding, which she shared with Daniel.

He was excited when she started telling him about the success of her online clothing business. But she was concerned about being away. Jevon, though more than capable of taking care of the orders and shipping, was absolutely hopeless when it came to sourcing new stock. "We have clients who buy from us on a regular basis as soon as they see something new on the website," she explained. "Without that flow of new merchandise, we could lose a lot of business."

Daniel reassured her that she would be going home soon, without being entirely convinced himself that either of them would, at least not for the moment. He was also extremely concerned about Pia despite her and Jane having police protection. He just wanted the whole matter to be over and done with so they could all get on with their lives. Whether he would ever be able to live a normal life again was a continual matter of concern. As so often in his life, he knew he was procrastinating again, shying away from making difficult decisions. This one, he realized, would be the hardest of all.

Yet it could wait for another day, he finally decided, avoiding the problem once again. Today they had both found immense happiness in one another's company. He had no intention of spoiling that, he thought, as want for an excuse. As they were preparing to leave, Brianna, who was grinning, told him what the woman had said at the next table. "We're movie stars!" she exclaimed; she clung on to him tightly as they exited the pub.

Like two naughty children, their first inclination was to run and hide. But it was too late for that. Frank had already spotted the pair walking up the hill heading for the wooden style leading to the coastal path. He was glaring at them from the car. He drew up alongside them in the car and told them to get in. A constable was waving his arms frantically from the other side of the road, trying to warn them that cars were not allowed in the village.

Frank ignored the uniformed policeman and drove away with his two rebellious charges in the back of the car.

CHAPTER 58

ILL MET BY MOONLIGHT – Flinders Island
17 October 2017 (AEDT)

It was turning dark and Jane drew the curtains whilst Pia went to make a cup of tea. They had already finished their dinner, consisting of a store-bought leek and bacon quiche, and the freshest salad Pia had ever tasted. All the ingredients Jane had grown herself in her little veggie patch by the water tank at the side of the house. They both had two large glasses of Mateus Rosé with their meal and were feeling rather relaxed.

Earlier in the afternoon they had sat together looking through some of Jane's old photographs. She had them stored in a shoebox in no particular order, spanning decades and two husbands. Her aboriginal partner, who came late to her life, was her only true love. He was someone she still missed every single day. On certain days she physically ached from her longing to be with him one more time, cradled in his arms, snuggled next to one another listening to the waves pound the shore as gale-force winds rattled the windows of the house.

They went through more than a hundred photos, one by one; seven of the earliest were of the most interest to Pia. One was of Jane when she was fifteen, proudly holding her new baby brother.

"Daniel was about six months old when that was taken," she said. "Must have been late 1953 or early 1954."

Pia was fascinated. "You were both so blonde," she commented. "I see Daniel had his curly hair even back then."

"And here's the only one I have of our mother," Jane said quietly, passing it to Pia sitting beside her on the sofa. The woman in the photo looked Scandinavian, slim and with the blondest hair Pia had ever seen. She was smiling as she stood next to Daniel, who looked about two, and holding his hand. Jane was on the other side hugging her mother around the waist.

"You all look so happy."

"I guess we all were back then before she disappeared. Even Dad," Jane said and showed Pia the next picture of her father. It seemed to have been taken at the same time; he was standing alone displaying a cheerful grin. He appeared tall and in contrast to the others his hair had a reddish tinge.

"The war affected him a great deal, but there were times he seemed normal and happy whilst Mum was still around. Once she had gone, he started drinking. Then I left and poor Daniel was shipped off to that dreadful school in England." Jane paused for a moment and sighed. "I really should have been there for Daniel, but living with my father was too difficult. I had to get away."

———◆———

Louis checked the two guns for the last time. He had screwed a silencer on the one he intended to use and was keeping the other strapped to his leg in reserve. The third weapon he was carrying was attached to his waist. It was the world's deadliest knife, the *Jagdkommando*, named after the Austrian Armed Special Forces Operations group, this version made in the USA. They were banned by the Geneva convention for use in war, yet any American ten-year-old could own one as long as they had eight hundred dollars. It had a seven-inch, corkscrew blade and a hollow titanium handle with a solid titanium *glass breaker* on the end designed for breaking and entering. This part was especially useful if you needed to kill someone sitting inside a car; or it could punch a hole through a man's skull into the soft tissue of his brain if sufficient force were applied.

He spent some time in the waning light applying special face paint, camouflaging it with green and black streaks. Later he changed into lightweight combat fatigues that he had bought at an army surplus store in Parramatta, a suburb of Sydney. The knife he had purchased on the dark web, along with the two guns and silencer and several clips of ammunition he had tucked inside the multitude of pockets in his military jacket and pants.

He had on a pair of Ryno Gear combat boots he had worn since leaving England; they were favoured by the US Marines. Satisfied that he was fully prepared for just about any eventuality, he sat on a rock as the sun was setting over Prime Seal Island. Once he had completed what he had come to do in Leeka, assuming all went according to plan, he would focus on finding a secure park for the night as close as he could to the Whitemark airport to spend the night in the van. In the morning he would leave it where it was parked and walk a couple of kilometres to catch the six-forty flight over to Launceston. So late at night it could be hours before someone discovered the bodies, and when they did, he would be long gone. From Launceston he would take a flight over to Melbourne and then onward to the UK via Qantas. With a little bit of luck, he would be in the air heading towards Singapore and home before the plods on the island had the slightest clue of what had occurred.

Louis had driven unnoticed along West End Road earlier in the day, just another tourist driving another camper van. From the corner of his eye, he caught sight of the police car parked in the neighbour's carport before driving past the sister-in-law's house. Four or five police at most, he guessed. As someone who had been part of a relatively small force, way outnumbered by the Argies at Goose Green, he had no concerns about taking on a few policemen on a sleepy island on the arse side of the world. He had not hesitated to execute two teenage Argentinian conscripts back then. A handful of out-of-shape, poorly trained policemen would be no problem whatsoever. Of course, he needed to avoid coming in to direct contact with them if possible.

If he could complete the job tonight as late as possible, or in the very early hours of the morning well before the police would do a physical check on the women, then with perhaps an hour to get away from the area, he would never be caught. One hour was all he needed from the time he got back to the van. Even in the worst-case scenario and it was too dangerous to leave the island on the early flight in the morning, with his survival skills he had absolute confidence he could remain on the island for days undetected until he had found another way to get off Flinders safely. Of course, that worst case would only occur if the police could get their act together by early morning to monitor the port and airport. This, he decided, was highly unlikely. They simply did not have the resources.

Superintendent Chase was restless and frustrated; he continually looked at his watch as the hours dragged by interminably. He had made a big mistake volunteering for the protection unit rather than allowing a subordinate to handle it, someone who would have jumped at the chance of a mini-vacation on an idyllic island, if only to escape the pressures of the office for a few days. But seeing that the request had come from the Met in London, his immediate superior, Commander Kershaw, had also suggested the feds should have someone on the spot with rank. So, Chase volunteered before he was ordered to!

Breaking his own golden rule not to drink on the job, he went into the kitchen fridge and pulled out a can of VB. He then quickly made a cheese sandwich with two large dill pickles on the side. Bugger it, he thought! He returned to the living room and switched on the TV to watch the ABC News.

Louis had a small torch with him but turned it on only briefly as he scrambled over the rocks wrapped around Bun Beetons Point. In the darkness they reminded him of the Giant's Causeway in County Antrim, which he had seen on manoeuvres when he was stationed in Northern Ireland after the Falklands. There was more cloud about than had been forecast for this time and the moonlight was intermittent, making his progress slower than he had calculated but less likely to be seen from the road. Once over the rocks, he could see well enough. As he approached West End Beach, he turned off the small torch.

It was still over a kilometre to the house. He kept close to the rocks as he jogged quickly on the hard sand until reaching the dunes that stretched the full length of the beach. His movements were disguised by the waltzing shadows of the scurrying clouds filtering the moonlight. It was perfect cover for him in his camouflaged outfit. Even a man standing on the shore might not have seen him, let alone someone standing above with an interrupted line of sight.

Louis paused for a moment and pressed the side button on his watch. The phosphorescent glow told him it had taken him less than twenty minutes to get from the camper on Tanner's Bay. He was making much better time than he thought he would.

There were some lights ahead set further back from the beach; they told him that he was almost there. As he drove past earlier in the day, he had noticed there were five houses along that stretch of the coast, with two of them on the beach side, including the targets, whilst the three other homes were a little further down on the far side of West End Road.

Cautiously, he moved ahead and took out his gun from its holster just in case an unpleasant surprise was lying concealed in the dunes watching his approach. There was no one. All was quiet apart from the constant rhythm of the ocean's waves trying to reach the shore, then draining in specks of white foam beneath the sand. Louis looked upwards and saw a light flickering from inside the house. The old dears were watching TV, he thought, just as he discovered a partially overgrown path. He'd known he was in the right place when he saw two houses at the top of the rise. The one on the left-hand side was in total darkness; it must have been the one he had seen with the parked police vehicle.

Now his military training and innate intuition took command. He became entirely focused and vigilant as he slowly made his way up towards the house, like any animal on the hunt.

CHAPTER 59

ANGEL OF DEATH – Flinders Island

17 October 2017 (AEDT)

Jane was at the kitchen sink washing the dishes by hand and Pia was drying. It was early still, not quite eight, but Jane was feeling tired and had decided to go to bed once they finished. Her afternoon's journey travelling back in time, looking through old photos from the early 1950s, had left her exhausted and extremely sad. How different all of their lives might have been had her mother not vanished all those years ago, leaving behind so many unanswered questions. It would have been better, she thought, to have kept those mostly dark memories hidden within the photo box. Now the damage was done, too late to repair.

Pia's mood had also been affected by seeing Jane's photos. Rather than feelings of sadness, she was experiencing an inexplicable rising tide of anger as she dried the dishes. Her anger was not directed towards anyone in particular, for there was no one in particular to blame. No one was directly responsible; rather it was a random sequence of events that had destroyed an entire family from the very day Peter Hannaford had embarked on the troopship carrying him and thousands more to someone else's war.

It could have been so different for them all, including herself. For the first time since her marriage to Daniel, Pia understood this. Had he opened up to her fully, perhaps she could have helped him. Then again, perhaps not. Daniel himself had been denied access to most of the facts of his past; his mother had vanished and Jane had left home and Daniel had unwillingly been dispatched overseas whilst his father had continued to embrace alcohol.

Life had not been kind to the Hannaford family, nor to Pia. It was their history, not hers, that had denied her children.

They were both quiet as they finished off in the kitchen. Jane gave Pia a brief hug and then went to her room. Pia retired a little later after she had taken one more look through the seven photographs that had captured such fleeting moments of happiness for a family that had deserved so much more. She popped them back inside the box before going to bed. Twenty minutes later the two were still wide awake, both restless with thoughts and images conjured from their afternoon's travels to a place that perhaps should not have been revisited.

Suddenly, a loud explosion invaded what had been total silence shrouded in a blanket of darkness! There were no streetlights here on the street, and the moon had been hidden by more thick cloud for the last fifteen minutes. A second shot then echoed again through the night, silent only to its target.

Pia threw back the covers and scrambled from her bed and ran into Jane's room, where she found her collapsed on the floor. Jane's eyes were open; she was attempting to speak and grasping hold of Pia's hand. Pia could just make out the terrified expression on Jane's face, illuminated briefly by the moon before additional racing clouds extinguished the light and left the room and the two women in total darkness once more.

———

Louis moved slowly up the incline towards the house. The clouds were more numerous and there was no moonlight now to show the way. He could barely make out the silhouette of the house and could no longer see any lights coming from inside.

They must have just gone to bed; he realized he would now have to enter the house to take his shots. It was something he had anticipated and planned for, but he was concerned about the extra time it would take. The longer it took the more chance there was of discovery. Louis moved silently along the outside wall until he came to what appeared to be a back door. He gently turned the knob and, somewhat to his surprise, discovered the door was not locked. He began to open it slowly but then stopped short for a moment when he heard noise coming from the TV.

The two women must have only closed the curtains. He swore to himself. He should have considered this beforehand. Very sloppy for a highly trained professional soldier. He found himself in a kitchen when he entered and could hear the soft hum of a refrigerator. Taking extreme care not to knock into anything, he could only see his way forward from the light emanating from the TV in the next room. With both hands grasping his gun before him he inched very slowly towards the archway separating the kitchen from the living room.

Pia was one hundred per cent focused after Jane appeared to have stopped breathing. She was kneeling on the floor performing CPR chest compressions. Despite the urgency, Pia maintained an utterly professional composure, just as she had been trained. She had to remain icy cold and smother her emotions if, as it seemed, Jane's life was in danger. It was the only way.

Pia was too fixated on what she was doing to realize someone else was now inside the house moving towards the bedrooms. Suddenly Jane's eyes briefly fluttered open and it was then Pia felt the presence of someone else in the room. She turned and saw the outline of a man holding what looked like a gun pointing towards the floor.

Superintendent Chase turned on the bedroom lights and took immediate stock of the situation. He replaced his gun in its holster and dialed triple zero. "Medical emergency," he said. "I'm with the federal police. We have a situation on West Point Road in Leeka, north of Whitemark, and require an ambulance immediately."

"I'm a former nurse, Superintendent," Jane said without looking at him. "Tell them the lady may have suffered a possible stroke and is having difficulty breathing."

Pia found a weak pulse but continued the compressions for a while longer, now anxious that Jane remain conscious until the ambulance arrived. "How long, Superintendent, how long will the ambulance take?" she demanded, desperately working on Jane.

"Half an hour at best," he said.

"She'll never make it if she's having a major stroke!"

Chase knew there was probably no time left for an ambulance. Using his UHF radio, he spoke to one of the policemen over at the other house. He and his partner had sprinted to it from their car after the first shot was fired. Chase ordered them to come over to take Mrs. McArthur to hospital in the back of their police car. Time was running out, he told them.

Chase then turned to Pia and told her one of the two policemen would drive them to the Flinders Island Multipurpose Centre Hospital in Whitemark. They had the facilities there to look after her, he assured. He then rushed from the house and ran over the road to Jane's where he had been encamped for the past two days.

For their safety Pia and Jane had moved over to the rental house further down the street intended originally for the superintendent. He had driven them the short distance in his rental car along with a few personal items they would require for the night and the box of Jane's old photographs. She had packed their dinner in two Tupperware containers and then put them in a shopping bag along with the wine.

Leaving the car behind at the rental house, Chase walked quickly back to Jane's hugging the shadows trying not to make any noise. When the moon was out, he knew he would have a fairly good view of the beach below and possibly detect movement from anyone heading up from the dunes along the overgrown path he had slid down in his city shoes earlier in the day.

Now, two nights later peering through the curtains below to the beach as the moon reappeared, Chase had detected brief movement by the sandhills a few yards from the path leading up to the house. Then another cloud obscured the moon and he thought perhaps he was mistaken. He maintained his vision trained on the spot where he thought he had seen the movement. Suddenly, for an instant, he saw the outline of a man trapped for a second in the light of the moon. He was crouching low advancing slowly up the beach path between the dunes.

The clouds scurried across the moon again and then Chase lost sight of the man. It was of little consequence by then because he knew the man was on his way and he only had seconds to prepare. He unlocked the back door of the house, by the side of the beach path, hoping he was choosing the man's point of entry for him. He did not want him moving around to the front or to start checking any of the windows, as he would no longer know the man's precise whereabouts.

He fully understood, as he had been trained, that the best chance for survival in a situation like this was to have the tactical advantage. One thing was certain, he would definitely have the element of surprise should the assailant enter by the back door, an assailant who was expecting to find only two elderly ladies.

Chase had imprinted in his mind the full layout of the house from the standpoint of its defensive strengths and weaknesses. Unlike the man about to check whether the back door was locked, Superintendent Chase was absolutely certain there was someone on the other side, armed and deadly dangerous.

As soon as the ceiling lights in the living room were switched on, Louis realized he would never see Colchester again. His luck had finally run out! He fired off just one shot using the gun with the silencer at a jacket hung around a lampstand in the corner of the room. It was a perfect shot that, had he been wearing the jacket, would have killed Chase immediately. Before he could even realize his mistake, Louis was unconscious and bleeding to death. Chase had intended his first round to be a headshot. His aim was too low, though, and the bullet severed Louis's carotid artery on the right side of his neck. His second shot hit Louis in the chest.

One minute later the ex-Para who had survived combat in the Falklands War was dead.

CHAPTER 60

DEATH AT PENDOWER COURT – Cornwall

15 October 2017 (GMT)

Frank Chambers, the Royalty and Specialist Protection (RaSP) officer assigned to Brianna and Daniel, was polite, but he maintained a stony silence as he drove them back to Pendower Court. He was not annoyed with them as much as he was with himself. He should have anticipated they would take off like that to spend time together. In their position he would probably have done the same. Yet it was his responsibility and his job to remain vigilant at all times. They could just as easily have been killed. He knew he had failed them. Moreover, he realized, he had failed himself.

"I hope there are no hard feelings, Frank?" Daniel asked, feeling a little sheepish, much like a young boy caught doing something terribly naughty. He and the others had just got out of the car and were heading around to the front of the building and flat #4. Frank looked more embarrassed than anything else. He had not expected an apology.

"That's very kind of you, Mr. Hannaford, but it's unnecessary and undeserving. I should have been doing a better job looking after you both. There may be someone out there trying to kill you, and this morning I gave them a perfect opportunity to do so."

"Well, I disagree," Daniel responded, "and I am certain Ms. Williams does as well."

Brianna nodded and gave Frank one of her radiant smiles displaying her two perfect rows of pearl-white teeth. Frank opened the door with his spare key and quickly checked inside to make sure everything was as it should be. Brianna and Daniel followed him.

Before Frank left Brianna asked if he would like to come over in half an hour and have a drink with them both. She never thought about whether he was allowed to drink on duty or not. After all, she had grown up in Jamaica where rules and regulations were tenuous at best.

"We have beer and wine," she said, tempting him.

Frank smiled. "I am certain a couple of beers won't impair my judgement. Sure, I'd love to pop over. Look forward to it." He was about to close the door behind him when he leaned back in. "You are not planning on going anywhere else in the meantime, I hope!"

Brianna was telling them all about the business she had started in Mandeville and how she intended eventually to expand by sourcing clothes elsewhere as well as the local markets. This would be easy enough once it was safe to do so, which Roger had assured it would be after she flew back home to Jamaica. There were plenty of discount shops in Jamaica and a number of wholesalers importing from several African countries as well as other places in the Caribbean. She and Jevon had already decided to check out Santo Domingo in the Dominican Republic for a week before she was hustled off to England

Daniel had not heard all the details and he sat there quietly, fascinated and proud of her accomplishments. She told them how her best friend, Jevon, had recently started searching for a proper warehouse, somewhere with sufficient space to maintain their stock and pack orders. They had been using both of their apartments until now and there was little room to move in either of them, and it was only going to get worse. A warehouse would also require a loading dock with easy access for pick up by various shipping companies – including the post office now that they had acquired their own Pitney Bowes franking machine, courtesy of Jamaica Post and their MegaMail service.

"Jesus, and you managed all this in the space of less than a year. That's unbelievable!" Frank commented as Daniel went to top-up Brianna's wine glass, as amazed as Frank at how quickly she established a profitable business. Now she was talking about warehouses and expanding her sales base to include a number of countries other than the UK and North America.

Brianna placed her hand over the top of her glass indicating she'd had enough. She had never really liked to drink and when she did it was usually only a Red Stripe or perhaps a rum and coke. Nor did she ever smoke ganja, even though her brother, Beanie, was a small-time dealer.

One of her uncles had done five years in Florida for attempting to smuggle a commercial quantity of cocaine inside two large cans of Blue Mountain coffee and two cases of Jamaican jerk seasoning. That was ten years ago, yet time would make no difference to her uncle, because for the rest of his life he would not be allowed to re-enter the United States.

"Have you eaten, Frank?" Brianna asked. "We don't have much in the fridge, but I could scramble you some eggs, Rasta style."

"Rasta, style! Sounds different, what is it?

"It's a bit like a Spanish omelette, only spicy," Brianna said. "Eggs, spring onion, coconut oil, red pepper, cayenne and chilli flakes."

Brianna had been in Cornwall only a few days by the time Daniel showed up at her door. She had spent her time walking the beach and wandering around the property. It was very quiet at this time of year because all the other holiday flats were left empty approaching winter.

She was accompanied most of the week by an armed, plain-clothes policewoman from Falmouth. Her name was Liz and she had done all of the shopping online for them both from a Tesco five miles down the road. Otherwise, most of the time they sat watching TV with doors and windows locked, or Brianna would tell the policewoman all about Jamaica and her life growing up there. Liz was quite young and she had lots of questions about Jamaican men and reggae music.

"I'd love to try it, Ms. Williams," Frank replied. "However, I really must go and check in with Inspector Sage soon. But thank you, perhaps next time."

After finishing his beer Frank said he was calling it a night and would check in on them in the morning. "I guess that's why my boss wants me to call him, to confirm when he'll be arriving."

———•———

Instinctively, on hearing the shot that came from the rear of the building, neither of them hesitated for a second. They knew immediately what they had to do. There was only one thing they could do! There was no time for discussion; the massive adrenaline rush, each simultaneously experienced, precluded all thoughts other than to survive.

Daniel pulled Brianna by the arm, threw open the front door and they both leapt down the few steps to the grass. Daniel tumbled to one side. Brianna immediately helped him up and they began running wildly down the steep lawn that led to the steps to the beach.

"No, Brianna," Daniel warned softly, pulling her over and almost dragging her through some hydrangea bushes that grew as a hedge all the way to the cliff edge."It's dark and we'll kill ourselves just trying to get down those steps. Whoever it is will probably have a torch and will soon spot us in the open before we reach the rocks."

They crawled most of the way through the hedge and then remained completely still on the other side, trying hard to breathe as quietly as possible. A short while later they caught sight of a torch beam sweeping from one side of the garden to the other and heading towards the steps. Whoever it was came within a few feet of where they lay prone almost tasting the dirt. At that point they stopped breathing entirely, yet each was concerned the person might still hear the pounding of their hearts deep inside their chests.

Then they heard the scuffing sound of shoes descending the steps. "Now!" Daniel whispered, urging Brianna to stand up and to keep low as he pulled her by her hand back up the hill. He knew exactly where they should go if they were to have any chance of survival at all.

Glancing over his shoulder, he saw the beam from the torch heading up the steps. It would seem the man had suddenly had the same thought as Daniel; without a torch, only a bat could see its way without light from the moon, which was hidden by deep cloud. Guided only by the lights of the car park, the pair turned the corner at the back of Pendower Court, just before Daniel suddenly stumbled.

To their absolute horror they saw he had tripped over the sprawled arm of someone lying flat on his face. Even in the dim lighting they could clearly see a gaping exit wound in Frank's back. He had been shot directly through the heart.

Briana placed her hand over her mouth to stifle an exclamation of horror.

"Come on, Brianna, we have to go. I can see the torch beam heading in our direction!" Still tugging her arm, Daniel ran as fast as he could holding on to Brianna.

They continued a short way along the drive and then veered to the right and began pushing their way through the dense foliage that Frank and the police driver first imagined only grew in the tropics. Brianna never uttered a word and followed Daniel with her hand in his, trusting him implicitly.

Daniel was yet to notice that in her other hand Brianna was holding Frank's gun, which she had found beside his body.

He warned her to be as quiet as possible from now on. They ascended a fairly steep grassy bank and then went through yet another tangle of jungle-like vegetation until they came to the clearing of an old track covered in weeds. It was too dark for Brianna to see where she was, whereas Daniel would have known the way had he been blindfolded. None of it had changed since he and Richard had played here all those years ago.

CHAPTER 61

KNIGHTSBRIDGE – London

16 October 2017

The Falcon taxied to the private-jet terminal located close to Heathrow's Terminal Four. Signature Flight Support provided ground handling services for all types of aircraft, from helicopters to B747s. There were VIP lounges for royalty and heads of state, and Customs and Immigration was available twenty-four hours a day.

Viewed from above on the plane's approach to Heathrow, London appeared at its very worst. Dark clouds hung low over the city like a blanket of brown puffballs. Rain was lashing in streaks against the windows as strong headwinds continuously buffeted the executive jet. Through breaks in the clouds now and again, he could make out long lines of snarled traffic, creeping slowly along wet and dismal streets with headlights blazing in the middle of the day. This was the first morning he had not been greeted by the sun since leaving the country after his birthday bash back in February.

Geoffrey Elm had a growing sense of unease. He had received no progress reports from Australia for ten days or so and, with no word from Louis, he was also in the dark regarding any developments in the UK involving Richard Wagner. To make matters worse, Michael had been ignoring his text messages and calls for over three weeks. He had tracked down Matthew by calling his mother in Spain. As usual their conversation was brief and frosty, although she had told him Matthew was home in London at his place in Notting Hill. She never asked how her ex-husband was, nor did he have any pleasantries to exchange with her.

His arrival in England was noted by Customs and Immigration who passed it along to the Met as they had been instructed. No reason had been provided, only orders to inform them if Lord Geoffrey Elm should return to the country. Geoffrey had not organized for anyone to meet him on arrival, instead taking a black cab directly to his three-bedroom flat in Knightsbridge in central London, opposite Harrods. He had purchased it for just over three million pounds two years before. The transaction had been conducted in absolute secrecy and only one of his trusted lawyers knew he owned it. For the sake of his privacy none of his children had any inkling, and certainly his ex-wives were kept ignorant of the fact. Apart from somewhere to entertain his carnal urges now and again, always with the same trusted professionals he paid well for their silence, his electoral ambitions had also required that he have a place of residence in central London. But his aspirations of becoming an influential politician had ended forever on receipt of the email he'd received from party headquarters on Matthew Parker Street in London.

He intended to phone Matthew in a little while and suggest they meet for dinner at the Harrods restaurant, a venue where he was unlikely to be recognized. No one could really confuse Lord Geoffrey Elm's penchant for fine dining with one of the restaurants at Harrods. There was nothing wrong with the food; indeed, it was rather good. But the ambience, rather like its customers, was far too plebian for his liking. He decided he would dress casually for dinner, slumming in jeans and an old jacket along with a scruffy baseball hat they had been handing out at the Queen's Jubilee forty years ago.

The final straw had come just as he was about to depart Rarotonga for London. A few minutes before taking off he had received an email from Paul Tamarua, the Minister of Immigration. It was just five lines of text informing him that they might have to rescind his permanent residency due to several serious allegations concerning him that the government of New Zealand had passed on. Being responsible for the island's foreign affairs, the Beehive in Wellington was obligated to inform the appropriate minister in the Cook Islands. There was no further explanation other than to say that an occupancy permit for his new house would not be issued until the situation had been clarified.

Coming so close on the heels of the letter emailed from the Conservative Party Assessment Board in London, informing him that he had not met the criteria for the approval list, it had instilled within Elm a gathering foreboding, suggesting worse things yet to come. Something had gone dreadfully wrong. People who had been in regular contact, including Michael, appeared to have vanished into thin air. These matters were obviously not coincidences.

He had to get through to Louis McPherson somehow. He could almost taste his rising sense of dread. It was a sensation he had experienced years ago, when he first started in business and was taking chances he would never dare take today.

Lord Geoffrey Elm was a conceited and arrogant man with few endearing qualities, except when he wanted something. Then he would mount a charm offensive to obtain whatever that something was. Whether it was a business advantage he was after or a young woman he wanted to bed, he always managed to get his way and, if not, he had always had his minions to ensure that eventually he did. His money had guaranteed him access to everything. Even his ex-wives continued to remain servile to his excessive demands – excluding those of a sexual nature, which were catered by much younger women now his wives had passed their prime. His exes understood only too well that they would be left without any financial support, and possibly a home to live in, if they opposed him. Just like the current president of the United States, Elm could manipulate the law to his advantage. It was much easier for his opponents to walk away than spend hundreds of thousands of pounds they did not have to stand up to someone who would win in the end.

The one person he feared and disliked the most was his ex-wife living in Malaga. She had found out about his indiscretion with the child on the Essequibo River in Guyana and the subsequent murder of the reporter as *El Gordo* lay at anchor. Geoffrey had the money to silence her, whether through an apparent suicide or even in a random accident. Then, of course, he was never quite certain what she had told his son, Matthew, or if she had some form of insurance buried in a bank vault somewhere.

Matthew was by far the smartest of his children. It was Geoffrey's bitch of a wife in Spain who had always prevented him from making him his successor. Elm knew that as soon as he was out of the way Dorothy would become her son's consort. She would be constantly by the side of her adoring boy. Then she would have direct access to the billions his lordship had always intended to keep far from her reach via the carefully crafted prenuptial agreement he made all his wives sign.

"Your call came as a bit of a surprise, Dad," Matthew said from one of the bar stools at the Grill, located on the ground floor at Harrods. "Why here? Wouldn't have thought this was your type of place," he added sarcastically as he brushed at his jacket. It was still pouring down outside, and he was quite wet despite the relatively short walk from the Knightsbridge Underground. He loathed carrying an umbrella, unlike his father who had deposited his six-hundred-pound Burberry in a stand by the entrance.

His father seemed tired. He looked dishevelled and was unshaven. Lord Elm had seen his reflection in a mirror as he entered Harrods from the Brompton Road and was stunned by his appearance. The old jacket and faded blue baseball hat displaying grey tufts of hair protruding over his ears, made him seem much older than the very youthful seventy-five his birthday party guests had all proclaimed back in February. Now he looked over eighty, especially as he was not wearing the signature steel-rimmed glasses that shaded the dark bags beneath his eyes. To avoid recognition, he had purposefully left his glasses behind at the flat and put in his contacts instead.

Matthew was shocked by how much he had changed since he saw him last, only a few months ago. "You are okay, Dad, right?" he asked, appearing genuinely concerned. Had Michael expressed the same concern about his health, he would have detected an undercurrent of optimism that his father might soon be dead and buried. Once again, Geoffrey Elm was reminded what a terrible choice he had made proclaiming Michael his successor.

"I'm just fine, Matthew," he lied. For one of the few times in his life he was feeling quite alone and somewhat flummoxed. This was new territory for someone who had always been so self-assured and laser-focused, earning his first million pounds before he turned thirty. He felt lost.

He ordered a 350g aged-on-the-bone ribeye with creamy spinach and dauphinoise potatoes on the side. He asked for hot English mustard for his steak rather than the Grey Poupon he disliked. Matthew ordered the Wagyu hamburger, and his father could not resist commenting that at a cost of thirty-five pounds the hotel must be flying it in directly from Japan. Matthew ordered a beer and his father an Irish whisky.

Matthew asked where his father was staying in London. Avoiding the question, Geoffrey merely told him he would be at a hotel for a few nights and then would be flying back to Rarotonga. Matthew did not ask which hotel.

"Must be an important meeting to fly all that way to England in November. Who is it?"

Looking at his watch, his father responded, "the meeting convened exactly twenty-one minutes ago!"

Matthew felt perplexed. Why would his father, who had paid scant attention to him the majority of his life, choose to fly close to twelve thousand miles to see him? Matthew managed a string of fitness centres associated with hotels his father owned in the UK and on the European mainland. It was not a demanding job at all, requiring perhaps one or two visits a month. He was currently going most often to Italy and Spain where they were only now incorporating the centres in the hotels. It most certainly did not require the attention of his father.

Not one to beat about the bush, Geoffrey came right out with his news. "Matthew, I want to nominate you as the new CEO of the entire group of companies at the next board meeting. It'll only be a formality as I have the deciding votes and so there will be no problem. When I turn eighty, when I plan to formally retire, you will then become chairman assuming all my responsibilities. At that time, you will have full and complete control without the slightest interference from me."

Matthew did not respond for a minute or two whilst the waiter was placing their meals on the bar in front of them. Later that evening, when he returned home to Notting Hill, Matthew would describe it to his girlfriend as an out-of-body experience. It was totally surreal, and he had been supremely angered by the offer.

"Christ!" he shouted at his father.

Geoffrey looked shocked by his son's immediate reaction and stopped cutting his steak. "There's a problem?" he inquired.

"You're damn fucking right, there is! How dare you! You, miserable old bastard! I am your eldest son, your smartest son in case you are not aware, yet you completely overlooked me in favour of that half-wit, half-brother of mine! You never even explained why you chucked me overboard for someone who seems to be only good at drinking and fornicating."

Geoffrey Elm was furious. He threw his knife and fork on his plate, disgusted by how ungrateful Matthew seemed. "Where's all this coming from, Matthew. That bitch of a mother of yours in Malaga?"

Matthew remained calm but seriously considered leaving there and then. "No, father, it did not come from her. It's the consequence of your behaviour and how you treat people, especially your family. As many here in the UK will attest, you are one of the most despised individuals in the entire country."

Matthew paused and thought a moment and then finally got off his bar stool. "Fuck off, Dad!" he yelled so all could hear. The barman looked concerned but said nothing. He knew exactly who the elderly gentleman was sitting there with an uneaten steak in front of him. Yes, indeed, he thought, his son is absolutely correct. Lord Elm was viewed in many circles no differently than Robert Maxwell, a thoroughly despised and hated human being, a person many had travelled thousands of miles just to spit on his grave in Israel.

Matthew started to leave the Harrods dining hall but then hesitated and turned. "You really thought you could buy me like you bought your fucking peerage? And whatever you may think of my mother, she really loves me and was always there for me when I was growing up. Where were you? Fucking a whore or some innocent child!"

The entire restaurant fell suddenly quiet. This last remark stung Geoffrey to his very core. Leaving no opportunity for his father to interject, words tumbled from Matthew, finally revealing his true feelings. "You love no one except yourself and your piles of money. You're a fucking sad human being, Father. You simply don't get it! You could never buy me even with an offer of ten times as much. I am not for sale!" Matthew turned and stomped from the restaurant. By then many of the customers had stopped eating to witness the dreadful altercation between father and son.

Before he was even out of the door leading to the Brompton Road, several of the customers were standing from their chairs and applauding the sentiments he had expressed. They all knew by then who the arrogant prick at the bar was. They all loathed this self-proclaimed philanthropist whose charitable causes always revolved around a return on his investment – if not in money, then in benefits of some other nature. Geoffrey Elm always had an angle to make himself look good in the eyes of others. Now he was exposed, by his very own son. His ability to manipulate people to his own advantage would be vastly reduced once one of the junior editors of the *Times* wrote the story about one of the wealthiest and most corrupt billionaires in the United Kingdom. The editor had been sitting at one of the tables close to the bar, within earshot of Matthew and Geoffrey Elm.

CHAPTER 62

RETURN TO LONDON

16 October 2017

She was sleeping with her head resting against Daniel. He had his arm around her and could feel the rhythm of her gentle breathing, continually rising and falling. Her body quivered briefly from her restless dreams and he held her closer. Then she was still again.

His arm had started to go numb and he had to remove it slowly in order not to wake her. Meanwhile, he continued staring out of the side window of the car travelling at high speed along the M4 Motorway over the Berkshire Downs towards Reading, and London beyond. Considering how close they were to one of the world's largest cities, he was surprised by how clear the night sky appeared. There were no clouds about and any light pollution from other nearby cities did nothing to diminish the brilliance of the myriad of stars studding the massive canopy above.

Apart from the hum of the engine it was quiet inside the car. The two men up front had barely said a word since they had left Pendower Court. Brianna had been awake at that point and was still visibly shaken after shooting another human being. If she hadn't had the foresight to pick up the gun and the courage to use it, he knew neither of them would be still alive.

Daniel had eventually discovered the row of four garages by following the track that had become almost completely overgrown with thick vegetation. It seemed almost as if no one had been there since he and Richard had walked it more than sixty years before. The garages looked abandoned and derelict in the faint light provided by a moon partially obscured by a thin layer of clouds. Most of the windows were broken, and peeling paint revealed the original timber, now weatherworn and splintered.

One of the garage doors was hanging off the top hinge and leaning at an awkward angle; two others were locked. They quietly moved on to the last one, which was not locked. Daniel pushed it open slowly, to avoid making a noise, and then only far enough that they could both squeeze in sideways. He pulled the door closed and slid across the small bolt he felt in the dark. The bank of clouds had drifted past and the moon briefly illuminated the inside of the garage through two broken windows. It smelled of fresh grass; they could make out the outlines of a sit-on mower parked at the back with a small trailer hitched to it. There were some tools lying in the trailer, including a long rake and a pair of sheers. There was also a can of oil and an old military-coloured jerry can. Daniel shook it on the off-chance he could use it somehow to defend themselves. It was completely empty.

They knelt behind the mower fully aware they would be seen if someone forced their way in. But there was nowhere else to hide. Daniel began to regret that he had brought them inside the garage, but it was too late to move elsewhere. He had no idea how far behind them the man with the torch might be. He just hoped he had given up by now and was driving away, afraid that someone had heard the shot that had killed Frank.

The pair remained completely silent for the next several minutes. All they could hear were the chirps of crickets and the leaves of a plant or small tree brushing against the outside of the garage. Far below them the waves continued to pound the beach, just as he remembered from all those years ago when he heard the roar of the ocean for the first time;

the smells and sounds still excited his senses as they had back then. For reasons he could not determine, it somehow made him feel whole again, part of something much larger than himself. Briefly, he had become one with the trillions of other atoms connected to the one body of nature.

Then they heard it and he squeezed Brianna's arm to warn her. It was the rustle of foliage being brushed aside further back along the track. The man hunting them had finally discovered it was leading to what looked like a row of old sheds. They could hear him approaching, then they saw the brief reflection of his torch beneath the garage door. The man kicked at the first door that was hanging off its hinge and then quickly moved to the second garage, which he found open but deserted. The next one was also unlocked. He swung both of the doors open forcefully, crashing each in turn against the sides of the garage. Once again, he discovered it empty apart from a few paint cans stored along the back wall.He moved on to the last garage. This time the doors did not budge when he pushed against them. They were locked from the inside! Using all of his brute force, he smashed both doors' inwards.

There, at the rear of the garage he could just make out the man and the woman huddled behind a rusty old tractor. These were the two he had been instructed to kill, an older white man with a black woman!

What neither Richard Wagner nor Daniel had noticed was the gun Brianna was holding. She fired it without warning!

Luckily, Inspector Sage had alerted the police in Falmouth that one of his officers protecting a couple at the Pendower Court flats was not answering his phone and appeared to have gone missing. Twenty minutes after Brianna had fired the gun, three police cars drove at speed down the narrow lane towards the flats.

The first thing they saw in their headlights was Frank's body lying face down on the ground. The police were trained in uncertain situations like this, which might involve hostages. It was also possible they'd driven into a trap with one or more gunmen hidden out there with high-powered rifles and night-vision, precision scopes. It would not be the first time it happened.

They swept the immediate area with powerful torches; five minutes later the inspector in charge declared it was safe to spread outwards looking for the killer and the couple who had been under official police protection; two of the police immediately began checking the flats, smashing the doors of the locked ones with solid steel enforcers. Three more went around either side of the building and headed down towards the beach.

Not realizing there was a much easier route, the remaining three clambered over a retaining wall of rocks and with difficulty pushed a path through the undergrowth to see if there was anyone concealed behind the flats. Ten minutes later one of the policemen found a man lying at the entrance to one of the garages. He was in excruciating pain and unable to speak. Then, holding his gun and torch clasped together, the same policeman saw a black woman and a man in his sixties. The woman was pointing a Glock 22 directly at him.

"Drop the weapon, ma'am, and both of you get down on the ground, NOW!" he ordered. "This is the police, and we are armed!"

Richard Wagner was bleeding extensively, and it was decided to place him in the back of one of the police vehicles and rush him to Falmouth Hospital. He would have been dead before an ambulance had time to arrive. One of the policemen made a strong cup of sweet tea for Brianna who was in a state of shock. They had taken her around to her flat with a blanket draped over her shoulders. Once inside Daniel had poured himself a large whisky. He could hear one of the men talking on the phone to someone he assumed was Inspector Sage.

When the policeman had finished his call, he came over to speak to Daniel. "There's no immediate rush, sir, but I am instructed to drive you back to London as soon as possible."

"But it is very late, officer, and you can see my friend is extremely upset."

"Yes, sir, I do realize the lady is very distressed, but for your safety and hers the inspector believes we should drive you both back to London tonight. We are not certain if the man your partner shot was acting alone. So, we need to leave once you have packed your things."

Despite the lateness of the hour, Roger Sage met them at the entrance to the Covent Garden Hotel, about a fifteen-minute walk from the new Met building on the Embankment. The hotel was expensive, but the commissioner had personally decided cost should not be a factor after what these poor people had been put through. Daniel and Brianna were Crown witnesses from overseas, foreign nationals who should not have been obliged to put their lives at risk for something of such little consequence to them personally.

Brianna looked exhausted and Daniel was pale with dark shadows under both eyes. He stumbled getting out of the car and Roger caught him by the arm to steady him.

"Are you sure you are all right, Daniel?" Roger asked, looking concerned.

"I believe so. I'm just tired and my vision seems rather blurred."

He tried to make light of it, but Roger insisted he would have a doctor check them both tomorrow at the hotel. "You have both had a terrible shock and it can affect people in many different ways. You can't be too careful."

Roger told them he would come and visit them tomorrow morning before he flew to Falmouth to question the man Brianna had shot. She was extremely relieved to hear the man was not going to die. Roger Sage explained that it was important to speak to him as soon as he could in case he had not been acting alone. Quite possibly there was still someone else out there who might pose a danger to them both.

Too tired to speak further, they nodded their appreciation to Roger Sage and then followed a hotel porter who was carrying their two small cases. He watched them disappear through the entrance of the hotel. They were certainly an unusual couple, Roger thought, and he envied them. The difference in their ages apparently meant nothing at all to two people so obviously in love with one another.

It was going to be a long and difficult day Roger was thinking as he walked briskly along the deserted streets back to the Met. He was lucky to have been allocated a real office since returning from Lucaya rather than one of the regular workstations. Now he could catch a little shut-eye at his desk before morning. It was too late to go home to Highgate.

Before he had met them at the hotel, Roger had spoken at length to Superintendent Chase in Australia, who had called him informing him about the incident on Flinders Island. It was good news, including the update on Daniel's sister; however, he had decided to wait until morning to brief them on this aspect of the situation.

Apparently, Jane had suffered a transient ischemic attack (TIA), the symptoms of which Pia had mistaken as a full-blown stroke or even a heart attack. Given the desperate situation at the time any medical professional in attendance would have been be forgiven for her misdiagnosis.

Daniel and Brianna did not need all this detail now, Roger was thinking. The important thing was Jane was safe and currently resting at the small hospital in Flinders for the night. She would be released in the morning.

CHAPTER 63

COVENT GARDEN

16 October 2017

The next morning, he took a quick shower in one of the men's bathrooms at the office. With only four hours sleep on an old army camp bed the Met had on hand for overworked detectives, he felt remarkably refreshed. The bed was nothing more than a simple narrow strip of kaki threaded on an aluminium frame. He required no blanket as it was sufficiently warm inside the building and he had slept soundly in his skivvies. A sofa cushion served as a pillow.

It took him less than twenty minutes to walk to the Covent Garden Hotel along Whitehall with a couple of detours where access was restricted for security reasons. Surprisingly for November, it was a beautiful day and fairly warm. He loved London on days like this. Unlike in summer the air was fresh, and the normally grey sky was a clear baby blue. It was a few minutes after eight and the city was already bustling; tourists strolled down Whitehall as earnest civil servants and others scurried on their treadmills to work.

He turned onto Monmouth Street and entered the Covent Garden Hotel. Inside, the reception area was covered in expensive Persian carpets, plush curtains and aged wood panels. Nearly all the furniture were genuine antiques. Copies of paintings from the 18th century were hanging in ornate wooden frames illuminated by bronze wall sconce lighting.

Table lamps were lit day and night, intended to convey an ambience of wealth and elegance.

Being so close to the theatre district, notable American actors would often choose to stay at the Covent Garden. For them it represented the essence of what they believed England was all about, at least in their American imaginations.

Roger found Daniel and Brianna already up and dressed for the day and drinking coffee at a small table by one of the windows. Like everywhere else throughout the hotel, it seemed, their room was exquisitely furnished. It even had a real four-poster bed with the palest pink curtains matching those at the windows. Paintings depicting pastoral scenes of the English countryside and various old castles and monuments decorated the walls adding to a sense of history that the hotel's transatlantic guests craved.

"How are you both feeling, this morning?"

"A little shell-shocked," Daniel responded. Brianna nodded in agreement. She looked tired and expressionless.

"I won't keep you too long as I realize you both need a quiet day and a good rest after everything you went through last night." He moved over to one of the chairs and sat down. "It would have been equally terrifying for me had I been in your shoes. To come face to face with a man holding a gun with every intention of killing you, I am sure will remain etched on your minds for a very long time." He looked sympathetically at Brianna, "And it must have been particularly hard on you Ms. Williams. Shooting a man, even one trying to kill you, is not something you will easily forget."

Brianna nodded again but remained quiet. It was all still too surreal. "But I am very pleased to tell you," Sage continued, "that the man you shot is expected to make a full recovery." Brianna's eyes suddenly sparkled. She looked over at Daniel and at last smiled.

"Thank you for telling me," Brianna said. "I wouldn't have wanted the death of someone weighing on my conscience for the rest of my life."

Roger reminded them that he would be going down to Falmouth to question the wounded man but should be back by evening. "Before I forget, here's my card with my work and home mobile numbers," which he handed to Daniel. "He's still in intensive care but alert, so they tell me," Roger said. "I'm flying down by helicopter in a couple of hours, but within the next few days I'm hoping we can finally sign the witness statements and then you'll both be free to return to your homes, at least once it's certain he acted alone. In the meantime, I can almost guarantee no one is going to try and kill you. Your ordeal is finally over," he said. "I'll stake my career on it."

"I suppose we'll never know if you lose," Daniel said with a hint of sarcasm.

Roger smiled. He decided, for now, not to tell Daniel what had happened on Flinders. There would be time enough for that, he had decided. Let them rest for a few hours.

"I have to dash, I'm afraid", he said excusing himself. I have a helicopter to catch and then once I have had a word Mr. Wagner, in the next couple of days I hope to have another meeting, one perhaps of far more interest with Lord Elm".

When Sage had gone, both of them went to make phone calls to their respective family and friends in Australia and Jamaica. Brianna moved to the bedroom to call Jevon who was an early riser and would have already been up for a good hour. They had not spoken to each other since Brianna went off with the two policemen just over two weeks ago. Jevon started crying when she heard Brianna's voice.

Daniel remained in the living room, sitting in a winged high-back chair. Roger had mentioned earlier, without further explanation, that Pia and Jane were now together in Eden. It was past eleven at night in New South Wales and he was hoping they would both still be awake. He was curious to find out why Jane was in Eden.

"Hello" Pia answered, speaking softly.

"It's me, Pia, calling from London," Daniel said. "The inspector suggested I phone as soon as possible. I would have called our time last night but it simply wasn't possible. I'll explain in a minute. Just wanted to find out how you both are first. You are okay, right?"

There was no immediate response from Pia and he thought the line had been disconnected for a moment.

"Are you still there? Are you all right, Pia?"

She continued speaking softly as she had previously, explaining to him that Jane had not been well and was currently sleeping.

"I have a lot to tell you, Daniel," she began saying, "but I need to explain first why I made the decision to bring Jane with me home to Eden. I really thought she was dying the other night. She needs to be with someone for a while and not on her own. It was a very scary experience for her".

"I completely understand, Pia. It was a very thoughtful and kind decision. We'll talk more about it after I get back".

Jevon was so excited to hear from Brianna and had so many questions. She had known her friend was okay because the police in Mandeville had contacted her the day after Brianna's mysterious disappearance with the two policemen. They had assured her that she was completely safe and being well looked after.

The local police had not mentioned, nor were they aware, that Brianna was on her way to London. At first Jevon refused to believe their story. Several days later, however, she was given a note, in Brianna's handwriting, confirming what she had been told. She knew it was true when she read Brianna's 'to do' list attached to the letter: instructions about several rush orders that had to go out immediately, the bills that had to be paid – and could Jevon please let her mother know she was away on business for a week or two, and that she would send more money to her as soon as possible?

Now, at long last, she had spoken to Brianna directly! She was so happy! Perhaps only another week and her best friend would be back and she would find out all about her mysterious trip. She poured herself a glass of red wine and turned up a Beyoncé song on the radio and began dancing to the music, drinking from her glass at the same time.

Mon did shi evah happy! Brianna did di bess damn fren shi did hav evah did hav eena har life.

Almost eight thousand kilometres away in London, Brianna was likewise thrilled she had spoken with her friend. She had missed her and her bubbly personality. Brianna could hardly wait to tell Daniel how well Jevon had managed things in her absence. The awful memories of last night were slowly beginning to recede.

Fifteen minutes later Daniel finished his call and went into the bedroom to tell Brianna his sister had suffered a minor stroke. He was in a sombre mood as he told her everything that had happened. Brianna hugged him close as she sat on the bed next to him. He told her how someone who had been paid to kill his sister and Pia had been shot dead by the police. "Their story was eerily similar to our own, Bri," Daniel said. "I suspect the police will determine the lord or his son had something to do with it. I'd kill the pair of them with my bare hands if I could!" He finished by telling her that Pia and Jane were together in Eden now after the Federal Police had flown them both back to New South Wales.

Soon there was a knock on their hotel room door. Daniel opened it and a man introduced himself as a police surgeon with the Metropolitan Police. He explained that Roger Sage had asked him to provide Daniel and Brianna with a medical check given the very serious events of the previous evening.

CHAPTER 64

THE MORNING AFTER
19 October, 2017

"Is he all right, and when is he coming home?" Jane asked, anxiously wanting to know about her brother. She was sitting at the table out on the deck, still wearing her pyjamas under a thin cotton housecoat Pia had given her.

Jane had already gone to bed by the time Pia had finished her call with Daniel the previous evening. Now Pia was telling her sister-in-law everything he had said.

"I have no answer to either question, Jane," Pia replied, seeming worried. "It was like he was absent, somewhere far away in his mind…" She suddenly interrupted herself to ask if Jane would like another cup of tea.

"No, my dear, I'm fine," Jane replied and put aside the needlepoint she had been working on depicting an array of wildflowers. She was going to give it to Pia for their bedroom if she lived long enough to complete it.

"He was beside himself when I told him about your mini-stroke, though, and the awful event on Flinders. Yet, even so, there was something else troubling him. You can't live with someone all those years not to know when there is something troubling them, and especially in Daniel's case, who should have a PhD in worrying."

Jane suggested it was no wonder he sounded odd after what he and the girl had been through in Cornwall.

"My goodness, to be chased like that with someone trying to kill you! I can't imagine anything more terrifying. It was really nowhere near as bad for us. We didn't even know we were being hunted until after it was all over!" She patted Pia on her arm and told her she should stop worrying now. "He'll be home soon and you can start living your lives again."

Pia wondered whether it would be possible to pick up their lives as if nothing had ever happened. They had become different people. In a few weeks it would be 2018, almost four years since Daniel had left for Lucaya. Nothing had been quite the same since then.

There was also the question she had failed to ask last night because she was afraid of the answer. It had niggled her all morning. It was probably nothing at all, but she could not help wondering about the girl Daniel had known since the pair had witnessed the unspeakable attack on the young American woman. It was as if he was almost growing fond of this Jamaican!

There was a warm breeze drifting from the south and a scattering of clouds drifted lazily to the east, disturbing the monotony of an otherwise endless blue above. Jane was continuing with her needlepoint and Pia was reading an excellent book by Isabel Allende about a family that fled Franco's Spain after the civil war to live in South America as refugees. Jane startled her when she suddenly broke the silence and suggested she should be thinking of returning to Flinders Island.

Pia sighed and closed her book.

"I'm sorry, my dear, I didn't mean to interrupt your reading. Please, carry on," Jane apologized.

"You really think I would be so rude as to sigh because you started speaking to me when I was reading?" Two red and green parrots swooped in and perched on the balcony rail and stared at the two women briefly, then totally ignored them to begin preening themselves. "No, Jane, I was sighing because you would even consider going home!"

"But, of course, I'll stay until Daniel returns and then I really must get back home," Jane replied.

Pia sighed a second time and placed her book aside on the table. "Jane," she said, "you cannot go home and live by yourself in that house in the middle of nowhere. It's a ridiculous notion. You are eighty and you just had a lucky escape on Flinders. Often mini-strokes are an indication of perhaps a far more serious one in the future."

Pia went on to suggest something that had come to her the previous evening, that Jane should move in with them. "We have this huge house for just two people whilst you live entirely alone now since your partner died. Having you here would be company for us all," Pia said. "And Daniel will finally get to know his sister! You can't leave him again, not now!"

Jane bristled briefly at this reminder but said nothing. Pia was right after all; she had abandoned him, just as all of the family had done.

"Let me think about it, dear," she said after a while. "See what Daniel thinks first, but it's lovely you should want to include me in your life."

"And wouldn't you much prefer living with your brother and a sister-in-law who is a qualified nurse? Imagine moving from Flinders over to the mainland to end your days alone in some dreadful nursing home?"

CHAPTER 65

DERRIFORD HOSPITAL – Plymouth, Devon

16 October, 2017

The Commissioner of Police of the Metropolis, Dame Cressida Dick, allowed Sage authorization to use a National Police Air Services Eurocopter, based at Elstree, thirteen miles northwest of London. Because the case was classified as the homicide of a serving police officer, possibly involving a Peer of the Realm and his son, the commissioner deemed it imperative the matter was resolved expeditiously, with little or no consideration to cost.

The police had rushed Richard Wagner to Falmouth Hospital. He had been losing a great deal of blood from a wound below his left shoulder. An inch or two lower and it would have severed his aorta and he would be dead. One of the policemen staunched the blood flow with his jacket in the back seat of the police Range Rover as Wagner slipped in and out of consciousness. Once the Range Rover arrived at the seaside town, they were surprised to discover only two nurses and a girl in her late teens, who seemed half asleep, manning a switchboard.

The hospital was classified a regional, cottage type, and not entirely suitable to deal with this kind of emergency, especially late at night and with no qualified doctor on call until the following morning. However, had they first gone instead to a larger hospital with a fully equipped emergency department, undoubtedly Wagner would have died. It would have taken them longer to drive there and by then he would have lost too much blood.

A young nurse managed to quell the bleeding by taping a thick pad of gorse to the patient's wound. She instructed one of the policemen to maintain pressure on it after she had administered a local anaesthetic, warning that the patient would require immediate surgery to remove the bullet. He would likely die, she warned, if he was not taken straight away to Derriford Hospital in Plymouth. It was not the closest hospital but it did provide highly specialised care for someone with a bullet wound.

Luckily the roads were quiet at that time of night and they were able to drive from Falmouth to Plymouth in less than an hour and a quarter. The hospital staff had been anticipating the arrival of the wounded man and quickly wheeled him into surgery where they removed the bullet in a fairly delicate operation lasting over an hour. For a while it was touch and go, as the patient had lost so much blood. The bullet had not damaged any vital organ, though, and the surgeon later confirmed to the police that the patient would probably be available to question later. In the meantime, he remained heavily sedated and handcuffed to the bed rail. A local constable had been posted outside his hospital room as a precaution.

The Eurocopter settled on the hospital landing pad, not far from one other helicopter on a separate pad. Roger Sage climbed out with a female detective, also from the Met, and they walked quickly to a group of three uniformed officers waiting for them. The Eurocopter departed shortly afterwards, roaring upwards, nose down, and headed back to base. Roger and the superintendent would travel back later to London by car.

He was a little perplexed when he arrived at Wagner's room in time to see a tall man wearing a dark suit exiting. He must have been in his late sixties; he was extremely pale and was wearing a pair of rimless glasses that gave him a distinctly cruel appearance. He barely glanced at Roger as he continued walking away down the corridor.

"Who was that?" Roger asked the young constable sitting on a chair by the hospital room door.

"Said he was his lawyer, sir, by the name of Braithwaite. He gave me this card," the constable said in a broad and barely intelligible Cornish accent. He handed the card to Roger. What the devil? Roger thought. He opened the door and went inside the room followed by Superintendent Margaret Maloney.

How the hell did he manage that? A lawyer turns up from one of the most prestigious law firms in London within eight hours of the prisoner being admitted. It was impossible! The patient had no access to a phone and was unconscious most of the time. Furthermore, he must have been monitored every second since his arrival and would have been in no condition to communicate with anyone. How on earth would anyone even know he was here, and then why would his lawyer leave like that when he must have known the police were on their way? Wouldn't he want to sit in on the initial interview with the prisoner? It made no sense.

Roger pulled up a chair and sat close to the patient staring at him with cold eyes. Richard Wagner was finding it difficult to sit up. It was apparent that he was still in considerable pain despite the anaesthetic.

—————

What this dumb copper would never know was that in a semi-lucid moment, as they were wheeling him for surgery, Wagner had managed to ask one of the orderlies to phone a particular law firm in London and provide the patient's name and that of the hospital. Nothing more. Although he was in agonizing pain, he had also managed to whisper to the orderly, moments before the theatre doors swung open, that one of the lawyers would pay him five hundred pounds in cash for the thirty-second call. Wagner told the orderly not to forget to leave his name with whoever answered the phone at the other end.

This emergency contact procedure had been put in place by someone who worked for one of Lord Elm's many companies should Richard Wagner be compromised and find himself in legal difficulties. Leaving Wagner to hang out to dry and fend for himself was not an option if his silence was to be guaranteed. Braithwaite had flown down to Plymouth in the helicopter Inspector Sage saw when he arrived half an hour later.

The lawyer spoke with Richard Wagner for less than ten minutes, explaining that his firm would be representing him. This would be on the explicit understanding that Wagner emphatically denied any connection with Lord Elm, which, for all intents and purposes was true; he had never met nor spoken to Lord Elm directly, only to the son and later to some unknown person who gave him his instructions.

"You should be mindful that my client is well aware your wife and daughter have recently moved to Argentina," the lawyer said as a veiled warning. "So, when the police question you, make certain you mention only that it was Michael Elm who hired you and gave the instructions." The lawyer was thoughtful for a while before adding, "You might get twenty years, but with time off for good behaviour you could possibly see your daughter before her twenty-first birthday." He left the last sentence hanging for a while, giving Wagner time to absorb that he had no option other than to do what he was being told. "Young Michael will get life, of course, not forgetting an additional twenty years or so in the Caribbean for rape!"

The lawyer gave Wagner a wan smile as a precursor to his final warning. "Oh, and by the way, as of now the Americans have no way of connecting you with the girl you killed in Florida. It would be very wise therefore to keep it that way unless you want to face conviction in Florida for a crime subject to the death penalty."

Braithwaite's half-smile vanished and his narrow-shaped lips pursed in obvious dislike of his new client. "Just do as we suggest and within ten to fifteen years, you'll still be young enough to enjoy a future in Argentina with your family!"

As he was leaving, he said, "Someone else from our firm will contact you in the next day or so, once you are up to it. They will want to discuss your defence, which has already been paid for. No need to worry about money. In the meantime," he advised, "say as little as possible to the police when they come to question you."

Instinctively, the lawyer knew that the man heading down the hospital corridor was a policeman coming to interview his firm's new client. He could smell the 'filth' from a mile away. He walked past without looking at him and continued outside to his helicopter.

The pilot acknowledged that the orderly had made himself known and he had given him the five hundred pounds in a manila envelope as instructed.

Inspector Sage was not at Wagner's bedside much longer than the lawyer had been. "No comment," was the only reply he received to the questions he put to the prisoner. His frustration quickly mounted when the man later decided to close his eyes and made no attempt to respond at all. Sage glanced at Superintendent Maloney, who simply shrugged and shook her head. She could see their trip down to Cornwall was a complete waste of taxpayers' money.

"I understand you don't want to say anything that might implicate you," Roger said in a last desperate effort to get something out of the man. "Was Lord Elm the one who contracted you to kill Mr. Hannaford and Ms. Williams?"

Richard Wagner suddenly opened his eyes and looked angrily at the policeman. "I have already told you; I am not prepared to comment! And, no, I have never met, nor have I ever spoken to Lord bloody-high-and-mighty. He never contracted me to do anything!"

Wagner remained silent and so Roger gave it one last shot. "Then I suppose we will simply have to cooperate with the Americans, because it appears the police in Florida lifted a partial print off the syringe you dropped in the Irish pub. Once they confirm this after we send them a full set of your prints, there will be nothing to prevent us from extraditing you to Florida."

"But you couldn't do that, moron!" Wagner spat, becoming tired of listening to this useless copper. "Florida has the death sentence and Britain will never extradite a British citizen if there's the remotest chance of them being executed."

"Very good, Mr. Wagner. I'm impressed you know so much about the law!" He looked at Maloney again and winked. "Yes, you are quite correct, Britain would not extradite someone under those circumstances. However, there would be nothing preventing us from popping you on a US airline flight to Florida as a free man unescorted. Of course, we'll make sure there's a US Marshall onboard so you behave yourself."

Richard Wagner winced trying to lift himself from the bed. "You can't fucking well do that either," he shouted angrily. "It would be kidnapping!"

"Control your language, Mr. Wagner, there's a lady present!" Maloney grinned and Roger knew his gamble was paying off. "Seeing there is nothing left to discuss, we'll leave you now to recuperate," Roger said, getting up to leave. Maloney started for the door.

"It was someone working for his son, Michael," Wagner suddenly blurted, then lying back on the bed and closing his eyes again. Appreciating the fact the Americans must already have his print on the syringe he used to kill the woman in Florida, he knew his only choice now was to cooperate with the British police to avoid even the slightest chance of ending up in American custody. He knew the British could not put him on a US-bound flight as a 'free man', but who was to say he could not be bundled onto a private jet after being rendered unconscious by a powerful sedative? Then later he could be turfed out of the plane at some private landing strip in the middle of nowhere in Florida, police cruisers chasing towards him with lights flashing as he remained disorientated from the effects of whatever the damn police had shot into his veins. By then the private plane that had carried him over the Atlantic would be long gone.

With no passport on him nor any means to identify himself he would be arrested immediately as a possible illegal alien. Undoubtedly, sooner or later, they would discover his finger print would match the partial on the syringe. Better, he decided, to turn on Michael and perhaps get a plea deal of some sort that would insure he would not be extradited.

"Thank you, Mr. Wagner," Roger said. "That was all we needed to know", and then Roger and the Superintendent immediately left the room.

CHAPTER 66

WITNESS STATEMENTS – London

22 October 2017

A female police sergeant ushered them into the commissioner's office shortly before eleven. Dame Cressida Dick, or Dame Cressida as she preferred to be called (for obvious reasons), was sitting at the head of a large boardroom table. To the commissioner's right two lawyers, from separate prestigious law firms in London, meticulously checked over the documents for the umpteenth time to ensure every detail would survive scrutiny in court. Later they would append their signatures as witnesses to all documents signed by Mr. Hannaford and Ms. Williams.

Having two high-profile lawyers witness the documents would normally be unnecessary but for the unusual aspects surrounding the case. This was no minor matter to be served up by the tabloids until the next salacious story broke. The repercussions from this could bring down the government. It was also likely to further erode trust in British institutions, with Brexit looming on the horizon.

A police stenographer sat at the far end of the table with a pad and a pencil for taking notes; she was also responsible for monitoring the recording device that could be played in court to verify the witnesses were not coerced into signing their statements. Like everyone else she had been given a bottle of Fiji water.

Roger Sage sat facing the lawyers and Superintendent Maloney was next to him. Further down there were two men from the Foreign

Office with only their mobiles and the Fiji water in front of them. One of them was Bryce. Whether that was his first name, or even his real name at all, Inspector Sage had no idea.

They all stood as soon as Daniel and Brianna entered the room. Daniel was no stranger to boardroom meetings. Brianna, on the other hand, immediately felt intimidated by the aura of authority she could feel pervading the room, plus she was the only black person present once the female police sergeant had left the room. Brianna had detected a distinct Trinidadian accent when the officer had spoken earlier.

The commissioner shook their hands and personally showed Daniel and Brianna to their seats, each of them sitting next to one of the lawyers. They all introduced themselves in turn. Roger smiled at the pair and Margaret Maloney reached across the table to shake their hands. The two from the FCO merely nodded towards them but said nothing and did not attempt to shake their hands. The stenographer was invisible to them all, apart from Brianna who gave her a friendly smile.

"Ladies and gentlemen, thank you all for coming today," Dame Cressida began; she remained standing as the others took their seats. The stenographer began scribbling. "First, on behalf of the London Metropolitan Police, we would like to extend our very special thanks to Ms. Williams and Mr. Hannaford for being here today and for all the personal sacrifices they have made over the last two years assisting us. Not only have they had to endure time away from their families; both have also been subjected to grave dangers."

She paused and looked at each one in the room for dramatic effect. "Only two nights ago a man now in our custody came very close to killing them. In fact, had it not been for Ms. Williams, he undoubtedly would have succeeded."

The applause was spontaneous as the others stood up. Everyone in the room was aware that Brianna had shot the man using the gun belonging to the murdered detective. Brianna was mortified by the sudden attention. She sat there paralysed, not knowing where to look or how to respond to congratulations for almost killing a man. It would weigh on her mind for years to come. Considering her religious upbringing, she was thoroughly ashamed!

Daniel could see she was struggling. He had been clapping along with the others but now hugged her and thanked her for saving his life. He whispered something in her ear no one else could hear and she smiled.

"Thank you once again, Ms. Williams, we are all very much in your debt," the commissioner said. "Now, we must also not neglect to extend our deepest condolences to the family of Francis Chambers, the RaSP officer murdered a few nights ago protecting our two witnesses." She stopped speaking for a few moments and then proclaimed, "Francis Chambers did not lose his life in vain."

The commissioner went on to explain that the matter was considered of a highly sensitive nature because of the high profile of Lord Geoffrey Elm. To emphasize her point, she stressed that Daniel and his wife had already been subjected to various forms of intimidation and that his sister had almost died. Ms. Williams, she said, had been forced into hiding in Jamaica before the decision was made to bring her to the UK for her protection.

There had been several killings and a possible assassination, she continued, all connected to what they had witnessed in Lucaya that night in 2015. They'd been brought to the United Kingdom in the belief that the British authorities could better control the situation – until it all went horribly wrong in Cornwall!

It would have been premature and irresponsible if the commissioner had mentioned the Foreign Secretary at this stage. He remained under investigation, yet evidence gathered thus far seemed to indicate that he had indeed received personal benefits for procuring a peerage for Geoffrey Elm.

The two lawyers stood beside Daniel and Brianna and indicated where they had to sign and initial each page. It was all over in a few minutes. Inspector Sage came around the table and thanked them both again. The others in the room shook their hands for a second time, excluding the two from the Foreign and Commonwealth Office who had already left the room. They had been present as official FCO representatives of a government committee currently assisting the police with their investigations into the Foreign Secretary. Silence was necessary at this stage, so neither had said anything, but they would make a full report of the morning's meeting to the committee.

The commissioner came over to Daniel and Brianna before she left. "Thank you so much once again, the pair of you. You have been of tremendous assistance to the Metropolitan Police and to the country. I shall personally write to the prime ministers of both Jamaica and Australia and commend your actions on behalf of the United Kingdom as well as your personal sacrifices."

She saw some concern on their faces. "Don't worry, none of this will ever be made public, you have my word on that!"

Roger remained with them until the room was empty. "I know you're both anxious to return to your homes, but I wonder if I could make one last request. Please, don't feel bad if you don't want to, as I would completely understand. I was wondering if you would attend Frank's funeral on Saturday? It would mean an awful lot to his family."

Oddly enough, Brianna and Daniel had both been talking about it the previous day and were going to ask Roger whether they could attend. After all, Frank had lost his life protecting them.

"Thank you," Roger said. Just before he left, he told them the Met would he arresting Michael Elm in the next day or two. He would be charged with money laundering and other financial crimes in the United Kingdom. Separately, he would be charged in Lucaya for the egregious attack and rape of the murdered American, Vanessa Hall.

CHAPTER 67

BENJAMIN YULE – Texas

1864

Within Harrison County and most of north-eastern Texas, he had always been known as Benjamin Yule, a name borrowed from his maternal grandfather in Scotland. The only people in the country who knew him by any other name worked at the banks in Galveston and in Boston where he was known as Samuel Bethel.

He had considered waiting until the cotton was harvested in late July before departing, after the new owner had taken over the plantation. He had become increasingly anxious, though, as the Union forces once again regained control of Galveston. He could buy passage on a blockade runner carrying cotton to the Bahamas or Cuba – where goods were transferred to other ships bound for England or elsewhere in Europe – but that would be risky. He decided it would be better to find one sailing from Matamoros, the sister city to Brownsville, across the Rio Grande in Mexico.

So, placing caution before profit, he left the cotton to root rot in the fields and departed sooner. He had accumulated sufficient money since arriving in Marshall eleven years ago. He had tripled the size of that poorly managed plantation and his revenues had increased tenfold. He had also increased the mere handful of slaves he owned in 1852 to eighty-three, counting the pickaninny. Why take the risk? The inevitable Union victory would bring an end to it all soon enough. It was high time to leave and *plunge into a new life, living somewhere close to the sea and far from the shadows of his past, and from English-speaking societies.*

He craved variety in his food, especially fish, or anything other than the massive beef steaks that had been his primary diet for the past decade. A good claret would not go amiss either. Most of all he yearned again for someone young to attend to his needs and keep him company in his old age. Anton, the young negro boy, had become far too sullen as he'd grown older. Benjamin was concerned that his companion would cut his throat one night, once the slaves were freed and perhaps running rampant after the war. God forbid, he often complained to himself, they might actually want to be paid to work as well!

He was only able to see from the light of a small kerosene lamp by the bed, which was projecting shadows dancing along the walls in an eerie yellow glow. The man was grunting, struggling as he heaved the other one onto the bed. Moments before he had struck him in the back of the neck with the shoulder stock of his rifle.

The man on the bed was still breathing as the other laboured to place the unconscious man in a sleeping position on top of the blanket. He took off the man's boots but left on his worn socks. For good measure, just to ensure he remained unconscious, the man standing by the side of the bed hit him once more, this time quite brutally in the side of the head, yet without killing him.

The tall man in the full-length duster coat and black leather Stetson picked up a can of kerosene and began splashing the contents over the bed and the unconscious man, around the bedroom walls and onto the floor. After dropping the can he took the kerosene lamp from the table and walked towards the door. From there he threw the lamp back at the table where it shattered on the floor, immediately spreading a line of flame tracking towards the bed and up the walls.

Before the room was fully engulfed, he locked the door behind him and hurried from the house, now fully illuminated from the shafts of light of a full moon slicing the darkness inside through the windows. He quickly mounted the horse tethered to a small tree outside. Taking one last look behind him he noticed the first licks of flame at the back of the house and smoke belching from the front door. He lashed the horse, urging it into a full gallop, heading from the cotton plantation south towards Brownsville. He knew it would not be long before the alarm was raised and the other slaves were rushing from their beds in terror. They would frantically search for anything that would hold water in futile attempts to extinguish the flames.

After ten years working a cotton plantation, Benjamin Boyd no longer remotely resembled the corpulent owner of the schooner Wanderer *who had disembarked for that last time on Guadalcanal. He was now lean and muscular from his years of management in the fields, always acutely aware that leading by example was the only way to increase the productivity of his slaves. His hair flowed in golden curly locks, and his sagging jowls had vanished, giving him the distinctive appearance of a man much younger than sixty-two. His brother Mark could have passed him on Regent Street and would not have given him a second glance. Benjamin even seemed taller, no longer stooped as he used to be from carrying so much extra weight. Had he ever felt the desire, and were a man still in his forties, he could have had any young woman he wanted.*

It took him thirteen days of hard riding to reach Brownsville and the Rio Grande. Early the next morning, after a good night's sleep in a soft bed, he used the recently re-opened crossing into Matamoros, or the Port of Bagdad as it was also known. By 1880, the town was officially non-existent. At the end of the 19th century, it was invisible, completely covered over by the shifting sand. In 1864, however, Matamoros was a bustling port where ships of all nations, except those flying the US union flag, disgorged their cargoes of armaments from England, Germany and France to resupply the besieged Confederacy just across the river – before loading bales of cotton for export to Europe and beyond.

The blockade of Union ships was powerless to stop them without creating an international incident that might have led one if not all of the world's superpowers of the day to declare war. This was something the

Union could ill-afford when it was already embroiled in a civil war, the outcome of which was yet to be determined.

Boyd found an inexpensive hotel down by the quay and rented a room, initially for three nights, trusting in the meantime that he would find passage on a foreign vessel sailing to Cuba. The island served as the nearest trans-shipment hub for the Confederacy for all European imports and exports. Eight days later he booked passage on the Jane Cockeral, a British merchant ship bound for Liverpool via Havana loaded with four hundred bales of cotton. He sold his horse for two hundred and fifty dollars and spent his last day studying maps of Cuba he had found in a small shop across the road from his hotel. On 28 May 1884, the Jane Cockeral set sail with the passenger Samuel Bethel aboard, bound for Cuba and the Caribbean.

Texas Republican, Tuesday 3 May 1864

A plantation home southwest of the city was discovered burnt to the ground after one of its slaves raised the alarm to a passing citizen on horseback.

On investigation the police authorities in Marshall determined the house had been torched by one of the slaves called Anton. There was a strong smell of kerosene detected in an area where one of the bedrooms had been located. There were also the remains of a human being. Police presume the dead person was no other than Benjamin Yule, a prominent local citizen.

The police are treating Mr. Yule's death as an apparent murder and wish to question the slave, Anton, who has vanished and is nowhere to be found. An Indian scout tracked a horse the slave must have stolen for 20 miles until the tracks disappeared after an apparent rainfall in the area.

All efforts are being made to apprehend the negro for this terrible crime to face justice, which we hope he will receive shortly by dangling from the end of a rope.

CHAPTER 68

VIEW OF HARRODS – London
23 October 2017

He had been gazing from his apartment window for a full five minutes, his mood reflecting the decidedly dreary weather outside. The sky was a leaden grey and a steady downpour cascaded to the street below. Pedestrians were streaming from the Knightsbridge Underground on their way to work. Others quickly alighted from familiar red London buses, whilst some struggled to open umbrellas. The young or sufficiently fit dashed from the double-deckers to find shelter from the rain beneath the famous green awnings. Everything seemed sodden, even the two or three flags he could see hanging limply from their poles atop the façade of Harrods.

After all that had been happening, or had failed to happen, particularly his unpleasant meeting with Matthew, Geoffrey Elm was experiencing something he rarely had. He felt utterly despondent. He even regretted buying this flat. The view he had from his sixth-floor suite, of Harrods and the Brompton Road, was obscured on either side by the ugly red brick walls of the two buildings that fronted this very busy road in the borough of Westminster.

He started when there was a sudden loud knock at his door.

What the devil? It had to be something fucking important if someone dared knock at his door. The concierges down at the entrance were paid to announce guests using the intercom. Maintenance people were never permitted without prior notification, and deliveries were left downstairs. Who the hell could it be, he wondered? Perhaps one of the three other owners on the sixth floor who needed help? Good God, what if someone has died and a husband or wife needs my assistance?

He grimaced at the thought but was mildly surprised when he opened the door to a man of moderate height, perhaps in his late forties, who was wiping his glasses with a clean white handkerchief. His dark brown hair was slightly wet and his light grey suit jacket was speckled from the rain. Assuming his usual imperious manner, Lord Elm snorted his annoyance at being disturbed without an announcement from the concierge.

"Who are you?" he demanded, staring down with his piercing, cold blue eyes at the shorter man. People would normally turn away from his frigid stare, but this man failed to flinch. "I asked who you are! Do you want me to call the police?"

"I don't think that will be necessary, Lord Elm," the man said, handing him his card. "I am the police." Geoffrey's mask of superiority vanished for a moment and he appeared a little confused, allowing time for Roger Sage to brush by him after asking the peer if he could come in.

Just as I thought, Roger was thinking, another of life's bullies whose confidence is shattered by the sudden intrusion of a policeman into their life. Lord of the Realm he may be, but his lordship's behaviour was running true to form. He had reacted no differently from any of the countless thugs and criminals Roger had encountered in his career.

"I won't keep you a moment longer than necessary," he assured Geoffrey.

How dare this upstart invade my privacy like this, not even registering with the doorman and then barging through my door, Elm thought. Who the fuck does he think he is? No doubt someone from a working-class background who scraped through school and just managed to pass the five required GCSE's to get into police college.

"May I sit down?" Roger asked, which he did anyway without waiting for a reply.

"If you must!" Geoffrey spat at him contemptuously. "You do appreciate that I am an exceptionally busy man, Inspector, not only overseeing a dozen or more international companies, but I also have my responsibilities in my service to the state as a member of the House of Lords."

"Oh, I do apologize," Roger said. "I didn't realize. I thought I'd read someplace you were about to relinquish your peerage with the view to contesting the next general election as a commoner," he said, with heavy emphasis on the word, 'commoner'.

By now, Geoffrey was fuming and at the point of tossing this revolting little man from his flat. Of course, he knew he couldn't, and the frustration of realizing this made him even angrier.

"Yes, I won't keep you more than five minutes, Lord Elm," Sage assured, clearing his throat as he pulled a small photo from his inside pocket and placed it in front of Geoffrey on a large ornate coffee table. It was of a man who was quite obviously dead. He was lying on what appeared to be a stainless-steel autopsy table with his head on a disposable headrest. No attempt had been made to conceal that the dead man had been shot on the side of the neck and part of his jaw had been shattered in the process.

Roger watched Lord Elm very closely but detected no visible reaction to the rather gory photograph of someone Elm must have known, if only casually, during the man's time working on his motor yacht, *El Gordo*. By now Lord Geoffrey Elm was raging within. His immediate reaction was to baulk at the obvious, denying this photograph was even real. Acknowledging slowly to himself that it was – this was the only thing that saved him in the end from exposing his inner conflict with reality. The horrific photo was indeed of his friend, Louis McPherson.

Roger was impressed that Lord Elm had shown no reaction to the photo whatsoever. Not even the twitch of an eyebrow. "Do you recognize this man, Lord Elm?" he inquired.

Geoffrey sat quietly. He was outwardly calm, but inner turmoil was starting to collapse the composure of a man who had never expressed any form of emotion in all the years he had been at the forefront of public life – not even last night when Matthew was railing against him, screaming to all and sundry about the despicable father he had been. He slid Louis's photo towards Roger on the glass. "Yes, I recognize him. He was someone who used to help crew my yacht."

"The *El Gordo*, correct, Lord Elm?" "Yes."

"But only 'used to'?"

Geoffrey could always smell a trap and this one was no different from the hundreds of others he had to navigate throughout his business life. There was always someone trying to pounce when the truth was assumed to be hidden. He could see there was no point trying to conceal something that had already been confirmed by the police if they had done their job properly. He was starting to believe this policeman had been quite thorough in his investigations and was not quite the 'plod' he had first imagined.

"Well, not quite," Geoffrey finally began to explain, almost indifferently, as if Roger should have already known what he was about to tell him.

"He recently helped navigate passage of the *El Gordo* through the Panama Canal."

"But wasn't he hired as a security officer, nothing to do with navigating the boat? Wouldn't that have been well above his job description? He was in the army, I believe, not the Royal Navy."

He could feel himself taking charge again; he had subconsciously prepared responses to any question this infuriating policeman could possibly throw at him. "Actually, Mr. McPherson navigated through the Panama Canal once before under the supervision of the captain at that time."

"But surely your current captain would not have required any assistance?" Roger suggested.

"Probably not, but then the last time I went through we had local Panamanian line-handlers who caused some considerable damage to the boat," he said, this time telling the truth. "We needed someone else assisting the captain to ensure that didn't happen again."

Roger was quiet for a while and Geoffrey knew he was starting to gain the upper hand at last.

"Odd that Mr. McPherson a few weeks later ends up in Tasmania trying to kill the wife of someone who had witnessed your son rape a woman on the island of Lucaya!"

"Those accusations concerning my son are totally unfounded, Inspector," Geoffrey said in a determined yet measured tone. "The charges against him were later withdrawn."

"By the same woman who was murdered in Florida!"

"A mere coincidence, Inspector. Murder is almost a national sport in the United States and hundreds of people are murdered each and every day. You should not read anything into it."

"Then, of course, the only other witness was the former premier of the island who was also conveniently murdered."

Geoffrey Elm sat for a while on the sofa as the rain continued to teem down outside. Now that Louis was dead, he was thinking, there was nothing directly linking him to any of this, except Michael. Michael was the one who had first conceived of the idea of doing away with the girl in Florida and the two witnesses. And even though his son had not made arrangements to kill the premier, he was the only one who could be accused of having a real motive – to save his own skin.

Harrison would have tried to do a deal with the British – and probably had. Holding the girl down against her will, as he had, Harrison was just as guilty as Michael, though, sadly for his son, he had nothing to trade by way of reaching a deal to save himself. Michael never quite understood that it was not he that Geoffrey had been trying to protect, but himself. Walter Harrison possessed too much dirt on Geoffrey Elm and his nefarious business dealings on the island.

CHAPTER 69

THE SCAPEGOAT – *Hampshire*

24 October 2017

Michael Elm had ignored his father's incoming text messages and phone calls for almost a month. The last time they had spoken on Skype Geoffrey Elm had presented him with the bad news.

Michael had been promised by his father long ago that at the next AGM he would be officially confirmed CEO of the group, and eventually made chairman on his father's retirement. The actual succession of the new CEO was scheduled to occur the same day Geoffrey won his seat in North Yorkshire.

That any item referencing the succession had been excluded from the next AGM agenda was disconcerting, but not so much as to cause Michael significant alarm. Urgent, last-minute additions to the AGM agenda often meant that less-pressing issues were deferred. Some matters could just as easily be announced or discussed at a regular board meeting. These things happen, and so he had simply placed it at the back of his mind to ask his father about it the next time they spoke.

But that Skype call from the Cook Islands was a cataclysmic event in Michael Elm's life. Something he believed was his birthright, despite being the younger son, was suddenly snatched from his grasp when his father revealed he was having second thoughts. Michael had quarrelled with Geoffrey many times in the past, but never in his wildest dreams could he have imagined his father would, for all intents and purposes, disinherit him simply for demonstrating some youthful exuberance. The girl was a black and a nobody. What did it matter? Who cared? It certainly did not merit this reaction from a man whose proclivities for much younger women were almost legendary.

There was no mention of Matthew, yet Michael could only assume his hateful half-brother would be handed everything that rightfully belonged to him. He screamed and ranted at his father, reminding him that he had always been there when his brother had not.

"I have made no decision who will take over, Michael. Don't forget you have a sister as well, who is just as capable, if not more so, than the pair of you."

"That fat bitch?" Michael screamed. "Are you completely insane, old man?"

It made no difference how much he cursed his father, or how many times he tried to change his mind; his father was adamant in his decision. "It's no use, Michael, it's entirely your own fault. You should have kept your pecker inside your swim shorts!"

"Christ," Michael exclaimed, "that was just a bit of fun. You're still obsessing over that!"

At that point of the conversation, Geoffrey Elm disconnected the call, in case his son began saying too much over an open line.

Before he became too inebriated, Michael decided to drive from his flat in London to his house in Hampshire in the picturesque village of Chilworth, a few miles from Southampton. His name was on the title but his father had paid for it. He dropped in at the Chilworth Arms once he got there. There were always a few single women about, often wealthy ones who could afford to live in the area – or at least whose parents were. He had yet to meet a woman who could refuse a ride in the Bugatti Chiron he had parked conspicuously in front of the pub door, leaving little space for customers to enter or exit.

That evening he entertained two sisters who'd been already on their way to getting drunk when he had joined them uninvited at their table.

One was nineteen and the other only seventeen, the younger one appearing older than her sister. Later, he drove the girls back to his house. None of the three had slept until after dawn, when they all sprawled naked across Michael's four-poster bed, exhausted. Used condoms had been thrown carelessly on the outrageously expensive Axminster carpet. There were empty bottles of champagne tipped over on their sides on the furniture and the floor. On the coffee table down in the main living room, three neat lines of cocaine on the glass top remained to be inhaled. The maid would clean everything later.

For the next several weeks, it was very seldom that Michael was alone in the house. There was always some girl, or often several girls, drinking to excess and revelling in debauchery with the son of one of the wealthiest men in the United Kingdom. Occasionally he would drive to Southampton a few miles away and take a chartered jet to Paris with some of his friends and several girls. On one occasion he took three of his old school chums to Frankfurt to entertain them in the notorious red-light district by the central train station. None of his friends was aware that he had brutally raped a woman, but they would not have cared. He had not been publicly linked to the murder of the woman in Florida yet and, curiously, he had continually insisted to his father that he had had nothing to do with her death whatsoever.

The silver, blue-and-yellow-chequered police car drove slowly down the lane and into the cul-de-sac where a set of wrought iron gates sat guard on the entrance of an imposing house of red reclaimed brick, with a gingerbread spine decorating an L-shaped roof. The house was twelve years old, yet at first sight one would think it had been nestled there within two acres of manicured lawns and flowerbeds since Tudor times. Council regulations strictly controlled the architectural integrity of one of the wealthiest villages in Hampshire. From the rear of the house there was a far-reaching view to the English countryside at its spectacular best. Along both sides of the house two cultivated small forests of pine trees provided complete privacy.

The gates were open and the police car came to a crunching stop on the gravel before the large wooden garage doors. The occupants of the car, two armed police officers and Inspector Sage, stepped out and walked quickly to what they took to be the front door of the house. One of the officers banged on it as loudly as he could.

"Would you mind awfully coming around to the front of the house to identify yourselves?" a woman's voice called from somewhere. Roger led the way around the house to the front.

"Up here," the voice shouted.

Whatever surprise they may have felt at seeing a naked woman standing on a roof terrace above them, none of the police officers gave any indications that they were there on anything but serious police business. "Could you please let Michael Elm know the police are here?" Roger Sage called back, appearing oblivious to one of the most beautiful bodies he had ever seen. The girl had such a glorious tan; she was an utter delight to behold.

"Sorry, officer! Just freshening my tan in the sun trap up here," she said and gave Roger a sly wink. It did seem warmer this side of the house, he thought wryly.

The three returned to what was in fact the back door and waited for a minute or two until the woman appeared wearing a colourful Hawaiian sarong and a pair of slip-on leather sandals. A cool breeze whistled down the lane to the house and she shivered.

"Thank you, Ma'am," Roger said as he pushed past her. "Please stand back."

Meanwhile, Michael Elm had appeared at the top of the stairs wearing only a pair of shorts.

"Michael Elm?" Roger demanded.

"Yes," Michael replied; he slowly descended the stairs, like someone who needed to demonstrate he was lord and master in his own house.

"How can I help you, gentlemen?" One of the policemen quickly took hold of Michael's wrists and put them behind his back for hand-cuffing. The young woman suddenly looked scared, but her almost naked boyfriend began spewing out a series of expletives at Sage and the officers, most of which were directed at their mothers or suggestive of what they could go and do with one another.

"Michael Elm," Roger began, "I am hereby arresting you for the aggravated rape of a US citizen named Vanessa Hall on the island of Lucaya on or thereabouts of 8 December 2015. I hereby formally caution you that anything you say may be taken down and used in evidence against you!"

"You can't fucking well arrest me – a British police officer in England!"

"I am a serving officer in the Royal Lucayan Police Force, sir, working in conjunction and with the full compliance of the British police authorities and approval of both the British Home Office and Foreign Office," Roger explained, showing him a copy of a warrant authorized by the courts in Lucaya. "As a dual citizen of the United Kingdom and the Dependent Territory of Lucaya, you shall be deported tomorrow morning from Gatwick Airport on a direct flight to the island of Lucaya where you will face trial."

Michael Elm began to struggle but there was little use. The officers had him well restrained as they walked him reluctantly to the car and placed him in the back seat of the BMW. One of the officers went to the opposite side of the vehicle and sat next to him.

"Could you go and fetch him some clothes, please?" Sage asked the girl. "He probably needs rather more than a satin pair of shorts to wear in London."

There were far too many practical and political considerations to address to allow for a speedy trial. London and the Lucayan government agreed to an extension until matters on the island were somewhat calmer following the assassination of the premier. The last thing either party wanted was to further agitate the locals by placing Michael Elm on trial for rape prematurely. Such a decision could very well re-ignite the social unrest that had prevailed for weeks after Walter Harrison's death.

The FCO also needed a delay in proceedings whilst the involvement of Lord Geoffrey Elm was under investigation in the UK. By now, contrary to statements provided by Richard Wagner, few within the establishment actually believed Michael Elm was directly implicated in murder. It therefore served no purpose to rush to convict him whilst the father many believed to be guilty of murder remained free.

The two cases were irrevocably linked, and the British authorities required concrete evidence of Geoffrey Elm's guilt before they could proceed against him. The rape at the Premier's had subsequently hatched the need to commit those murders and it was that connection that could prove Elm guilty of the crimes. Without it, or if the evidence from the rape trial was found inadmissible, which should determine the reasons behind the murders, then there would be no case for Geoffrey Elm to answer.

The witness testimonies of Daniel and Brianna might very well convict Michael Elm only to be rejected in evidence in any subsequent trial to convict Geoffrey. After all, the authorities in the UK were far more interested in convicting the father in a British court than his son on a remote island in the Caribbean. The rape trial could always be delayed. Michael Elm was certainly going nowhere.

Meanwhile, the island and its people would have that precious commodity of additional time, allowing recovery from the dramatic events of 2017. After all, it was only a matter of weeks since their former premier was found dead on the beach, his brain tissue splattered on the soft white sand.

CHAPTER 70

THE FAREWELLS – London

25 October 2017

Recently promoted Chief Inspector Roger Sage ushered Daniel and Brianna to one of the pews at the rear of the Anglican church of St John's Notting Hill, already almost full to capacity. The front pews had been reserved for family and friends, with the remainder occupied by members of the London Metropolitan Police Force and representatives from many of the other forty-three police forces located around the country. The first ten benches on the left-hand side of the nave were allocated for various dignitaries, including the prime minister and the leader of the opposition in the front pew.

Behind the government officials there was limited space for the general public wishing to pay their final respects to Sgt Francis Chambers, loving husband and father of two, who had been murdered in the line of duty. No specific details of his death had been released to the press, as there was an ongoing operation involving national security.

As Sgt Chambers' commanding officer, Commissioner Cressida Dick once again had the unenviable task of delivering the eulogy, much as she had done nine months previously at the funeral of Constable Keith Palmer who had been killed on Westminster Bridge in a terrorist attack. She even repeated her reading of the WH Auden poem *Funeral Blues,* leaving few dry eyes in the congregation.

She went on to praise the sergeant's service and bravery on behalf of the London Metropolitan Police Force and offered her sincerest and deepest condolences to his wife, Susan, and to Antony and Mary for the loss of their father. Dame Cressida then spoke at length of the many sacrifices being made by the men and women of the security services whose dedication still maintained Britain as one of the safest countries in the world, selfless and professional individuals without whom there would have been a far greater loss of life over the years.

Brianna lowered her head in respect as the coffin draped with the flag of the London Metropolitan Police was slowly wheeled past her pew to the waiting hearse outside.

Yuh save fi wi lives! God be wid yuh, Frank, and grant yuh eternal peace.

Later there would be a private burial service for Sgt Chambers at the historic Kensal Green Cemetery where he would be interred close to a row of horse-chestnut trees, which would whisper peacefully in summer breezes as guardians of the dead.

The following day, Sunday, Brianna and Daniel had entirely to themselves before they were both scheduled to fly home the next day. Roger had already said his farewells to them directly after the funeral. He told them he had a plane to catch early Sunday morning to Lucaya. Once back home, he said, he would be assisting with the police interrogation of Michael Elm, along with other senior officers of the Royal Lucayan Island Police and someone from the governor's office, who would liaise with the Foreign Office in London. Elm had already arrived on the island and was being held in a special cell located at the airport, which, unlike the local prison, was fairly new and less likely to create claims of inhumane conditions by the defence lawyers at trial.

Once again, Roger thanked them profusely for everything. He gave Brianna a long hug and Daniel an affectionate pat on the arm as he walked away. He said they would be picked up early the next morning, taken to Heathrow, and personally escorted to their separate departure gates for their flights home. Brianna had a flight booked for Montego Bay, and Daniel was flying in the opposite direction, via Dubai and Singapore to Sydney.

They had both anticipated being together longer than just over a week. Daniel felt he had to get home as soon as possible though after the events on Flinders and Jane's sudden illness. He also had a lot to talk about with Pia now that she had invited Jane to remain with them indefinitely. Brianna also needed to get back to Jamaica to keep the business alive and was looking forward to being with Jevon again.

The thought now of having to part so soon left them both feeling subdued on what was to be their last day in England. They were both quite exhausted after the events of the past ten days. So, rather than walking too much about the city, Daniel suggested taking taxis to several of the well-known tourist sights.

Brianna was excited to see Buckingham Palace and the Tower of London and Tower Bridge, especially from inside a real London cab whose driver gave them a running commentary in a broad cockney accent she could barely understand. She thought she recognized Piccadilly and Trafalgar Square, but was uncertain, and the Albert Hall meant nothing to her at all.

She had been pleasantly surprised by England though, and she had to admit that the little she had seen of the country was very beautiful in its own right. Obviously, England was a lot richer than Jamaica, yet even with its copious display of poverty her beautiful country remained the jewel in the crown of the islands of the Caribbean.

They walked hand in hand in Hyde Park and fed the ducks on the Serpentine and had lunch at a cosy pizzeria in Soho. Afterwards, they walked up Regent Street and went to Hamleys, where Brianna bought several small toys for her nieces and nephews. In Liberty's she tried to dissuade Daniel from buying her a red Marlborough Iphis canvas tote bag, insisting it was far too expensive. He purchased it anyway because, he said, he loved her and it might be a long while before they saw one another again. Brianna also bought a bottle of Byredo, Mojave Ghost perfume for one hundred and seventy pounds as a gift for Jevon. She christened her new First Caribbean Visa card to buy it.

Remembering that she would be flying home alone the next day began to ruin what so far had been a wonderful day, adding to the anxiety of watching the hours slip away. It was too sad for her to accept the inevitability of life without a part of her soul.

CHAPTER 71 – PART 1

Flt 39 to Montego Bay, Jamaica
26 October 2017

A small package had been left on a narrow shelf below the business class window adjacent to her seat on the Boeing 777-300. It was wrapped in blue and white paper and tied with silver ribbon. Slid beneath the ribbon was a small gift card.

Accompanied by a female officer from the aviation division of the London Met, Brianna had been able to avoid normal departure protocols. She had to show her ticket and passport only once, to an immigration official seated behind a locked door in the departure concourse. The policewoman had opened it with her own set of keys and then continued to lead the way once the passport had been stamped. Brianna followed, pulling her small carry-on and a Liberty's shopping bag containing the gifts she had purchased the day before.

They walked for what seemed to be miles to the boarding entrance, where an American Airline steward was waiting for them. It would be twenty minutes or longer before other passengers began to board. Wishing her a safe journey home, the policewoman shook Brianna's hand and left.

Once she was settled and the steward had put her case and shopping bag in overhead storage, a stewardess came and offered her a glass of champagne. Brianna had never been keen on alcohol but she made an exception, taking the glass along with a packet of tiny cheese crackers.

She sat there for a long while simply staring at the blue and white giftwrapped package, not in the least bit interested in opening it. She was elsewhere, still clinging to Daniel's presence, as she'd felt it until that moment they had walked away from each other in the company of their assigned security escort.

Daniel had hugged her for a long while, kissing her eyes, her nose and her mouth. She noticed his eyes were moist and his mouth trembled as he tried to smile.

"I've loved you ever since I first saw you smile that night we first met," he said. "That and your perfect pearl-white teeth are what I shall always remember most about you, Bri." He was pensive for a moment before speaking the truth of something he had only admitted to himself. "Since that moment on the island, my life has never been the same, nor do I imagine it will ever be the same again. Thank you for making an old man so happy." Daniel sighed, kissed her once more, then turned abruptly and walked away quickly before she could see his tears.

"Goodbye, Daniel," she called after him, now shedding her own tears, which slowly meandered down her cheeks. "I shall always love you, always!" He had already melted into the crowds and he did not hear her. But he already knew. They were one entity, and nothing could ever separate them, not even when each had been released from the loneliness of their existence. They would remain together in life and in death, forever one.

She was still staring at the package when the other passengers started coming aboard. Reality disturbing her reverie, she decided to open it. Inside she found an armorial plaque with the crest of the London Metropolitan Police. Engraved beneath it on a brass strip were the words, *In appreciation of Brianna Williams for her singular bravery. LONDON METROPOLITAN POLICE.* The gift card was a handwritten note from

Roger Sage expressing his personal thanks and hoping their paths would cross again one day.

After dinner had been served, she went to sleep for several hours as the Boeing sliced through the sky at thirty-five thousand feet. She had left most of her meal uneaten. The champagne had disagreed with her and made her feel slightly nauseated.

She dreamt of them both together when Daniel was much younger. She was in her twenties and he in his thirties. They were sitting in a psychedelic painted bus as it struggled along a winding road from Browns Town to Nine Mile in the Parish of St Ann. Black fumes belched from the back of the bus as it laboured upwards, rattling and spluttering around each steep bend in the road.

Bob Marley was sitting at the back of the bus singing a song he had just written:

> *'Cause – 'cause – 'cause I remember when we used to sit*
> *In a government yard in Trenchtown,*
> *Oba – obaserving the 'ypocrites – yeah! –*
> *Mingle with the good people we meet, yeah!*
> *Good friends we have, oh, good friends we have lost*
> *Along the way, yeah!*
> *In this great future, you can't forget your past;*
> *So dry your tears, I seh. Yeah!*

Everyone on the bus joined in the chorus, NO WOMAN, NO CRY. It was a beautiful day, and they were all so young and happy. Daniel was just telling her how much he loved her.

Then there was shot and Bob Marley fell forward clutching at his chest, and suddenly the bus was following a hearse driving up the hill where Bob's open grave was waiting for him. Brianna turned to look at Daniel who was staring at her. Blood was also pouring from a wound in his chest.

Brianna woke with a start, feeling desperate and utterly lost and alone.

Damn yuh, Daniel, mi luv yuh fur too much.

She had sent a text to Beanie during her three-hour layover in Miami where she had to change planes for Montego Bay. The new aircraft was smaller than the one over from London, but she was still seated in business class. This time she declined the offer of a glass of champagne. She was still feeling unwell, although she managed to sleep until shortly before the plane touched down at Sangster International Airport in Montego Bay.

Beanie was there to meet her after her gruelling flight. He seemed genuinely pleased to see her again and kept poking and prodding his sister to make sure she was real. *"Such ah fancy gyal dees days, sis. Nearly didn't recognize yuh until mi did si dem damn teet ah yours."* Brianna laughed and gave him a big hug. She told him she was very tired after her long day and was hoping it was not too far to her mother's new house.

Smoking his usual spliff with the window down, Beanie drove to the residential suburb south of the city where her mother had purchased a new home with the money Brianna had been earning in Mandeville. Everyone she knew was there to greet her: her mother and her siblings and cousins. Jevon had sent her a text to say she was too busy with the business to get away but looked forward to seeing her soon in Mandeville.

Brianna excused herself after an hour catching up with her family, explaining she had to go to bed because she was so tired. She was so delighted to see them all. It had been over three years since she had last seen them together, when she first went to work in Lucaya. Much of that time away from her family had been spent with the one person she loved, who was no longer by her side.

Perhaps one day, she hoped.

Flt QF2 to Sydney, Australia

Brianna was already in Miami waiting for her next flight by the time Daniel boarded his Qantas plane to Sydney. He had spent the entire time since they had separated inside the brand-new Qantas International Lounge in Terminal 3, which had only just officially opened. The Airport Authority had not as yet even revealed the covered signs directing passengers to its location.

Chief Inspector Roger Sage had personally arranged a private VIP room for Daniel to use during the long wait for his flight, slightly over twelve hours. He could have remained in central London for the day but he had wanted to accompany Brianna to the airport and say goodbye to her there. The VIP room was quite small, but cosy enough to relax and stretch out on the sofa if he wanted to sleep. There was a blanket and two pillows provided on the sofa just in case.

It was an impossible situation, especially for someone who had always struggled to make life-altering decisions. Of course, he loved Pia and would always continue loving her. He had been faithful all their married lives, until that fateful evening he had met Brianna. Perhaps it had been the soft music drifting on a warm breeze, recalling exotic memories of the alluring scents and sounds of the Caribbean in the early seventies. He was very young back then, and the magic of Jamaica had ignited fires within him that smouldered for the remainder of his life. It was in the Caribbean that he first understood the pure joy of living – and it was why so many years later a beautiful Jamaican woman rekindled something inside him that he thought was lost long ago.

It had little to do with sex and all to do with the sensation of being alive and young once more. Youth had escaped him and Pia; they'd focused on their separate careers as their dreams and hopes for the future dissolved slowly over time. Not so long ago he had been a young man with a full life stretching endlessly before him. In 2015, facing his own mortality, he'd found the temptation too strong; he could not reject the extension of youth Brianna had offered him at the premier's party. It was all about recapturing the exotic magic of Jamaica when life still seemed never-ending, excitingly fresh and held so much promise.

He had never made promises to Brianna and it would have been dishonest of him to do so. Any promise would have been a lie, as it would have involved hurting Pia, the only other person he had ever truly loved. His life had become a dichotomy: of the sixty-four-year-old man and his much younger self. To follow in either direction would inevitably lead to consequences he wished to avoid. It was less to do with being a coward, which he reluctantly considered himself to be, than that he did not wish to cause anyone pain. Yes, he knew he should have thought about it before he had surrendered to the younger man he once had been. Now he was paying the penalty for making his first major decision in life in haste.

Was he the bad man he was beginning to see in himself? He knew he would see her again at the trial in Lucaya next year, but it was wrong for him to have given her false hope of anything else. Beyond that, if the doctor's diagnosis was correct, he might very well be incapable of travel again on his own. Had he lied to her just as he had been lying to Pia? Was he in fact trapped in that proverbial *'tangled web we weave when first we practice to deceive'*?

He had little appetite but took the elevator to the second floor of the lounge to get a drink. The bar was circular, formed out of white marble patterned with grey swirls like an exotic ice cream. Above, hanging from a recess in the ceiling, and the same shape as the bar, were two enormous chandeliers, a smaller one suspended below the larger. Atop each was a circle of thirty or so small candle lights.

For old times' sake Daniel ordered a Corona and nibbled from a bowl of assorted nuts. Looking at his watch he realized she would be well on her way by now, possibly flying over Ireland on her way home. God, how he already missed being with her!

After the beer he decided to find the private room, which was on the same floor as the bar. He took just a few steps from his seat and suddenly stumbled and fell over. The barman rushed over to help him up. "I apologize," Daniel said. "Just tired, I guess." The barman escorted him to one of the small tables and said he would bring him a coffee. Daniel said it was not necessary, but the barman insisted.

The doctor at the Covent Garden Hotel had told him to visit a specialist as soon as he arrived in Australia. There was every indication that Daniel could be displaying the early signs of multiple sclerosis. Dizzy spells on their own were insufficient evidence, but Daniel had told the doctor that he also had tingling sensations in his hands and was often easily fatigued. Daniel had long suspected something was not quite right with him but had never said anything to either Pia or Brianna.

Daniel smiled when he opened the small package, he found waiting for him on the plane. It was wrapped in the same blue and white paper and ribbons as Brianna's. Inside he found a stainless-steel hip flask encased in reversible tweed with the insignia of the Metropolitan Police. The card from Roger wished him many years of happy drinking 'down under' and thanked him for signing the witness statement. He promised to be in touch with updates on the case.

Daniel found the long trip excruciating, even in the more comfortable seat in business class. After ten years of schooling in Leicestershire, he hoped this would be the final time he would ever have to fly from the UK to Australia.

He thought a lot more about Brianna on the flight. He remembered their last conversation in Covent Garden when she had told him she only wanted to be part of his life, not own it – perhaps a Skype call every so often, and the chance to see each other now and again.

She tried to convince them both it would not really be so bad. They would still be close to one another, even if not in the physical sense, due to distance and circumstance. She said it was the best solution for everyone. True happiness, she reminded him, could not be found at the expense of others. She was extremely wise for a young woman who had grown up in a poor family, he thought. This was something no expensive education could have taught her. Her worldly wisdom and appreciation of life well beyond her years were God-given. She had never studied philosophy and yet she had conceived what she considered the perfect solution to a split triangle relationship. In a society such as Jamaica it might work, yet it seldom could in other countries or between people of such different ages.

Especially now, however, it was not something he would dream of committing to, not when she was still young and had the prospect of a full life ahead of her long after he was gone.

"Better just having a part of you, Daniel, than no part at all," she had explained. "Please don't expect me to walk away and find some Jamaican man, or any other man to replace you. This will never happen. Love is not just some meaningless word, Daniel. I would never ask you to leave Pia, nor would I ever want you to, and I would think less of you if you even suggested such a thing. She is a huge part of your life and you have been with her for many years. It would not be right for you to ever consider leaving her. We both know it would crucify you if you did. Please, Daniel, if you can just continue to love us both the way you are doing."

After the plane had taken off from Dubai he managed to sleep for an hour or two. He was tired of trying to resolve an impossible situation. Breaking up with Brianna, being cruel to be kind, was only that, cruel! And likewise, if he were to abandoned Pia so late in life, when she had always tried to be a good wife.

Finally drifting off to sleep, he thought there might be only one real solution to it all if he had a terminal condition, the same one his mother had chosen all those years ago.

CHAPTER 72

HOME AGAIN – Jamaica

28 October 2017

Jevon opened the door and let out a piercing screech that could be heard all the way to the university. It was so loud a man came from his apartment to check whether someone had been murdered or raped. He slammed the door behind him in disgust when he saw the two women in what he thought was a passionate embrace, apparently kissing one another as only lovers do.

"*Yow gyal eff mi did ah ah fish lady mi stick fi mi tong rite dung yuh choat,*" she exclaimed, jumping up and down in excitement to see her friend again. They hugged for the longest time, until Brianna pushed her gently back, beaming and pinching her friend's cheeks in affection.

"I almost threw up a while ago in that stinking taxi, so please don't even think about carrying out your threat by sticking your tongue down my throat!"

Jevon howled and pulled her friend inside her apartment still hugging her in disbelief. Brianna was genuinely thrilled by her friend's reaction at seeing her again, submitting herself to a further barrage of hugs and pinches as Jevon continued to demonstrate how sorely she had been missed. She eventually went off into the kitchen to put the kettle on for a cup of tea.

"How's your mama doing, gal?" she called. "Everyone loving their new home, I bet?"

They sat at the dining table drinking their tea whilst Jevon listened intently to her account of everything that had happened in England. "Mon, you were so brave," she said, captivated by Brianna's account of what sounded like a movie.

"Not really," Brianna replied, "if I hadn't picked up that gun, we would both be dead now! You would have done exactly the same thing." Jevon quite clearly disagreed and said had she been Brianna she would probably have wet her panties and hidden behind Daniel with her eyes closed.

They chatted for a long while and had two more cups of tea. Jevon told her the business was doing almost too well, as they were running very short of stock. Last week alone they lost forty per cent of orders that were not possible to fill because the items were already sold and very little could be back-ordered.

"It's OK, I am here now," Brianna assured. "First thing in the morning I'll be back at work. I have lots of good ideas where we can source new clothes. I think we should expand our horizons and look on other islands. How would you like to take that trip with me to the Dominican Republic in a couple of weeks? I spoke to a friend of mine on the phone at my mum's who said she could help us."

"The waitress who overheard those men planning to kill you?"
"Yes," she said, "Rosa!"

They spent the next hour discussing the business in detail as well as working on an itinerary for their buying trip to the DR. Rosa had already agreed to meet up with them for a few days in Santa Domingo whenever they decided to come. Jevon agreed she would be invaluable to help source new items.

"And how's your man, Daniel?" Jevon asked, changing the subject with a huge smile. "Keep you awake all night like a Jamaican man would?"

Brianna smiled but at the same time looked anxious. "What's up, gal, he need a pill to climb inside?"

"No, not at all," she said slapping the back of her friend's hand in feigned disgust. "No, I am worried about him," she said. "He saw a doctor in London but never said anything about it afterwards. He just shrugged and said it was nothing."

"Well, perhaps it was nothing. Lucky the pair of you didn't end up in intensive care after what you both went through."

"Yes, I hear what you're saying, Jevi, but he told me earlier in the day he was having problems with his eyes and then he went dizzy on our walk to the prettiest fishing village you have ever seen."

"Oh, I am sure it's nothing, Bri. He'll be OK," she said, asking, "Will I ever meet your Australian man?" She was patting Brianna's arm affectionately.

"You certainly will, girl! He and I have to attend the trial, probably next year on Lucaya, and he's promised to come to Jamaica for a while and meet my mum and my family. Surprisingly he's looking forward to meeting you too. Don't worry, won't say a word about your suggestion of putting your tongue down my throat earlier!"

After they had finished laughing Brianna said it was getting late and she should try and get to bed early for their busy day tomorrow. Jevon hugged her again at the door and watched her friend walk over to her apartment and unlock her door.

She turned and blew Jevon a kiss.

Instead of going inside Brianna suddenly stumbled against the door and slid sideways on to the floor and lay there without moving.

"BRIANNA!" Jevon screamed.

CHAPTER 73

SURPRISING NEWS – Mandeville, Jamaica
29 October 2017

When she finally opened her eyes, she was relieved what had concerned her so much was just a dream; why was Daniel not calling her as often as before? In the dream it was already 2018 and they had only spoken on Skype once immediately after he arrived back in Australia in early December the previous year. Later he had left just a voice message wishing her a Merry Christmas, as he did the following week wishing her a Happy New Year. It seemed he was avoiding her!

Brianna's head began pounding with pain once she was fully awake. Realizing she had no idea where she was, she became agitated and her heart began racing. The blinds at the window allowed only faint streaks of light between the louvres, revealing what looked like a hospital monitor recording someone's vital signs.

She sat up from the bed and was horrified to see the monitors were attached to her! What had happened! Had she been in a car accident? Where was she, in England? And why was her head in so much pain? For a terrifying moment she thought she might be dying. An alarm in the distance went off, and in less than a minute a nurse rushed into the room to check why Brianna's heart rate had increased.

"Lay back, please, miss," the nurse advised and fiddled with something on the monitor that switched off the alarm. "You have concussion, and you need to rest!"

What on earth is going on, Brianna wondered, finding it impossible to keep her head off the pillow.

"Please, miss, it's for your own good," the young nurse warned. This time Brianna did as she was told but only because the pain was becoming more intense than she could bear. "I'll tell the doctor you are awake. You have a friend outside who is waiting to see you." The nurse went off to look for the doctor after beckoning Jevon, who had been waiting on one of the plastic chairs reading an out-of-date copy of People magazine. She was sipping from a styrofoam cup of tepid coffee.

"Hey, sister, you gone make me have a heart attack!" Jevon exclaimed as she entered the ICU. "You really misbehaving, banging your head to get out of work this morning!"

Brianna only managed a brief smile because she was still in acute pain. She was trying to sit up but her friend coaxed her to remain as she was. "Don't fuss yourself, Bri! I just came to see you quickly. I am not staying long."

Jevon was there barely three minutes before she was manhandled out of the ICU. She had been standing by Brianna's bedside, exchanging a few words with her friend, when without warning alarms went off on the monitor. Other alarms screeched simultaneously at the nurses' station in the centre of a ring of ICUs, separated by a corridor connecting to the main body of the hospital. Red lights were flashing outside Brianna's room as two nurses barged in, followed closely by a female doctor.

"Leave," the doctor ordered as one of the nurses clutched Jevon by her arm and pushed her from the room.

"What's happening?" Jevon pleaded to the nurse.

"Please, miss, just do as the doctor told you," the nurse warned and then slammed the door shut.

CHAPTER 74

BACK ON LUCAYA
10 November 2017

It was mid-December before either of them was able to find the time to get together again. Roger had been too involved assisting the Crown Prosecutors to prepare their case against Michael Elm, whilst Harry was as usual overworked with his own caseloads as a defence lawyer. Three weeks had passed since Roger returned to the island before they finally met for lunch one weekend.

Roger arrived at the Bistro Restaurant early. It was a Saturday, and he was living at a condo not too far down the beach. He was wearing blue shorts and a white polo and had been walking in bare feet, kicking up the soft sand. He stopped to put his flips-flops on before he entered the bar-restaurant by way of three weatherworn steps.

He overheard two English people speaking loudly to one another; they were lounging on deck chairs close to the steps like two tubs of lard. The pair sounded Cockney, but Roger knew they were not, at least they were not born within the sound of Bow Bells in the City of London. He had been raised in London and could easily detect a true Cockney. These two were *Towies* (The Only Way is Essex) whose accent had become the Cockney of the times, spoken by the descendants of emigres to other London boroughs in search of more affordable housing after the war. Roger guessed they came from somewhere near Romford, or some equally ghastly place.

He had been in the bar once or twice since his return to the island. Even so, Jimmy greeted him effusively as if he had not seen him for years. Roger ordered a Pinot Grigio and bantered with Jimmy about Jamaica's poor showing in the cricket series against England. "You see, Jimmy, had you not forced independence in August '62, you might very well have stood a small chance of winning the series this week. With us still around you might actually have learned to play the game properly by now."

Jimmy laughed loudly and dropped a full glass of wine he was about to hand to Roger. "Whoa, mon, now look what you have made me do," he accused Roger in feigned anger. "Yeah, mon, independence was the worst thing that ever happened to us. Now the economy is so bad we can't even afford proper cricket bats!"

Just then Harry Charlesworth was walking in with his usual gifts of two bottles of champagne. He'd overheard Jimmy: "But then, dear boy," he said, "the Brits would have stolen all your beautiful women!"

All three laughed after Jimmy pulled a face of despair. Harry ordered a Scotch before they went to find a seat at the front of the restaurant overlooking the ocean.

They were both genuinely pleased to see one another again. Other than being loosely connected by the law, the lawyer and the policeman were in many respects quite different. Roger, a good deal younger by more than thirty years, had only been married once whereas Harry had recently divorced his sixth wife, a gorgeous young woman from the Dominican Republic who turned out to be a lesbian.

"And how is your dear wife," Harry asked, without anticipating Roger's rather glum response.

"Not good," he said. "She wants a divorce. Sick of being married to a policeman!"

"Has she met someone else, then?" Harry asked, apparently quite shocked by the news. He had always thought Roger was the perfect husband and father. "And what about your kids?"

"She met an accountant and wants full custody of the kids!"

"And an accountant is an upgrade on a policeman?" Harry chuckled. "My thoughts exactly," Roger responded. "But then I guess she deserves a bit of boredom in her life so she can at least schedule dinner so everyone eats at the same time. Most nights I didn't get home until eight-thirty, often much later" he admitted. Then he lamented that he would miss the kids. "One day they will be teenagers and they will need more than an absentee father in their lives."

"Well, I am truly sorry to hear all this, Roger," Harry said. They clinked their wine glasses to better things to come. "Perhaps I should set you up with one of the young ladies I know," Harry suggested with a broad grin.

"I am a policeman, Harry! It would not look good consorting with someone who looks seventeen but who is probably only fifteen!"

"Touché, my friend," Harry responded.

It was a splendid day and the beach was not too crowded. There were no clouds about, only blue sky, miles of powdery white sand and a turquoise ocean. The two bloated white specimens sitting on their beach chairs just below where Roger and Harry were sitting, were arguing about something but Roger could not quite make out what they were saying.

"You know those two?" Harry said pirouetting some linguine onto his fork. Just as he was about to pop the delicious portion into his mouth, the unravelling knot of pasta slipped off the fork and slid slowly down his Tommy Bahama silk shirt. "Fucking hell," he swore, trying to lift the linguine off with his pudgy fingers, making an even worse mess. "I can see the day rapidly approaching when I will require a nurse to feed me, preferably eighteen with an incredible body!"

Roger laughed, then tilted his head towards the pink heaps of blubber below, "Should I know them?" he asked.

"Oh, I'm sure you will if you don't already," Harry replied. "Apparently they are under investigation by the Serious Fraud Squad for flogging uncut diamonds on the island."

"Oh, those are the two!" Roger exclaimed. "Yes, I have heard about them, but couldn't fit a face to a name until now. I thought they were regular tourists," he said.

Roger peered down to get a better look at the couple. The woman noticed him and gave him a look to kill, said something to her husband who called to Roger to stop peering down his wife's bikini top.

"Shudder the thought," Harry whispered. Then loud enough for the couple to hear him, he said, "My goodness, Roger, you make friends quickly."

After they finished their lunch, with the evidence of what Harry had eaten still quite visible down the front of his shirt, they moved closer to the bar to get away from the coarse couple on the beach. Sinking down into the comfort of an old worn armchair covered in brightly coloured Caribbean fabric, Roger began to reply to Harry's question, why the two witnesses in the Michael Elm case had been flown to England rather than having them sign their statements on Lucaya.

"Would have made a lot of sense in hindsight, I suppose," Roger agreed. "No doubt the FCO would probably think twice before suggesting the same again after what transpired in Cornwall. However, I think everyone, including the Foreign Office and the police, all agreed the matter was too sensitive, at least politically. Seeing that it involved the son of an English peer and one of the richest men in the UK, they believed it was up to London to command the narrative."

A long-legged Dominican girl in a tight-fitting black dress came up and bent down to give Harry a passionate kiss on the lips. She said something in Spanish Roger could not understand and Harry laughed loudly and slapped her behind gently. Waving Harry goodbye and giving Roger a warm smile, she then went to the bar to sit next to her friend, who was also an exceedingly good looking *Dominicana*.

"Difference between you and me, Harry, is if I had done that, she would have slapped my face and I would lose my job."

"Ah, my boy, that's because you have a job maintaining the law, whilst mine is to find the cracks for my clients to break it. Legally of course," he added, smiling!

They had paced themselves over lunch, consuming the two bottles of Veuve Clicquot slowly before ordering two coffees. Roger was the first to surrender to further temptation about an hour later to get himself a glass of Pinot Grigio. Harry asked for another Scotch. It was Saturday and they were both settling down to an afternoon of some serious drinking! Roger was off duty and Harry could work anytime he dammed well pleased. He was enjoying the younger man's company. Plenty of time later in the evening to wander around Morgan's Cay.

Harry and Roger always respected the boundaries of the other in their relationship; Roger was a policeman investigating possible crimes committed by Lord Elm and Michael Elm. Harry Charlesworth on the other hand was one of the lawyers protecting their corporate interests on the island, yet had not been appointed counsel involving any criminal matter. It had been suggested he may act in an advisory capacity when Michael Elm was put on trial where local knowledge and experience would be essential in assisting a team of the very best lawyers from London, who had already begun preparing a defence before charges had even been laid against the peer's son.

The one interesting point Roger did pick up in their conversation was Harry's seemingly sarcastic remark wondering whether Lord Elm was setting up his son to take the fall for everything. In fact, this suggestion had already been discussed with his immediate boss at The Met in London. Both of them had agreed it was a distinct possibility. Perhaps Harry's reference was a head's up confirming it to be true without blatantly crossing their self-imposed borders.

The other matter bugging Roger was how Michael Elm had been released from a perfectly adequate jail at the airport and was now under house arrest in a luxury penthouse, a three-bedroom suite on the Coral Bay strip. He was even allowed to wander down to the beach with his guard, who was so overweight he could never have kept up had Michael Elm simply walked away slowly.

"Yes, it would be interesting to know who arranged that," Harry responded without feeling compromised. "Perhaps his father is still pulling strings so Michael doesn't feel abandoned altogether."

"Dearest Daddy can't make it too obvious he's going to leave his son hanging out to dry!" Roger retorted sarcastically whereas Harry remained silent. "He'll probably get ten to fifteen years here and possibly life when he's tried in the UK; that's if of course he was directly involved with any of the murders".

"Did you realize I know your star witness very well?" Harry suddenly said. "He and I would often have a drink together. Considering he is Australian, he seemed a thoroughly decent fellow, but somewhat troubled, I always thought."

"Yes, I still think there is something bothering him. He and Miss Jamaica seemed incredibly happy together, but underlying that, I agree, there is something not quite right with him."

"Guilt, perhaps, because he's snagged a woman most men would die for," Harry joked.

"Perhaps," Roger said, sounding unconvinced.

It was coming up to five o'clock by the time they decided to head home. Roger was feeling a little worse for wear and wanted to make it a very early night. Harry, on the other hand, had other plans and needed a quick shower and a change of clothes before heading out on the prowl in Morgan's Cay. "Before you go, Roger," he said, "you may be interested to know the position of Detective Superintendent with the Criminal Investigations Division will be vacant in a couple of months. I believe the governor would very much like you to apply for it!"

"How on earth would you know that!"

"You forget, Roger, I have friends in very high places!" He winked at Roger and then excused himself because he was in a hurry. "Great afternoon, Roger, one of the best!"

Roger was thrilled by the possibility of remaining on the island indefinitely. He had no wish to return to London and its dismal climate now his wife had left him. He would miss the kids, but then they could always come and visit him on the island, and he would probably see more of them than he would back home.

He was so excited by the prospect that he decided not to go home immediately. He went up to the bar and called to Jimmy for a large rum and coke. The girl who had given Harry the kiss earlier smiled at Roger from the other end of the bar. Her friend was talking to someone else and the girl picked up her glass and came over and stood next to Roger.

CHAPTER 75

ROAD TO EDEN
5 January 2018

Australia was his very least favourite country to travel, bar none. Never mind that it virtually required hospitalization to recover from the long flight; driving on the roads in New South Wales, particularly in Sydney, was an excruciating and unforgettable experience. Sydney's roads had obviously been planned by someone lacking vision of the basic requirements of a city even back in the 1800s, let alone two hundred years later. Initial work had been supervised by the Superintendent of Convicts, who instructed his convict labour to build the roads to follow the ground contours and Aboriginal tracks surrounding Sydney Harbour. In future years, therefore, it would be next to impossible to construct roads on a grid system, such as in San Francisco, at least not without demolishing most of the existing buildings in the city. By 2018 Sydney's roads were chocked day after day by idling traffic gushing carbon monoxide into the atmosphere.

Furthermore, the mostly two-lane coastal highways, stretching almost three thousand kilometres from Cairns to Melbourne, was additional proof of the lack of any cohesive infrastructure planning in one of the wealthiest nations in the world. The roads remained totally inadequate to meet the demands of a burgeoning population. What had they been thinking?

Richard Crossly swore as some moron overtook him in a white Corolla at a dangerous bend in the road. Richard had just driven through the village of Pambula, 16 kilometres north of the port of Eden.

His trip to Australia had been planned weeks before as part of a campaign to recruit additional engineering staff for his company on Lucaya. He had interviewed three people at the Sofitel in Darling Harbour. Two of the applicants were unsuitable, but he had engaged a new quantity surveyor. He had decided to make Daniel a surprise visit. He desperately needed to talk to him to try and put things right. It had been gnawing at him for weeks and he needed to try and explain everything.

He had not chosen the path he now found himself on. He could once have made quite a different decision, one that would not have challenged his core beliefs. To have made that choice two years ago, though, would have meant the end to his construction business on the island; and it would have jeopardized the future of his family in England, quite possibly placing them all in danger.

I had no choice, he thought, no fucking choice at all. In the end I had to sacrifice my best friend for my wife and children.

Once in Eden he filled up his car with petrol and then continued two kilometres south until he found the turn-off to the house. He stopped the car on the grass verge and reached over to the back seat and his briefcase. At first, he could not find the photo, then, with a sense of relief, he finally located it between two sheets of paper in one of the files. He had begun to fear he had lost it.

He held it up between two fingers to look at it again. It was a copy of the photograph he had taken the previous August down at Morgan's Cay on Lucaya. Joseph Pierre Toussant was not looking directly at the camera, oblivious to the fact that his picture was being taken. The package he was carrying under his right arm was quite discernible. Richard slid it back in the file carefully.

CHAPTER 76

HARD DECISIONS – Eden

25 January 2018

D aniel was watching them from above as they slowly ambled back from their walk around the property. It was slightly over five acres, too large for a couple in their sixties to look after, he often thought. Four acres of it, situated on the side of a steep hill of solid granite, comprised two large fields with several grazing sheep. They were useful lawn mowers and so there had been no need for Daniel to invest in a sit-on tractor that would probably have tipped over on such a steep gradient.

The real garden, what there was of it, was fairly low maintenance. Scattered at the front of the house were growing at least thirty or forty tall yuccas, and a dozen or more cypress trees lined the driveway. In the summertime the yuccas blossomed for several weeks, each with a single cluster of large, white, bell-shaped flowers at the very top of the plant, reminiscent of an angel on a Christmas tree. There had been a number of times when Daniel had almost taken his eye out gardening close to the yuccas or had to dash indoors with blood streaming down his arms on coming too close to the razor-sharp leaves.

It had taken them well over an hour, with short breaks every now and again, for Jane to catch her breath. Even Pia seemed to be puffing a bit. They waved as they saw him standing on the upper deck leaning over the blue-bonded metal railings. He waved back at them and then returned inside the house.

Pia was getting along with Jane extremely well, better in fact than he did. There were times when he had to admit to himself that he felt awkward with his sister. He never quite knew what to say. They would discuss the weather and the news and he would always inquire how she was feeling, but very rarely if ever did they discuss their childhood in Western Australia. It was as if it had become a taboo subject.

The thought occasionally occurred to him that they had both for their own reasons retreated within themselves after their initial meeting on Flinders Island – or perhaps it was just him, because he simply did not want to be reminded so much of the past. Nonetheless, he was still pleased she was living with them, thanks mostly to Pia's persistence. It had been the right decision, and Pia enjoyed having another woman to talk to. She failed to elicit much interest when she tried to discuss her sewing projects or her cooking with Daniel.

Daniel was happy that they got along so well. When Pia had informed him in England that Jane was going to come and live with them, he was far from certain it was a good idea. After all, he did not really know his sister that well. But Pia had persuaded him that his sister should not be living on her own. Jane, she said, had a narrow escape, and next time she might not be so lucky. She might very well die alone.

Pia had witnessed plenty of old people dying during her nursing career, with only her hand to hold in their last moments. They either had no family or their loved ones were long past caring. Someone who perhaps once embodied the very essence of a close and loving family had become a frail old grandma or granddad and only reminded the living of their own mortality. Who needed that in the midst of life!

Not wishing to concern her unduly, Daniel had not informed Pia that the doctor in Eden had made an appointment for him to undergo some tests at the hospital in Bega.

He often went for walks on his own during the week, usually along one of the never-ending stretches of deserted beach a few miles north from Eden. He had been told it was unnecessary for him to stay overnight; he could drive to the hospital and have the tests without Pia being any the wiser. On the day of his appointment, he was longer than usual on his so-called beach walk, but he explained that he had gone to explore Potato Point Beach, about a two-hour drive north.

He was at Bega hospital for over five hours. He first sat down with the resident neurologist and answered a number of questions about his general health and the symptoms he had been experiencing. Although additional tests would be required in the coming month, by the time Daniel left the hospital the neurologist and other doctors were fairly certain the original suspicions of multiple sclerosis were correct. This was confirmed once they had the opportunity to study the results more closely. The MRI and lumbar puncture showed indisputable evidence of MS.

He intended to talk to Pia in the next day or so. Obviously, there was no way he could keep it a secret forever; the signs would soon become obvious to someone who'd been so long in the medical profession. But once he told her he knew she would argue strongly against him ever again travelling by himself.

He desperately wanted to see Brianna one more time. They had both accepted that it would be at least another year before the start of the trial on Lucaya. But now it seemed likely he would not be able to make the journey! The alternative was to try and persuade Brianna to visit Australia. Yet this was an option he already knew she could never accept. It would place her in an untenable position between himself and Pia, a husband and wife who had been married for over four decades.

At the end of the day, he was convinced Brianna would sacrifice their relationship to protect Pia. Brianna had a peculiar moral code, at least from his perspective, though it was one widely accepted in countries like Jamaica. It was perhaps understandable in a country where fathers were in the habit of walking away from their wives and children with hardly a backwards glance.

Steeped as she was in the Christian values of the Jamaican Baptists, 'borrowing' was acceptable to Brianna's conscience as long as no one was hurt – at least not in the way her own mother and countless other Jamaican women had been hurt.

Brianna would not accept Daniel behaving like a Jamaican man, because she knew he loved Pia as he loved her. Differently, perhaps, but just as much. If he left Pia, she understood, her own relationship with Daniel would also inevitably die.

CHAPTER 77

A SURPRISE VISITOR – Eden

26 January 2018 (AEDT)

"You go with him to the Seahorse Inn, Daniel," she said, speaking quietly in the kitchen so as not to be overheard. "Tell him I have to remain with Jane." Pia took a beer from the fridge and added it to the others on the tray. She had taken a dislike to Richard Crossly as soon as they had been introduced.

"So nice to meet you," she had lied, observing that he was unable to look her directly in the eye. He was a good deal taller than Daniel yet nowhere near as good looking, she thought, passing a judgement not without bias. It was difficult to refrain from staring at the rosacea on Richard's face, which had spread like an angry rash over most of it, making him appear like someone recovering from skin-graft surgery in hospital.

Normally she would have empathized with a patient suffering from such a condition, appreciating how it made many people terribly self-conscious. This man was very different, though! He wore his infliction like a badge of honour, providing the impression that he would aggressively challenge anyone who dared mention it. If that failed to dissuade, his guttural Yorkshire accent would almost certainly intimidate even the bravest who might consider broaching the subject.

But Pia's reason for disliking him really had nothing to do with his coarse accent or his nasty skin condition. Nor was it to do with his lack of eye contact or any other discernible aspect of his character. Perhaps it was unfair of her, she thought, but she had taken an immediate dislike to him for no particular reason.

"What's wrong, Pia, why don't you like him?" Daniel asked, shocked that she could be so quick to have an opinion of someone she had barely met.

He had been surprised when he opened the door to find Richard Crossly standing there. He was the last person he expected to see. Richard explained that he was on business in Australia and had decided to drive to his next series of interviews in Melbourne from Sydney, a road trip that was to take him directly through Eden. Pia and Daniel had escorted Richard outside to the deck. Jane remained in her room. It was a little too warm, but they had the shade of a large umbrella to protect them from the midsummer sun.

Daniel went for a couple of beers and a glass of water for Pia, who found it extremely difficult making small talk with a man she had instantly disliked. She quickly excused herself, suggesting that she had changed her mind and wanted a beer instead of water, and followed Daniel to the kitchen.

"My spirit doesn't warm to him at all," Pia whispered. "There is something about him I can't quite put my finger on, but let's just say he's not someone I would care to trust! I know you have both been friends most of your life. I'm sorry. I don't know what it is or why I simply don't like the man."

Later, while they were drinking their beers, Richard announced that the Rosminian religious order, which had operated their old school in England, had finally agreed to settle the civil action brought by the twenty-two abused former pupils, most of whom were now in their mid to late sixties.

"The fucking bastards didn't want the publicity," Richard explained without thought to his bad language in front of a woman he did not know. "They finally caved a week before the trial and have agreed to refund the school fees to each one of the litigants still alive who attended as pupils in the fifties and sixties. It will cost them several million, I suspect. Once the lawyers have taken their chunk, each one of us will receive a cheque for approximately thirty-five thousand pounds, which allows for the inflation rate in the value of the pound over five decades."

This had an immediate effect on Daniel, who without warning furiously exclaimed they could keep their fucking money. "Thirty-five thousand pounds for destroying so many lives. You have to be joking, Richard!"

Richard Crossly was taken very much by surprise at Daniel's sudden reaction, as was Pia. He thought Daniel would have been delighted by the outcome, certainly not angry.

"I'm sorry, Daniel, I thought you would be pleased!" "Why?" Daniel retorted sharply.

Richard did not respond, diverting the course of the conversation instead when he could see his friend was becoming increasingly upset. Pia never entered the conversation at all. A lifetime of living with Daniel had taught her to avoid any mention of his school days in England. She did detect that his friend seemed agitated and upset by Daniel's reaction, however. It could have been from the heat, or possibly it was her imagination, but his rosacea looked worse than before.

The conversation began to stall after Daniel's outburst and Pia suggested the pair of them should go to the Seahorse Inn for lunch. She said she would have to remain home to be with Jane who had not been feeling too well. This was not entirely true, but she had to make her excuse a plausible one for Daniel's sake. She could not exactly come out and say she would prefer not to accompany them because she could not stand the sight of Richard!

CHAPTER 78

REVELATIONS – Boydtown

26 January 2018 (AEDT)

First, they stopped at the Seahorse Inn, where each of them had a 'middy' of pale ale and shared a large basket of potato wedges. They were sitting outside at a trestle table under a sunshade awning; Daniel had spread out an old map depicting how Boydtown looked back in 1843. Pia's enthusiasm for writing a book about Benjamin Boyd had been infectious, encouraging Daniel to explore more about the history of the region. But he was having difficulty sharing his newfound passion with Richard, who seemed disinterested.

Not a great deal had changed since Boyd commenced his ambitious project one hundred and seventy-six years ago. The inn was larger than it used to be, but there had been additional buildings scattered within the site that no longer existed. In those days there had been a salting house, two kilns, a wool house and a three-hundred-foot jetty where they loaded Boyd's ships bound for London and Sydney with wool from his extensive grazing flocks. The buildings had fallen into disrepair and been demolished; the wharf was completely destroyed over time from the relentless action of the tidal swells.

Boyd had also built a small church perched on a hill overlooking the inn; a year after completion its graveyard already held half a dozen souls. Today the church sits in ruins barely visible through the trees that have been growing there for almost two centuries, shading those buried and now long forgotten.

Try as he might, Daniel could not stimulate Richard's imagination with the history of the area. He appeared distracted and remained as agitated as he had been back at the house. After a while Daniel surrendered and folded up his map. Now that he was calmer, he changed the subject back to the settlement with their old school's religious order, the Rosminians.

"I was serious what I said before, Richard, I don't want any part of it. They can keep their filthy money. No way in hell those bastards can buy me off with thirty pieces of silver!"

Richard merely nodded in reply, making no comment. "Are you all right, Richard? You are very quiet."

"No, not really, Daniel," he said, finally breaking his silence. "I have some rather disturbing matters to discuss with you."

They drove there in silence for about twenty minutes until they arrived at a square masonry tower that loomed high above the forest. The tower had been constructed in 1847 from large Pyrmont sandstone blocks brought by ship from Sydney and off-loaded on the southern headland of Twofold Bay, above the Seahorse Shoals. It was intended as a lighthouse, but the New South Wales government rejected the application, so it became a lookout for whales. There was a three-hundred-and-sixty-degree view from the top. Once the flukes of the huge mammals were spotted out in the ocean, the alarm was called, and the whaling boats stationed in the bay were launched.

Killer whales, or orcas as they are also known, are permanent residents of the surrounding waters. They would work with the whalers to herd the migratory whales into Twofold Bay where they were slaughtered by harpoon before being dragged by the boats to the whaling station. There they would be cut into large chunks for food or boiled to produce tallow to be exported to England for candles. The tongues of the whales were tossed to the waiting orcas as a reward.

One hundred and seventy years later, the original purpose of Ben Boyd Tower had long been abandoned; it was now preserved as a monument in memory of the early pioneers of Australia. The sixty-two-foot tower sat on a promontory of rugged cliffs with a clear view of Twofold Bay over to Eden on the far shore. To the southwest the wild coastline stretched for miles skirting the Ben Boyd National Park as far as the Green Cape lighthouse and the state border with Victoria.

Stunted eucalyptus and windswept bush had grown around the tower as if to feature it for future generations; some of the more adventurous visitors commenced a thirty-kilometre bush hike to Green Cape along the cliffs. The sweet calls of the bellbirds pervaded their forest walks, with the boom of crashing waves of the Tasman Sea far below.

Daniel and Richard were sitting on a wooden bench at an observation point perched on the cliff about one hundred yards from the tower. The wind had started to pick up and would soon prevent any attempt at a meaningful conversation. For the time being the musical accompaniment of the bellbirds could still be heard about them.

"It is very beautiful and peaceful here," Richard said, breaking his long silence. He had hardly uttered a word on the drive to the tower from the Seahorse Inn.

"It really is," Daniel agreed. "And we are so fortunate the tourist industry has so far not exploited it as they have other parts of the country. That's all likely to change, though. They are beginning construction of a new wharf over in Eden so the mega-cruise liners can dock here."

Richard failed to comment, but he proceeded to open a manila envelope, taking out a colour photograph that he passed to Daniel. He remained silent as Daniel studied the picture of a black man, obviously taken at night. Lights of many colours, emanating from what looked like bars and small stores, had blurred the background. The man was walking; he appeared oblivious that someone was taking a photo of him. His features were sharply defined, and Daniel was guessing he was someone from the Caribbean, possibly a Haitian, about thirty. He seemed well-nourished and healthy.

"Who is this, Richard, I don't understand?"
"Do you see the package he's carrying under his arm?"
"Well, yes, so what?" Daniel said handing back the photo to Richard.
"That package contained the gun that assassinated Walter Harrison!"

CHAPTER 79

PIA'S CONCERNS

26 January 2018 (AEDT)

"Where did they go?" Jane asked, collecting the empty glasses from the table outside.

"Leave those, Jane!" Pia snapped, unintentionally. It was seldom she displayed feelings of irritation, and it was only on the rarest of occasions that she revealed she was angry about something. These days she was generally quieter and kept her feelings to herself; she was skilled in the art of diplomacy after a lifetime of dealing with difficult patients or unpleasant situations at the hospital.

"I'm sorry, Jane, I really didn't intend to be rude," she apologized. "It was that friend of Daniel's who was just here. He didn't say very much but I found him quite offensive."

"Why was that, dear?"

"It was something in his off-handed manner; he was barely listening to a word Daniel was saying and seldom even glanced in my direction. All he wanted to talk about was the wretched settlement," she said, immediately regretting the reference to Daniel's old school. He had purposely made no mention of his school days in England to Jane. It was a chapter of his life he had no intention of sharing with her.

"Oh, and what was that all about?"

"I'm not sure, Jane. You'd have to ask Daniel."

"My goodness, I hope it had nothing to do with abusing boys by priests! I have been reading about that dreadful Cardinal Pell the other day, the one going to trial later this year for molesting altar boys."

"Like I said, Jane, you'll have to ask Daniel," Pia replied, refusing to take the bait to pursue it further in conversation.

For reasons she was unable to explain, Pia had this uneasy intuition that she was starting to lose Daniel. Since his return from England, he had become even more withdrawn and introspective than usual. He seemed deeply troubled about something yet disinclined to discuss it with her when she would inquire if he was all right. He would simply tell her he was perfectly fine, and then often abruptly leave the room. He also seemed less spritely and energetic these days. It was as if the young man who had always inhabited him was preparing, like the nymph of a cicada, to vacate its shell before flying away forever.

She heard the familiar tone of a Skype call coming from Daniel's computer in the office and hurried downstairs to answer it. By the time she got there, however, the caller had rung off. She noticed the call was from Jamaica, although not from the girl who had saved Daniel's life in England. Had it been, it would have been good to talk to Brianna and thank her for protecting her husband; Pia believed she was exceptionally brave.

But the call was from someone called Jevon. She had no idea who that was; she would let Daniel deal with it once he returned from his sightseeing tour. Shortly after that, she prayed, Richard Crossly would be on his way to Melbourne.

CHAPTER 80

CONFESSIONS – Boyd's Tower

26 January 2018 (AEDT)

"What the hell are you talking about, Richard?" Daniel demanded to know. He leaned forward and took the photo from him to get a better look at it. "How would you know what's inside the package?"

Richard sighed in exasperation. "Because I had given it to him five minutes earlier, before I took the fucking photo!"

"Richard, you are not making any sense at all. Why would you be giving this man a gun, which of course begs the question of where you even got it from."

"I brought it aboard Elm's motor yacht, that small one he owns, *La Codicia*, or 'the Greed' in English! Appropriately named, don't you agree?" he smirked. "Well, *La Codicia* was moored in Port Everglades at the time I was over there in Florida. His lordship had asked me to meet someone, an Englishman who he had dealings with. I was never told what it was I had to collect, only given instructions to hand it over it to someone in Morgan's Cay after we returned to Lucaya on *La Codicia*. Elm had already left for the Cook Islands weeks earlier on *El Gordo*."

"ENOUGH!" Daniel snapped, finally losing patience with Richard's account of something that clearly had nothing to do with him. "I don't need to know all this. It's the police you really should be speaking to, not me."

"Just hear me out, Daniel. Let me tell you the whole story," Richard said, growing impatient.

He explained that he had only discovered it was a gun once he was back on Lucaya. From the weight and size of the package he already had his suspicions, but he wanted to confirm it before he took on the role of Elm's errand boy. The evening he got home, he carefully opened the package and discovered, as he had suspected, a handgun inside. He had sat simply staring at it for a long while pondering what to do. He had absolutely no idea it was going to be used to assassinate the ex-premier of the island; he only realized this later when all the pieces began falling in place after Harrison had been shot on the beach.

"You must understand, I had no choice! Geoffrey and his son had always made it quite clear what would happen to my business if I didn't toe the line, long before Michael even raped that American woman."

Daniel sat there listening in growing apprehension of what was to come, of what Richard had not as yet told him.

"He could have pulled my loan anytime he chose, and the business would have gone overnight. Everything I have is tied up in that!" he said, wallowing in self-pity.

"My wife and children live in a heavily mortgaged house near Whitby in Yorkshire. If the business goes bust, there goes their home. And I am too old now! No one would lend me a penny to start over again!" A sudden blast of wind prevented him from being heard. "In any case," he continued, when it had died down, "my credibility would be down the drain. I would be ruined and my family would be left without so much as a roof over their heads."

Richard got up from the hewn wooden bench, clearly becoming more agitated as he continued providing details of what he had been bottling inside for almost three years. He began pacing back and forth, dangerously close to the edge of the cliff.

Below them the Tasman Sea was now roaring, battering against rugged ironstone cliffs. Spray from the impact of the waves drifted high in the air, suspended for a moment in a mist of rainbow curtains. Like the fingers of God, the last rays of sunshine poked through clouds scurrying across the blackening sky; they heralded an approaching storm to the east.

Then Richard Crossly began to confess! Becoming visibly angrier, thumping his fist into the palm of his left hand over and over again, he continued pacing wildly in front of Daniel, who was still sitting on the bench. Richard was too distraught to stop, one minute looking out to sea, then at Daniel, whilst directing his mounting fury at him of matters Daniel knew nothing about.

It began teeming down with rain that neither of them seemed to have noticed. Richard continued ranting from within his own particular hell whilst Daniel, dumbfounded, remained sitting there with rain lashing his face and soaking his clothes.

"Your fucking problem was you always told me everything! Thanks to your big mouth, I always had a good idea where you were and what you were doing!"

Richard stood, silent for a moment, glaring at Daniel as if he had hated him all of his life. "Did you never wonder how someone tracked your wife to the beach the day the dog attacked her?"

Daniel did not respond, bewildered that this could be the same person who had been his friend for most of his life.

"You, you mindless idiot! You told me she liked to go for walks on that particular beach, even at what time of day. No problems identifying her either, thanks to all the photos you kept sending of her and the fancy house you live in, and no doubt fully paid for," he added spitefully.

Richard became even more agitated as he rambled on, more or less incoherently, perhaps hoping, yet not believing for one minute, that his friend would absolve him as the priests used to at school after fumbling inside his trousers, blaming him for their perverse predilections.

"Same with the house, when you let me know you were going off to Tasmania on your own," he continued, screaming above the noise of the wind and the rain. "Then later, when you rang to say you would be flying to England to finally sign that statement, something you continuously avoided like most other things in your miserable little life."

He bent down and stared at Daniel like a madman, his eyes wide and the veins on the sides of his neck bulging. The guilt that had haunted him for so long was now fully on display as he attempted, like the priests, to transfer all blame to someone else.

"I could always read you like an open book. Never once could you make a clear-cut decision. Even took you close to three years to decide to do the right thing and sign that bloody statement," he snarled, as someone would walking along the edge of insanity! "If it had been anyone else, I could have lived with all this. But why, why you of all people!"

Daniel was unsure what Richard meant by this last remark. Even if he could understand the ravings of this madman, someone he had always considered his one true friend in life, he was past caring.

"And look at you now! Got yourself into a fine mess," Richard laughed insanely, wiping the rain from his face with the back of his sleeve. By then they were both drenched from the violent squalls sweeping across the bay. Boyd's Tower, only yards away, was already obscured by walls of rain from the thunderous downpour. The surrounding forest of eucalyptus looked as if they might snap at any minute as the storm continued to rage; leaves were shredded off branches to be caught up in a swirling vortex of debris and carried out to sea.

Richard continued shouting, leaning much closer now to Daniel so he could be heard over the constant roar. "You absolutely have no fucking idea who you want or what to do! Who's it to be, your wife or that Jamaican cunt?"

Daniel suddenly bolted from his seat and lunged forwards.

With the shock of such an unforgivable betrayal, Richard had unwittingly unlocked Daniel's labyrinth of dreams, freeing them from their box and leaving them to scatter freely and rattle around inside his head. Luckily, the sudden overwhelming confusion of emotions paralysed what could have been an instinctive impulse to kill. After all, Richard was the first to have managed to invade the darkest recesses of Daniel's soul, which guarded the stranger that Daniel had never wanted to be.

Yes, unquestionably, he loved them both, at least that was what he firmly believed. His conundrum had always concerned how to move forward and retain his self-respect, at the same time ignoring the darkness that had always beckoned from inside his box of dreams. Would any gentle soul have behaved differently, he often wondered, especially one whose early life had been suffocated, who had been trapped between a domineering father and an abusive school?

Perhaps he was not the hypocrite or coward he sometimes believed. Perhaps he simply lacked the ability to release the person he was born to be after that day long ago when his mother and the centre of his universe had mysteriously disappeared. He had spent far too much time in his own company since then, repressing those feelings. Until he did no longer, they would never allow him to be completely free. When he had met Brianna, he began to grasp a lifeline, at least for a short while. There were genuine moments of pure joy – yet they were always tempered by the realization of how much he had missed during a life of mostly loneliness. There were times over the last few years when he saw himself as neither a bad man nor a hypocrite. He was merely lost, still that seven-year-old boy looking for the right path no one had ever bothered to show him.

Daniel's great conflict of emotions abruptly resurfaced and erupted inside him as soon as Richard called Brianna that awful name. He rushed towards him, but Richard quickly stepped to one side with an arm outstretched.

Daniel lost his balance and began sliding on the small stones loosened by the downpour. In the roar of the storm, Richard failed to hear Daniel scream for Pia as he slithered towards the cliff edge.

CHAPTER 81

THE ARREST
March 2018

The Lucayan Airways plane taxied towards the main terminal at the Owen Roberts International Airport in George Town. As it approached, it passed a group of six smaller aircraft parked on the tarmac by the private jet building. Chief Inspector Roger Sage spotted Lord Geoffrey Elm's Falcon Dassault, sitting smugly apart from the rest. Larger than the others, it wore a livery of white except for the registration numbers on the two cowlings. As his plane passed the peer's executive jet, the sun reflected off the fuselage of the gleaming aircraft, briefly blinding him.

Two uniformed officers of the Royal Cayman police met him as he exited the plane and escorted him to a waiting police car. He had no luggage apart from a small overnight bag. He would be flying on to Jamaica later in the day and staying there until the following afternoon before returning to Lucaya.

An official from the British Foreign Office dressed in a dark blue suit with a pale blue tie sat in the back seat of the police car. He had a ruddy complexion and appeared as if he drank too much. His nose was snaked with tiny purple veins making it his most prominent feature, a fact Roger had noticed as soon as he got inside the car.

"You realize, officially, this is a Cayman police operation?" the man asked without any formal greeting. He had been in touch with Roger the

previous day by phone and considered any additional pleasantries unnecessary. Roger said he understood but asked for confirmation that he
would be the official arresting officer. "Yes," said the man with the problem nose. "Of course, I will accompany you, along with several armed
police officers, just in case!"

"I am certain that will not be necessary, Jim," Sage replied.

Jim promptly responded by informing Roger that every precaution
had to be taken to ensure absolutely nothing went wrong. Although
Cayman was a British Dependent Territory, it had its own laws and regulations, which had to be respected, even by the British Foreign Office.
Everything had been kept tightly under wraps until Elm was formally
charged back in the UK – lest unsubstantiated leaks or 'fake news' reports prejudice the case they were still building against Elm. Even the
press had no knowledge of the seismic events that would soon dominate
the international news and British politics for months if not years to
come.

"They have bent over backwards to assist, possibly fearing a local
backlash as occurred over on Lucaya. Essentially, they have been extremely cooperative and have made it possible for us to legally circumvent certain extradition provisions to avoid delays. We certainly didn't
want a repeat performance of the Ronnie Biggs fiasco when he was
caught in Barbados years ago."

The Barcadere Marina was situated adjacent to the international
airport. In minutes the police vehicle was drawing up alongside a thirty-
eight-foot fast interceptor police boat moored at the quayside. The crew
had been forewarned; they were preparing to cast off as Jim and Roger
stepped down into the boat. Four heavily armed police officers from the
firearms response unit were already waiting onboard, each wearing a
balaclava mask and equipped with a semi-automatic carbine.

"Surely not!" Roger exclaimed in disbelief. "He's over seventy. He's
hardly going to resist!"

"He's responsible for several murders, Chief Inspector, and we are
not prepared to take any chances."

Roger reluctantly accepted these precautions, although he continued to think it was all a bit over the top.

The *El Gordo* was moored approximately two hundred metres out in North Sound. Leaving a wide wake splaying out behind it, the speeding police boat took less than ten minutes to splash down as it came alongside the luxury yacht. One of the police crew immediately attached a line to the yacht's retractable boarding ladder and the first of the police officers clambered up on deck followed by the three others and the plainclothes detective. Roger was next, then the man from the FCO, who was not quite as agile as the others. He missed his footing on the first rung of the ladder and almost fell into the sea.

"Lord Geoffrey Elm, I am arresting you in connection with the murder of Francis Chambers in the Duchy of Cornwall on or about the 15th of October 2017 as well as the attempted murders of Brianna Williams and Daniel Hannaford on the same day. Have you anything to say?"

Geoffrey Elm was standing facing Inspector Roger Sage encircled by the police officers still wearing their balaclavas and holding their weapons, together with the man from the FCO and the detective. Standing on the periphery of this astonishing spectacle were several of the crew, including the captain of the vessel.

As Geoffrey Elm failed to respond, Roger Sage continued by informing him that he would be charged separately for the murders of Walter Harrison and his driver Lloyd Bailey in Lucaya at an appropriate time. He would also be charged in the random killing of Jack Nielson, more commonly known on the island as 'Cowboy Jack'. However, until the State of Florida agreed to take the death penalty off the table as a possible sentence, as would first be required under British law, he could not be transferred to American custody for the murder of Vanessa Hall in Naples, Florida.

All these additional charges were conditioned on his ever being released from prison in the UK – which was unlikely: if found guilty he would likely die in prison. Perhaps realizing that Geoffrey Elm would never be deported beyond England's shores, the Commonwealth of Australia had not as yet indicated how they would proceed in the matters of the attempted murders of Jane McArthur and Pia Hannaford in Tasmania.

Geoffrey Elm sat ramrod straight in the back of the police car with his handcuffed hands held in his lap. He showed no expression whatsoever, assuming the haughty demeanour he had always presented to his peers in the House of Lords, staring vacantly at the headrest in front of him through rimless glasses. He seems such a cold, cruel bastard, Roger was thinking as the car came to a stop by the side of the Falcon.

"You can't commandeer my own plane, Inspector," he claimed in a cultivated and imperious manner, as if he were still in control of world events. He had always liked to give the impression that his background was aristocratic, rather than that of a middle-class, grammar-school boy raised in a semi-detached house in Basingstoke.

"I demand to meet my lawyer before you ship me off like some Gitmo detainee!"

One of the Caymanian police came to open the door. Roger raised a finger indicating he wanted him to wait a minute or two. "The Cayman government is deporting you, Sir Geoffrey, to the country of your birth, the United Kingdom. You should be grateful you are returning in the comfort of your own plane."

"It's all a waste of time and resources," Elm said. "My lawyers in the UK will have me out on bail as soon as we arrive."

"We will be opposing bail based on recent evidence provided by Richard Crossly and Richard Wagner, as well as messages we discovered on your satellite phone and various calls made to the Haitian who assassinated the Premier of Lucaya! Piecing all this information together," Roger said finally, "we believe we have sufficient incriminating evidence that will put you behind bars for the remainder of your life!"

Geoffrey Elm suddenly fell silent. He was surprised that either of the men would be offering evidence against him; one would now lose his family in Argentina, and the other would be financially ruined along with his family in Yorkshire. It would not be too hard to facilitate these arrangements even from a prison cell.

"Just in case it crosses your mind," Sage began to say, "Richard Wagner's family was moved to a safe location where your thugs will never locate them."

He went on to say, without trying to mask his contempt for this faux aristocrat, "Ah, and I almost forgot to mention that the police arrested the Haitian national in Port-au-Prince only two days ago. Silly man was still carrying the same cell phone Mr. Wagner had called him on when he arranged the initial meeting. We now know Wagner stopped off in the Dominican Republic before he flew on to Vancouver. Before he departed the DR, however, he had driven across the border into Haiti where he met Monsieur Toussant and paid him a generous fifty per cent advance for the assassination."

"You still can't prove that I had anything directly to do with that," Elm argued.

"But we can prove the man Wagner, who still believed he was a go-between for Michael was, unbeknownst to him at the time, actually working for you."

Roger let Elm absorb this information for a minute before continuing, "As you are already aware, your pal Louis McPherson was killed recently by the police in Tasmania. Your son may have met your trusted security man on your boat once or twice but beyond that there were no further communications with Michael, nor does it appear he has ever met or spoken to him since. The last time Michael had any discussions with anyone about this sordid affair, was with Wagner when they met at the gentlemen's club in London. Wagner, of course, believed he was being instructed by Michael, not you!"

Here Roger hesitated for a moment, thinking how much he could actually tell Elm without compromising the case in any way.

"Amongst a growing collection of additional evidence, even the pilot flying the Falcon today made a positive identification of Mr.

McPherson a few days ago. We have interrogated Michael at length and we are satisfied he was never in communication with Mr. McPherson. There were no messages between Michael and Mr. Wagner left on any of their devices, except one from Wagner indicating he had taken care of the problem in Florida when he injected an overdose of pure heroin into that poor woman. We already suspected, as he later confirmed, that Michael contacted you about the message without really knowing what it meant. No doubt you never enlightened him either; however, from that point on you made sure Michael was kept out of the loop when you had McPherson act as the go-between with Wagner."

Roger beckoned to the policeman indicating he could open the door now. As Elm was taken from his seat Roger got out and walked behind him and the two police officers holding Elm by each arm. Geoffrey Elm never uttered another word. He was escorted up the steps of the plane where another British plainclothes detective was waiting along with the man from the Foreign Office. The Chief Inspector watched him from below with a deep sense of satisfaction. It was almost all over.

"Your man Wagner must have eventually realised his orders were coming from you, right?" Roger called up to him. "But for some of the time he must have believed Louis McPherson was working for Michael. Sooner or later, Wagner will tell us everything when it dawns on him, if only to shave a few months off his sentence" Roger smiled "and if he's anything like his father, I am sure Michael will have plenty of Additional information to provide about you, certainly once he understands you were willing to sacrifice him to save your own hide!

The police allowed Elm to stand by the entrance of the plane to hear what Roger Sage was saying.

"It was all about saving yourself and your empire, wasn't it? Ultimately you hung your own son out to dry. He was your fall guy! Everything Michael thought you were doing on his behalf was really to save your own skin in case things started to sour so you could blame it all on him! Your plan would have worked had it not been for one thing, and it was your biggest mistake by far; it was a call Louis McPherson made to you from Colchester."

Roger then explained that Colchester is a major military garrison and as soon as a satellite phone connection had been established between Elm and McPherson, an alert went out to GCHQ over at Cheltenham. GCHQ, he reminded Elm, was the Government Communications Headquarters responsible for providing signals intelligence and security and information assurance to the government and armed forces of the United Kingdom. Louis's home was less than two miles from the Colchester Garrison and fell within the parameters of additional security established for any major British base whether at home or overseas. GCHQ was perhaps the foremost signals gathering operation in the world.

"It had managed to record enough of your conversation to prove conclusively you and you alone were managing all of the recent events," Roger informed him. "We know you set your own son up to save yourself and your financial empire! Your own son, Michael, for God's sake! Then Mr. Wagner and Mr. Crossly helped put it all together for us."

Lord Geoffrey Elm seemed to visibly shrivel at this point, hunching his shoulders in the grip of the two policemen, then lowering his head to avoid Roger's scrutinizing expression of thorough contempt.

"Goodbye, Mr. Elm," he said, purposely dispensing with the pretentious title the fake peer had purchased, which would surely be stripped from him once he was convicted of murder. "Have a good flight. I very much look forward to seeing you again one day in court."

Roger checked his wristwatch as the Falcon's door was pulled up and locked from within. He had just over an hour until his flight to Montego Bay departed.

CHAPTER 82

THE LETTER – March, 2018
Eden, December 28, 2017

My dearest Brianna,

As I write this letter thousands of miles from you in Jamaica, I am trusting in God, if indeed there is one, that you will never have to read these words, for your sake as well as my own. Undoubtedly, they will burden you with even further distress, perhaps far beyond what you have already endured these past weeks or even months.

If you are now reading this, though, some while ago Roger will have informed you that I am no longer alive. In preparation for that possibility, I have made this decision to write to you now, to avoid departing this life in regret of never having expressed how much you mean to me, or how much I love you.

You have only ever brought me sunshine and happiness, my sweet Jamaican girl. You awakened my soul to the true joys of life, at the same time reflecting your own abundant love as through a mirror, uniting us as one into something whole and beautiful. Be assured, my love, you will be with me in my final moments, resting your head on my shoulder, sustaining me as the night approaches.

For reasons not always of my own making, the road I travelled in this life has been quite hard. This is not to suggest I did not love my wife, nor could I ever deny the many good times I spent with her over the years.

I would be lying if I said otherwise, because even tonight as I look over the bay to the hills of eucalyptus beyond, I still love her and respect her as much as I always did. It was not her fault I could not escape the torments that denied me the essence of a normal and happy life.

  You, Brianna, succeeded in finally setting my spirit free when no one else ever could. I shall always be grateful for what you have given me, whether I live another twenty years or discover a consciousness beyond this life, perhaps in a place we can reunite one day, walking the beaches of an alternate Jamaica or through green fields to Portscatho in Cornwall. My biggest regret now is that I have left you only memories, nothing much of substance to comfort you during what I trust will be a long and happy life. I pray you meet someone else who will hold your gentle hand whilst I am away and love you as much as I have loved you, if that is even possible. Rest assured, Bri, I shall never be far away; perhaps in the breeze caressing your hair or in the sunlight as it gently kisses your cheek. I shall always be by your side one way or another.

  Do not weep for me, celebrate instead the gift we shared and will continue to share always. My love for you is eternal.

  Forever, Daniel

PS. When I finally close my eyes, I will be remembering your first smile and your perfect rows of pearl white teeth! LOL!

Goodnight, dearest girl. I must go now as the sun has started to set and it is becoming dark.

Roger Sage was smiling to himself on his return trip from Mandeville. He was driving the small blue Yaris he had rented on arrival in Jamaica earlier in the day before checking into the Montego Hotel overlooking Sangster International Airport.

From the hotel it had taken almost three hours to reach Mandeville, along often congested, narrow and winding roads. He finally managed to locate her apartment using the satnav; it was a few streets from the Northern Caribbean University in a pretty neighbourhood, reminiscent of someplace in southern Spain. Her whitewashed apartment building with its terracotta barrel tiles was the most distinctive on the street.

He noticed as soon as she opened the door, but thought best not to say anything. Behind Brianna he could see another woman sitting at a table in the kitchen; he presumed it was Jevon whom he had spoken to back in late January by telephone from Lucaya.

Brianna had been out the day he called. Before Roger even had a chance to speak, Jevon explained how they had both been attempting to contact Daniel without success for several weeks. They had not heard from him since the new year when Brianna had spoken briefly on Skype to him. Ever since Brianna had been sick with worry because, she said, Daniel did not seem his usual self.

It was at this point Roger was forced to interject to tell Jevon that ... Daniel was presumed dead!

Jevon had broken down almost immediately. She started crying and sobbing uncontrollably into the phone once Roger had finished, explaining Daniel that had died ten days earlier in what was believed to be a tragic accident, although the matter was still under investigation.

Jevon was utterly bewildered later, after Brianna came home. She told her friend the terrible news and tried to hug her to console her. Apart from a barely audible gasp, Brianna pushed her friend away and otherwise displayed no reaction whatsoever to the tragic news; there were no tears, no screams, no indication of grief at all. Instead, she merely thanked Jevon for telling her, then went to her room and closed the door and did not speak another word to Jevon for over twenty-four hours. Neither did she answer her telephone, and she refused to open her front door to Jevon. She did text her friend two or three times when Jevon became too persistent, knocking at her front door trying to get a response to make sure she was still alive. Her brief messages told Jevon she simply wanted to be left alone and not to worry about her.

Brianna had vacated reality and was lost in a world with only Daniel by her side.

Almost a week went by before she had any meaningful conversation with Jevon, yet even then she avoided saying anything about Daniel. It was as if she had locked him away in her heart where she could protect him and their life together, refusing to share a moment of it with anyone else, lest it somehow dilute the happiness of their time spent together. It was for her alone to remember him, not to share with others who had never known him.

Brianna finally broke down when she saw Roger standing there in the doorway. For a moment there had been an awkward silence, then she flung her arms around his neck and buried her head in his chest, sobbing uncontrollably, finally releasing some of the pent-up grief that had slowly been eating away for weeks inside her like a form of terminal cancer. Both Roger and Jevon tried hard to console her; eventually she became calmer, and she took Roger by the hand and led him to the sofa.

When she was fully composed, Roger gave Brianna the letter Daniel had sent him via FedEx. He thought she was going to break down again in tears. Instead, she calmly placed the letter on a sideboard to be read alone one day when she had the strength and privacy to face up to the fact that she would never see her dearest Australian again, at least not in this life.

Before he left, he had a cup of tea Jevon had made and then confirmed with Brianna that she still intended to attend the trial of Michael Elm now scheduled for next July. Roger made no mention that she might also be called to testify at Lord Geoffrey's trial in England for murder and attempted murder later this year. That, he thought, could be left for another day. Brianna confirmed she would attend Michael Elm's trial because she knew it was what Daniel would have wanted.

For reasons she could not explain, and despite his horrendous crime, Brianna almost harboured sympathy for Michael Elm when Roger told her how Geoffrey had attempted, almost successfully, to have his own son held accountable for all the sins of his father. The boy never had a chance, she thought.

They hugged one another before Roger departed, and Jevon hugged him too, not wishing to be left out. She had never even touched a white man before, and she giggled.

Roger had already spoken to Pia some weeks before. Like Brianna, she had severed herself from her old life, trying to forget, focusing instead on Jane, who was taking Daniel's death very badly. Jane feared her sister-in-law might have another real stroke if she did not constantly watch over her.

After he arrived back at the hotel, shortly before nine, Roger found the bar was still open and so he ordered a beer before heading to his room. "Here's to you, Daniel," he said, lifting his glass in a toast to one of the few people in his life he genuinely admired. "I truly believe your story will have a happy ending," he said out loud.

"What was that?" the barman asked.

"Nothing, nothing at all," Roger replied, toasting Daniel one more time and chuckling to himself.

CHAPTER 83

THE LAST PAGE – Boydtown

May 2019

It was a little over a week away and yet winter seemed unable to wait, stealing the last days of autumn with an invasion of cold air from Antarctica. She was wearing a thick woollen hat pulled down over her ears and Daniel's padded, goose-down jacket, two sizes too big, wrapped about her. Her jeans were too thin and her bottom was freezing from sitting on the special rock she liked to call her 'thinking spot'. She shivered as a sudden rain squall spattered her notebook. She closed it quickly but was reluctant to leave, despite the weather; instead, she pulled up the hood of her jacket.

Pia continued to speculate about exactly where Boyd's wharf had been. There were no visible remains of it, one hundred and sixty years or so later. It was so frustrating: she had been unable to find an old illustration or even any reference to it in the local library. Recently, however, a local person had informed her there were wooden sections of the wharf in the water but covered by sand. The man could not tell her exactly where though as he had not actually seen anything himself.

Then her mind wandered and she began thinking about Daniel again. He had been dead for well over a year and still there were many times she was angry at him; how dare he just walk out of the door with that awful friend of his and then simply vanish over the edge of a cliff!

The initial report of his death had a profound and immediate effect, slicing a gaping wound through her heart the moment a policeman and a policewoman had come to her door with the dreadful news. She had screamed that it had to be a mistake, even tugging on the sleeve of the policewoman's tunic and pleading with her to confirm it was not true.

Jane had overheard the conversation from inside the house and had hurried to the door and told them to go away; they were insane, she yelled, it could not possibly be true! Her brother was with his friend showing him some of the local tourist attractions.

Once Jane had calmed down a little, the policewoman mentioned the name of Richard Crossly. At that moment the sisters-in-law had to finally accept the devastating and undeniable truth. Daniel was gone from their lives forever! Pia continued screaming again like a wild animal caught in a trap, the steel teeth crushing and biting into bone. Jane was also crying but able to maintain a modicum of self-control for Pia's sake. After much coaxing, Pia let her sister-in-law gently take her by the arm and guide her back inside the house.

A flotilla of boats, including a local police launch and a similar craft from the Australian Border Force, had been dispatched to search for him as soon as the storm had abated the following day. After three days of intense searching, without finding a single trace of Daniel, they were forced to abandon their efforts as another storm blew in from the southeast.

Six months after the presumed accident, the police had issued a report to the coroner concluding that Daniel most likely had died by misadventure when he stumbled and then slid over the edge of a cliff. The weather at the time had been particularly violent and storms had battered that region for close to a week.

A referral from his doctor in Eden, addressed to a specialist at the hospital in Bega influenced the final judgement of the coroner's court, that in all probability Daniel's death had been an accident. Pia had discovered the letter in one of Daniel's jacket pockets one morning as she sorted through his clothes to donate to charity. She had given the letter to the police, who in their investigations a few days later discovered that Daniel had been diagnosed with multiple sclerosis.

Daniel had never intended to keep the news to himself, as Pia was left to assume. He had planned to tell her and Jane, but he had never had the right opportunity to do so before he died.

Richard Crossly remained under arrest in Australia until eventually he was extradited to Lucaya where he was initially charged for supplying the gun that killed Walter Harrison. Later he faced further charges for providing information, innocently passed to him by Daniel concerning Daniel's movements, including the name of the beach where Pia liked to walk and when she was left alone in the house the night Louis McPherson smashed all the windows and let loose a deadly Eastern Brown snake. All of this information was read out by the Australian Coroner in a statement prepared by Roger Sage and signed by Crossly from his jail cell on Lucaya. He remained adamant that Daniel had slipped in the loose dirt from the effects of the violent storm. He reached for him, Richard Crossly had written, but it was too late and Daniel disappeared over the edge.

———

Daniel died instantly and his body was carried out to sea, drifting unnoticed in the currents until it eventually floated to the surface and for days was violently buffeted by the action of the waves, later exposing what remained to scavenging seabirds. Within a matter of weeks nothing of Daniel remained but his bones; they eventually sank beneath the waves and scattered randomly in the currents over a vast area of the Tasman seabed below.

———

Having no body to bury was as if he had never existed. Pia would often think this in her darkest moments when she was grieving alone. She had tried to discuss with Jane the idea of placing a memorial plaque close to the spot where he had fallen, which Jane had immediately rejected out of hand. She thought it would be morbid, like those white crosses dotted along Australia's highways advertising fatal accidents.

Pia never told Jane about the exchange of emails she had discovered on Daniel's computer between him and Brianna, the woman she had initially held in such regard for having saved her husband from a bullet in Cornwall. That discovery had come later after the inquest on how he had vanished from her life. It had been a day like no other, far worse than when she was told he was dead. Nothing had prepared her for this, the sudden revelation of intimacy between a man she had lived with for almost fifty years and an obviously much younger woman from Jamaica.

It was as if an explosion had occurred inside her head, destroying all the wonderful memories of the man with whom she had shared her life and had loved so much. For Pia it was very much as if he had died twice.

It was now a year since she had discovered the emails. It seemed like a lifetime now; days and weeks and months of introspection, alone with her thoughts and the fury of being part of someone else's lie. Yet with the passage of time, very slowly, she found some relief on reading and re-reading the many emails between Daniel and Brianna.

The intimacy expressed there would always remain extremely distressing to Pia, although the more often she read his correspondence with his Jamaican friend, the more she began to rediscover the man she had always loved and respected. No matter how much the truth had hurt her, Daniel's exchanges with this woman unwittingly exposed the same tortured soul Pia had first encountered long ago.

Gradually it became evident to her that until the very end he had remained that gentle and deeply sensitive man she had always loved, one struggling with his demons, yet constantly and acutely troubled by the consequences his actions might have on others. She had begun to realize that there were two different Daniels; the man who had stood by her steadfastly all their married life and the other, the younger one, who had always wanted to break free from that separate person he had become, shaped by the cruel events of his childhood.

Pia understood now that he must always have been devoured by guilt from the day his mother had disappeared, blaming himself for it. The years locked away in an abusive environment in a foreign country were, to his subconscious, fitting punishment for the guilt he had assumed for his mother's abrupt departure.

One day, without warning, it suddenly dawned on Pia that the Daniel who had fallen in love with Brianna was a version of the much younger man who had briefly escaped his past. When he had first met Brianna, Pia surmised, it must have been like a sudden and overwhelming release, arming him with an absorbing sense of freedom to embrace a life he had never before experienced.

It must have lasted only a brief while, Pia thought, before he had continued to torment himself with doubt again, anguishing not only over Brianna but over her as well. The young man and the old one had fallen into the same trap; except this time, he could see there was no possible solution.

Daniel loved them both, that much was obvious now. Brianna had even said as much in her replies by warning him that he would never find happiness if he left Pia, something she made quite clear she would never expect of him. She only wanted to share a small portion of his life, not possess him fully at the expense of Pia.

Pia found Brianna's messages to her husband both disquieting and comforting, because it was almost impossible for her to cast Brianna as that 'other' woman to be vilified and despised for interfering in their marriage. In the emails, Brianna came across as someone wise beyond her years, thoroughly thoughtful and kind. Obviously, the poor girl had not connived or manipulated the situation, rather, she had discovered she simply could not help herself from loving Daniel, no more than he could have stopped loving her.

Neither had control over their feelings for one another. They had collided through no fault of their own and fate had decreed they remain together merely to survive. It had been the right thing to do; one or both of them might very well have been killed if they had not.

Somewhat begrudgingly at first, Pia began to develop a deep sense of gratitude towards Brianna. In a peculiar way she was happy for Daniel that he had found someone to love him before he died. She thought of Brianna and understood that she would be grieving over his loss as well; she hoped one day she too might find some happiness again.

The rain had stopped but it was becoming colder, so she decided to go home and cook something nice for them both for dinner. She enjoyed living with Jane and was thankful for her company, someone who would remain a physical connection to Daniel, providing some comfort that she otherwise might never have found.

The one matter that still disturbed her was how Daniel had died. Did he fall or was he pushed? Only one man would ever know that for sure, and he was currently serving ten years in prison for complicity to murder the premier of Lucaya. It was unlikely he would ever admit Daniel had been pushed and had not slipped as he maintained. He continually insisted it was an accident from effects of the downpour and Daniel was unable to grasp on to anything before he went over the edge.

The police later found a photograph in the dirt of a black man carrying something under his arm; behind him there were palm trees growing and people sitting at tables in small bars.

Perhaps they would open a bottle of Merlot tonight, Pia thought as she got up and started walking back to the car park. She wanted to celebrate. This afternoon she had finally finished writing her fiction al account of the life of Benjamin Boyd. She had entitled it *The Last Blackbirder*.

CHAPTER 84

HELLO, DADDY – Lucaya

July 2019

The security booth by the entrance was deserted as two men struggled to take a large FOR SALE sign down nearby. She had parked the car on the other side of a tall boxwood hedge, just before the turn-around at the end of the promontory overlooking Coral Sound. Beyond, tiny Coral Island shimmered in the heat of the day. From her vantage point she could see a number of tour boats idling across the turquoise water as their passengers, cameras at the ready, explored the island on raised wooden walkways, hoping to catch glimpses of Caribbean Rock Iguanas.

"Yuh too late, likkle darling, di yaad aready sell," one of the men joked as she walked past. Brianna laughed, briefly surprised to hear Jamaican patois spoken. She should not have been, but four years was a long time and she had forgotten how much Lucaya benefitted from the Jamaican presence; they were a people possessed of happy-go-lucky personalities that many of the sour-faced Lucayans totally lacked. Without Jamaicans, tourists would never have returned.

"Takes two of yuh tuh tek dung dat likkle sign?" she laughed, sashaying past as only a Jamaican woman could.

"Marry mi gyal!" one of the men called after her as Brianna continued walking towards the main house. She hurried because she could hear Jevon and the others getting out of the car on the other side of the

410

hedge. She told them she had wanted ten minutes alone, which Jevon could well understand.

The house was empty now. The expensive furniture had been seized long ago and sold towards the mammoth debt Walter Harrison had accumulated over the years as premier of Lucaya. The seven and a half million dollars the tech billionaire from Silicon Valley had paid recently for the house was a fraction of what the current government had been obliged to pay for the corruption trial, in excess of one hundred million dollars.

She finally came to the place where she had been working at one of the portable bars at the party. Her heart skipped a beat remembering that night and the first time she had laid eyes on him. For her it was very much love at first sight, and she still loved him with all her heart. It was four years since then, but she could still recall every detail of that magical evening, at least until she and Daniel had witnessed the brutal rape of the young American woman.

Mon, I miss you so much, she told him. I know your spirit is here right beside me, just as you promised in your letter.

A tear started to slowly slide down the side of her face. "I came here especially today to give you a beautiful gift I am sure will make you very, very happy, hon," she said out loud, wiping away her tear.

She could hear the others coming closer, all three of them giggling amongst themselves. Jevon called out wondering where she was.

"I'm over here, Jevon, over here, talking to Daniel."

Your present is on its way, my love, the very best present you can ever imagine!

Brianna had come to Lucaya as the main prosecution witness in Michael Elm's trial. Unknown to her, Richard Crossly was also going to provide evidence and would swear under oath that he had been complicit in the cover-up to protect Geoffrey Elm's son.

The prosecution lawyers had advised that her evidence was crucial to the outcome of the trial; no one could possibly dispute her testimony, unlike that of Richard Crossly, who could be accused of lying to serve his own interests. Brianna, on the other hand, never had anything to gain, and yet had lost so much.

Perhaps Crossly was hoping for a reduction in his sentence, not that the CPS on the island would ever have entertained such an idea, unless they wanted to re-ignite civil unrest. He would be serving his full sentence of ten years.

Lord Elm was still awaiting trial in the UK but was currently in hospital. It had finally been decided in consultation with the Home Office and the FCO to proceed with Michael Elm's trial first without waiting for an outcome in the pending trial of his father; Lord Elm had been diagnosed with pancreatic cancer and it was virtually certain he would not live to face justice.

Roger Sage had met them at the plane the day before and had taken them to one of the condo resorts on Coral Bay where they would all be staying for the duration of the trial. Then, when it was all over, they would return to Jamaica. Roger was taking them out for dinner tonight.

"Stop running you two!" Jevon called out. But the twins did not listen and ran towards their mother.

"Where's Daddy?" they were shouting.

"He's here! You can't see him, but he can see you. Say hello!"

"Hello Daddy", the two little girls shouted in unison.

"We're here, Daddy. Your two little girls, Pia and Jane."

Both Brianna and Jevon began to cry.

After five minutes or so Brianna told the twins to say goodbye to Daddy and the four of them returned to the car. She did not want to see the indoor pool and the scene of the crime. A sudden, tropical gust of warmth caressed the side of her face as she exited Tara. She shivered and smiled to herself.

"Bye-bye, Daddy," Daniel's two little girls shouted.

"Goodbye, my darling," Brianna said to him.

Pia was never to know about the twins, Brianna had decided this on the drive back to Coral Bay. She had been unsure until only moments ago when she re-visited the place where she and Daniel had met. Just before Jevon and the twins had found her in the gardens at Tara, she was positive she had heard Daniel telling her it was best not to say anything. It would be far too cruel for Pia to know that Daniel had given to someone else what she had always wanted most in her life. But Brianna would always remain in touch with Pia, one way or another; Daniel had also just asked her to promise this.

As they drove back to their condo, Pia was sitting on Brianna's lap, and little Jane on Jevon's. Between them on the car seat Jevon was holding Brianna's hand gently.

I never knew how to tell you, Daniel, Brianna was thinking. You see, my dearest, I also understood the torment of loving more than one person. But it changes absolutely nothing because I shall always love you until the day I die. I shall never forget you, ever!

EPILOGUE

BARACOA – Cuba, 1883

*B*enjamin Boyd lived until he was eighty-two, another nineteen years, in a small town called Baracoa, located in a remote part of eastern Cuba.

It had an insouciant feel and was set in stunningly beautiful natural surrounds. Verdant mountains and rivers encompassed a sweeping bay, with beaches of white sand brushed by the turquoise waters of the Caribbean.

The years in Baracoa were amongst the happiest of his entire life. In such a place he found the freedom he had always craved. The local inhabitants made no judgement of others and had no interest in whom they shared their beds with. It was a town where social conventions were an anathema, in conflict with the lives they all wanted to lead in freedom. It was the reason most had sought it out in the first place, somewhere so remote they could live in peace, where the state had little or no influence.

Benjamin Boyd died in 1883. During his Cuban years he had never thought of Stevens, whom he had murdered in Guadalcanal, nor the young negro boy he had burnt alive on his plantation near the town of Marshall in Texas. He had never dwelled on the past, only the future and himself. He had no regrets and he died peacefully in his sleep.

His funeral was attended by many of the townsfolk who followed his coffin carried by four young men from his house by the beach to a cemetery on a hill nearby with a spectacular view of the ocean.

Mark Boyd had died five years earlier at the Alexandra Hotel in Hyde Park in London, aged 74. He had never heard from his brother again.

THE END